MW01616597

HELIX

BOOKS 1-3

NATHAN M FARRUGIA

ANOMALY PRESS

HELIX: EPISODE 1

HELIX

CHAPTER ONE

DAMIEN WASN'T MEANT to be here.

'Thirty-five minutes and you haven't asked why you're in this room,' the border control officer said.

Damien was sitting in an interview room, although he used the term loosely since his wrists were duct taped to the chair's plastic armrests, with cable ties fastened over the tape just to be sure. If he had to be honest, this wasn't quite how he'd planned things.

They weren't taking chances either. Both his sneakers were missing their shoelaces and there was no partition glass. Just a single camera in the corner, bringing him little comfort.

The officer sat behind a table, directly under a sprinkler head fixed to the ceiling. On the table there was a single sheet of paper, face down. The linoleum floor smelled of ammonia, searing Damien's nostrils. Vents blew cool air; the room temperature was intentionally cold.

The officer prodded a tablet with an impatient finger. He was American, but his portly midsection pressed against his local Guatemalan uniform.

'Would you like to know why you're here?' he asked.

'You find my aura unusually calming,' Damien said.

'I find your criminal record unusually alarming.'

He held up the paper for Damien to see. It was blank.

But Damien was more interested in the officer's arm. There was a thin band of white fabric above his right elbow. He'd seen it before, yet couldn't quite place it.

'I filled out the immigration form wrong, didn't I?' Damien said. 'Should've put Casual Relief Teacher.'

'I hope you enjoyed your time in Guatemala.' The officer's attention was back on his tablet.

'Thank you…' Damien said, reading the surname on his uniform, '…Officer White. As far as being pulled off a bus and cavity searched goes, it's been a real blast. Some people pay for that kind of experience.'

'And I expect you'll pay for this,' White said. 'One way or another.'

'I'd prefer a little Shibari myself, but we have to start somewhere,' Damien said.

White's left eye twitched. 'And I know precisely where this will end.'

Damien focused with his enhanced hearing. There was light traffic in the corridor outside, and someone was talking about his possessions in the opposite room. White's breathing was a bit faster than it should've been.

'Level 181 is absurd,' White said.

Damien blinked. 'That's where I am?'

White looked up from his tablet. 'I mean on Candy Crush. This level is impossible to beat.'

'Why did you take me off the bus?' Damien asked.

White barely raised an eyebrow. 'That doesn't matter anymore.'

'When the other officers saw my passport, they seemed pretty keen to put me *on* that bus.'

'Believe me when I tell you I was doing you a favor.' White put his tablet down. 'What matters is where you *will* go. There are certain gentlemen from a department of the United States government who look forward to meeting you. They should be here soon.'

'And which department is that?' Damien asked.

'Do I look like I should know, or care?' White glared at him. 'Do you know who I am?'

'Well, I'm crossing off "romantic love interest,"' Damien said. 'Or am I not giving us the chance we deserve?'

'What we deserve?' He gave a self-assured nod. 'We deserve to be purged.'

'I was thinking of doing a detox myself.'

'Are you scared, Damien?'

He knew the answer. He could die here. Or worse, the government could take him. 'I'm a little concerned.'

'You have good reason to,' White said, hand on his holster.

Damien felt his skin crawl. Maybe it was the cold air, maybe it was White. 'What things?' he asked.

White lifted his hand from the holster and inspected

his fingertips. 'What did you do, exactly? Are you a terrorist, Damien?'

Damien felt his pulse race, a dull throb in his ear. He breathed slowly and focused on the officer. There was still a way out. 'Why would you believe anything I say?'

White shifted in his seat. His chair squeaked. 'That depends on what you say. Do you think you'll survive this?'

'That depends on who's pulling your strings.'

White's tablet buzzed. He checked it, then double-checked it. His lips shivered into a smile. 'I have some good news.'

The door opened and a pair of uniformed officers entered. Like White, they didn't appear to be local. And like White, they both wore white arm bands. One officer closed the door.

Their name tags read Price and Gray. Price had an oddly large head and thick eyebrows that twitched when he drew a fixed-blade knife. It didn't look government issue, and it didn't glint under the light because it was coated black.

Gray didn't reach for her knife, but she kept a hand close to her holstered stun gun. Her glass-green eyes focused on Damien's restraints. Damien pulled sharply on them, but it did little good. From opposing sides, both officers approached him.

'Change of plans?' Damien asked.

'No,' White said. 'Change of strings.'

TEN YEARS AGO

OLESYA

CHAPTER TWO

St Petersburg, Russia

'WAKE UP.'

Olesya rubbed her eyes. Zakhar, her older brother, was whispering in her ear.

'What are you doing?' she asked, sitting up.

Zakhar held a letter, typed and printed. She tried to read it but some of the English words were difficult. Zakhar giggled and folded the paper over to reveal the Russian translation.

'I'm … accepted? I have the scholarship?' she asked.

He grinned. 'Congratulations!'

'Where did you get this?' she asked.

'I took it from the kitchen,' Zakhar said. 'But you need to act surprised when they tell us tomorrow.'

Olesya looked at him. 'Where's your letter? Did you get in?'

'No,' he said. 'My letter's different.'

'But … I'm going without you?'

Zakhar smiled. 'You're fourteen now, you can do it. I know you can.'

She looked at her brother. He was dressed in jeans, a down jacket and beanie.

'Where are you going?' she asked.

'I'm going to build a snowman,' he said. 'And I'm not doing it by myself.'

She frowned. 'In the middle of the night?'

'All the other kids are doing it. And it's your last New Year before you go.' Zakhar wiggled an eyebrow. 'You don't want to miss out on the fun. Unless you're boring—'

Olesya pushed him to one side. 'I'll get my boots—'

'These ones?' Zakhar was already holding them.

She grabbed them. 'Lucky guess.'

Zakhar paced the bedroom while she pulled a thick sweater and jeans over her pajamas. He'd already picked out their scarves and gloves. She reached for the door. Zakhar put his hand on her arm.

'The window,' he said. 'Always go through the window.'

Luckily they were on the first floor, because she didn't like heights. The window creaked as he opened it, and she hoped their parents wouldn't hear. She could hear them with the other adults. They were in the apartment next door, sharing Olivier salad, champagne and loud stories.

Their voices were constant enough to cover Zakhar's movements as he helped Olesya out into the winter's night, holding up the window so she could wriggle through. She let him take her hand and steer them to the subway, avoiding next door's windows. It was only a five-minute trip into town and they didn't have to wait more than a minute for the train.

It was almost two in the morning, but the streets were filled with equal amounts of kids and grownups. She watched kids slide down a hill on a wooden sled and plough into a clump of snow. They disappeared into the white, their laughter muffled.

Zakhar's nose was already winter-red as he pulled her eagerly toward the bridge. He wanted to walk across the canal—the water frozen solid—but she chose the bridge instead, not wanting to slip across the ice. He didn't protest and instead they crossed the bridge and reached the Palace Square. This was their first new-year celebration outside of their hometown in Belarus and she wasn't prepared for so many people or decorations.

In front of the peppermint and cream Winter Palace, Olesya could see large crowds gathering. Grownups ate *pirozhki*—pies filled with cabbage, mushrooms or beef— while the kids nibbled on sweet gingerbread. Some of the families danced around fir Christmas trees that sparkled with gold ornaments and purple, blue, and green fairy lights. They were dancing for Santa Claus—*Grandfather Frost*—and his granddaughter, the Snow Maiden.

Olesya squeezed Zakhar's hand. 'Let's dance.'

'Nooooooo,' he said as she pulled him through the crowd.

They made it as far as the nearest glittering fir tree before Zakhar saw the circle of kids and dug his heels into the snow. He poked his tongue out and broke from her grasp. Olesya gave chase, cutting him off at the market stalls. By then he was distracted. He seemed to ignore the pies and go straight for the fireworks stall. She caught up and pushed him to the next stall where she could talk him into sweet cotton instead. He used his pocket money to pay for two pink balls of fluff, each on a stick, and handed her one.

'They call this cotton candy in America,' Zakhar said.

He bit a chunk off the sweet cotton so large it stuck to his cold nose. Olesya laughed as she watched him try to retrieve it with his tongue, going cross-eyed. He was just showing off, so she took the sweet cotton from his nose. He tried to stop her but she was too fast, shoving it in her mouth. It melted on her tongue and tasted exactly like pink.

'That's not fair!' Zakhar said.

This time, Olesya stuck her tongue out.

Together, they walked Nevsky Prospekt and ate their sweet cotton. Zakhar didn't seem to have a direction in mind, which was fine with her.

'You'll need to know words like "cotton candy,"' he said.

'I know,' Olesya said. 'I need to learn more English.'

'You're super-smart. You can do it.' He pulled her beanie over her eyes. 'I still get to see you on vacation, right?'

She nodded, breathing thimbles of cold air. The buildings on both sides of Nevsky Prospekt were high and dusted in snow, lit with pretty lights. Everyone seemed to be smiling tonight, eyes warm with hope for the new year.

'What should we do?' Zakhar asked.

Olesya wrinkled her nose. 'Build a snowman, obviously.'

His eyes lit up. 'Let's build a snow army!'

'I have a better idea,' she said. 'Let's build a snow dinosaur!'

'I'll make the horns!'

The street was busy and Olesya had to watch her step so the sweet cotton didn't stick to someone's coat. They crossed another frozen white canal. On either side of the road there were more aged buildings. Some were aglow with festive lights while others—candy cathedrals and apricot fortresses—gleamed with an enchantment of their own. Zakhar found a garden that was less crowded, but still coated in snow. Olesya scooped up a handful and smoothed it into a ball.

'I like this statue,' he said, standing before it.

With a scepter in one hand and olive wreath in the other, the Empress of Russia stood before them. Below her, a second tier of carved men and women—politicians, poets, swordfighters, and courtiers.

Olesya knew the Empress from her mother's history books. She was called Catherine the Great. Born Sophie Friederike Auguste in the eighteenth century, she was intelligent, kind, and ambitious. Sophie expanded the country's education, science, and the arts, bringing a golden age to Russia it had never seen before.

Olesya ducked just in time as a snowball almost struck her face.

'How did you—' Zakhar said.

She was ready, hurling her snowball at him in mid-run. It exploded over his ear. He spat snow and tumbled.

Olesya ran over to see if he was hurt, but he sprang to his feet with a new snowball that clipped her shoulder. He adjusted his beanie and looked up at her.

'You never miss,' he said. 'How do you do that?'

'Easy.' She wiped snow from her coat. 'I watch you move and know where to throw it.'

Zakhar collapsed on his back with a sigh. 'That's why they picked you.'

Olesya slumped down behind him, the top of her beanie touching his. She looked up at the sugarcoated spires. They pointed to the stars above.

'What if I come back and you're not here anymore?' she asked.

'I'll always be here,' Zakhar said. 'And if I move, I'll leave a secret message for you where no one can find it, except you.'

She laughed. 'That's impossible.'

'Nothing's impossible.' Zakhar, still lying down, pointed toward the statue of Catherine the Great. His finger aimed for one of the people carved under her. 'See that woman in the gown, holding that book?'

She followed his aim. 'The head of science.'

'Yeah, her.' He nodded. 'I'll hide a secret note in her gown that only you can find.'

'What if … I can't?' Olesya hated the words as she said them.

For a while, he was silent. It was the longest she'd seen him not talk. Above them, fireworks crackled, then trickled down the velvet sky. Olesya tried to imagine what this scholarship on the other side of the world would be like. What it would be like without her big brother.

The snow squeaked under Zakhar's jacket. He rubbed his face with a gloved hand and she realized he'd been crying. The fireworks had faded now, golden glitter in the night.

'I'm supposed to look out for you,' he said. 'How will I know you'll be OK?'

'You won't.' She squeezed his hand. 'Even I won't know that.'

CHAPTER THREE

Location: Classified

THE ENTIRE SQUAD stopped what they were doing and looked at Olesya.

'What are you doing here?' one of them asked.

This wasn't off to a great start.

There were nine recruits inside the compact living quarters. The quarters smelled of used socks and shoe polish. There was a pair of recruits to almost every metal bunk bed, the bed sheets folded with hospital corners and smoothed by a wooden ruler. The recruits wore nametags velcroed to their uniforms, a privilege reserved only for those in Combat Training.

A boy stepped forward, arms folded. Olesya recognized him as Ark, the squad leader. He was tall and thin, with curly brown hair and rounded eyes that looked too big for his head. He smirked as he approached.

'Take a wrong turn, Blondie?' he said. 'Which squad are you looking for?'

Olesya swallowed. 'Firebird.'

His smile dissolved. 'Uh, that's us.'

'I've been transferred,' she said.

'Not to Firebird, you haven't.' He lifted his chin. 'Must be some mistake. Where are you from?'

'English Squad.' Olesya noticed the empty bunk. 'Is that the spare bed?'

'Whoa, hold up there.' He stepped between her and the bed. 'That's for a proper recruit, not some little girl from English Squad.'

I'll show you a proper recruit, she thought.

'I don't know why they moved me,' she said. 'I'm just following orders.'

'From English Squad?' Ark laughed. 'Great, a recruit who can't even speak English properly.'

Someone else cleared their throat and moved nimbly forward. Her nametag read Xiu. Her large brown eyes flickered between Olesya and Ark. When she spoke, she was calm but sure.

'It sounds like she speaks better English than you,' Xiu said. Her accent was American, not Chinese. Her gaze lingered on Olesya for a moment, but not too long.

'I didn't ask you.' Ark focused on Olesya. 'I don't care about your language skills, I care about your combat skills. And you have zero.'

'I have basic training,' Olesya said. 'Did you forget?'

Ark almost laughed. 'Basic won't get you far in this squad, Blondie.'

The rest of Firebird were whispering in their bunks.

Olesya couldn't hear what they were saying. She spoke up, drowning them out.

'That's why I'm here, to learn,' she said. 'Everyone says you're the best leader of all the squads.'

Ark allowed himself a knowing smile.

She leaned in to whisper. 'But I think they're wrong.'

'What do y—' Ark said. 'What do you know, huh?'

'You can't handle one untrained recruit.' Olesya stepped forward. 'The best leader could do that, easy.'

For a fraction of a second, Ark flinched, as though he was about to be attacked from something high above. Then his bony arms locked at his sides. 'We have more important things to do than babysit you. We have training and tests to pass. You won't even last a day.'

'Then you have nothing to worry about,' Olesya said.

Ark smiled. 'Exactly.'

Olesya sidestepped him and threw her pack on the empty bed. She just wanted to get on with it and make this change as painless as possible. 'I'm from English Squad, remember? I'll only be here for one day.'

Before Ark could reply, an instructor in black fatigues stepped into their quarters.

'Firebird Squad,' the instructor said.

The recruits stood at attention, Olesya included.

'Today you move into your final phase of Combat Training.' The instructor eyed each of them with passing interest. 'Your first field exercise is tomorrow. Do you know what happens if you fail?'

'Corporal.' Ark cleared his throat. 'Those who fail to qualify go back to Basic.'

'Incorrect. Those who fail are disqualified from the

entire program. Do you want to be disqualified, squad leader?'

'No, Corporal!' Ark said.

'Any further questions, recruits?' the instructor asked.

'Corporal,' Olesya said.

The instructor inhaled sharply. 'If this is about why you're here, recruit, it is not an administrative error. You will keep pace with your new squad or you will be disqualified, which in your case won't be much of a difference. But since Firebird would be disqualified along with you, they might disagree.'

Olesya shook her head. 'No Corporal, my question is different.'

The instructor was already turning to leave. 'What is it?'

'Do you know when we can make phone calls to our family?' Olesya asked.

'Outside communication is prohibited during FPCON Bravo,' the instructor said. 'Once the threat is downgraded to Alpha, you might be allowed to have outside contact. Any letters addressed to you will be withheld until further notice. It might not have occurred to anyone here, but our security is more important than your temporary homesickness.'

With that, he left.

Another recruit shrugged. His nametag read Jay. 'I think he seemed happier than usual,' Jay said.

Olesya noticed Ark stiffen. He swiveled and closed on her. His nostrils and eyes widened as he stared her down, which was difficult since she was a bit taller than him.

'Let's make this clear,' Ark whispered. 'We're qualifying. You're not going to screw that up for us. On the field exercise tomorrow, you're a shadow. You follow us and you do nothing else. You got that?'

'More than you think. I've seen your scores in Combat Training,' Olesya said. 'They say Firebird is almost the best. And I can see why.'

Ark's fists opened slightly. 'Almost?'

Olesya tried not to mumble. 'Next to Helldiver.'

'Just 'cos they recently qualified?' Ark walked to his bunk. 'That'll be us soon. Then they'll be *almost* the best.'

Jay laughed. 'Yeah, we have a fresh recruit from English Squad and we still kick ass. Wouldn't that be something?'

Ark's lips twitched. 'She won't last.'

'She has to,' Xiu said. 'She's one of us now.'

Olesya met Xiu's gaze. 'If you'll have me.'

'We'll have you, all right.' Ark stepped between them. 'If you need to aim your weapon, you aim it. If you need to fire your weapon, you do what little English Squad girls do and pretend to fire.'

'What if she needs to, you know, actually shoot something?' Xiu asked.

Ark held up a finger. 'I'm trying to save our squad.' He focused on Olesya. 'Do you understand me?'

'I understand you're insecure,' Olesya said. 'And I understand that someone used to hit you when you were younger. Older brother, bully at school, maybe your father.'

On his face, she noticed an almost imperceptible eye twitch. It was a flicker, and nothing more.

'So it's your father,' Olesya said.

Ark strode toward her, his lips curling to reveal a chipped tooth.

Olesya stood her ground and spoke without pause. 'My father did the same to me. I think a lot of recruits here had that problem.'

Ark stood, almost nose to nose with her, unblinking. '*You're* going to have that problem in a minute.'

'Ark, don't.' Another recruit placed her hand on his shoulder.

Olesya read her nametag: Val. His shoulders relaxed. He seemed to listen to her.

'You're one of the best performing recruits here,' Olesya said to Ark. 'But you could be *the* best. If they see how much a recruit like me improves—under your command—they would be very impressed. You pull off the impossible, that guarantees your squad qualifies. Maybe that's the real test.'

'Wait, she has a point,' Jay said.

Ark glared at him. 'She does not.'

Xiu folded her arms. 'But what if she's right?'

'You're the squad leader,' Olesya said to him. '*You* have to be right.'

Ark straightened up. 'Xiu, you like this new recruit so much, how about you train her in your free time?' He watched Olesya carefully. 'You only have today, Blondie. Don't waste it.'

OLESYA STEPPED into the mess a few minutes late for breakfast. It smelled of instant coffee and overcooked scrambled eggs. She was the last recruit from Firebird to arrive, and after what happened this morning, she preferred it that way.

Her appetite was almost zero, so she skipped the over-cooked eggs and dry bacon that most recruits shoveled down their necks and settled for a liquid breakfast: a bland-tasting coconut shake, purposely missing all the chocolate so the recruits wouldn't go crazy on sugar. So no one would question her appetite, she placed a cup of coffee and a snack-sized packet of cashews on her tray.

By now, all of Firebird were halfway through their breakfast and chatting among themselves. She felt Ark's stare as she walked to an empty table. Another recruit shifted from Ark's table to hers, sitting opposite her.

'So you're Olesya?' Xiu asked.

She was reading off Olesya's nametag, but Olesya nodded anyway.

'Welcome to Firebird Squad, I'm Xiu.' She pronounced it as *she-you*. 'Where are you from?'

'Russia,' Olesya said. 'Technically I'm from Belarus, but my family moved to Russia. And you are from—'

'America.' Xiu grinned. 'Technically from China.'

Xiu didn't say anything more. Instead, she ate her eggs in silence, her eyes wide and focused. Under the fluorescent light, Olesya could see freckles scattered across Xiu's pink cheeks and threads of amber in her brown eyes.

Xiu's movements were smooth and quick, so quick that a mouthful of scrambled eggs slipped from her fork onto her lap. That would've annoyed Olesya, but Xiu didn't seem to care. She wiped her chin with the back of her hand and collected the egg with her fork. It looked funny, but Olesya was careful not to smile. Xiu caught Olesya staring.

'Your father never hit you, did he?' Xiu said.

Olesya swallowed. 'No.'

Xiu tucked a strand of raven-black hair behind her ear. 'So why did you say that to Ark?'

'I was just … trying to make a connection.'

'What you said to him, no one's ever gotten away with that before.' Xiu seemed almost amused. 'But you said it better than most.'

'Thanks.'

Xiu chewed thoughtfully. 'So, English Squad, huh? All this time and then they just throw you in with us.'

Olesya nodded. 'I don't know why they decided to move me.'

Xiu's small lips curled into a smile. 'I was born in America and your English is better than mine.'

'But I have an accent.' Olesya felt her cheeks warm. 'And I think you overestimate me.'

'We're all here because we're special,' Xiu said. 'You don't think so?'

Olesya sipped her shake. 'We're different.'

'I saw your test results last year.'

That seemed so long ago, Olesya could scarcely remember that. She couldn't even remember arriving at the base. 'Nothing out of the ordinary.'

'What I saw this morning, you ran rings around our squad leader and he didn't even know it,' Xiu said, leaning in. 'That wasn't ordinary.'

Xiu stopped talking when Jay sat next to her and

started eating from his tray. He had high cheekbones, an amber complexion and an ever-present smirk.

'Sorry about our squad leader,' he said, between mouthfuls of bacon. 'He can be a bit of a dick.'

Olesya looked down. 'I don't think he likes me much.'

'Ark can be a bit difficult,' Xiu said. 'But we're family.'

Another recruit sat next to Jay with his own tray of food. His nametag read Damien. He had pale olive skin, scruffy hair, and a nose slightly too big for his face.

'So you've met our squad leader?' Damien asked. At least he still had a slight Italian accent.

'Unfortunately,' Olesya said.

Damien shook his head. 'There was this one time at the range, the rear sight on my pistol was stuck and I couldn't adjust it.'

Jay elbowed him. 'Yeah, I bet Helldiver sabotaged it on purpose.'

'My point is, we had this big test and my shots were off,' Damien said. 'I wasn't going to qualify. I told the instructor and he just blamed me, told me there was nothing wrong with the sights. He didn't even bother to check.'

Damien paused to sip his juice.

Jay cleared his throat. 'When the instructor wasn't looking, Ark swapped his pistol with Damien's.'

Damien nodded. 'I just scraped through.'

'What about Ark?' Olesya asked.

'His shots before that were dead center, tight grouping,' Jay said. 'Even with Damien's messed-up pistol, he just managed to qualify.'

'Ark looks out for us,' Damien said. 'Give him time and he'll look out for you too.'

'What if I'm not good enough?' Olesya asked. 'Then I get all of you disqualified. What happens then?'

Xiu, Damien and Jay exchanged glances.

'We don't know,' Damien said.

'I can tell you my theory,' Jay whispered. 'When you're disqualified, they—'

Xiu held up her hand. 'No one wants to hear your theory, Jay.'

'Fine, whatever.' Jay accidentally spat bacon into her shake. He looked at the table behind them and ran off the names of every recruit in Firebird Squad and their 'inherent abilities'.

'Sitting next to Ark, that's his sister, Val,' Jay said. 'She has really good night vision and she can see ultraviolet stuff. Ark's ability is magnets or whatever it's called. Pretty lame ability. I never said that though.'

Val had the same curly brown hair, but longer, and her face wasn't narrow like Ark's. She was actually quite pretty, Olesya thought. Hard to believe she was Ark's sister. Val caught them looking at her and smiled. She seemed friendly.

Olesya watched as she turned to Ark and rattled her fist. He did the same. They both shook their fists three times, then she opened her palm while he opened his fist into a finger gun. It looked like they were playing some sort of game and he'd lost. It showed on his long face as she pinched the last of his bacon.

'Val keeps him in check and he looks out for her, just

like the rest of us,' Jay said. 'But they're super tight.' He paused. 'Tight is like close. They're real close.'

'I got it.' Olesya nodded. 'Tight.'

Xiu followed her gaze to the table across from Firebird.

'Who are they?' Olesya asked.

'Helldiver Squad,' Xiu said.

Olesya noticed the girl a few shades darker than Jay. She had tightly drawn lips and dark springy hair tied in a bun.

'That's Nasira, their squad leader,' Xiu said.

Jay risked a glance. 'She never smiles.'

'Don't stare,' Xiu said.

Olesya averted her gaze and caught a smirk from Xiu.

'Not you, Olesya.' Xiu nodded to Jay. 'I meant him.'

Jay nudged Damien. 'Tell her your ability. It's a good one!'

Damien had just started to delicately eat his breakfast, one food group at a time. He cleared his throat and looked up. 'Um, they call it thermogenesis.'

Jay groaned. 'That's too complicated, I told you to call it *Thermo*! It sounds way cooler.'

'How does it work?' Olesya asked.

Damien leaned forward and wrapped his hand around Olesya's cold cup of coffee. Nothing happened for a while. He released it and she could see steam rising.

Jay grinned. 'We make him do that all the time, it's real handy.'

'What's yours?' Olesya asked.

'I can electrocute stuff,' Jay said, reaching for her cup.

Olesya quickly moved it from his reach.

Jay looked dejected. 'I call it *Electro*.' He moved his

hand toward Xiu but she was quick to intercept it, gripping his wrist.

'Shock me again and I'll shave your eyebrows while you sleep,' Xiu said.

Jay pried his wrist free and rubbed it. 'Xiu's ability is she's a total ninja. Reflexes like a cat. The testicle system—'

'Vestibular system,' Xiu said. 'Balance, agility. The scientists here call it *Hyperequilibrioception*.'

Damien chewed on his eggs. 'They're pretty keen to take that ability and give it to all of us.'

'If we qualify,' Jay said. 'So what's yours?'

Olesya's mouth went dry.

'Jay, not everyone has one.' Xiu glared at him. 'We were picked because of our special genetics, not whether we have party tricks. Plus, it's rude to ask.'

'Yeah, sorry.' Jay leaned over to inspect Xiu's breakfast. She slapped his hand, sending him into retreat.

'Olesya doesn't have to tell anyone her ability, unless she wants to,' Xiu said.

Damien nodded in agreement. Jay did too, although he was busy peering over Damien's breakfast. He spied a sausage on Damien's plate and poked it with his fork.

'Are you eating that?' Jay asked.

The sausage was already in Jay's mouth by the time Damien replied.

'No, I'm not.' Damien looked over at Olesya. 'Just give Ark some time. He'll come around.'

Olesya flicked the straw in her shake. 'He reminds me a lot of my brother.'

'Your brother tried out for this?' Jay asked.

She nodded.

'Was he eligible?' Damien asked. 'It's totally the whole genetic thing. I'm an only child, but there's heaps of brothers and sisters here.' He nudged Jay. 'Didn't you say you had a brother?'

Jay rubbed his nose. 'No.'

'My brother should be here, not me,' Olesya said.

'Why would you say that?' Xiu asked. 'So you don't want to be here?'

Olesya didn't want to offend Xiu or the boys, they'd been so friendly. 'Not as much as my brother did.'

'He didn't pass the trials?' Jay asked.

'Don't talk with your mouth full,' Damien said.

Olesya wet her cracked lips. 'He passed everything but the stress tests.'

'Yeah, they suck big-time,' Jay said. 'He buckled under pressure, hey?'

'My parents were disappointed in him,' Olesya said.

Jay smirked. 'But *you* got in, right? You're here.'

Olesya drank the last of her coffee. 'Yeah.'

Xiu clapped her hands once, sharply. It made Damien jump and Jay choke on his food. Xiu ignored them. 'Olesya, have you used a weapon before?'

'A gun? No.'

Xiu leaned over her breakfast tray. 'OK, so first rule is you don't call them guns. They're pistols, rifles, carbines, things that go boom,' she said. 'Second rule, you probably don't get this in English Squad but we have two hours of free training after lunch. I'm no expert, but maybe I can show you a thing or two.'

'Nice,' Damien said.

'Yeah, Xiu's our best shooter.' Jay grinned. 'After me, anyway.'

Xiu tilted her head. 'Jay, do you even remember our scores in close quarters?'

'In my head,' Jay said, 'And I exaggerated the numbers a bit.'

Damien and Xiu laughed, and Olesya laughed with them. It was the first time she'd laughed in a while.

'How about it?' Xiu arched an eyebrow and Olesya saw a glint of mischief in her eyes.

'You really want to help me?' Olesya asked.

Xiu smiled. 'We have to.'

Olesya's packet of cashews rustled. She looked down to see Jay's hand over it.

'Are you going to eat those?'

CHAPTER FOUR

'DRAW YOUR WEAPON.' Xiu's voice sounded distant through Olesya's earplugs.

Olesya flipped the stud on her holster. She drew her pistol along the side of her body. When it reached her chest, she took it with both hands and extended it out toward her target. The pistol's front and rear sights wobbled. It was a Glock 19, Xiu had told her. It was gray and blocky, but small enough for her sweaty hands.

Xiu walked behind her, watching closely.

Olesya noticed the rangemaster peer over his newspaper. Maybe it was a bit funny to see a teenage girl teach another teenage girl how to fire a live pistol. She wondered if he might intervene, but he seemed more interested in his crossword puzzle.

'Relax,' Xiu said. 'And you can breathe, by the way.'

Olesya inhaled sharply, which made Xiu laugh. The

shooting range was indoors and smelled of rubber. Xiu smelled a lot better.

'Two shots, one after the other,' Xiu said.

Olesya gripped her pistol with clammy hands. She lined up the sights and carefully squeezed the trigger. The pistol kicked with a dull pop. She sighted her target again, tried to keep her arms still. The pistol was light, but she was getting shaky. The longer she gripped it, the harder it was to aim. She squeezed again.

Xiu was standing beside her, looking at the target. Olesya felt embarrassed. She wasn't very good. She peered over her pistol and noticed both shots were slightly to the right and lower than the target's center.

'Not bad for your first try,' Xiu said.

Olesya swallowed. 'I don't know if I can do this under pressure.'

'We'll find out tomorrow.'

'What happens to me if I'm disqualified?'

Xiu adjusted Olesya's fingers for her, wrapping the secondary hand further around to support the pistol. 'You repay your debt.'

Her new grip felt strange. 'What's the debt?'

Xiu checked Olesya's thumbs: now one rested behind the other. 'No one knows,' Xiu said. 'Maybe you work for them or maybe they just kill you.'

Olesya waited for her to laugh or admit she was joking. She didn't.

'Relax your shooting hand,' Xiu said. 'But keep your supporting hand firm.'

Olesya did as she instructed. 'Do you really believe that?'

'It doesn't matter what I believe.' Xiu took a step back. 'Two more rounds.'

With her new grip, Olesya focused on relaxing her shooting hand. She sighted her target and sent two more rounds into it. The recoil was light and the pistol snapped in her grasp.

'Holster,' Xiu said.

Olesya pulled the pistol back to her chest, down along her body, into the holster. Xiu must have noticed the smooth movement because she raised her eyebrow.

'You told me you've never handled a pistol,' Xiu asked.

'The draw and holster?' Olesya said. 'No, but I was watching you.'

Xiu blinked. 'That was perfect.' She turned her attention to the target at the end of the range. There were two new holes; they were in the center this time. 'Better grouping. Last time, your shooting hand was too tight. Your wrist was putting torque to the rounds as you fired.'

'Torque. What is that word?' Olesya asked.

Xiu frowned. 'It's like turning or twisting. So you're twisting the pistol with your wrist. Throws off your aim, just enough to miss. It's a common problem.'

Olesya nodded. Today, she'd learned a new word and how to shoot a pistol.

'Now you are relaxed.' Xiu's hand touched Olesya's for a moment. 'Your supporting hand gives you stability.'

'What if I'm shooting one-handed?' Olesya asked.

A smile tugged at the corners of Xiu's mouth. 'If we make it through tomorrow, I'll teach you.'

'Why are you helping me?' Olesya asked.

Xiu folded her arms. 'You want the truth? I want to help you.'

'Do you think that's why I'm here?' Olesya asked.

'I don't know why they put you in our squad. But if we're all disqualified from the program, I won't blame you.'

'But it will be my fault.' Olesya felt sick at the thought of it. 'Maybe I'm not cut out for this sort of thing.'

'Maybe you're too scared to step out of line,' Xiu said.

'I don't want to make a mistake.'

Xiu smiled. 'I think that's exactly what you should do.'

CHAPTER FIVE

THE WHISTLE SOUNDED through the forest.

In the darkness, the recruits drew their compact Glock 19 pistols. The objective of this exercise: at least one Firebird recruit must cross the beacons at the finish line without being hit. Stopping them from doing so: trained special forces soldiers.

With her thumb, Olesya flipped the stud on her holster. She drew and aimed low. The pistol's slide was pale blue, chambered with electro-rounds. They didn't penetrate their target, but they were tipped with four-pronged electrodes that delivered a nasty electric shock, enough to cause what their instructors called *neuromuscular incapacitation*. It was enough to drop the target—and disable their firearm for the remainder of the exercise—but not enough to kill them.

Olesya breathed in the winter air. It smelled of the giant trees around her, their trunks surfacing from damp undergrowth and twisting skyward. She looked up to see them disappear into the midnight fog.

From the front of the squad, Ark shot her a stern glare through his mask before nodding to the rest of Firebird. Everyone wore safety goggles and a blue vest that identified them as members of the same squad, although in this darkness the blue seemed almost gray.

They assembled into a line and Ark closed his eyes. Everyone remained still, waiting. Firebird didn't have compasses to guide them, and there was no visible moon to orient themselves. Thankfully, Ark's magnetoception afforded him a precise sense of direction. He closed his eyes for a moment, found his bearing and then opened them. He pointed ahead.

Xiu moved behind Olesya, taking rear security, while Damien took the scout position ahead of the squad. Everyone else moved in single file with space between them. Olesya watched as Damien slipped into the darkness and Ark followed him, leading the squad carefully in his wake.

Olesya listened to the soft squishing sound of their boots on moss and undergrowth. The forest itself was silent, making her skin prickle.

Ark issued a slight correction and Damien adjusted his bearing. Ark's hand fell to his side. It was shaking.

Olesya strained to listen for sounds around them, half-expecting an ambush. Her nose was cold and she resisted the urge to sniff. It wasn't long before Damien led them to the edge of the forest and a road. Without a word, he lay down quietly.

Firebird Squad followed suit and flattened out prone,

inching forward to him. Ark's sister, Val, was looking ahead with her enhanced vision. Olesya crawled forward, her elbows moving over damp ground.

'What can you see?' Ark asked quietly.

'Small town in the distance,' Val said. 'Gas station, some abandoned shops. Taller buildings ahead.'

'How tall?'

'Three levels, I think.'

'Did they say anything about a town in the middle of the forest?' Damien asked.

Jay shook his head. 'They don't say much of anything.'

'It doesn't matter,' Ark said. 'What's here is here and we get through no matter what.'

Jay nudged Damien. 'We're not out of the woods yet.'

'That was terrible,' Damien said.

'Quiet,' Ark told them. 'Right, open ground from here to the gas station. We make a run for it and use the station as cover. Once we see more of the town, we can plan from there. If anyone disagrees, now's the time to say so.'

No one disagreed.

'Good,' Ark said. 'Move in groups, cover your front and sides.' He paused and turned to Olesya. 'Don't screw this up.'

She said nothing and watched as the first group of four broke the line, then crossed the road.

Ark got to one knee and tapped Xiu and Val. 'Let's go.'

They moved in a compressed line of three, then dissolved into the long grass. When Olesya checked over her shoulder, she was relieved to see Damien and Jay still lying behind her. They watched different areas of the forest in case someone snuck up behind them. Jay scratched his chin.

Olesya inched herself to the edge of the forest, ready to move. She watched as the second group reached the gas station, collecting along the back wall with the first group. Val and Xiu watched from each corner. Everything they did was thoughtful and calculated. She admired them.

Damien was beside her now. Jay was on her other side. He gave her a nod—the same nod that Ark gave his squad because he trusted them.

Does Jay actually trust me?

Jay was first on the road and then Damien dropped down the slope behind him, facing right. Olesya slid carefully in their wake, reaching the road and moving behind Damien. She held her pistol low and to the left, and scanned the distant road. Jay looked over his shoulder, checking that she was with him. He seemed pleased that she was.

'Let's roll,' he said under his breath.

He started into a run. Damien was two paces behind. They didn't wait for her to catch up, they just expected her to be there. She liked that.

They crossed the road and moved into the night. Her boots hit the grass and for a moment she worried about their rear being exposed, but Ark and the others had that covered.

Just focus on getting this right, she thought.

All she could hear was her own breathing and the grass whipping across her legs. She looked down, surprised to find her legs moving in perfect rhythm with Damien and Jay. Maybe she could do this.

They reached the gas station and pulled up against the wall. Olesya took a moment to catch her breath but Ark wasn't waiting. He was already on the corner with Val, directing his squad to the town. They moved low and spread out.

A breeze ruffled through the grass as Ark strung them into an empty parking lot. Some of the Firebird recruits aiming their pistols high into windows as they passed them. Olesya had no environmental training with firearms, let alone for an urban scenario like this.

Firebird collected along the rear brick wall of a two-story shop. They were just around the corner from what looked like the center of an artificial town.

'If there's gonna be an ambush, it's on the main street.' Jay thumbed in the direction of the shop.

Ark was silent for a moment. 'If I was them,' he said, 'I'd mount the ambush at the very end of town. When we think we've won and our guard is down.'

'Maybe we can recon the street,' Damien said.

Xiu adjusted her mask. 'You won't know until you step out there and get shot.'

'Nope,' Jay said. 'Not doing that.'

Ark snapped his fingers and pointed at Olesya. 'You can scout it out.'

Olesya swallowed. 'You want me to go out there?'

'Not a good idea,' Xiu said. 'She doesn't have the training. It's a waste.'

'That's the thing, right?' Ark shrugged. 'She's a waste, so she's the perfect choice.'

Xiu stepped in front of him. 'I'm fast, I could run it. Maybe I can get you some useful information.'

Ark chewed his lip. 'Fine, you run it. If you see movement, call out their—'

'I'll do it,' Olesya said.

Everyone stared at her. They seemed surprised, except for Ark.

'Good.' He nodded his approval. 'We need people on both corners, ready to check the street while she's running. If there's any movement or shots fired I want their location called out, you got that?'

Firebird Squad nodded.

Ark turned to Olesya. 'Just run for the other side and find a place to hide. If you're not covered in electro-rounds by the time we cross, we'll come get you.' He glanced down at her pistol. 'Don't even think about shooting. Just run as fast as you can.'

Xiu winked at her. 'Good luck.'

Olesya was nervous, but she kept it to herself as she moved for the corner. Damien and Jay were behind her, ready to catch up and watch for movement. Jay tapped her on the back and gave an enthusiastic thumbs up. They were ready. She wasn't.

Don't think about it, she told herself. *Just run.*

With her pistol in one hand, Olesya sprinted across the main road, across the intersection. Her boots hit asphalt, echoed through the empty town. She reached the other sidewalk. She didn't stop. She kept going until she found an alley to duck into and press herself against a brick wall, hiding her profile. The brick pulled at strands of her hair. She leaned forward and listened. She heard more footsteps.

Firebird were crossing the main road.

Pistol in both hands, she risked a glance out of the alley. Xiu was running across the road, followed closely by Damien.

Then she saw it.

Something high, on a rooftop. Her heart rate doubled.

That's why I haven't been shot.

They were waiting for the entire squad to walk into their trap. They were waiting for *now*.

Olesya leaned farther around the corner and saw all of Firebird crossing the road. She had to do something.

'Rooftop!' Olesya yelled.

Firebird kept moving. Some recruits heard her and looked up. Others, like Xiu, sprinted as fast as they could to get clear. Olesya saw helmets and rifles in the windows, taking aim. Firebird Squad was about to fail.

The opposing force's soldiers opened fire.

Electro-rounds struck the recruits. They shuddered violently, their vests carrying the current, then they crumpled to the asphalt, gasping.

Olesya extended her pistol with both hands, just as Xiu taught her. She tried to sight a soldier as his helmet rose from a window frame. She fired. Twice. Her electro-rounds struck under the window, off to the right.

Then she remembered something else Xiu had taught her. She adjusted her grip, relaxed her shooting hand. Sighted the soldier's helmet again. Shot three rounds. One after the other. No torque. One of them struck his helmet, jolting him and disabling his weapon. She couldn't believe she'd hit him at this distance.

But there were more soldiers shooting at Firebird. Olesya turned the corner, pistol aimed. Ark was running toward her, his big eyes wide with panic. Electro-rounds ricocheted around him. A soldier moved from the corner behind him and took aim.

Olesya didn't think. She punched out—both arms extended—her pistol aimed just over Ark's shoulder. She ignored the horror on his face and sighted the soldier's chest. Two to the chest, followed by two more. The soldier jolted, raised his arms. Her first pair of electro-rounds struck the soldier's chest. Target down.

Ark stumbled. Her second pair of electro-rounds struck his shoulder. He collapsed on the sidewalk and shuddered like Jell-O. Olesya turned and saw a soldier on the street behind her. He was moving, taking aim at her and—

He slipped to the asphalt, writhing.

'Go!' Xiu yelled. 'Don't stop! Never stop moving!'

She was running down the street. Olesya noticed the two blinking beacons at the end.

The finish line.

It was almost within reach. Olesya broke into a run, parallel with Xiu. A soldier appeared from a window above Xiu, aiming down at her. Olesya fired as she ran. She got him. Kept moving. Another soldier appeared. She didn't think, just kept moving, kept shooting. Xiu fired across the street and he dropped, convulsing.

She hit the beacons. Xiu was with her all the way. They made it through. She couldn't believe it. Firebird passed the exercise.

She turned to see the rest of the squad. They were lying on concrete, out of action. A whistle blew and soldiers walked out to check their vitals. Olesya and Xiu were the only survivors.

'Are you OK?' Xiu asked.

'I just had a thirty-minute long heart attack,' Olesya said, 'but yeah, I'm OK.'

Xiu grinned. 'Remind me to teach you how to reload.'

Olesya looked down to see the slide on her blue pistol locked to the rear. Her chamber and magazine were empty and—during the chaos of their gauntlet run—she hadn't even noticed.

Xiu guided Olesya's pistol into her holster. Her hand felt electric on Olesya's skin.

'Thanks,' Olesya said.

Xiu smiled. 'Maybe you are cut out for this sort of thing.'

TODAY

DAMIEN

CHAPTER SIX

Tecun Uman, Guatemala

'RELAX,' White said. 'The knife's only to cut your restraints. They get a little excited with high profile resistance members.'

'Resistance?' Damien surveyed the three border control officers. 'I'm not with any resistance.'

The other two officers, Price and Gray, exchanged glances.

'No?' White arched an eyebrow. 'No plans to overthrow your government?'

Damien swallowed. 'I'm here for the coffee.'

White folded his arms. 'I prefer Starbucks.'

'And I preferred that bus,' Damien said. 'The one you're supposed to put me on.'

'We're not putting anyone on that bus.' He approached

Damien and leaned in to whisper. 'We're changing things. You should be honored, the change starts with you.'

'So I'm a terrorist now?' Damien asked.

'No,' White said. 'You're worse.'

Standing off to the side, Price sliced his own forearm. Damien watched blood well across the laceration on his arm.

'Let me guess,' Damien said, 'I attacked you with a knife.'

'And we responded appropriately.' White removed the radio from his belt, ready to make the call.

Price took a knee beside Damien and tugged on a cable tie around Damien's duct-taped wrist. Gray stood nearby but she didn't assist, her hand resting on her belt. Damien gripped both plastic armrests and tried to pull free, but it was no use.

'Is this what you call responding appropriately?' Damien asked.

Price and Gray ignored him. White stepped back and placed his radio on the table. Price slipped the knife blade under Damien's cable tie. Under Damien's fingertips, the plastic armrests felt soft and hot.

White smiled. 'Tell me, what would you call responding appropriately?'

His gaze shifted to the wisps of smoke coming from Damien's hands. Damien's wrists were still fastened to the armrests, but Price dropped his knife and cursed.

'This,' Damien said.

He pried the gooey armrests from the chair. White went for his pistol. Molten plastic splattered his face and he screamed.

Above White's head, a globule of liquefied plastic hit the sprinkler, melting the glass bulb underneath. The sprinkler blasted water into everyone's faces. Damien flicked his armrest, hoping to spray molten plastic in Price's face. Both armrests fused rapidly, becoming jagged batons in his seared hands.

Well, that didn't work.

Price and Gray spat water and reached for their projectile stun guns. The guns were black and shaped like spiked cow bells.

Damien slapped a jagged armrest down on Price's arms. The gun dropped to the wet linoleum floor. Damien bent his other elbow and knocked Gray's aim off. She fired her gun. Two electrode darts missed Damien's nose by an inch and struck Price.

Damien stood between them. Through the downpour, White drew his Heckler & Koch pistol. But Gray's arms were in the way, still sending an electric current through to her partner. By the time Gray had realized what she'd done, it was too late. Damien whipped the armrest over her arms and sliced across her neck. Simultaneously, he rammed the other armrest into the back of her leg. Gray shrieked until her voice cracked.

White sidestepped, searching for a clear shot. Damien kicked Gray in the hip, sent her crashing into White. Damien's sneaker, missing its shoelaces, went flying.

Price, with conductive wires dangling from a bleeding cheek, regained control. He lunged for Damien, his wet knife gleaming. Damien retreated quickly. The knife cut air. Damien moved closer. The knife cut below his ribcage. He stepped around it, used an armrest to guide the knife and sent Price stumbling forward. Damien pushed him into White. Damien's other sneaker loosened and he almost tripped. White circled around Price and aimed.

Damien discarded both armrests and charged behind Price. He snatched a dangling conductive wire from the stun gun and looped it over Price's neck, then slammed him into White, pinning them both to the desk. They struggled for oxygen. White dropped his pistol and Damien saw it skitter across the water-slicked table.

White clawed for his firearm. Damien pushed harder. White's fingers knocked it farther across the table, past the radio and tablet. It wobbled near the edge, just out of reach. White gave up on his firearm and shoved Price back into Damien.

Damien slipped, lost his other sneaker completely. He moved around Price, his wet socks sliding on the linoleum. Blood and water stung his eyes. He blinked to clear his vision and saw Price slump to the floor. White rolled over the table to rescue his pistol. He faced Damien and exhaled sharply, unclogging his nose. Between them, his radio and tablet on the table.

Damien and White—soaked from sprinkler water and diluted blood—watched each other. He knew White might try to shoot him at close range. Or he might call for assistance. But he couldn't do both. Not before Damien got to him.

White dived for the radio.

Damien slid feet-first under the table. White yelled into the radio. He was mid-sentence when Damien kicked his ankles out from under him. There was a hollow clonk as White's head struck the table. Damien got to his feet behind White and saw the radio bounce across the floor.

He closed on White, squinting through sprinkler water. White grasped his pistol and turned to strike. Damien ducked and grabbed the tablet. It was slippery in his grasp. He slammed its edge down on White's wrist, then into his elbow, then across his neck. White's grip on the pistol loosened, but he didn't let go.

Damien knocked White's legs out from under him and slammed the tablet flat on his head, pinning his head to the table. He twisted the pistol and White's index finger broke inside the guard. From underneath the tablet, White roared in pain. Water spilled off the tablet and Damien pressed harder, hard enough so White couldn't even think of resisting. Just the right amount of pressure on his skull and White stopped wriggling.

Damien leaned over and spoke loud enough so White could hear over the sprinkler.

'Where does the bus go?' he asked.

White grunted and wheezed. 'You're wasting your time.'

Damien discarded the tablet. 'Who takes the people on that bus? Where do they go?'

White spluttered water, mixed with blood. 'I don't know!'

Damien pressed his bare hands into White's head.

'Thermogenic genes,' Damien said. 'I can fry your brain in seconds.'

'Get bent,' White whispered.

Damien could feel the twitches and muscular contractions along his arms, transferring hundreds of degrees of heat through his fingertips and searing White's face. His mouth was open and he gurgled something.

'Three days ago, someone on that bus route disappeared,' Damien said. 'His name was Jay.'

White caught his breath. 'His passport ... flagged like yours. But I didn't touch—'

'No shit. Where was he taken?'

White's skin turned purple and red. His gasps became ragged under Damien's burning fingertips. Damien looked over at the other officers. They were crumpled on the floor, soaked in water and blood.

It took White a few breaths to respond. 'Facility.'

Damien pressed down on White's skull.

White dribbled blood. 'Colombia.'

'Where in Colombia?'

White's body convulsed. There was a clear red imprint of Damien's fingers on his face that looked like sunburn. Damien removed his hand, peeling a layer of pink skin from White's neck. There was something small and dark with a hard corner. Damien peered closer. It looked like some sort of tracking chip.

CHAPTER SEVEN

DRESSED in White's wet border control uniform, Damien stepped through the evacuating personnel in the corridor and entered the evidence room. He had to admit it felt good to be armed again, even if he was soaked. He carried a stun gun, an unconcealed pistol—standard issue Heckler & Koch P2000—and a strong urge to get out of here as soon as possible.

The evidence room was vacant, but the evidence bag containing his phone and earbuds was still on the table. He fished out the phone, keyed in his passcode, and dialed.

The first thing he heard was Nasira, swearing. Judging by the background noise, she was driving too.

'Good to hear your voice,' Damien said.

She sighed. 'I take it you're not on the bus I'm following right now.'

'No, but I dropped my tracking device before they

yanked me off the bus,' Damien said. 'Which I guess is why you think I'm still on the bus. That's a good thing, right?'

'You're in the middle of the goddamn border control station, ain't you?' Nasira said.

'I wouldn't say the *middle* of the station,' Damien said. 'Maybe the south-west corner.'

Nasira sighed again. 'Well, shit.'

He heard her make a fast turn, wheels screeching.

'I might need your help.' Damien said. 'Getting out of here could be tricky.'

'Understatement of the century,' she said. 'Can you get to the south entrance? Near vehicle inspection?'

'I'll try.'

'You better do more than try, I'm already rescuing one stupid son of a bitch,' she said. 'Ain't gonna make that two.'

'I'm keeping you on the line,' Damien said.

'So I can hear your ass get shot?' Nasira said. 'Yeah, I look forward to it.'

He took his earbuds from the evidence bag and popped one in each ear, then threaded the cable under his wet shirt. It was already beginning to dry. The upside to having thermogenic genes—otherwise dormant in most humans—was the high body core temperature. Most viruses burned out before they could make him sick, and he rarely felt cold. Plus, he could quick-dry a uniform in less than a minute. Damien slipped the phone into his hip pocket and checked the corridor before stepping out. It was mostly clear. He passed the other interview rooms and holstered his pistol. He matched a passing officer's stride and received a strange glance. His uniform was mostly dry, but his hair was still wet.

He made it to the south entrance as quickly as possible. Through the front vestibule, he could see a row of patrol cars parked out front. He could steal one and drive it out of the station to Nasira. Or he could if heavily armed officers weren't walking through the vestibule in jungle camouflage.

'This could be tricky,' Damien said.

'Almost there,' Nasira said through gritted teeth. 'Keep 'em busy.'

Four officers: two with long-nosed M4 carbines, one with an angular UMP submachine gun and another with a sleek black Remington shotgun. White's backup had arrived, and they were already raising their weapons. The only advantage Damien had was that he was still hugging the wall on the side and they were focused ahead. These officers weren't like White, they were special-operations trained and wouldn't be as easily subdued.

Damien reached for a fire extinguisher on the wall beside him and pulled the pin. The nearest officer turned and saw him. Damien squeezed the fire extinguisher's handle and doused him in a thick cloud that obscured all four officers. It effectively blinded them, but wouldn't last long. Damien lifted the fire extinguisher from the wall and moved into the cloud, swinging it like a club. The extinguisher caught the shotgun officer in the stomach and cracked his ribs. The shotgun dropped to the floor and Damien kicked it away. A carbine-wielding officer slipped on it. Damien closed on that officer and slammed the extinguisher down onto the carbine, then sprayed carbon dioxide into his face, coating his goggles and freezing his lips. He dropped.

Two down, two to go.

The cloud dispersed quickly. The officer wielding the UMP retreated for a better shot. Damien hurled the empty extinguisher at the UMP officer. It struck him, but not heavily enough to knock him over.

Damien closed on the other carbine officer and grasped the rail of his weapon. He lifted the stock up, catching the officer in the chin. Using the carbine's sling, Damien pulled him forward by his neck, right into Damien's knee. The officer stumbled and rolled across the linoleum floor.

That left the UMP officer. He was out of reach, somewhere in the fading cloud of carbon dioxide. Damien had nothing but a holstered pistol and stun gun. That lingering officer poked his barrel through the cloud. Damien drew his stun gun and fired. The electrode darts hit the officer and punctured both sides of his nose. He collapsed, writhing and jittering.

The UMP officer was standing nearby so Damien moved quickly around him. The conductive wires wrapped around the officer's legs and sent him tumbling onto his face. Damien discarded the stun gun and reached for the—

'Don't move!'

At the edge of his vision, Damien noticed a new group of special forces officers training their weapons on him. He had nowhere to run and nothing to use. The UMP submachine gun lay promisingly close but still too far.

Following their orders, Damien raised his arms high in

the air and lowered himself to his knees. The officers moved behind him in a loose semi-circle. One officer moved closer, but not close enough to endanger himself.

'On the ground!' he shouted.

Damien did as instructed.

An explosion detonated behind them. Damien felt a wave of heat roll over him as the standing officers were knocked from their feet. Glass blasted inward from the vestibule, lacerating the officers, and sending the officer issuing instructions right into Damien. They collided and tumbled together across the floor. The officer came to rest half lying on top of him, but the UMP was almost in reach. Now was his chance.

Damien wriggled out from under the dazed officer and collected the UMP, then quickly crawled behind a transaction booth. Rounds cracked on the glass, but the glass didn't break. Damien crouched, noticing the tiny speaking hole in the center.

That will do nicely, he thought.

He checked the long magazine that protruded from under the UMP—it was still full. Safety off, cocked, round in the chamber.

He jumped to his feet and poked the stubby barrel through the hole, then peppered the officers with rounds. Three dropped. A fourth was quick enough to circle around the bullet-resistant glass and take aim at his side. Damien withdrew his UMP from the glass hole, or tried to. A protruding lip under the barrel kept it stuck in place.

The vestibule door exploded behind the officer, kicking out another spray of glass. A border control 4x4 crashed through the processing center as the officer rolled

NATHAN M FARRUGIA

to one side, just clear of the impact. Still holding the trapped UMP with his left hand, Damien drew the subcompact pistol with his right and stared down its three-dot sights. He squeezed the heavy trigger and fired his last four rounds into the officer. Then he jiggled the UMP, pried it from the glass, holstered his pistol and aimed the submachine gun.

Behind the wheel of the 4x4, he could see Nasira, eyes narrowed with concentration. Her copper skin was shiny with sweat and her dark coiled hair was pulled back in a ponytail. She held the steering wheel with one hand and changed gears with her pistol hand.

'Get your goddamn ass moving!' she yelled, taking aim at an officer.

Damien saw the officers sprinting into the processing center. He ran from the booth, firing on the move, and jumped into the passenger's seat. Nasira was already in reverse, grazing nearby parked vehicles. She blasted her way through the parking lot.

The officers appeared in front of them. Damien aimed and fired, punching holes through the windshield. He saw another vehicle just before it rammed into the 4x4's side. The door crumpled but held.

Nasira pulled hard on the wheel, moving with the impact and spinning their vehicle around. She rammed the stick to second, peeled from the intercepting vehicle and accelerated for a set of reinforced steel gates. They were open, but that was changing now that someone was closing them. Nasira changed gears and pushed the 4x4 harder.

'Watch this,' she said.

He double-checked his seatbelt. 'I'd rather not.'

Nasira's foot was to the floor and even if he wrestled the wheel from her, she wasn't about to slow down. The gates were already half closed. They were committed.

In the side mirror, Damien saw two 4x4s hurtling from the parking lot and accelerating toward them. He dumped his UMP in the footwell and pinned it with his shoe.

Nasira aimed for the gap between the closing gates and punched through. The side mirror popped off and the gates scraped the doors, ripping their rear bumper off. But they made it. Damien looked behind and saw the pursuing vehicles pull up short.

'Holy crap,' Damien said.

He patted himself down, checking for wounds. As Nasira steered the 4x4 into a bus depot, weaving around buses, he looked over at her and was relieved to see she wasn't bleeding. She whipped the 4x4 onto the southbound and floored it again.

'Have to say it, we are kicking ass,' Nasira said. 'Or we might be once we catch up to the bus again.' She shot him a sidelong glance. 'You good?'

Damien saluted her. 'Border control officer, at your service.'

'Fucked up border control officer,' she said. 'Bleeding all over my upholstery.'

He looked down at his blood-stained seat. 'It's not your upholstery.'

Nasira focused on the road ahead. 'Doesn't matter.'

He loaded a new mag into his pistol and flipped the mirror under his sun visor. His face was covered in blood.

Once he saw it, the pain kicked in. He stung all over from shattered glass.

At least Nasira didn't look injured. There was no blood or lacerations across her face or limbs. Only sweat. He saw the muscles shift in her arms as she weaved between traffic.

Damien had to admit, he felt slightly embarrassed that he needed to be extracted like this. All it took was one minor complication for everything to go to hell. Those nutjob officers with white armbands had derailed everything. He wanted to explain to Nasira but he knew that would make it worse. He kept things simple, the way she liked it.

'Thanks for getting me out,' he said.

'You got the tracker on the bus, that's all that matters,' Nasira said. 'Now we just follow it and find Jay.'

'I should've been on the bus.' Damien shook his head. 'That was the plan, right? So you could track wherever they take me.'

'Plans change.' Nasira looked over at him. 'The important thing is you found who took Jay.'

'I didn't find who took Jay,' he said.

Her grip on the steering wheel tightened. 'Bullshit.'

'If I knew, I'd tell you,' he said.

'My money's on the covert multinational agency who trained and programmed us.'

'It's not the Fifth Column,' Damien said. 'Someone else took Jay.'

Nasira refused to look at him now. 'That's not helping. You're supposed to help. That's the whole freaking point.'

Damien clenched his fists. 'I am helping.'

His hands felt like they were on fire, which told him his adrenaline—or epinephrine—was rapidly wearing off. He opened his fists and noticed the top layer of his palms were seared red.

Nasira nodded to her rucksack in the back seat. 'Bandages. And there's some—'

Damien already had her rucksack, a slim black military-grade backpack, in one hand.

'—morphine,' she said.

He injected half a dose into one palm, then tried to focus through the pain. It would take a few minutes for the drug to cut off his pain receptors. He injected his other palm, then dropped the rucksack between his feet.

'Don't take too much,' Nasira said, watching the road. 'I don't need you crashing on me.'

'We can swap injuries if you want.' Both of his hands trembled and he had trouble pushing the last of the morphine into the muscle.

'I'm good,' she said. 'You … take what you need.'

He capped the needle and tried to put it back in her medical pouch, but it fell loose into her rucksack.

'What about your fancy regeneration genes?' Nasira asked. 'That chameleon thing'll heal you up soon, right?'

'Salamander,' he whispered. 'Takes a while.'

It was a nice little upgrade and he was glad to have it. He rested his hands on his knees, palms facing up, and focused on the road ahead.

Nasira moved swiftly around traffic. 'We need new wheels. You up for that?'

Damien looked between his legs at the open rucksack. 'I'm up for not being killed or captured.'

'I'm taking that as a yes,' she said. 'I got what we need in that rucksack, including a passport that won't get you caught.'

Damien looked up and realized they were in a small town already. Nasira pulled into a side street and got them away from traffic. She stopped behind an old pickup and cut the engine. Damien moved his hand carefully through the rucksack's strap, shrugging it onto his shoulder without touching his raw hand on anything. Half the missing skin from his palm was likely still attached to his pistol grip.

Before she stepped out, Nasira took a set of jiggler keys from the rucksack. Through the gunfire-peppered windshield, he watched her move for the pickup. She examined the ring, flicking through and trying one key after another. The second key was a good enough match and the door opened. She jumped inside and a moment later the engine coughed.

Damien lifted himself into the driver's seat of the 4x4 and drove it ahead, taking the first left. He parked it there and waited for Nasira to catch up. Once she did, he grabbed the UMP and jumped in beside her.

'Thanks,' Nasira said.

'You don't need to thank me,' Damien said.

He looked down and realized his hands had stopped shaking. The pain was still there, dulled by opioids. The cuts on his face itched as they slowly healed, but he suppressed the urge to scratch them.

'I mean it,' Nasira said. 'I really didn't know who else to ask.'

'There is no one else to ask,' he said. 'Not on this side of the world anyway.'

'Yeah.' She actually agreed with him.

Damien felt suddenly tired. He leaned back in his seat with his palms still open.

'This bus,' she said. 'They load people on there with flagged passports, just like Jay?'

He nodded. 'Yeah. There should be two other people on the bus right now. Whoever abducted Jay is taking these people somewhere. We just need to keep on the bus trail and follow whoever picks them up.'

'So why did they kick you off the bus?' she asked.

Damien looked down at his own uniform. 'These border control guys were different. They had white armbands. I think they called the Fifth Column on me, then they decided it was better to kill me.'

'That makes no sense.' Nasira looked at him, her eyebrows pressed together. 'Is that the morphine talking?'

'I wish,' Damien said. 'But they weren't the ones who took Jay.'

'There some kind of auction price on him now?'

'Rogue operatives with activated pseudogenes.' Damien shrugged. His body ached. 'Maybe we're in high demand.'

Nasira was watching the road ahead. They couldn't see the bus, but the GPS tracker he'd stowed onboard was transmitting loud and clear from just over the hill. The tracker was heading for the northeast coast of Guatemala, pushing GPS data at five-second intervals over a cellular network. It was only the size of a micro USB stick, small enough for him to wedge into a seat where no one would notice. He'd managed to shove it in before border control climbed aboard and pulled him off the bus. The tracker carried its own Nano SIM and a tiny battery that could keep it alive for four days. He hoped it wouldn't come to that.

Nasira rubbed her eyes. 'Don't matter who's waiting for us at the end of the bus trip, whether it's Fifth Column or some human trafficking ring or a boy band reunion.' She sighed. 'As long as there's someone who can lead us back to Jay. Else we got shit.'

'Jay was on a bus just like this one, I know that much,' Damien said. 'We stay on this bus like glue and we find him.'

Nasira blinked. 'He better be alive.'

TEN YEARS AGO

OLESYA

CHAPTER EIGHT

Location: Classified

'YOU'RE lucky you made it across,' Ark said.

Olesya turned from her bunk bed to see Ark standing in the doorway of their quarters. It was just the two of them. Ark's bed looked unkempt today. No hospital corners.

'The only reason you're here is to test my squad.' Ark pointed to himself. 'They want to see how I handle an untrained civilian.'

'That's what I've been saying,' Olesya said.

'No.' Ark stepped into the quarters. 'You don't get it. In the real world, when they send me to get a hostage or something...'

Olesya nodded. 'I'm the curveball.'

Ark raised his hand. 'Let me explain. You're the challenge. My squad almost failed today because of you. *That* was the real test. Not to train you. They don't care about training you. They want to see if we can still make it through with you slowing us down.'

Olesya felt her cheeks flush. 'I put myself on the line so *your* squad could make the right decision.'

'And you couldn't even do that right,' he said.

'You're blaming the ambush on me?' Olesya asked.

'You shot me.'

'I didn't mean—'

'I told you not to shoot,' Ark said.

'I shot the soldier,' Olesya said. 'You got in the way.'

'No, you got in the way,' he said. 'This is why you do everything I tell you. And why you don't shoot at all. Can you get that through your thick skull?'

Olesya nodded.

'Our final qualification is tomorrow and you'll get through with us. I will make sure of it. And once we qualify, you'll be out of here so fast you won't know what hit you. Or maybe you will.' He walked for the door.

'Is that your plan?' she asked.

Ark paused in the doorway. 'Xiu sees something in you. If she's wrong, then you're dragging us down.'

'And if she's right?'

He turned to face her. 'Then you're dragging *me* down. And I won't let that happen.'

'My father never hit me,' Olesya said. 'I told you that to make you feel better.'

'I don't need you to make me feel better.'

'The path of least resistance,' she said. 'I can choose the easy way out. I can adapt to the way you do things and shut my mouth. It's better than making waves.'

He nodded. 'Now you finally get it.'

'If it goes on long enough, the resistance adds up,' Olesya said. 'It's not worth it anymore. But you don't realize that until it's too late. Sometimes, the path of *most* resistance is actually the least.'

His eyes narrowed. 'What are you trying to say?'

'The person who hit you.' She took one step toward him. 'They were taller.'

'No one hit me,' he said.

Olesya took another step. 'You flinch from above. And there's a slight twitch when I mention your father.'

Ark closed the gap between them. 'You say anything about my family again and you'll be the one flinching.' He wet his lips. 'Tomorrow, you're not firing a single round. I'm taking your magazine and I'm keeping it until it's over. You got that?'

Olesya stared through him. 'You're not taking my magazine. Because I'm not giving it to you.'

She waited for him to say his final words and then storm off, but there was something different in his eyes now. She'd miscalculated. He lunged forward and grabbed her arm, tight.

'You do what I say,' he said in a low growl.

'Disarming me is against the rules of engagement.' Olesya tried to pull free. 'You'll get us disqualified if you do that.'

His grip tightened. 'No! I'll get us qualified.'

'You're not thinking—'

Ark held both her upper arms and shook her. 'I'm the squad leader! You hear me?'

Olesya tilted her head back, focused on the ceiling to slow the dizziness. 'Stop shaking me!'

He banged her head against the bunk. 'Then. Stop. Resisting!'

Olesya fought through the pain. She slammed her forehead into his nose. The cartilage crunched under the impact, dispersing across her forehead. Ark fell backward and landed on the linoleum floor, blood coating his face.

'What ... what?'

'The path of most resistance,' Olesya said.

CHAPTER NINE

DENTON PAUSED THE CAMERA FEEDS. Two recruits—teenage girls—ran through the street, firing blue pistols. He checked their records. Their names were Xiu and Olesya. He leaned back in his chair. It creaked, making Dr Cecilia McLoughlin wince. He secretly enjoyed it.

McLoughlin was motionless, a folder under her arm. She studied him like she would study the Project GATE recruits. McLoughlin was different from most of the staff at Project GATE. While she was easily bothered, she lacked the psychological imperfections of most people, and that granted her clarity and focus. She carried only the necessary emotions.

Denton recognized this in her. Just as she recognized it in him.

'I assume you have something to show me,' Denton said.

McLoughlin placed the folder before him. There were

only a few pages inside, paper-clipped. He didn't pick it up, just leaned forward and read the title.

'Ah yes, the Human Genome Project,' he said. 'An ideal cover story.'

One that had allowed him to build the Fifth Column's DNA database of the human race, entirely in secret. Thanks to the clandestine sample collection of the genome project, Denton had 1.4 billion records he could filter for particular genetic markers; 0.4 percent of those records carried the markers he was looking for, and those underwent further DNA testing to determine those who possessed rare abilities.

Denton oversaw the testing of 7,000 candidates for Project GATE, children from countries around the world and often from impoverished families. Less than 1,000 of those children passed the tests and were admitted into Project GATE under the guise of a lucrative scholarship. Denton expected that over the coming years no less than 80 percent would fail their Special Forces and Intelligence training. The 200 or so who passed were the nucleus of Project GATE: to create the most formidable operatives the world has known. Remarkably trained and genetically enriched. And they would all be his.

All the more reason to have the world's best computer geneticists on his team. McLoughlin was *the* best, here to study the genes that made each recruit special, and learn how to switch them on in other recruits.

Denton opened the file. On the first page, he noticed a dark image of the human body, lit brilliantly with green fluorescence.

'You were successful?' he asked.

She took a step closer. 'You seem surprised that my zinc finger modules worked.'

'Impressed. That is different from surprise.' Denton ignored her stare. 'And you deliver these inside a virus: adeno-associated virus,' he read off her papers. 'Why this one?'

'Serotype eight. By far the most efficient vector,' she said. 'We inject it into the operative's bloodstream. We're talking systemic expression within twenty-four hours.'

Denton was impressed. McLoughlin had achieved the unachievable inside of two years.

He tapped the green fluorescent image with one finger. 'And it's permanent?'

'We can resurrect pseudogenes,' she said.

'Can we can take a recruit's ability—say, Damien's thermogenesis—and copy it to another recruit?'

'Yes, but we are limiting ourselves to existing mutations,' McLoughlin said. 'We can create our *own*. The genes are there, they just need the right kick. Sometimes, the right twist.'

Denton met her piercing gaze. 'Let's not get ahead of ourselves.'

'That's what I do,' she said evenly. 'That's why you hired me.'

Denton waited for her to blink. She didn't.

'Do you have something in mind?' he asked.

'I have multiple things in mind, I always do. But as you said yourself, let's not get ahead of ourselves.' She almost smiled. 'For our own safety, I recommend we implement some sort of control system in the recruits.'

'They will be programmed,' Denton said. 'We have the best programming.'

'I don't doubt that.' She paused, just for a moment. 'I was thinking control of a more genetic nature.'

Denton leaned back in his chair again, disappointed when it didn't creak. 'Go on.'

'I'm talking about encoding loyalty directly into their DNA,' she said. 'And one step closer.'

'Closer?'

'We encode a fail-safe.'

Denton raised an eyebrow. 'Define *fail-safe*.'

'We have to consider the scenario where an operative fails to comply. Or is turned by the enemy,' she said. 'They would become a formidable weapon in the wrong hands.'

Denton thought for a moment. 'You're proposing a kill switch.'

'Part of the package,' she said. 'A seemingly harmless protein that fuses with the pseudogene and lies dormant. Something we can trigger at a later time, if necessary, to terminate the operative. Final measures, of course.'

'I'll take it under consideration,' Denton said.

McLoughlin glanced over at the camera feeds. 'Olesya. She interests you.'

'She warrants my interest.'

'Are you certain?' McLoughlin said. 'She shot her own squad leader by accident.'

Denton allowed himself a smile, knowing it would irritate her. 'It wasn't an accident.'

Her eyebrows lifted a fraction. 'Olesya is not one of your precious candidates.'

'Yet we had a difficult time programming her. Just like my candidates.'

'Her DNA doesn't qualify,' McLoughlin said. 'If you insist, I can run a new analysis on her bloods for you, but then I'd have to push viral testing to next week.'

'No.' He paused a camera feed as Olesya ran through the beacons. 'Test the candidates we have. We need to know.'

He could feel her gaze weighing on him.

'What are you looking for?' she asked.

'Perfection.'

CHAPTER TEN

ARK DREW HIS PISTOL.

The forest was dark and cold, but this time there was no fog. His squad stood around him, still and patient. This was the final exercise. This time, he needed three recruits to pass the beacons in less than sixty minutes. Olesya was enough of a problem, but this was worse. He checked his watch. It was 0300. No night vision monoculars, no red filtered torches.

He wasn't going to be disqualified from the program.

He was going to lead his squad to victory.

A whistle sounded through the forest. He pointed out their bearing and Val took point with her natural night vision. He fell in step a distance behind her, the rest of his squad behind him in single file. Even with his squad, he felt alone.

They reached the road and he checked his watch again. Fourteen minutes. He lay down and shimmied to the tree line, keeping one eye closed to save his night vision.

'Holy crap,' Jay whispered from beside him. 'The town's lit up like a Christmas tree.'

He wasn't wrong. From the gas station to the center of town, street lamps burned hot, swarmed by frantic insects.

'What do we do?' Damien asked.

Ark held a hand over his eye. 'Wait, I need to think.'

While the rest of his squad waited for his master strategy, he tried to think of a master strategy. They were relying on him for that, he couldn't let them down. He felt his chest press harder against the grass with each breath. He licked his dry lips.

'Are we skirting around?' Damien asked. 'We need to keep out of the light.'

'What are we, vampires?' Jay said. He made a hissing sound.

Ark tucked his shaking hand under his chest. They could shoot through the middle, avoid as much light as possible. But they'd have to move through the grass, in the darker patches. And then they would need to cross the main street, but they had to do it at a safe distance from the intersection. He didn't know if that would work. What if they walked into an ambush? No, they needed to circumvent the town entirely.

'Is that Olesya?' Val asked.

'Where? What's she doing?' Damien whispered.

Val was watching the road ahead with her superior vision. Ark saw movement and couldn't believe it. Olesya was running across the long grass. By herself.

He swore. She was ruining everything.

'Olesya!' Xiu called out.

'Don't,' he said. 'She's on her own now.'

He hoped she would get picked off by the enemy. And if not, he could deal with her later. After what she'd done, he had good reason to shoot her.

'That doesn't look good,' Val said.

She was looking past the gas station, where headlamps bled through the night. A jeep with a searchlight on the back. Someone was washing the light over the grass. Ark returned his attention to where he'd last seen Olesya. She was gone.

'They're not the same soldiers,' Val whispered.

Ark inched himself closer to the edge of the forest. With his exposed eye he looked directly at the patrol. Val was right, they were wearing different vests.

'The driver is a soldier, but the ones on foot are our age,' Damien said.

'Helldiver,' Val said. 'Squad leader is Nasira.'

Ark's stomach churned. Nasira's squad was the only squad so far to *complete* Combat Training. They were no longer just recruits. Promoted to the rank of private first class, they were now in Special Operations Training. Which meant—

'We are so screwed,' Jay said. 'One time, Nasira stepped on my toe and didn't say sorry.'

'That's nice, Jay,' Xiu said. 'But her squad's objective is to hunt us down, not step on toes.'

Helldiver took a right turn at the road and started in Ark's direction. The searchlight swiveled to the trees. The large beam cut through the forest, turning night into day.

'Slowly withdraw,' Ark hissed. 'Now.'

OLESYA KEPT to the long grass and moved low. In the darkness, her vision was monochrome. Avoiding the blind spot in the center of her vision, she watched the edges for movement.

She made her way in a slow curve to the left. The main street continued out of town and passed before her. She rested on one knee.

On the other side of the road, an unnatural shape shifted in the long grass. Olesya looked through the edge of her vision and noticed somebody's elbow. She watched, listened to her breathing and the rustle of wind through leaves. She picked out the detail of bodies. Many, many soldiers in black, lying in wait.

Once she was sure they weren't looking in her direction, she carefully returned the way she'd come. She made a deliberate arc to the gas station they'd run for last time. She was almost there when a breeze tickled the grass. Something flashed ahead of her. She paused, ready to draw her pistol. A recruit.

'Olesya.'

It was Xiu. Olesya followed her to the wall of the gas station and then the rear of a shop on the main street.

Through Ark's mask, his nostrils flared. 'Are you *trying* to disqualify us?'

Olesya just glared at him. 'While you were hiding in the forest, I was scouting the opposing force.'

Ark drew his pistol and aimed at Olesya. He was ready to fire, but Val stepped in his path.

'Don't,' Val said.

'Why not?' Ark pushed her aside.

Val shoved his barrel into her own vest. 'If you want to shoot someone, go right ahead.'

'You too now?' Ark lowered his pistol slowly. 'Unbelievable.'

Val turned to Olesya. 'Helldiver is out there with those soldiers. They should be behind us, patrolling. Which means we're in the clear, right?'

Olesya hadn't expected Val to ask her a question. 'I don't think they're patrolling.'

'You can think what you like,' Ark said. 'We need to make it to the beacons or we're disqualified.'

'No way I'm getting disqualified,' Jay said. 'We'll get through this.'

Damien returned from a quick peek around the corner. 'Um, so this time they've blocked off the street.'

'We're screwed!' Jay said. 'We can't get through this.'

'There's no way they've blocked it off,' Ark said.

Olesya ignored Ark's drawn pistol and walked over to have a look for herself. The intersection she'd run across last time was completely blocked. Burned out cars were pushed into a cluster. Behind the cars she could see a high wall made of concrete blocks. The instructors must have shifted things around before the qualification started.

Ark shoved Olesya aside to have a look, then turned back to his squad. 'OK, I've got it.'

'Really?' Jay said. 'What do we do?'

'We detour.' Ark pointed back to the gas station. 'We

can't go around from here, we have to pull out and circle the town.'

'I wouldn't do that,' Olesya said. 'I was just on the left side and they're waiting in the grass.'

'How many?' Damien asked.

Olesya thought for a moment. 'I don't know exactly, but there's at least five to six of them. Could be double that.'

Ark paced around them. 'It's a trick. They want to funnel us in here and push us over that wall. If we fall for that, we deserve to be disqualified.'

'But I saw them waiting for us outside the town,' Olesya said.

'On the left wing?' Ark said. 'Fine. So we go on the right wing.'

Xiu shook her head. 'If they're on one wing, they'll be on both.'

'Then they'll be weaker. Just half force,' Ark said. 'Not counting the large numbers they'll have covering this wall. I say we ambush the small team on the right wing and push through. Fast, aggressive.'

Val raised her hand. 'How about I scout the right side, see how many are waiting? We pick the weakest side.'

'No,' Ark said. 'We have a time limit on this. We need to choose a side and commit, or we miss out completely. We need three of us to make it through and it's a pass.'

'They *want* you to choose a side!' Olesya said. 'There's a wall here, which means they need less soldiers here.'

Ark jabbed a finger at her. 'Are you suggesting we scale the wall and risk what will definitely be an ambush?'

'I don't know, I'm just saying—'

'Olesya,' Xiu said, 'now's the time to take your shot.'

'Fine.' Olesya swallowed. 'Over the wall.'

Ark blinked. Everyone was looking at Olesya now.

'You for real?' Jay said.

'They'll have some soldiers at the beacons, but that's it,' Olesya said. 'The rest are waiting on the left and right wings. That's where I'd put my strength.'

Ark looked less than impressed. 'Yeah, well that says it all, doesn't it?'

Olesya heard the jeep in the distance. Helldiver was coming back for another sweep.

'They'll have a couple of soldiers covering the wall,' Xiu said. 'But if we get to higher ground we could deal with them.'

'Scale the wall, if you want,' Ark said. 'I'm taking Firebird Squad down the road to the right. If there are soldiers there, we take them out. We move around and that's it.'

Ark started for the intersection. Most of his squad followed.

Jay hesitated. 'You know what? Screw it. I'm scaling the wall.'

Ark growled softly to himself. The jeep's searchlight splashed over the gas station in the distance. They couldn't turn back now.

'Helldiver is coming,' Val said. 'Ark, whatever we do, we do it now.'

Damien nodded. 'I'm going over the wall.'

'I need you guys at the wing,' Ark said.

Damien and Jay didn't move.

'Fine.' Ark turned to Olesya. 'Good luck.'

He didn't sound sarcastic this time, which caught her off-guard. 'You too,' she said.

Ark didn't linger. With Helldiver approaching, he moved with the rest of his squad, Val included.

Xiu was looking at Olesya. 'I said take a shot, not a gamble.'

Jay frowned. 'Can you get to the roof? I don't want a sniper shooting me when I go over.' He nodded to Damien. 'We'll clear the street.'

'On me,' Xiu said. 'Olesya, let's go.'

Olesya gripped her pistol in both hands and followed Xiu around the wall, to the intersection. The street lamps lit the pavement, Olesya avoided looking directly at them. Xiu slipped inside a building. Olesya followed her to the staircase.

She kept her shoulder against Xiu's back. When they moved apart, she kept her hand on Xiu's shoulder. Together they climbed the second flight of stairs, pistols aiming in tandem. There was no time to check the entire floor. They kept moving.

Once they reached the third level, Xiu moved into a corner room that smelt of mold and spotted two windows that gave enough light. There was no one in here. Xiu crouched under a window. Olesya left the door ajar and took a position under the window next to her.

Xiu was silent, her head tilting as she looked out the window and searched the other buildings. Olesya took the other window and checked the rest of the rooftops, looking for movement and silhouettes. Between them they had the intersection covered.

Then she heard the jeep.

Xiu held a finger to her lips.

Olesya nodded. On the street below, Damien and Jay darted into a shopfront. A searchlight washed over the shopfront. The jeep was closer now. Helldiver was heading right into the center of town.

Xiu gestured for Olesya to get down. She ducked under the window. The jeep turned the corner, accompanied by Helldiver on foot.

It seemed like an eternity before the jeep and Helldiver Squad moved again. When Olesya looked again, Damien and Jay were doing the same. And she saw something else. Two soldiers in the windows above them, pistols ready. But Olesya couldn't shout to warn the boys, Helldiver might hear.

'There's two,' Olesya whispered. 'One in each window.'

Xiu took aim. Olesya didn't hesitate. She lined up her front and rear sight, inhaled partly, and fired. One round, then another. Xiu did the same with the other soldier, then gave a thumbs up to the boys.

They ran for the wall. Jay threw himself onto the roof of a burned-out car. Damien followed. The cars were against the wall, giving them some extra height. Jay holstered and ran up the concrete while Damien kept his pistol out to cover them.

Jay managed two quick steps then gravity kicked in, but not before he gripped the top of the wall with both hands. Jay stuck his butt in the air. As silly as it looked, Olesya knew that was their technique to climb a wall. He would drive one leg up the wall, using the momentum to launch him high enough so he could throw his forearms over the top. He hoisted himself over the wall and a moment later reached down to offer Damien a hand.

Olesya kept her focus, scouring the windows and rooftops for more soldiers.

'Anything?' Xiu whispered.

'Not yet,' Olesya said.

'You were right,' Xiu said. 'They put most of their forces out on the wings. Then they have the patrol come in to flush us in either direction.'

'But why not one direction?' Olesya asked. 'They could concentrate their forces if they blocked one side off.'

Xiu nodded. 'Sure, but we'd get suspicious and back out. That's why they give us two choices—'

'The illusion of choice,' Olesya said.

'Exactly. And Ark fell for it.'

Olesya watched Damien climb over the wall and disappear from view.

'You think they'll cover us?' Olesya asked.

'They can't until we're over the wall,' Xiu said. 'We have to make it there first.'

Xiu moved for the door and nudged it open with her foot. Olesya covered her as they took the stairs down. Olesya's vision had improved, but she still kept her hand on Xiu's back.

They stepped out onto the sidewalk and faced opposite directions. The street was deserted. A moth flew past her pistol, drawn to the street lamp.

Xiu moved for the wall. Olesya followed, scanning every window and corner she could find. Xiu was on the car, her hand out. Olesya took it and stepped onto the roof with her.

Gunfire echoed in the distance. It came from the right wing.

Xiu's hand tightened over hers. 'That's our squad,' Xiu said. 'With Helldiver right behind them.'

'Should we go help?' Olesya asked.

'No, we need three past those beacons. That's the objective,' Xiu said. 'You go, I'll cover you.'

Olesya hesitated. 'What about you?'

'I'll see you on the other side.'

Olesya holstered her pistol and jumped onto the wall. Xiu boosted her up. She managed one foot but the next one slipped and she caught the top of the wall with the fingertips of her right hand. The concrete was rough, cutting the circulation to her fingers. Using what little energy she had left, she raised her left hand up and gripped the top of the wall. She looked below. Xiu was taking aim down the street.

'Go!' she said.

Olesya drove her knee high, bringing her boot up the wall. She used the thrust of her knee as momentum and threw her elbows over, hugged the top of the wall. On the other side of the wall, there were no cars, it was a sheer drop. She clung to the top, lungs burning, and peered back over at Xiu.

'I can help you up!' she called out. 'Quickly!'

'Keep going.' Xiu looked up at her. 'You're family now.'

A Helldiver stepped under a street light. Nasira.

Xiu started firing, but she was too late. Nasira fired first and Xiu caught the electro-round in her chest. She slumped off the car and rolled onto the road. Olesya watched her spasm.

'Xiu!' Olesya whispered.

Xiu's hand trembled, reached up to Olesya.

Nasira took aim.

Olesya dropped from the wall. She landed, grazing the skin on her hands. The beacons flashed ahead. Ark's team wouldn't have made it through. She was Firebird's third surviving member. She needed to make it. Her stomach coiled into knots. She had only a short distance. She sprinted, pistol in her holster, didn't look back.

She crossed the beacons, lungs burning.

Firebird Squad had qualified.

Damien and Jay were busy adjusting their holsters so she left them alone and sat on the grass near the beacons. She couldn't go back out there, so she waited for Xiu. No one climbed over the wall, but eventually Nasira approached from a nearby street. She gave Olesya a slight nod, then walked over to Jay and elbowed him softly.

'Nice one,' Nasira said.

Jay nodded quickly. 'Uh thanks. You too.'

She smiled and touched his arm, then walked ahead, handing her pistol to a pair of soldiers in black fatigues. The soldiers approached Jay and Damien and took their weapons too, then directed them after Nasira. The soldiers wanted them all moving. Olesya stood and brushed herself off. She checked the wall again but Xiu was nowhere to be seen. The soldiers pointed Olesya in a different direction.

'I'm not with them?' she asked.

'No, this van,' the soldier said. 'Your weapon, please.'

Olesya handed them her pistol. The soldier ejected the electro-round and the magazine. Olesya made her way to the van. A driver stood by the van and flicked the cigarette into the night air.

She lifted the rear door for Olesya. 'In the back, recruit.'

Olesya was too exhausted to say anything; she climbed inside and took a seat. It smelt of tobacco and pine air freshener. She hadn't wanted to leave Xiu behind like that.

The driver climbed in the front and closed her door.

'Is there anyone else coming?' Olesya asked.

Either the driver hadn't heard her or chose to ignore her. Was she in trouble? She hoped she wasn't being transferred to another squad. She didn't like Ark but she wanted to stay with Xiu.

The driver was talking on her radio. 'Have them wait. I'll come around.'

A soldier closed the van's rear door. The engine started and the van turned and drove past the beacons and soldiers. She didn't see the instructors anywhere. Maybe the qualification wasn't over yet.

The van stopped again. This time, when the rear door opened, Val climbed inside and sat opposite. She didn't say anything, but her hands were still shaking. Before the door closed, another recruit climbed inside.

Ark.

He sat next to Val and glanced over at Olesya. This time, he didn't look angry. He just looked tired. She felt much the same, her adrenaline ebbing away with every moment.

The rear door opened once more and more recruits filed in. These recruits wore purple vests. Olesya made room for four Helldivers. The door closed and the van was almost at full capacity. Street lamps flashed past as they left the perimeter and took the long road back to the training center.

Except this wasn't the right road.

Olesya looked around at the squad members' faces. Ark was the only one who seemed to notice their bearing was off. He caught her gaze. This qualification hadn't ended yet and he knew it.

The van suddenly accelerated. Olesya stopped herself from falling onto the Helldiver next to her.

'Listen up, kids.' The driver switched her headlamps off and reached for her helmet. 'This is no longer your qualification. We're undergoing some restructuring. Which is a nice way of saying we're about to start fighting each other.'

'Helldiver Squad?' one of the Helldivers asked.

'Your squads don't matter anymore, you're in this together,' the driver said. 'I'm talking about the entire Fifth Column.'

Olesya had no idea what she was talking about.

The driver put her helmet on and flipped the night vision monocular down over one eye. 'We'll explain everything to you once you're out.'

Olesya noticed headlamps in the distance. The driver took the van off the road, rushing to a stop, then watched through her monocular, waiting for the car to pass.

The driver looked over her shoulder at Olesya and the

other recruits. 'Effective now, Russia and China are out of Project GATE. That includes all of you.'

'What's Project GATE?' Olesya asked.

'The phony scholarship you're all in,' the driver said. 'They didn't even tell you the name? Jesus.'

'So we're disqualified?' Ark asked.

'The project doesn't matter anymore,' the driver said with a heavy sigh. 'You're out of—look, all you need to know right now is you have two options. Option one: sit tight in Project GATE and see what they do with you. Maybe they hold you hostage. Maybe they brainwash you. Maybe they make you disappear.'

Olesya's mouth went dry. 'You're kidnapping us?'

'Option two,' the driver said. 'We kidnap you. Take you back to your country of origin.'

Ark's hands trembled in the near-darkness. 'So we have to choose?'

'We already made that choice for you,' the driver said. 'But the door's right there, if you want to change that.'

The driver waited for them to open the door. No one did.

'Option two it is then.'

She drove the van to a narrow road that fed into a forest. Olesya could hear rapid breathing as the other recruits tried to process what was happening.

'This could get rough,' the driver said. 'Seatbelts are in the back. I suggest you use them.'

Olesya found a seatbelt in the darkness and buckled up. 'Are we the only ones? Are there more?'

'We have a few vans on the move,' the driver said.

'What about Xiu?' Olesya leaned forward, held in by

her seatbelt. 'She was in our squad but you didn't pick her up!'

The driver didn't take her eyes off the road. 'We're not picking up a Xiu.'

Val reached over and put a hand on Olesya's leg. 'She's Chinese-American, Olesya.'

Olesya felt her hand tremble. 'But she should be with us, right?'

'If she's American then this is where she belongs.' The driver risked a glance in her direction. The monocular gleamed at her. 'She's safer here. But you're not.'

Olesya felt her eyes well with tears. In the darkness, only Val would see.

Val squeezed her hand. 'I'm sorry.'

'She'll be OK,' Ark said. 'Whatever happens.'

Olesya imagined not seeing Xiu again and it hurt.

'You were right, you know,' Ark said. 'We all should've gone over the wall.'

The driver was right. The exercise didn't matter anymore.

'Your American accent is good,' Olesya said. 'I didn't know you were Russian.'

He shrugged. 'My name's Arkadiy.'

She forced a smile, even though he couldn't see it very well. 'I thought you were Polish.'

'I know it doesn't mean much now,' Ark said, 'but how many of us got over the wall?'

'Three,' Olesya said. 'Damien, Jay. Me.'

'You did good.' Ark's head hung low. 'I was too scared to notice.'

'You don't have to be,' Olesya said.

'I know.' He nodded. 'It's just us now.'

Light flooded the windows. Tires screeched. Something smashed into the side of the van. They spun wildly. Olesya held onto her seatbelt. The van rolled. Gravity pulled at her. Everyone clung to their seat-belts, bumping and colliding into each other. She shut her eyes. No one thought to scream or yell. They tumbled in silence.

TODAY

DAMIEN

CHAPTER ELEVEN

Guatemala

DAMIEN COULD BARELY SEE Nasira's face in the cold glow of the speedometer, but he knew the fire in her eyes had extinguished hours ago. It was past midnight and she was running on fumes. There were no street lamps on this lonely stretch of Guatemalan road and all Damien could see outside were distant mountains, flat ground, and occasional spots of jungle. Sometimes he wished he had Jay's pentachromatic vision rather than enhanced hearing.

'How are you holding up?' Damien asked, swallowing a metallic aftertaste.

'Your new passport's in the rucksack,' Nasira said.

'Right.' He reached down with bandaged hands, plucked the Greek passport from the open zipper and stuffed it in his pocket. 'You didn't answer my question.'

'I'm all right.' She winced. 'Could be better.'

Damien cleared his throat. 'Since when have you and Jay been—'

In the darkness, she glared at him.

'—on good terms?' he said. 'You used to hate him.'

Nasira resumed her focus on the road ahead. 'He grew on me. Unfortunately.'

'We'll find him,' Damien said. 'We'll get him back.'

'Don't need your words of reassurance.'

A passing car illuminated her face. He could see tears on her cheeks. She wiped them quickly.

'Just want the son of a bitch back,' she said.

'Wherever he is, whatever's happening to him, he knows you're out there looking for him. He knows you won't give up.'

She shook her head. 'He doesn't know that.'

'You're the reason he has hope.'

'He's the reason *I* have hope.' Nasira swallowed. 'I know you know who took him. Just spit it out.'

'Facility in Colombia,' he said. 'One of those border control officers told me. Right before I killed him.'

She didn't look at him. 'The Fifth Column are holding him there.'

'That's not logical,' Damien said. 'The Fifth Column only control Central America and the United States. They don't hold much ground in Colombia.'

Nasira stared ahead. 'That's rare these days.'

'If it was the Fifth Column, they'd take him back to the States. Like they were about to do with me.'

'Colombia's a nice out-of-the-way place to interrogate Jay,' Nasira said. 'Give him a lobotomy and throw him in the ocean, Bin Laden style. Or Bin Laden stunt double style, whatever.'

Damien hoped she was wrong. Rescuing Jay from some sort of shady underworld was one thing. Rescuing him from the Fifth Column was another entirely.

With one hand, Nasira shoved a cigarette in her mouth and lit it.

'Do you have to smoke?' he asked.

'Yep,' she said. 'You know, there's one thing he said to me that I'll never forget.'

'What's that?'

'He told me you were his brother.'

'He lost his brother when he was young,' Damien said.

Under the whisper of moonlight, he watched the jagged mountains on their left.

'No, I mean he said it for real. That's how he sees it.' Nasira sucked on her cigarette, then opened her window a crack. 'And it made me think. We're all family now. We're not programmed zombies running jobs for the Fifth Column anymore. We're on our own and we're all we've got.' She breathed sharply. 'I don't want to lose that.'

Damien watched her silhouette. 'That's probably the most emotional thing you've said in your life.'

She flicked ash out the window. 'If you tell anyone, I'll shoot you.'

Damien wound his window down a fraction and breathed in the night. 'You know, there is someone else who can help us.'

'Sophia?' Nasira laughed. 'She's on the other side of the planet right now. Doing something … more important. I'm not gonna drag her all the way down here just for this.'

'She'd do it in a heartbeat, you know,' he said. 'You said it yourself, we're all we have.'

'I don't want to be the one calling Sophia every time we screw up,' she said. 'We just got to find out who has Jay. Then we get him the hell out. We can tell her after.'

'And if we can't get him out?' he asked.

'Then all hands on deck.' Nasira closed as much distance as she could, but the bus still had an hour on them. They'd tracked it on a northeastern route to the coast, passing a large lake and forest. They needed more time to catch up, but Damien wasn't sure they had it.

'Puerto Barrios,' Damien said. 'That's where the bus is going.'

'Putting 'em on a ship to Colombia.' Nasira sounded uncertain. 'But where in Colombia?'

Damien checked her phone. 'I don't know, but we're not too far behind them now.'

Nasira was already accelerating. They needed to close the gap fast. If they missed their chance to see where in Colombia the two occupants on the bus were transferred, they'd miss their shot at Jay. And Damien wasn't too keen on going through another processing station again.

'Do you ever wonder what happened to all those Chinese and Russian recruits?' he asked.

'No,' she said. 'I already know what happened.'

'Thrown in prison?' he asked.

She snorted. 'The official story is bullshit and you know it. Fifth Column had them put down.'

'I don't believe that. The Fifth Column put a lot of

money into Project GATE. Millions into each of us. They wouldn't waste that unless they had to.'

Nasira shrugged. 'Maybe they used them for testing. Made sure the pseudogenes worked before they activated them in us.'

'What if we aren't the only ones who escaped?'

Nasira drew on her cigarette. 'The Fifth Column wouldn't allow them to exist.'

'They don't allow us to exist either,' he said.

'Yeah, and it shows.' She drove in silence a while longer.

Damien kept an eye out for the bus as Nasira played catch up, but even after an hour he still couldn't see a thing.

'I'm sorry,' he said.

'What the hell for?' Nasira discarded her cigarette out the window.

'I should still be on that bus. It was the one thing I had to do.'

'Damien.'

'Yeah?'

'Shut up. Not your fault. And we ain't got time to feel sorry for ourselves.'

He opened and closed his bandaged hands. The pain was dull. 'I know, I just … yeah. You're right.'

'I'm always right,' she said. 'Except for the part where Jay got captured.'

'Take your own advice. It's not your fault.'

Her fingers tightened over the steering wheel. 'It *is* my fault.'

'What are you talking about?' Damien asked.

'We had an argument and I told him to get out of my face. "Get out of my face" wasn't supposed to mean "Take your passport and get your ass kidnapped by the Fifth Column."'

'Some argument,' he said.

Nasira drove over a bridge, crossing the narrow gap in a lake. For the first time, he could see the bus in the darkness ahead. Its headlamps splashed two cones of light on the asphalt.

Damien checked her phone. They were only a fraction behind the tracker now.

'Just in time,' he said. 'We're at the port.'

Nasira slowed down, giving the bus a chance to enter the port.

'We need to watch the transfer,' she said.

'Assuming it's a vessel like you said,' Damien said. 'How are we going to tag it?'

'I have one more tracker.' She stopped the vehicle just outside the port and opened her door. 'And a waterproof Pelican case with magnets.'

Damien wasn't sure if she was joking. 'You're going underwater?'

'Don't got much choice,' Nasira said. 'Someone didn't stay on the bus like a good boy, did they?'

'Yeah, well someone got cavity searched.'

Nasira stifled a laugh as she got out of the car, then leaned in. 'That's totally worth the swim.'

TEN YEARS AGO

OLESYA

CHAPTER TWELVE

OLESYA WAS ALONE.

She was lying on a hospital bed, wearing pajamas that weren't hers. The room was bare and on the other side there was a closed door and a long window with dark glass she couldn't see through. There were no bunks, no Firebird Squad, no hospital corners. She climbed from her bed. She remembered being inside a van. And then nothing. The grazes on her hands from climbing the concrete wall—they were completely healed. She remembered Xiu's face.

How long had she been here? And where *was* here? Was she committed to some sort of mental asylum in Siberia? The room was heated through a fat, vertical pipe in the corner. She walked over to the door and reached for the handle. It turned freely. She wasn't locked inside.

The corridor was long. She walked down it, her feet

freezing on the tiled floor. There were more glass windows along the right-hand wall. The rooms beyond them were dark. She could hear noise at the end of the corridor, behind another door. Footsteps, talking, keyboard typing. She reached the end and stepped into an open space buzzing with people and activity. There were desks, monitors, a whole bunch of people standing and sitting, wearing jackets and hoods, carrying papers or pointing at screens. The area smelled of instant coffee and cigarette smoke. She looked from one face to another, recognizing none of them. And one by one, they looked back at her.

Something was very, very wrong. She had to get out. Next to her, an external door opened and someone stepped in with a gust of cold air. It smelled of the forest, but not of the night.

Olesya ran.

Past the figure. Barefoot, into the snow. She heard them calling her name. They knew her, but she didn't want them to. She kept running, down a hill. She plunged through snow, tripped and rolled. Recovering at the bottom, she got back to her feet and kept going.

But Firebird Squad wasn't out here. It was just white.

Smeared across her face, the snow numbed everything. She could see the forest ahead. Fog lifted from the treetops. She stopped. Her memories came back, falling inside her like icicles.

Firebird drawing their Glock 19s.

Xiu leaning over her breakfast tray and raising an eyebrow.

Gripping her pistol at the range, her palms sweating.

Clinging to the concrete wall, pushing air from her lungs.

'Keep going.' Xiu looked up at her and smiled. 'You'll find me again.'

The van rolling. Glass shattering.

Olesya felt her eyes warm with tears.

She dropped to her knees. Her nose dripped into the snow. There was no point in wiping it. It was all white around her. It was all nothing. She pressed her hands into the white and let them sink deeper. The cold burned and she focused on it. Her body shivered.

'Olesya?'

The voice was deep, but not unwelcoming.

She wanted to ignore the man, but he called her name again. She didn't say anything, and instead slowed her breathing so she didn't look so pathetic by the time he circled around her. Failing, she slumped into a cross-legged position, ignoring her bare feet.

He didn't seem to mind. He took a knee before her. She didn't want to look at him but she could see from the edge of her vision that he wore a fur jacket and held a spare over one arm. He handed it to her.

'Your feet must be cold,' he said in Russian.

She looked down at her feet, pale and covered in snow. She didn't care.

'My name is Illarion,' he said. 'It's nice to meet you.'

She looked up. Illarion had closely cropped hair and whiskers, a mix of silver and coal. His nose pointed like an arrow toward a scarred chin.

Olesya took the fur jacket from him.

'You can put the jacket on,' Illarion said.

'No.' She put the jacket on.

'How about you come inside and I tell you everything?' he asked.

She pulled the hood over her head and wiggled her hands back inside each cuff. She could feel his gaze, patient and calm. 'No.' She would stick to English.

He frowned. 'You'll get frostbite if you stay here.'

'Fine, I'll get frostbite until you tell me.'

'The project you were in wasn't a scholarship.'

She looked into his eyes. They were a pale, frosted blue.

'Project GATE,' she said. 'I know what it was.'

'You don't know everything.'

Her hands clenched into fists. 'So what … what was it for?'

Illarion looked at her. He was a bit older than her father, and the cold didn't seem to bother him at all. 'They were training you to become operatives.'

'Not anymore, I guess,' Olesya said.

He cleared his throat and looked around. 'Do you want to know where we are?'

'I don't care,' she said.

'We're thirty kilometers north of St Petersburg,' he said.

'I said I don't care.'

He smiled. 'And I don't care that you don't care.'

'And I don't care that you don't care that …' She looked away. 'Shut up.'

Through the corner of her vision, she watched him shift from crouching to a sitting position.

'I have a question for you,' he said.

'You already asked me a question.'

'Two questions. What's the last thing you remember?'

She looked away and sighed. 'I don't like that question.'

'No, you don't like the *answer*.'

She glared. 'Fine. Being taken away. By your people.'

Illarion unlaced his boots and peeled off his thick woolen socks, one after the other.

'What are you doing?' she asked.

He handed his socks to her. 'Put those on. I didn't rescue you from halfway around the world so you could get frostbite.'

She dusted off her feet and pulled on the socks. Her toes began to thaw.

'The van was hit,' she said. 'I guess *you* did that.'

'No.' He inhaled slowly and paused for a moment. 'That was the Blue Berets. The Fifth Column's soldiers, they're drawn from special forces units around—'

'I know who they are, they helped train us,' she said. 'But why did they want to hurt us?'

'Because we're not on their side anymore,' Illarion said.

Barefoot, he placed his boots neatly in front of her.

'China had a South Blade unit from Guangzhou on location,' he said. 'They were able to extract everyone under threat, including you. We were lucky.'

'I don't feel lucky.' She snatched one of Illarion's boots. Her foot slipped inside with room to spare. She put the other boot on and hugged her legs. 'I can't go back, can I?' she asked.

He shook his head. 'No, you can never go back.'

CHAPTER THIRTEEN

OLESYA LOOKED through the glass at Ark, sleeping in a hospital bed.

'Is he in pain?' Olesya asked, speaking in Russian.

'He sleeps for now,' Illarion said. 'He needs time to recover, time to process. To understand that everything he's been taught about the world is a lie.'

Illarion didn't wait for her. He was already moving across the white tiles in the corridor. She had to hurry to catch up. He paused to scratch dark whiskers, then looked through the glass to the next room. Inside she could see Ark's sister, Val. She was sleeping peacefully.

'So we're all you've got,' Olesya said. 'Everyone in that one van?'

'There was more than one van, but it would be unwise to have you all in one place,' he said. 'There are many places like here.'

She wanted to ask about Xiu, but she already knew the

answer. She wasn't coming. She didn't belong here, or in China.

'How long have I been here?' Olesya asked.

'A little over a month,' he said. 'You were the quickest for us to deprogram. Congratulations.'

She stared at him. 'What do you mean, *deprogram*?'

He clasped his hands behind his back. 'The Fifth Column programmed your mind. Fortunately, the programming at your stage was preliminary,' he said. 'Think of it as a framework. All the wooden beams put in place so at a later stage in your training they can build on it.'

She frowned. 'I'm a ... house?'

'The land on which your house is built, that's the real you. It's called the *archeopsyche*,' Illarion said. 'Your house has no rooms yet, it's big and it's empty. This new, empty house is called the *neopsyche*.'

Olesya crossed her arms. 'What's the point of an empty house?'

'The Fifth Column's plan is to build rooms,' he said. 'Each one has a specific purpose. The living room is for assassination and combat. The cloakroom is for adopting undercover personas. The bedroom is for developing them. The study is for surveillance and gathering of intelligence. And the attic, that's for self-destruction.'

'To kill yourself,' Olesya whispered.

Illarion nodded. 'The Fifth Column use a simpler framework for their suicide bombers,' he said.

'They ... turn people into bombs?'

Illarion ran one hand through his hair. 'Do you know

how hard it is to find a real suicide bomber?' he said. 'The Fifth Column's demand is larger than the supply.'

'So they make their own?' Olesya asked.

'Two rooms. The living room and the attic. It's all they need.'

'So we're just like them? We're ticking time bombs?' she said.

'No. Your programming was intended to be more complex. And you were trained to do more. You can move from one room to another as the situation requires,' Illarion said. 'Each room feels different. Each window has a different tint, a different color. Things outside appear … altered.'

'How?'

'The man on the street walking his dog; through your window, he looks like the world's most dangerous terrorist, because that's what the window reveals to you. That's what the Fifth Column reveals to you for your operation. Does that make sense?'

'So I don't know if he's a terrorist or just a man?' she asked.

'To know for sure, you need to leave the house,' Illarion said. 'Right now, Val is trapped inside her own house. We need to dismantle it piece by piece until all she has left is her mind.'

It looked like Val was dreaming. Her eyelids and arms twitched.

'You can't just open the door and she walks out?' Olesya asked.

Illarion paused at another room to check on a boy

inside. He lay in his bed with his eyes closed, breathing slowly and calmly. He was from English Squad.

'We opened the door for this boy too soon,' Illarion said. 'He refused to step outside.'

'Why?' Olesya asked.

'The house—his *neopsyche*—was real to him. He didn't believe what was outside,' he said. 'When we forced him out there, he rejected it. It was not real to him anymore. The man walking the dog was *still* the terrorist, even without the window.'

'What happened?'

'He rejected reality. He went back inside and the man was a terrorist once more,' Illarion said. 'So we continue to dismantle his house until there is nothing left. When there is no house—when the illusion is destroyed—only then will he see the real world. Only then will he see himself as he really is.'

'And the man walking the dog,' she said.

'Of course,' Illarion said. 'Seeing ourselves as we really are, that is humanity's greatest challenge. One that most of us will certainly fail.'

'What about these recruits, will they fail?' Olesya asked.

'It's my job to ensure they succeed.'

'If you knew all this, then why didn't you get us out sooner?'

'We've been planning your rescue for two years,' Illarion said. 'Believe me, if I could have gotten you out sooner I would've done so in a heartbeat.'

'I don't have to believe you.'

He studied her with arctic eyes. 'In the real world,

belief is worth nothing.'

'What about my family?' she asked.

'They're safe,' he said. 'We relocated everyone's families and helped fund them. When the Fifth Column come looking for you in Russia—and they will—they'll go for your family first. We won't let that happen.'

'Can I see them?' Olesya asked.

'As long as the Fifth Column exists, it's not safe,' he said. 'Your parents still believe you are completing your scholarship.'

'You just said belief is worth nothing.'

'Nothing to us. But it's everything to the Fifth Column. They run the entire world on belief.'

'Why aren't we on their side anymore?' Olesya asked. 'Because of Project GATE?'

'And so much more.'

'I want to know,' Olesya said, folding her arms. 'Everything.'

'Some say it happened in the 1940s. Others say it was the '60s. Others say it was now,' Illarion said. 'I don't know when, but I know at some point in history the Fifth Column quietly and gradually took over the United States of America.'

'So that's why you broke it off?' Olesya asked.

Illarion shook his head, slowly.

'They didn't stop with America,' he said. 'They took Russia next. Quietly and gradually. And once they had Russia's resources and America's military industrial complex, the Fifth Column tripled their power in just a few years. We were the pipes that fed the machine and it was killing us. We lost millions of people to the cold, to starvation, to suicide. Russia could no longer provide for its people. But over the years we formed a splinter faction inside the Fifth Column.'

Illarion led her into a larger room where others were busy working. They looked up at Illarion and Olesya then resumed their activities.

'We called it the Sixth Column,' Illarion said. 'Comprised of Russia, China, some of our neighbors, and a growing resistance inside the United States. But the alliance did not hold. It fractured the day after we rescued you.'

'Why did you rescue us?' Olesya asked. 'Are we really that special?'

'We were planning a major operation to strike at the Fifth Column from within,' Illarion said. 'But we underestimated our enemy. They saw us coming and took measures to stop us. They dismantled everything we were doing. They captured many of us before we could free ourselves of their dominion.'

'What about all the other kids from Project GATE, from all the other countries?' Olesya asked. 'I could help the Sixth Column rescue them all.'

Illarion's gaze drifted to the floor. 'As I said, the Sixth Column dissolved. Now, we work solely for a clandestine Directorate. Our objective is to protect Russia—and hopefully the world—from the Fifth Column.'

'If we're protecting the world then I'll help the Directorate rescue the kids.'

'I want you to help, Olesya. It's why we're having this conversation,' he said. 'But you need to know the reality of the situation. We aren't even a fraction as powerful as the Fifth Column. If we tried to rescue your friends we would all be dead before we hit the ground. The remaining children of Project GATE will be trained as planned. They will become black operatives, as planned.'

'Then what am I supposed to become?' Olesya asked. 'If I agree to help, you're training me to be an operative as well. Is that your plan?'

'No.' He met her gaze. 'I'm training you to hunt them.'

TODAY

DAMIEN

CHAPTER FOURTEEN

Cartagena, Colombia

DAMIEN WOKE SUDDENLY, Nasira's elbow catching him in the ribs. She was in the back seat, peering through a window with her night vision monocular. Damien was beside her, sitting so low that he'd fallen asleep. Driving in shifts through half of Central America would do that to you. Even with regular changeovers, they'd clocked thirty hours and seven vehicles before they'd even reached Colombia. Her latest steal was an old midnight blue Chevrolet sedan. Damien found the blue an odd choice but didn't comment. Until they figured out who'd flagged Jay's passport, they weren't going anywhere near an airport.

'They're here,' she said.

Damien rubbed his eyes and checked Nasira's phone. The GPS locator she'd fixed to the vessel was blinking close to the port. Their guess had been right, this port was where they were heading. He looked past the front seat and saw a large lumbering freight vessel approach the Colombian port of Cartagena.

He checked his watch. The sun would rise soon, but for now the bay was dark and still. On the other side, wafer-thin skyscrapers sparkled in the night.

'They have a bus ready?' Damien asked.

'Nothing yet,' she said.

Damien reached for a fresh bottle of water and slowly opened it. It fizzed, and he cursed. He'd purchased carbonated water by accident again because his Spanish was terrible.

Nasira kept her eye glued to the monocular. They waited for the vessel to dock.

She spoke quickly. 'Standby,' she said. 'I think I see the captives.'

She handed the monocular to him. He peered through and saw four armed guards in civilian clothes guiding two people with hands bound behind their back. They weren't blindfolded or hooded, but they looked sluggish, sedated.

'OK, I see two of them,' Damien said.

'Front seat. After me.'

Damien waited for her to wiggle forward, into the driver's seat, careful not to bump the wheel and hit the horn. Then he climbed through to the front passenger seat.

'I don't see a—'

'There it is,' Nasira said, looking over the dashboard.

She didn't point, but he could see she was watching a

small silver van as it pulled up in front of a shipping crane mounted on rail tracks. The van's headlamps bathed Nasira's Chevrolet in blue-white light. Damien slid down, just in time to avoid the light catching his pale skin. In the driver's seat, Nasira slouched low.

Risking a glance over the dashboard, Damien counted two men in civilian clothes, armed with carbines and rifles, climb out of the van and wait.

Damien cracked his window open a fraction. The air was still warm and heavy, and he could smell the sea salt. Putting his enhanced hearing to good use, he listened as someone orders to put the two passengers in the van. The engine growled. Nasira flinched. She wanted to move but she couldn't just yet. Damien rolled up his window.

He held their last GPS tracker in his hand. 'I could try and sneak up, slap it on there.'

Nasira shook her head. 'I want you to tag them more than anyone. But if their security is half decent, you'll blow our chances.'

'I know, but if I pull it off, we can follow from a distance and then—'

'And then they get spooked, switch vehicles and we lose Jay forever,' Nasira said. 'No way.'

Damien nodded. 'Then we follow by eye.'

Nasira didn't respond. She waited in silence as the van drove right past them, oblivious to their presence. Damien remained in the footwell, knees to his chest, listening to the van recede into the distance. He heard Nasira counting to ten, before pulling herself back up and turning the screwdriver in the ignition. Lights off, she made a quick turn. Damien reached for the monocular.

Dawn was starting to break over the bay.

Nasira accelerated hard, catching the van as it slipped onto a busy highway. From there they tracked it for fifteen minutes before the traffic slimmed to two lanes and the highway became a one-way freeway. On either side there was paved stone for pedestrians. On the left, gleaming white condominiums and on the right, the stone walls of old town.

'Chute one of two,' Nasira said.

She reported the lane as *chute*, using the surveillance terminology they'd learned as recruits in Project GATE.

'Heading for the coast,' Damien said, watching the map on her phone. 'Or maybe Centro.'

The sky warmed orange. The Chevrolet's air conditioning wasn't working, and Damien's t-shirt was already damp under his arms. He could see beads of sweat collecting on Nasira's neck, under her coiled hair.

'Uh, we have a problem,' she said.

Damien looked over to see the van in chute one, the left-hand lane. It was two vehicles ahead of them and the traffic was starting to thin. But that wasn't the problem.

A white Renault 4x4 overtook Nasira and aimed for the van. In his side mirror, Damien caught sight of a second Renault. Their shared distinctive feature: very dark windows.

'Really contrasts against white, huh,' Nasira said.

'Subtle.' Damien reached down into the footwell. He opened the folding stock on his Heckler & Koch UMP submachine gun.

'Count?' Nasira said, remaining calm.

Damien already knew. 'Thirteen rounds.'

She sighed. 'Pistol?'

It was tucked in his waistband with a new magazine. 'Ten.'

The foremost Renault accelerated.

'First Renault in front, chute two of two,' Nasira said.

Damien looked over to see a taxi push past, oblivious. 'Second Renault is behind us, chute one of two.'

It was still in the other lane. He watched in the side mirror as it crept forward, its front wheels lining with Nasira's rear. He knew why.

'Third vehicle, stacked two back,' Nasira said. 'I think they've seen us.'

Damien noticed a gunmetal gray Daewoo sedan with equally blackened windows.

Nasira tried to nose her way into the traffic ahead, only to be blocked by the front Renault. Both 4x4s were keeping her boxed in, at the speed they wanted. Damien gripped his UMP in both hands, low enough so no one could see. He wondered if the tinted glass was also bullet-resistant.

'They're going to spin us out,' Damien said.

Nasira growled. 'The hell they are.'

She hit the brake, dropping them back suddenly. The Renault overshot and their side crunched into Nasira's Chevrolet. Damien held on as they turned to the pavement. Nasira corrected it, keeping them in chute two.

The Renault lined up for another shot. Its front wheel drew level with her rear wheel. Nasira touched the brakes and let them overshoot. She slammed into the side of the Renault, striking its rear wheel. She accelerated into it.

Damien felt the crunch.

The Renault driver wasn't ready. He was already turning the wrong way and it was too late to correct his mistake. His rear wheels lost traction. Damien watched the 4x4 fishtail, then lose control in the high-speed traffic. It spun through the one-way freeway and smashed side-long into a row of metal bollards.

Bong bong bong bong.

The Renault rolled over the bollards and went flying upside down. Glass and metal sheared off in fragments. The car landed on its roof and scraped across the freeway; Nasira jerked her Chevrolet into chute two, narrowly missing it. The Daewoo pulled in behind her, then lurched back into chute one.

Damien saw it. Nasira saw it. But it was too late.

The Daewoo clipped Nasira's rear wheel. She tried to counteract, pulled her wheel in the opposite direction. It wasn't enough. Damien braced himself, both hands on the dashboard. The Chevrolet fishtailed. They lurched side-ways across the two lanes.

'Hold on,' Nasira said.

She flicked the wheel right, then left, slipped the stick into reverse.

The beaten up Chevrolet roared along the freeway, only now it was backward. Damien was face to face with the tinted windshield of the Daewoo. The sunroof slid open and a man with shiny long hair and imitation Ray-Bans emerged. He braced himself with widened elbows and aimed an AK-103 rifle.

Nasira's Chevrolet didn't have bullet-resistant windows.

She pumped the brakes. The Daewoo crunched into

her. The shooter's elbows slipped and he smacked his head on the roof. Damien lined the UMP's sight and fired a burst through his windshield. The UMP was wonderfully accurate, each round catching the dazed man just below his throat. He slumped back into the Daewoo.

The driver accelerated, ramming Nasira's car. She couldn't match his speed. The Daewoo pushed them in reverse along the freeway.

'Let's see if their car is armored.' Damien squeezed off a round.

It punched a small hole through Nasira's windshield, but it hardly dented the enemy's.

'Armored.' Nasira grappled the steering wheel. 'Chute one of two.'

Damien knew that even a small movement from the Daewoo would spin them out of control. Her rucksack was slim enough to wear while sitting, so he slipped it over both shoulders. This ride wasn't going to last long.

'Get us out of here,' he said.

'Where?' Nasira yelled.

In the rear-view mirror, Damien could see the white condominiums parting to reveal wider ground. He hoped that would give them some options. There was a marina on one side and thick fort walls on the other. He checked the side mirror. The leading white Renault dropped back and rode beside them. All they needed to do was open fire and the rounds would snip through the Chevrolet like it was made of tin foil.

There was a large open plaza coming up on their left. It narrowed toward a clock tower. Underneath the tower were archways for pedestrians. Nasira saw it too. She accelerated suddenly, pushing the Chevrolet as hard as it would go in reverse. For a moment, her bumper separated from the Daewoo. She had the space. She turned the wheel sharply. Her Chevrolet peeled off, crossing to the next lane.

The Renault dropped back, poised to ram them as they made their escape. Through his side window, Damien saw the Renault's rear coming right for them.

Nasira kept her foot to the floor, bouncing them onto the paved plaza. The Renault came after them, swerving off the road and onto the pavement. Damien covered his face as the Renault screeched along his door, tearing off the side mirror. But they weren't quick enough to block Nasira's escape. She scraped through.

In their wake, the Daewoo overtook the Renault and accelerated across the plaza. She watched through the rear-view mirror and she hit her horn to scatter pedestrians.

'Faster,' Damien said through clenched teeth. 'Faster.'

Nasira tore the Chevrolet under the archway. It was barely wide enough but they scraped through, right into Cartagena's old town. She spun the car around, switching to second gear and accelerating again. The Daewoo crashed into Damien's door. It buckled from the impact and almost sent the Chevrolet straight through a shopfront. Damien felt dizzy.

'You OK?' Nasira yelled.

'Yeah.' Things moved past him in a sickening blur.

He patted himself down, checked for injuries. No blood. Nasira turned hard and plunged the car into a cobbled side street, sending locals scattering. Nasira weaved around taxis, riding up on the sidewalks. The Chevrolet's tires weren't going to hold up for much longer.

Damien peered in the rear-view and saw the Daewoo. It was momentarily caught behind a maneuvering truck.

Nasira gripped the steering wheel. 'This some crazy shit he got us into.'

'Who?' he mumbled, straightening up.

'Jay.' She almost choked on his name. 'We lost the van.' She hit the wheel with her fist. 'We lost the goddamn van.'

Colonial buildings streaked past in candy blue, orange, yellow, and aquamarine.

The white Renault 4x4 appeared on one side, moving like liquid under the sun.

'Shit,' Nasira said.

She accelerated, tearing from the side street into a large, open plaza. The Renault crashed into their rear and accelerated, pushing them forward.

Nasira wrestled the wheel, but the Chevrolet turned, turned some more. The Renault eased off for a moment, waited for them to expose their side, then rammed them. Nasira's Chevrolet skidded through tables and chairs toward a restaurant. Everything smeared around Damien as the car rolled onto one side. He hung from the side, his UMP falling past Nasira and clattering under her seat. The Renault's engine was a low growl, approaching. That wasn't encouraging. He pushed up at his door but it was jammed shut.

Beneath him, Nasira kicked out the windshield. It came off in one fractured sheet. She gripped her pistol, but before she could climb out, the Renault rammed the

Chevrolet's underside. They both held on. The Chevrolet slid roof-first through the restaurant. Damien covered his face as metal screeched and glass shattered around him. The Renault finished its charge and backed off, probably so they could get out and open fire. An unarmored vehicle like Nasira's Chevrolet offered no protection against even small calibers.

Nasira was already out and running for the kitchen at the back of the restaurant. Damien had lost his UMP, but he still had the pistol and Nasira's rucksack on his back. He wedged the pistol farther down his waistband before climbing out into the restaurant. He landed on broken tables and flatware.

Gunfire erupted behind him, punching through the Chevrolet. Damien ran toward Nasira, through the kitchen and into another side street. Even in the shade, the air was warm. Nasira had stopped. The Daewoo with the tinted windows was barreling toward them. Nasira didn't hesitate for long. She sprinted right for it, then darted sideways into the open doors of a luxury hotel. Damien slipped in behind her.

He ran through a shimmering lobby, tracking Nasira into an open courtyard. She picked up a small marble statue on the way and held it against her as she pushed through a pair of spindly women in black skirts. Damien caught up with her and climbed the flight of stairs. He picked a front-facing room and sidestepped so Nasira could slam her statue down on the door handle. He pushed the door and ran through to the timber balcony.

'They're coming up now,' Nasira said.

'Which way?' Damien asked.

Without thinking, she pointed to their right.

Damien took the lead. The balconies ran seamlessly down part of the street, and he sprinted along them. He could hear Nasira's steps behind him, and shouts from the street below. There were three more balconies ahead, but no more. He took a running leap over the railing and landed on the next one. Nasira landed behind him.

'Stop!' she whispered.

He turned to face Nasira. Her copper skin was flushed red. Quietly, she pointed under their feet, then launched herself into the street below. She landed right on top of the Daewoo and aimed her pistol into the sunroof.

The gunshot echoed down the alley. The driver's head splashed the windshield.

'Well, that's one way of doing it,' Damien said.

A small yellow taxi slowed behind the Daewoo, its driver confused by the chaos. More cautious than Nasira, Damien hung from the lip of the balcony and dropped neatly onto its roof, sinking into a crouch to absorb the impact. He slid off and moved along the sidewalk, close to the wall. As he reached the hotel entrance, he drew his pistol.

A woman stepped out in front of him, an AK-103 in both hands, looking in the direction of the Daewoo. Right behind her, another armed man. They saw Nasira and raised their rifles. Damien kicked under her barrel, whipping it skyward. The rifle's iron sight smacked her in the nose. Damien drove his foot into her stomach. She fell back into her accomplice. They both dropped to the marble floor, entangled.

With his pistol, Damien shot the woman in the chest,

then in the head. The man beneath her struggled to free his weapon. Damien closed the gap quickly and, with his knee, pinned his rifle to the floor. Damien kept his pistol on the survivor, but not too close.

'Who are you?' Damien asked in Spanish.

He repeated in English just to be sure.

The man didn't reply, but tried to shift from under the dead weight. Blood spread from the man's stomach. Damien didn't know whose blood, so had to act fast. He locked the man's elbow and levered it up. The man winced.

'Who are you?' Damien asked again.

The man stared at him, his chest rising and falling.

'Who do you work for?'

'No one,' he whispered in an American accent.

There was a white armband around the man's upper arm. The same armband those border control officers were wearing. Damien lifted the man's elbow higher, almost to breaking point.

The Daewoo reversed behind them. Damien turned to see Nasira now at the wheel.

'Why are you after us?' Damien said, his gun pressed into the man's head.

He could hear yelling in the distance, a vehicle accelerating.

'What do you want?' Damien shouted.

He managed a weak smile. 'You can't protect them.'

'Damien!' Nasira called from the Daewoo.

'Protect who?' Damien shouted.

The smile faded. 'Aberrations.'

'Don't make me leave your ass behind,' Nasira said.

Damien leaned in. 'What was your job?' he asked. 'Who do you think we are?'

The man's chest stopped moving. Damien swore and climbed into Nasira's new ride.

She hit the gas. 'Damien, if you're going to interrogate someone, the key is not to kill 'em first.'

NINE YEARS AGO

OLESYA

CHAPTER FIFTEEN

St Petersburg, Russia

OLESYA BLINKED SNOW from her eyes. Flakes fell from the sky and collected on the street lamps. The garden was empty, except for the monument of Catherine the Great. The empress wielded her scepter above her flowing gown and stared out over the treetops. She wasn't scared, like Olesya.

Underneath the empress, Olesya could see Ekaterina Dashkova, the first woman in the world to lead a national academy of sciences. She clasped a book in both hands and almost seemed to smile at Olesya.

People walked the street of Nevsky Prospekt, but no one paid Olesya much attention. She wasn't cold but her arms were shaking. She folded them, climbed the steps of the monument and crawled over the bronze sign. Using it as a foothold, she reached up along the smooth surface. She was just tall enough to reach Ekaterina's feet.

Removing a glove, she used her hand to check the folds of the gown while holding onto Ekaterina's foot with her other hand so she wouldn't fall off. Each fold in the bronze gown was hollow. But there was nothing inside. It was only after her second thorough search, when her fingers started to feel numb, that she discovered a fold she'd missed before. She reached as high as she could and her cold fingers brushed something that wasn't metal. A scrunched ball of paper.

She crawled back down off the monument, making sure no one was watching her. Her heart pumped faster as she unraveled the note. Sure enough, scrawled in faded ink, there was an address, one not terribly far from her old home. Her brother's handwriting.

Olesya scrunched the paper and shoved it in her pocket. She hoped he hadn't given up on her.

ILLARION FOUND Yuri halfway through demolishing a sandwich of cold meat and salad. The security outpost smelled of hard-boiled egg.

'Have you seen Olesya?'

Yuri raised an unruly eyebrow and picked lettuce from his black mustache.

'The young one? She hasn't been through here.'

'The watchtower hasn't seen her either,' Illarion said.

The phone on Yuri's desk rang. He carefully placed his sandwich on the table and answered with spidery fingers. 'Yes? I see. How long ago?' He hung up, puzzled. 'How could she make it so far without being noticed?'

'Because I trained her to,' Illarion said. 'Who was on the phone?'

'One of our drivers. He just found your gloves in his truck,' Yuri said. 'And the truck is in St Petersburg.'

Illarion had given his gloves to Olesya.

'Assemble your Spetsnaz,' Illarion said. 'I want everyone at the gate in five.'

'Just for one girl?' Yuri asked, reaching for his rifle. 'Does she have superpowers?'

'Not yet,' he said. 'But your team isn't to handle her.'

Yuri hit a button, which Illarion knew would trigger the alert for Yuri's team.

Illarion walked out into the snow.

'Her family are in St Petersburg, aren't they?' Yuri asked, calling out from the doorway.

'It's why she's there,' Illarion said.

'Sure, but the whole team? What's the worst case scenario?' Yuri asked. 'Her family find out she's back? I'm sure they can keep it a secret. We can manage this.'

Illarion turned sharply. 'It's too late to manage. The family's ability to keep a secret is the least of our problems right now.'

'You relocated every single one of those families,' Yuri said. 'They're safe.'

'No one's safe.'

OLESYA WHISPERED into her older brother's ear. 'Wake up.'

Zakhar rubbed his eyes. 'What are you doing here?'

'Visiting is good, but home is better,' she said. 'I'm going to build a snow dinosaur, and I'm not doing it by myself.'

He sat upright and poked her in the face.

'Ow!'

'You're real,' he said. 'You're here! What about your scholarship?'

'I know.' She shushed him. 'But I wanted to … I needed to see you.'

'You never replied to any of my letters!'

'You sent me letters?' Olesya swallowed. 'I never got them.'

Zakhar had grown quite a bit since she'd last seen him. His face was longer and his hair was shorter. He smelled of toothpaste. Even though this bedroom was new, she felt at home for the first time in a while.

'It's the middle of the night,' Zakhar said. 'How did you find me?'

'Your note on the monument. Catherine the Great.'

'I never thought you'd see it!' Zakhar was speaking loudly again. 'I put it there just in case.'

'Olesya, darling?' It was her mother's voice.

'Great. They know I'm here,' she whispered.

Zakhar leaned close. 'You don't want to see them?'

'Yes, but I'm just not ready. I need a second.' She tried to calm herself.

What was she going to tell them? Could she tell them anything?

'Can you come out, please?' her mother asked.

Zakhar walked to the door, but he waited for Olesya to open it. Something didn't feel right.

Always go through the window.

Olesya opened the door.

'Come in,' Denton said. 'Don't be a stranger.'

Her body iced over.

Denton stood with four men in dark winter coats, overshadowing her mother and father. They were soldiers. Her mother sat in her chair by the window while her father paced.

'Olesya,' her father said. 'We need to talk about what you've done.'

The blinds were drawn and only a single lamp lit the living room, casting nightmarish shadows over Denton's face.

'We were very worried about you,' Denton said.

Olesya's heart raced. She'd never heard him speak Russian before. He did so almost perfectly.

'You're the man from the scholarship,' Zakhar said.

'Yes, I am.'

'I'm sure Olesya is very sorry for her actions,' her father said, looking from Denton to her. 'And she will do whatever it takes to resume the program.'

'Luckily, we implanted trackers into *all* of our candidates.' Denton eyed Zakhar as he stepped inside, beside Olesya. 'Yours has been removed, but what about the children who weren't selected for Project GATE?'

Denton glanced between the two of them. His smile vanished.

'Since your disappearance,' Denton said, 'we've been

keeping an eye on your family and anywhere you were likely to turn up.

'Olesya, why did you leave?' her father asked. 'Zakhar would never have dishonored our family.'

There was only one way to play this, Olesya thought. *There was only one way out.*

'I was abducted,' Olesya said. 'They interrogated me and then I escaped.'

Denton stepped forward, into the center of the room. The lamp lit him evenly, across his hooked nose and shaved head.

'Children three that nestle near, pleased a simple tale to hear,' Denton said.

She didn't know what that meant, so she maintained her confusion.

Denton took another step forward and repeated the phrase. His hand reached for something under his jacket. 'This is curious,' he said.

He nodded and two of his soldiers closed on Olesya. They reached down and grabbed her by both arms, holding her in place just below her shoulders. She could smell the leather of their gloves. The other two men seized her parents, whose shouts of protest drowned out everything else.

'Let them go!' Olesya shouted.

Denton threaded a long tube-shaped suppressor to the barrel of his shiny black pistol.

'What are you doing?' her mother shouted. 'She's just a girl!'

Denton shot Olesya's mother. It sounded like a staple

gun; polite and soft. Blood splashed on the window. She fell in front of the sofa.

Olesya pried one arm free, but the soldiers grabbed it, held her fast. Blood trickled down the window pane. Olesya looked around, saw her brother standing there, inanimate. He didn't move. But her father collapsed over her mother, screaming and sobbing. Olesya collapsed to her knees.

Denton lowered his pistol. 'You're not a very good liar, Olesya.'

This wasn't real. She tried to breathe. Her mother lay dead on the floorboards and her father sobbed. This wasn't really happening. She was in the wrong world and she had to get back. This was a nightmare she had to escape.

Her father screamed, hands trembling.

Denton cringed. 'Please, we're trying to have a conversation.'

He aimed his suppressed pistol and shot her father. Olesya got up on one knee and launched to her feet, but the soldiers got to her first. Her father dropped to the floor with a thud. The soldiers held onto her arms. Tears clouded her vision and her body started to shake. She couldn't control herself any longer.

One of the soldiers released her to seize Zakhar as he tried to run for the bedroom. He screamed as the soldier dragged him back into the living room. She didn't want to look at him.

This was her fault.

She never should have come back.

Zakhar screamed again. His scream didn't sound human.

Denton aimed his pistol at her. 'The Sixth Column have stolen *my* children. Where are they?'

Olesya's hands were shaking. The other soldier didn't let go of her wrist. She focused on his shoes. She could think of nothing, nothing but the man who killed her parents.

'Are my children in St Petersburg?' Denton pointed his pistol at her, then lowered it. He pressed a button near his collar. 'Bring the rest of the squad back.' Then he turned to the soldiers holding Zakhar. 'Get him out.'

Two soldiers walked out of the apartment, one carrying her brother. That left one standing by Denton and the other holding Olesya's wrist.

Denton leaned forward. 'Your brother will be safe. If you tell us where the Sixth Column are hiding.'

She felt rage coil inside. Her fingers trembled. They felt numb, icy.

Denton didn't notice. 'You don't need to be scared.'

'I'm not.'

The soldier let her wrist go and cried in pain. His fingers were black.

Olesya lunged forward and grabbed Denton's pistol. Before the nearby soldier could intervene, she pushed Denton's wrist back onto itself and squeezed the trigger. The top of the soldier's head exploded across the ceiling. He slumped onto Denton, who released the pistol and dived clear of Olesya's aim. He disappeared behind the sofa, then moved for a nearby wall. She screamed at him, firing through the sofa and through the wall. Her scream filled the apartment.

She barely noticed the window shatter and something roll across the carpet. A stun grenade. She covered her eyes but the flash still stripped her vision. The sound exploded through her.

White snow.

ILLARION SHOT the first of the Fifth Column's Blue Berets: two rounds into the back and two into the skull. The Beret wobbled to the hallway floor. Illarion fired again and again, didn't stop until there were no more targets. The others were destroyed in moments by his Spetsnaz team, crumpled across the hallway. His Spetsnaz team breached the apartment. Illarion followed them in and saw Olesya.

She was lying on the ground, curled into a ball. Her hands came away from her face. She was alive. He felt her body for injuries and was relieved to find none.

'We have you, Olesya,' he said. 'We have you.'

She squinted, seemed to recognize him. Sprawled around her, the body of a Blue Beret and the bodies of Olesya's parents. They were all dead.

'Where's my brother?' she whispered. 'Denton's soldiers took my brother.'

'I didn't see your brother,' Illarion said. 'Where are they now?'

Olesya looked around with bloodshot eyes. 'Gone.'

The cheeks of the dead soldier were black and lilac,

their eyebrows flecked with ice. The fingers on his right hand were also black. Illarion said nothing and picked Olesya up. She wrapped her arms around him. In one hand, she carried a USP Tactical pistol with an attached suppressor. He recognized it immediately—Denton's pistol. He tried to take it from her but she held tight. It was cold to his touch. She wasn't letting go so he kept his hand near the suppressor to control the muzzle.

His team finished their search—Illarion motioned for them to check outside.

He waited for them to clear the area before carrying Olesya to his red Lada sedan. He lowered her to her feet and she finally let him take Denton's pistol. He opened the passenger door, then stopped. Something stirred under the snow behind them. He saw the barrel first, then the single Blue Beret hiding in the snow, covered entirely in white camouflage.

'Don't raise your weapon. Turn around slowly.'

Illarion faced the Blue Beret. He aimed a slender white carbine with a magnified scope and attached suppressor. He was not part of the assault team. He looked young, mid-twenties, African American male. He shifted his aim down to Olesya.

'The Sixth Column base,' he said. 'Where is it?'

'The Sixth Column does not exist anymore.'

'The base location,' he said. 'Or she dies.'

'You won't kill her,' Illarion said. 'You need her.'

The Blue Beret blinked. 'Where are all the children you abducted?'

'I never abducted them. I rescued them.'

The Blue Beret's left glove wrapped over the carbine's white rail, inscribed with two letters.

'DC,' Illarion said. 'Is that your name?'

'Close enough. How far are the children from here?'

'My soldiers have secured the area,' Illarion said. 'You're running out of time.'

'You're the one running out of time, grandpa.' DC's hands twitched around the carbine.

Interesting.

'Nine out of ten men in this world have a conscience,' Illarion said. 'If you shoot this girl, you'll see her face in your nightmares. Every night for the rest of your life. Is that something you want?'

'What makes you so sure I'm not the one out of ten?' DC asked.

'Because you would've squeezed the trigger already.'

Illarion turned away and opened the door for Olesya. She climbed in without protest. He walked to the driver's side and opened the door. Only then did he look back at DC.

The soldier was gone.

Illarion heard his men shouting in the distance, then the sound of suppressed gunfire. They reported back to him a moment later. DC had escaped. Illarion gave them orders to withdraw. He climbed into his Lada and started the engine. It was time to take Olesya home.

ILLARION DROVE IN SILENCE, unable to think of

anything he could say to Olesya. She sat in the passenger seat, silent. She wasn't crying and that worried him.

'I betrayed Denton.' Olesya wiped her face. 'And I paid the price.'

Illarion's grip tightened on the steering wheel. 'Denton is different.'

'How?' Her voice was strained.

'He's a psychopath.'

'I've read about them.' Olesya sniffed. 'But in the end, we're all the same.'

'No,' he said. 'Denton cannot feel the way you feel, Olesya. His brain is different.'

She watched the road ahead. 'You said one in ten men.'

He was surprised she'd remembered that. 'Those are your odds,' he said. 'Denton might look human, he might act human, but he has no humanity. He's the type of psychopath you've never read about in your school books.'

She looked at him. 'I should have known.'

'If everyone knew what a psychopath was, they would lose the power they wield over this world,' Illarion said. 'That's why your school books will never have men like Denton. No one can know they exist.'

TWO YEARS LATER

OLESYA

CHAPTER SIXTEEN

St Petersburg, Russia

OLESYA WAS DROWNING.

Water splashed her face, soaked the black hood. Breathing sucked the hood into her mouth and made her choke. She inhaled through her nose, desperate to draw air from inside her hood. There wasn't any.

Panic flashed inside her. She slowed her breathing. Focused. She heard the loud crackling in her ear. For a moment, the darkness lit under her hood. She knew what was coming.

Silence.

She breathed slowly. Listened for movement.

The stun gun made contact. Ark screamed. His body shuddered beside her. She could hear him sucking the damp hood into his mouth with each heavy breath.

The electrodes struck Olesya this time. They bit hard

under her ribs and the current surged through, locking her every muscle. Her plasticuffed hands pulled tight against her back. The pain stopped. She slumped back. A pair of boots paced around her.

Val screamed.

Olesya flexed her fingers. Her hands were shaking. Every time an electric current snapped through her, her body jerked and drew the plasticuffs around her wrists tighter. Her fingertips were tingling. Soon, she would lose feeling altogether.

The footsteps receded. A door opened and closed. They were alone now. Three teenage captives, unarmed and with no one to save them.

Ark whispered, 'Now.'

Olesya kept her breathing slow and reached into the back of her pants. Hooked to her underwear, a long flat sliver of metal: an improvised shim she'd made herself. She straightened the thin wedge with almost numb fingertips and worked fast, rotating one wrist. Using her index finger, she probed for the ratchet in her plasticuffs.

She found the gap where the teeth fed into the ratchet and lowered her shim. It took a few attempts until she lost the ratchet completely. Her breathing was heavy again, she tried to slow it. Her body ached and her fingers trembled. In any high stress situation, fine motor skills were the first to deteriorate, skills she needed desperately right now.

On either side of her, frantic breathing and curses told her Ark and Val weren't having an easier time. She concentrated, used her index finger to find the ratchet. Once she was sure she had it—and she wasn't entirely sure—she tried the shim again. The more she rotated her wrist the more the hard plastic dug into her skin.

And then she started losing feeling in her fingertips.

'Come on,' Olesya whispered.

The shim hit the tiled floor with a tinkling sound.

Inhaling, she sucked fabric into her mouth. She tried to calm herself, she was running out of time. Running her fingertips across the wet tiles, she searched for the wafer-thin shim.

Then she heard the teeth on Ark's plasticuffs tear free.

'I'm out,' Ark whispered.

She could hear him pulling at his hood. 'Get Val,' she said.

The door burst open. Color inside her hood shifted. Ark was moving, then he landed hard. The stun gun crackled. Ark yelled, then spluttered.

'Not fast enough.' Illarion circled the trio.

He fastened a hood. Then plastic teeth clicked through a ratchet, binding someone's wrists.

The stun gun fired. Ark screamed. It echoed inside Olesya's head. Next, Val screamed. The stun gun stopped and her groan was twisted, breathless.

'Again,' Illarion said. 'You will make it out of this door in under five minutes.'

The door slammed shut.

Olesya's shim was gone. She felt for a spare, deeper inside her clothing, then stopped. There was a quicker way. She leaned back into an arch until her shoulder blades touched the wet tiles. Pointing her feet to the ceiling, she pushed her bound wrists under her hips, over her butt and under her legs. She bent one knee, then the other. Now her wrists were in front of her.

She only had one shot at getting this right. If she screwed up, it would pull her plasticuffs so tight she would cut off her circulation. Olesya held her wrists up high and pulled them back, hard, across her midsection. Pain flashed through her wrists as the plasticuffs tightened, then snapped. She ripped off her hood and saw the room for the first time. It was lit by a single light bulb, walls peeling, a single door in front. Her nostrils seared with the smell of bleach. Before her, Val was hooded, a shim in her plasticuffs as she wriggled her hands. Olesya moved to help Ark.

He felt her hands on him and pulled away. 'I can do it myself.'

She didn't bother arguing. She was on her feet, moving for the door. Illarion's footsteps fell on the other side. The door handle turned. She sidestepped quickly and pressed herself against the wall behind the door.

Illarion stepped inside. Olesya kicked him in the back of one knee. He dropped, and she closed her arm tightly over his neck. He lifted his stun gun up, the electric arc sizzling angrily. Olesya grasped his elbow, and guided the stun gun into his body. Illarion jolted beneath her, collapsed.

Olesya knelt on his arm, pinning it. She knocked the stun gun clear and drove her knees high into his armpits. He spluttered, trying to knock her off. She pressed her palms over his cheek and clamped his head against the tiles. Leaning in, she applied just enough pressure.

Illarion tapped out.

Olesya released him. Ark and Val had removed their hoods and were watching from their seated positions on the wet tiles.

'Congratulations.' Illarion cleared his throat. 'You're now the team leader.'

'But I cheated,' Olesya said. 'And we didn't escape.'

Illarion smiled thinly. 'This was never about escape.'

TODAY

DAMIEN

CHAPTER SEVENTEEN

Cartagena, Colombia

DAMIEN FLIPPED the sun visor down, cutting out the glare. Water lashed the rocks outside Nasira's window as she tore the Daewoo along the jagged coastline. Whatever the speed limit was, she was way over it. Then again, so was everyone else.

Nasira was heading for the destination programmed into the Daewoo's GPS—north, on the outskirts of another port town, Barranquilla. As far as she saw it, this destination was one of two places: the direction of the van they'd briefly seen before their attack, or where the Daewoo was heading after intercepting the van.

Nasira had stopped the Daewoo once they were clear and swept it. The only thing of use inside was the GPS. Even the corpse was sterile, so they dumped it. Nasira got behind the wheel again, insisting on taking the first shift.

While she didn't have his enhanced healing, he could see the tiny cuts on her face from their border control escape were already healing. The fibrin in Nasira's blood had hardened into slivers of carmine red over copper skin.

Damien turned the air conditioner to maximum and relished the cold air blasting on his skin. 'We need to swap cars.'

'What for? They know where we're going.' Nasira accelerated into the curve. 'What they gonna do, report it stolen? Think we're a bit past that now.'

'Well, that and there's brain on the windshield,' Damien said.

'It's on the inside,' she said. 'Nobody can see through the tinted glass.'

'Yeah, but I can see it and it's gross.'

'You just killed two people in a hotel lobby.' Nasira sighed. 'I'll stop for wet wipes.'

'Do you have another screwdriver in that rucksack?' Damien asked.

'Still in the Chev,' she said. 'But there's a crescent wrench in there if you plan on stealing another ride.'

Damien checked to be sure. 'They weren't after us. Those men.'

'What makes you think that?' she asked.

'The vehicle in the lead, it went right past us,' he said. 'Its target was the van we were following. At least until they saw us.'

Nasira's fingers drummed the steering wheel. 'They attacked us, not the van.'

Damien zoomed into their destination on his phone. 'They missed their shot at the van.'

'No,' Nasira said. 'They didn't.'

The van was ahead of them, pulled over on the side of the road. It was battered and broken, flanked by police cars. Nasira dropped to a reasonable speed as they passed. Damien absorbed what details he could. The driver's side window was smashed. He could see a body sprawled across the wheel.

Nasira picked up speed again. 'That would be the driver.'

The side door was open and there was no body inside. 'They took them.'

'Great,' she said.

'We could've saved them,' Damien said.

'Just stay focused on Jay. We barely saved ourselves.'

'You think they might be mercenaries?'

'Don't matter either way. The van was heading in this direction. The Daewoo was heading in this direction. And so are we.'

'I have someone checking the address for us,' he said. 'Could use the intel.'

'I got intel for you,' she said. 'The van was heading in this direction! The Daewoo was plotted for this direction! We have an address for this direction. There's your goddamn intel.'

'Look,' Damien snapped, 'I don't want to, you know, cramp your style. But I came down here because you needed my help.'

'No, you came down 'cause Jay needed your help. Who do you think he was going back to? He was off to see you.'

'What are you trying to say?' he asked.

'Don't pretend you're doing this for me,' she said. 'You don't owe me shit. But right now, two's better than one.'

'All I'm saying is any help is good help. If I can find out more on who took Jay and why, we can prepare. Make sure we're not walking into *another* trap.'

'Another trap? What do you want, Damien? A briefing book with pictures and color coding?' Nasira pointed at the GPS touchscreen between them. 'Jay could be there right now. And if he is, we need to get him out as fast as possible.'

'I just want to be sure we're making the right move,' he said. 'We can't screw this one up.'

'There is only one move!' Her hands clenched on the wheel. 'We don't have time to sit around and think about who's doing what!'

'Maybe if you did think, we wouldn't be here in the first place!' he yelled back, surprising himself.

Nasira slowed the Daewoo to a stop. When she spoke again, she was calm and measured. 'I didn't want to lose him.'

Damien wasn't angry because of her. He was angry because even now Jay was slipping through their grasp. 'I didn't mean it that way.'

'Yeah, but that's how you said it. And you know what ticks me off?' she asked.

'Well, a lot of things.'

She laughed, surprising him. 'We've been traveling together for two days and not once have you asked me why he left.'

'You said he was coming to see me.'

She cut the engine, kept just the air conditioning running. Her hands dropped to her lap.

'He wasn't coming to see me, was he?' Damien asked.

'No. He left 'cause I told him to leave. I've been pressuring him this whole time.'

'To do what?'

'Go see his extended family. In Rio,' she said. 'Tell them what happened. Who he was, who he *is*.'

'Closure. We could all do with some of that.' He turned to look at her. 'He didn't want to go?'

'He did. To start with. Then I pushed. Too hard.'

'It's not an easy thing to say to your family,' Damien said. 'That kind of … confession.'

'Yeah, what do you do? Turn up on their doorstep? "Hey, I was programmed by a secret multinational agency and when I graduated I was ordered to kill my own parents to pass my training. Oh, but then I was rescued and now I've declared war against this big agency. So anyway, we're all terrorists on the run now, bye."'

'It's a lot to take in,' Damien said.

He found himself staring at his hands. They'd mostly healed since his escape from border control.

'And a lot to ask,' Nasira said. 'I told him to stop running away. And what did he do? He ran away.'

'It's not your fault.'

She snorted. 'I just made a real convincing case otherwise.'

'Did *you* kidnap him? No. Did he kidnap himself?' Damien asked.

'No. I get it,' she said. 'It was their fault. Whoever the hell *they* are.'

'It was just odds. Odds that he was picked up. Odds that I wasn't. I still don't understand that. But it's odds that we get him back.'

'Suddenly all optimistic now?'

He smiled. 'I've been hanging around you too long.'

Nasira took the wheel again. 'So it's Barranquilla, or bust.'

Damien looked at his phone again, hoping the satellite view of their destination would inspire him. 'It's a facility. Just like the officer told me.'

'Yeah, that's real helpful.'

'We need to figure out our plan,' he said. 'How we approach this place, what we do once we're—'

'Here's our plan.' Nasira started the engine. 'We go inside the facility. I start shooting people in the head. We see how that works out.'

TODAY

OLESYA

CHAPTER EIGHTEEN

Moscow, Russia

OLESYA STEPPED INTO THE DARK, stale armory and found Ark and Val already inside, cigarettes glowing between their lips as they muttered to each other while the armorer wrote down the items they withdrew.

Having grown up alongside the brother and sister, they'd become like a brother and sister to her as well. The three of them had come a long way since their training in Project GATE. Their teenage years were long gone, even the special forces soldiers they passed in the corridors looked younger. Now, Olesya's team was assigned to hunt the very operatives they were supposed to become.

Olesya shed her charcoal coat and folded it over the table. 'What's the brief?'

'Three operatives in Moscow,' Val said. 'They're on the move.'

Olesya picked up her thin bullet-resistant gel vest. It comprised layers of Kevlar and a type of liquid that hardened on impact.

'That's one each,' Ark said.

Val tucked a curl of dark hair behind her ear. 'Still more than we're used to.'

Olesya removed her shirt and slipped the vest over her head, then fastened the straps across her stomach. At barely two kilograms, it didn't weigh her down like Kevlar, yet it could absorb knife attacks, most rounds—including armor-piercing—without crushing her ribs or lungs.

'When was the last time we had three in our backyard at once?' Val picked one of the new pistols, a polymer Strizh chambered with seventeen 9mm rounds. It was angular like a Glock, except for the grooves on the slide that looked like shark's gills.

'They're getting more confident,' Ark said.

Olesya considered her options for a moment.

'Whoa, hold up a sec,' Val said. 'Olesya might actually try something different.'

Olesya picked out her favorite, the Gyurza—Russian for *blunt-nosed viper*—an ultra-compact pistol from the early '90s. It was small and shiny in her hand, with a tapered barrel that never snagged on her clothing. Despite its size, the Gyurza carried eighteen armor-piercing rounds.

Ark exhaled cigarette smoke. 'And hell might freeze over.'

'That happened already.' Olesya took three magazines and loaded one. She fed a round into the chamber and pulled the slide just enough to see the glint of brass inside, then holstered it under her arm.

Val and Ark were competing over who got to choose the non-lethal weapons on the table. Typically, that was decided by a game of Rock Paper Scissors — or as they called it, Assassin, Drone, Suicide Bomber.

Val's hand closed into a fist with a thumb nestled between her fingers, while Ark's remained flat, with his little finger and forefinger tucked underneath to mimic the shape of an arrowhead.

'You cruise, you lose,' Val said.

'How does a suicide bomber beat a drone, anyway?' Olesya asked.

'Easy. The drone can't kill what it can't see,' Val said.

'That might be the worst explanation I've ever heard,' she said. 'And I've heard Ark explain hot yoga.'

'Fortunately I missed that one,' Val said.

'But you are fighting over a Glue Gun.'

'Firstly, we call it the *Ejaculator*,' Ark said. 'And secondly … OK, there's no secondly.'

Val gave Ark the sort of look that a sister occasionally gives her brother when she can't believe she's related to him, then took the Ejaculator and clipped it to her belt.

Olesya turned her attention to the knives section. She secreted a fling knife on her thigh and a survival knife inside her boot. On her belt, she holstered her combat knife, a Kizlyar Raven with a glass-breaker on its hilt. She almost forgot the compact titanium prybar, which she slipped inside her boot.

She put her shirt back on and clipped the radio unit to her belt. Then she shoved the near-invisible earpiece a little too far down her ear canal. All that was left were two sticky cams and her allowance of Russian currency. The amount had increased since the Fifth Column launched sanctions against Russia. She slipped the bills into her navy blue wallet along with her false identification for the FSB—Federal Security Bureau.

'Do you mind explaining why you're smoking in the only room you're not allowed to smoke?' Illarion said, from behind Olesya.

He was cleanly shaven today, which usually meant he'd received a visit from his superior. His steel-gray hair looked slightly more silver.

Looking down his pointed nose at Ark's cigarette, he said, 'By all means, feel free to continue your game while the clock is ticking.'

Behind Illarion was his recently assigned assistant, an intelligence officer by the name of Gleb. He had short, sandy hair and he blinked a lot. Olesya hadn't met him before, but he seemed excessively polite.

Ark crushed the cigarette under his boot. 'We're ready to move.'

'I'll expect you to clean that up later,' Illarion said, 'if you live through this operation.'

Val quickly took the Ejaculator before Ark could pinch it. She clipped it to her belt. Ark begrudgingly took the explosives detector instead.

Gleb extended his hand to Olesya. 'It's an honor to meet you, ma'am,' he said. 'I've read all about the Snow Maiden.'

Val cleared her throat. 'I wouldn't call her that.'

'Olesya is fine,' she said.

Gleb looked away. 'I'm very sorry.'

Olesya picked up one more item. She chose it every time and thankfully no one fought her for it. A black aluminum flashlight-sized device, the NetGun fired a lightweight tensile steel net, wrapping its target at a range of twenty meters and optionally delivering repeated electric shocks, subduing the target until they could be captured and removed. For every deployment, Olesya kept the electric shock enabled.

She pulled her charcoal coat back on and closed the studs to her neck.

Illarion led them to the garage for their transport. 'Gleb identified three operatives in Moscow yesterday. They went to ground overnight but they're on the move again.'

'What do they have planned?' Olesya asked.

'We don't know yet,' Gleb walked fast to keep up with her. 'Facial recognition tech is by no means foolproof, but these operatives came in at a seventy-percent match.'

'That's not enough to go on,' Val said from behind.

Gleb was quick to respond. 'Certainly, but in this case we matched the cluster of three operatives all together.' He handed Olesya a print of their low-resolution faces recorded from CCTV cameras.

Olesya looked at them. 'A little more than a coincidence.'

'It's unprecedented,' Illarion said.

Two females, one male. Olesya only cared about two things. Was the male operative her brother, Zakhar? No. Maybe they were other operatives she knew from Firebird Squad. What if the male was Damien or Jay? She wondered if they were still alive. If they were, it was possible she might encounter them again. And she would have to stop them, just like every other operative.

Hopefully not today, she thought.

She inspected the print closely. The woman stood side-on. She had straight black hair and wide eyes. There was a slight possibility this woman was Xiu.

Any operative out there could be Xiu.

Olesya tucked the thought away and handed the print to Val as they entered the garage, an underground level lined with an assortment of shiny armored cars and more commonplace sedans and bikes. It was loud and bright. The clamor of elite Zaslon soldiers—ultra-black Russian special operations—made her stomach knot. They were assigned to support her operation and that only happened when the situation was bad.

Illarion escorted them toward a three-door Lada Fora 4x4. It was silver and had seen better days.

'Don't engage until the operatives have separated,' Illarion said. 'Take them one by one.'

'Sure, but they might have other plans,' Olesya said.

On her left, two groups of Zaslon soldiers tucked themselves into white vans. They were staying mobile, a short distance from Olesya's team in case things went very wrong, but their essential purpose was to collect captured operatives.

'Once you take the operatives down,' Illarion said, 'keep moving and let our Zaslon teams transport them. Don't waste time. You need to capture as many of these operatives as possible.'

'Something tells me they aren't just going to shoot a politician and call it a day.'

Ark opened the back door to the Fora and climbed in. 'Not if we get there first.'

Val looked at Gleb for a moment, seemed about to say something, then climbed in after her brother.

'What about the rest of your team?' Gleb asked.

Olesya climbed in beside them. 'We *are* the team.'

Gleb stared at her. 'Don't you have *full* teams?'

'We did,' Olesya said. 'They were killed.'

CHAPTER NINETEEN

SNOW COATED MOSCOW LIKE ICING.

Olesya brushed flakes from her face as she followed the trio of Fifth Column operatives. They moved as one, slipping between snow-powdered Christmas trees that shimmered with violet lights. She kept a careful distance as the operatives moved around a carved ice display, toward the center of Pushkin Square. She could only see part of their faces and she seared those into memory.

Olesya closed the gap quickly. This was one of the busiest squares in the world, and during Christmas it glittered with fairy lights and sculptures, attracting crowds of people. It was pretty much the worst place to track someone. The operatives had chosen it for counter-surveillance. Once they'd shaken off any trackers—like Olesya—they would proceed to their objective.

Val broke the silence, her words clear in Olesya's earpiece. 'Ten-thousand rubles says it's assassination.'

'My money's on proxy suicide bomber,' Ark said.

All three operatives reached the crowd and abruptly separated.

'You're both wrong,' Olesya said. 'And I'm taking center.'

Her target had straight dark hair and wore a black padded jacket with a shiny hood. Like the other operatives, she carried a slim black rucksack.

Ark was the first to respond. 'I'm on left.'

'I'll take right,' Val said.

Olesya kept her attention on the shiny hood of her target. The operative turned her head slightly, as though looking over her shoulder, enough for Olesya to see the line of her jaw. Her nose.

Following her target, Olesya stepped through a wall of white fairy lights suspended from above. They parted like a luminous cobweb and she walked through, into the night.

The operative moved sharply away from the crowd and started for one end of the square. Olesya walked along the crowd's edge, keeping a low profile. In the corner of her vision, the operative stepped under a row of snow-coated power lines and disappeared down a flight of stairs to a subway station. Olesya started after her, feeling for the Troika card in her pocket.

She held her pressel switch. 'Under Pushkin Square, walking to Tverskaya Station.'

'Heading north-east,' Val said. 'Not going into subway.'

'Same here,' Ark said. 'North-east on Strastnoy, above ground.'

All three operatives were still moving in the same general direction. Olesya felt an itch between her shoulder blades. She didn't like where this was going.

She descended the stairs. The operative was still visible and there were plenty of civilians walking in both directions. She kept her distance and used nearby people to obscure herself.

A civilian might see your face three times before recognizing you were following them. A soldier? Maybe twice. An operative, once. She couldn't burn herself, but this vestibule made that hard. Last time she was in a place like this, eight people died. She should have saved them, but she didn't.

The Fifth Column, inspired by the suicide attacks of the ancient Chera dynasty and the Kamikaze pilots of the Second World War, started using this unconventional tactic a decade ago. And they used it because it worked.

The victim's programming was simpler than the programming of the operative who handled them. These victims were cheap and easy to produce, yet difficult to recruit because there was no reliable method for assessing who was susceptible to programming—short of inviting the entire resistance group to see a stage hypnotist. But the victim was easy to blame and the operative would slip away unseen.

And she'd let that happen.

Olesya moved through the vestibule, hearing phantom screams and car alarms from years ago. She remembered Illarion's debrief; he told her she couldn't stop everything. She felt the weight of disappointment in his words and could do nothing with it.

Today was different. The way these three operatives moved, this was coordinated. And it would take place in the largest, busiest underground transit system in the world: the Moscow subway.

Ark and Val reported in again, their voices crackling. Soon Olesya would be in the subway, losing contact completely.

Every so often, the operative in front would turn her head to the side and check for threats. Olesya watched her face intently, but couldn't see who she really was. If only Olesya could move closer, she could be sure.

The operative pulled her rucksack higher and, with her Troika card, moved through the metal turnstile. She disappeared down the escalator to the subway platform. Olesya reached for her own card and swiped it over the turnstile's yellow circle. The turnstile blinked green and the clear plastic barriers parted, allowing her into Tver-skaya Station.

Olesya stepped through, pocketing her Troika card and moving for the escalator. In mid-stride she noticed abrupt movement over the turnstile's shiny metal surface. Someone behind her. She ducked as two suppressed gunshots popped overhead with the sound of exploding popcorn. She dropped between the turnstiles and ripped down her coat, pulling the studs open. She drew her Gyurza pistol.

The operative was close behind. Olesya circled a turnstile for concealment. She didn't know whether this operative was Ark's and Val's, but it was her problem now. The crowd moved onward—not hearing the suppressed shots—and only a few lingered to watch a man stumble. He'd incurred a gunshot wound to his arm.

The operative launched over the turnstile. His elbow connected with Olesya's head and his knee knocked her Gyurza clear. It skittered down the escalator. The operative put distance between him and Olesya, then aimed his own pistol—a compact Glock with suppressor.

Olesya recovered more quickly than the operative calculated. She closed the gap before his finger was in the trigger guard and kicked his knee out. He sidestepped her kick.

Around them, the crowd widened. They didn't flee in terror like those she'd seen in Hollywood disaster movies. Olesya had been trained to react instantaneously, but the majority of the crowd stood around and watched, unable to process the danger and unable to look away. One person panicked and fled, then another, and another.

The operative tried to regain his balance, his right arm extending to shoot. Olesya stepped to one side and slammed her shoulder into his arm, breaking the joint. She grabbed his Glock by its long suppressor and pried it from his grasp, then threw herself backward. She slid on her back across the polished granite, away from the operative, aimed the pistol with both hands and fired. Nothing happened. She came to a stop on the granite. There was a blinking red diode on her pistol grip. Fingerprint restriction. She couldn't shoot.

'You're out of your league.' The operative advanced.

Olesya got to one knee, held the pistol by the barrel and used it as a club, knocking his attack off alignment. She stood and weaved around him. He held a knife in one hand. She drove her knee at his spine. He twisted, avoided her knee and countered with his knife. The blade cut her firing hand and her pistol went flying down the escalator.

Olesya slid back into a turnstile aisle and drew the fling knife from her thigh. She slapped her throwing arm down on her other hand to trigger a crisp release. The operative raised his broken arm to protect himself. The knife embedded into his forearm.

Olesya wriggled under the plastic barriers of the turnstile and climbed to her feet. Operatives were always a tough match, but this one seemed different. He pulled the knife from his flesh and cast it aside. It struck an onlooker in the shoulder. The onlooker saw the knife, then passed out. Nearby commuters screamed and finally everyone pushed against each other to flee. That gave her more room, but it also gave the operative more room.

Where are the others? This is their operative.

He closed on her, knife in his left hand.

Olesya drew her Raven knife. She needed help.

Behind the operative, an escalator delivered the suppressed Glock back to this floor. He went straight for her, reached the barriers and thrust his blade at her neck.

She deflected the strike with her own knife. His arm came back in for another attack. With a strong flick, she cut the knife from his grasp and sliced his wrist. His knife bounced off the turnstile and landed in the next aisle. He pinned her knife hand to the metal surface of the turnstile and head-butted her. Her vision crackled. The turnstile beeped in protest.

Olesya kicked off the barriers and launched herself up.

Her boot caught him in the face as she flipped over the turnstile and into the next aisle. Her wrist turned with her, but the operative kept it pinned.

Olesya landed in the adjacent aisle. His knife was between her feet. She grabbed it and stabbed at his good arm, but he pulled clear. She took the knives in both hands. Just one artery would be enough to bring him down, she thought, as she—

The operative vaulted the barriers with unexpected agility.

He must be wearing an exoskeleton.

The operative was in her aisle, one boot coming for her. She didn't have room to avoid the kick and the plastic barriers blocked her retreat. She reached quickly for the NetGun on her belt, but she was too late. His boot sank into her stomach, expelling air from her lungs and lifting her off her feet.

The kick sent her crashing through the barriers, through the air and across the polished granite. Releasing both knives, she brought her elbows up to protect her head. She struck the corner of the escalator. One elbow absorbed the impact and went numb, and the back of her skull banged hard on the step. Light flashed across her vision, then vanished.

CHAPTER TWENTY

Barranquilla, Colombia

DAMIEN BREATHED DEEPLY, filling his lungs. The industrial district smelled of old engine oil. He swiped his ID on the turnstile and waited for the elevator with Nasira. Underneath their feet was a sterile production facility that supposedly manufactured hormone replacement therapy and birth control medication.

With their stolen IDs, Damien hoped no one would notice Nasira's name was Pedro Herrera. A glass elevator finally arrived and they took the plunge.

Nasira chose the level in the middle, labeled CLIN-ICO. 'Barranquilla or bust.'

Her hand rested on her holstered Sig Sauer P226, as issued to Pedro Herrera. Back when they were operatives, the P226 was Jay's preferred pistol. It seemed a long time ago.

Damien checked his own utility belt. In addition to a P226, it contained everything the guards had been carrying, but like Nasira he'd made a few additions of his own: a knife, a shim and handcuff key, a small diamond saw, a flashlight and a sachet of combat gauze.

'Uh,' Nasira said.

She pulled him by the shoulder, turning him around. The elevator descended through a glass shaft, granting them a high view of the facility's floor below. Different sectors were broken by corridors and chambers, many lined with hospital beds. More than he could count. But most importantly, the beds were occupied.

'This might take a while,' Damien said.

'We don't have much time.' Nasira took a moment to steady herself. 'Christ, they're test subjects, aren't they?'

'Nothing Jay can't handle, right?' Damien forced away images of Jay being tested, possibly dissected. He hoped they weren't too late.

Nasira's eyes were glassy.

'You and Jay, you've been … close lately,' he said.

She swallowed. 'Just focus.'

The elevator reached the clínico floor and the doors opened. The corridor smelled sharply of ammonia and was oddly quiet. Nasira moved fast through the corridor. They passed the occasional nurse and doctor who wore pale blue scrubs over sneakers and civilian clothes. Nasira cornered a nurse.

'¿Falta algún paciente?' Nasira asked.

The nurse shook his head. 'No … I don't think we're missing any. They … there's no way they could—'

Nasira pointed to a security camera on the ceiling

behind the nurse. 'We have reports of a patient walking around unsupervised in this area.'

'I can check everyone immediately.' The nurse's wide eyes moved between Nasira and Damien. 'Do you know the patient's ID? Do you know what they look like?'

'Male, light brown skin tone, short black hair,' Nasira said. 'Dressed … like a patient.'

'That doesn't really narrow it down,' the nurse said.

Nasira snapped her fingers. 'He was threatening to electrocute other patients.'

The nurse blinked. 'Oh yes, that's 165. The ward is this way.'

He walked quickly but Nasira was already overtaking him.

'He's become very aggressive lately,' the nurse said. 'We've had to sedate him more often than the others. But he's never tried to escape before—'

The nurse swiped his ID and opened a glass door. Nasira drew her Sig, and Damien followed her through to a long, narrow ward with hospital beds that lined both sides. Nurses and doctors paced the center, collecting blood samples and writing on tablets. Damien noticed a small logo on the back of their tablets: two merged left and right arrows, like a misaligned X. It was an angular drawing of a DNA strand.

The nurse continued down the aisle and stopped by a curtained bed. Nasira ripped open the curtains to find a young man lying in a hospital bed. Damien couldn't see from his angle, but he didn't need to. Nasira's eyes told him everything. She moved forward, pistol lowered.

Damien sidestepped the nurse to see for himself. Relief

and anxiety pulled inside him. The patient wasn't awake, but the sensors alongside the bed showed his heartbeat and blood pressure. Unlike the other beds, this bed frame was made from hard polymers rather than metal. And unlike the metal restraints on the others, this patient was secured to the bed with plasticuffs. He had high cheekbones, an amber brown complexion and cracked lips.

They'd finally found him.

Jay opened his eyes.

Nasira gasped, coughing to cover her reaction. She turned to the nurse. 'Where is the supervising doctor for this ward?'

'I think she's on break at the moment,' the nurse said. 'I can find her.'

The nurse disappeared. Damien closed the curtain behind them. Jay looked confused, but tried to sit up in the bed. That was a good sign.

'You're … here?' Jay asked.

Nasira kissed him, her lips pressed firmly against his. When she withdrew, he gasped for breath.

Jay grinned. 'Definitely not hallucinating then.'

'Can you walk out of here?' Nasira asked.

Jay looked down at his cuffed arms. There were IV lines embedded in his veins. 'I'll crawl out.'

'What are they all doing here?' Damien asked. 'These patients?'

'They have abilities,' Jay said. 'These people are picking them off the street and copying their pseudo...'

'Pseudogenes,' Damien finished. 'They can do that?'

Nasira pried the plasticuffs loose with her knife. 'Not to Jay, they're not.'

The curtains parted and a doctor stepped through. 'Is everything OK?'

Nasira reached for a new line of plasticuffs, her voice suddenly deeper. 'We're tying the patient up. He was uncooperative and in possession of a knife. Any idea where he might have gotten that from?'

She tossed the knife to Damien and checked Jay's vitals. She looped the plasticuff around the bed frame and pulled the doctor's wrist onto it, fastening with a sharp flick.

'Kinky,' Jay said, 'but strangely not part of my fantasy.'

Damien cut Jay's other arm free and tossed the blade back to Nasira. She held it to the doctor's throat.

'What are you doing to these people?' Nasira asked.

'Ensayo clínico,' she said with a whisper. Clinical trial.

'What the hell is this place?' Nasira asked.

The doctor tried to respond but her voice cracked under pressure. She finally said, 'I-Intron.'

'Intron? Who are they?' Nasira asked. 'Private military?'

The doctor shot Nasira a disgusted look. 'Certainly not. This is pharmacology, biotech—'

'How many of your security guards are coming?' Nasira asked.

'Just two guards,' the doctor said. 'Usually.'

Shouts came from the corridor outside the ward. Someone yelled, 'Drop your weapons.' Then gunfire.

'Security?' Nasira asked.

The doctor stared through her. 'I don't know those voices.'

That wasn't pistol fire either, Damien thought.

'Friends of yours?' Jay pointed upward.

Damien followed his finger through the open ceiling. Another elevator descended the glass shaft. Inside it, a cluster of athletic looking men and women, masked, black fatigues.

'Are they here for you?' Nasira asked.

'I'm popular,' Jay said, 'but not *that* popular.'

Damien counted five of them. They wielded sand-colored carbines and black suppressors. They also wore white armbands.

'This doesn't look like a friendly visit,' Damien said.

Nasira made her decision. 'Then we leave now.'

Damien moved carefully ahead of her, listening. More footsteps. He held up a couple of fingers: two armed intruders in the corridor, just outside their ward.

Nasira drew her pistol.

CHAPTER TWENTY-ONE

OLESYA WAS LYING in the grass. Xiu stood over her and Damien and Jay were there too. They were all wearing their blue vests and safety goggles.

'We made it over the wall,' Damien said.

'Hell yeah!' Jay punched the air.

Xiu crouched beside her. 'All thanks to you.'

'I did it for you.' Olesya reached out for her hand.

'Then why did you betray me?' Xiu asked.

The whistle sounded through the forest.

Olesya woke up. She was sprawled across the escalator steps as they descended to the subway platforms. The operative gripped his pistol and descended the steps toward her, pushing past commuters.

Olesya's right arm was numb so she reached across her body with her left. He saw, raised his pistol toward her. His arm trembled. Blood dripped from his wrist.

Unclipping her NetGun, Olesya pressed the firing button with her thumb. Compressed air punched a featherlight steel net into the operative. It ballooned with weighted talons and wrapping around him, fixing his shooting arm to his neck and knocking the pistol clear. Tightly wrapped in the net, the operative toppled back onto the steps, shuddering as the net delivered repeated electric shocks.

The escalator pushed Olesya onto the red granite floor of the subway platform. She got to her feet, retrieved her Gyurza pistol and stepped clear of the entangled operative. She didn't know how long he'd been following her, and if he'd had the opportunity to report her presence to the other operatives before entering the subway. At least in here if she couldn't communicate with her people, he couldn't communicate with his.

She left him on the floor. The electric shocks would only zap him if he tried to move, plus the Zaslon teams would collect him from the platform as soon as she could make the call. She snapped the studs on her coat closed and walked the platform, feeling a cool breeze on her face. A train pulled in beside her. The doors opened and commuters moved on and off the platform. The operative was at the end of the platform. She jumped inside the rear car and slipped between the closing doors.

Watching Olesya through the glass, the operative smirked.

The train started moving again. Olesya swore under her breath. Thinking quickly, she slapped a sticky cam above the doors of the next car. It was small enough that no one would notice, but the lens would be wide enough to see the operative leave the train.

Olesya ran from the station, her lungs burning. At the surface she called in Zaslon to collect the captured operative, then checked on Ark and Val.

Ark swore. 'I lost mine. Think he doubled back to Pushkin Square.'

'Don't bother, I got him,' Olesya said. 'Val?'

'Still on mine, but he's boxing me,' Val said. 'We're about to go around the same block a second time.'

'Don't follow or you'll get burned,' Olesya said. 'Ark, we need you in there.'

'On my way.' Ark slammed a car door. 'I need directions.'

'Corner of Vorotnikovskiy and Degtyarnyy,' Val said. 'Bearing north on Vorotnikovskiy.'

'Olesya, what about you?' Ark asked.

'I'm working on it.' She waved at the oncoming traffic.

Many cars in Moscow acted as taxis, outnumbering official taxis. A bruised silver Chevrolet Optra pulled in almost immediately. Olesya considered stealing it at gunpoint, but she didn't know this city well enough yet. A local driver would be faster.

'How fast can you get me to Mayakovskaya?' she asked the driver.

He scratched a gray eyebrow. 'That depends on how much.'

'Ten thousand rubles.' She reached for her folded bills.

He stared at the bills. 'Very fast.'

Olesya jumped in the front seat. 'Give me faster.'

He stepped on it.

While Val directed Ark to her operative, Olesya knew she couldn't outrun the train with the hooded operative, and she wasn't going to try. But she didn't want to be too far behind either. Firing up her phone, she checked the sticky cam feed. It was black except for three words: no signal detected.

The wheels screeched as the driver took the corner almost as hard as she would have. Then the feed sparked to life. Through the sticky camera's fish-eye lens she could see the train stopping at Mayakovskaya; it had been quicker than she thought. The doors opened just below the camera. On the edges of the extremely wide lens, she could see the other car doors open as well. The resolution was reasonable, but she needed to squint to scan the crowd that flowed between steel columns.

Jacket with a shiny hood, black hair. Moving from the car on the right. A rucksack on her back. In the center of the platform, police officers appeared and started directing commuters out of the station. A lot of police officers.

'That's not good,' Olesya said under her breath.

The driver crunched the Optra to a halt. 'It is very good, we're here!'

She dropped the rubles in his lap. He wished her a good day as she slammed the door and sprinted for the station, muddied snow crunching underfoot.

Police officers were standing outside, leading commuters out but denying entry. Olesya watched the crowd filter out onto the winter streets, checking everyone's faces. The last few people stepped out, followed by more officers.

She checked her camera feed. The train was still at the now-empty platform, Empty except for a glimpse of shiny hood. The operative was still down there, alone. Whatever she was doing, now was the perfect opportunity to do it.

Olesya opened her wallet for the pair of officers guarding the entrance. The officer with two stripes on her shoulder—a junior sergeant—looked at her Federal Security Service ID. It was a perfect forgery, from her false name and number to the hologram in the center.

'What's the situation?' Olesya asked.

'Bomb threat,' the sergeant said. 'Special Rapid Response will enter now.'

Olesya turned and saw the blue and white armored van unloading a six-person team of rapid response officers in black fatigues and helmets. One of them moved like an astronaut in his bomb suit, layered generously in Kevlar, foam, and plastic.

'Give me ten minutes,' she said to the sergeant.

Before the sergeant could react, she moved quickly through the entry hall.

'I'm heading into Mayakovskaya station,' Olesya said into her throat mike. 'Call if you need me.'

'You're only a block away. Maybe you should call if you need *us*,' Ark said. 'We'll play tag in the meantime.'

'Speak soon,' Olesya said.

Leaping over the interior turnstiles, she strode under the colorful yellow and blue mosaic ceiling and onto an escalator. It fed her down through a white tunnel lit by globular lamps. The tunnel was so long that she could barely see the end.

'Val,' Ark said in her earpiece, 'do you see her? I've lost the eye.'

Val replied, but her words started to fragment as Olesya moved deeper underground. She thought of going back to help—they weren't far—but she couldn't let the hooded operative escape. Running down the escalator, Olesya only slowed when she neared the bottom, popping her coat studs slowly so they made no sound, and carefully drawing her Gyurza.

There were two figures in the distance, not one. The noise of the escalators covered Olesya's footsteps. She moved slow and whisper-soft on the outer edge of the platform, concealed by the shiny steel and marble columns. She stepped over the bodies of two dead police officers, parts of their heads shot through.

She moved close enough to hear them talking. They spoke English with American accents. Olesya stood behind a column and checked her phone. It had reception and the sticky cam was able to connect. She was rewarded with a view of both women, pistols aimed at each other. One was the operative with the hooded jacket, but she wasn't sure of the other one yet. She wore dark jeans and a black leather jacket over a gray t-shirt. She had dark bronzite hair and a pale complexion.

'If we're caught,' the hooded operative said, 'I'm the one with valuable intelligence to trade and you're the terrorist mastermind caught in the act.'

Olesya had just found the missing operative.

'Tell me where the explosives are and I'll get you out unscathed,' the new woman said. 'Relatively speaking.'

'With me as your prisoner,' the hooded operative said.

'Better than being dead.'

'It's me or the explosives. You can't have both.'

If the top brass wanted proof that operative hunters were effective—that *Olesya* was effective—they were going to get it. She aimed her pistol and stepped out behind the hooded operative, directly facing the new woman.

'Actually, there's a third option.' Olesya lined up her sights with the new one.

She didn't even flinch.

Both the hooded operative and the new woman kept their pistols trained on each other. Neither tried to aim at Olesya.

'I can drop you both without even calling for backup,' Olesya said. 'If you want out of this alive, then I suggest you slowly point your weapons to the ceiling and remove your magazines.'

The new woman stared back at Olesya with smoke-gray eyes that burned through her. They seemed to see everything; to read everything.

'Listen to me,' the new woman said. 'This operative has placed explosives on the platform.'

'Don't listen to her,' the hooded operative interrupted, speaking in Russian. '*She's* the suspect and I'm trying to stop *her*.'

'Last chance.' Olesya kept her aim on the new one with gray eyes. 'Both of you: aim your pistols at the ceiling.'

The new woman pointed her pistol to the ceiling. Slowly and deliberately, she released her magazine.

'Who are you?' Olesya asked.

'My name is Sophia. You might have heard—'

'No, I haven't,' Olesya said.

Sophia did look familiar, but Olesya couldn't recall a photo of her in Illarion's collection. Some of those photos were recent, they were adult operatives. Some were outdated, from back when they were still children. Maybe Sophia had grown some.

'Your turn,' Sophia said to the hooded operative.

Olesya shifted her aim. 'Remove your magazine!'

The hooded operative remained still.

Olesya needed to see her face. She needed to know…

Then Sophia spoke. 'Children three that nestle near. Eager eye and willing ear, pleased a simple tale to hear.'

The operative stood between them and twitched, then hung forward, limbs dangling. 'Access permitted.'

Sophia spoke to Olesya in calm yet stilted Russian. 'Ask her again. She will obey basic commands.'

Olesya kept her pistol trained on the hooded operative. 'Point your barrel to the ceiling, remove your magazine and clear the chamber.'

The operative did as she was instructed. The magazine clattered by her feet. A single round bounced across the marble. She remained standing and stared ahead.

'How did you do that?' Olesya asked.

Sophia arched an eyebrow divided with a fine scar. 'It's a long story.' She lowered her pistol and aimed at Olesya. There was one round still in her chamber.

Olesya aimed at the same time. Stalemate. 'You only have one round.'

'I can work with that,' Sophia said. 'Who are you? GRU? SVR?'

'FSB,' Olesya lied. 'Maybe that was your third guess.'

'Maybe.'

'Speaking of threes, how many of you are there—here in Moscow?'

'You tell me,' Sophia said.

It clicked into place. Olesya remembered where she'd seen Sophia. It was right in this very station, three years and one month ago. She'd slipped through the crowd before the explosion. Olesya tried to catch her but the detonation cut her off and she'd gotten away.

Not this time.

Olesya hit her pressel switch. 'I have two operatives.'

'You have one of them,' Sophia said, nodding to the hooded operative between them. 'And it's not me.'

Olesya kept her pistol trained on Sophia's face. Twenty meters. She could take the shot. 'You're one of them. I remember you.'

Sophia shook her head slowly. 'Whatever you think I've done, that wasn't me. I can explain.'

Olesya's finger curled over the trigger. 'Give me one good reason why I don't shoot you right now.'

'Because I'm not like them,' Sophia said.

'Why should I believe anything you say?'

'I'm not programmed. Not anymore.'

Olesya shook her head. 'That's not possible.'

'Then how would you explain what I just did?' Sophia asked.

Olesya's comms crackled. Ark's voice, dropping in and out.

'—can you—me? Val is—last seen—north from Tverskaya—'

Olesya held down her pressel switch. 'Unreadable, say again.'

Ark called her phone. Carefully taking a hand off her pistol, Olesya answered.

'I'm at the north entrance, can you hear me?' Ark yelled. 'Shit! I think they grabbed Val!'

Panic sheared through Olesya.

'White van!' Ark breathed rapidly and read out the number plate. 'Bearing north on Tverskaya Street! Shit, shit shit. You're closer, can you get there? Tell me you can get there!'

Olesya kept her gaze on Sophia. 'Yes.'

'The van has tinted glass, roof racks and a hatch with a small window on the rear!' Ark yelled.

'Let me guess.' Sophia didn't blink. 'You have to run?'

'My team know exactly where we are.' Olesya ended the call and pocketed her phone. 'If you were to make the wrong move.'

'Understood.' Sophia slowly lowered her pistol. 'I take it you want me to disarm the explosives.'

Olesya holstered her own, wishing for a moment her NetGun was loaded.

'Whatever you do with that operative, do it fast,' Olesya said.

She broke into a run, heading for the southern entrance. Her earpiece crackled.

'I repeat, white van. White van. Tinted glass,' Ark said. 'Two in the front seat.'

Olesya flashed her ID at the police outside and read out the number plate to them. 'The terrorists are inside and they've taken a police officer hostage.'

She ran for the corner. The street flowed with four lanes in both directions. She needed to steal a car if she was going to intercept this van, which could be passing her at any moment—

She saw it. Driver and passenger. Tinted glass.

It was almost here and she was on the wrong side of the road. She moved without thinking and ran for the double lines in the center. The van was heading right for her. She drew her Gyurza, knowing she couldn't shoot without risk of hitting Val. Even if she managed to shoot the tires, she'd end up killing half a dozen motorists from ricochets. There had to be a better way of stopping them.

She held out her ID and stepped boldly into the first lane. There was a blue two-door Jeep driving in front of the van. She aimed her Gyurza at the Jeep. The driver hit the brakes, but Olesya was already stepping into the next lane, aiming at the driver of a small red sedan. If she couldn't stop the van, she would stop everyone in front of the van.

The ground beneath Olesya shook. She widened her stance and felt it rumble through her body. A low, deafening roar. Glass and marble spewed from the station entrance on the other side of the road.

The van's driver swerved around the traffic into the adjacent lane, clipping the red sedan. The impact slowed the van, but now it had a clean break.

'Olesya!' Ark's voice was breathless in her earpiece. 'Can you see the van?'

Tinted glass—bullet resistant. One driver and a passenger in the cabin. Roof racks on top. The van accelerated toward her.

Olesya holstered her pistol and stood her ground. 'I see it.'

The van aimed right for her.

She jumped clear with a fraction of time to spare. The van passed by her, plain and featureless with nothing on the side for her to grab. She reached out and her fingers caught the rear hatch. It pulled her off her feet. She gripped the handle and hauled her boots onto the step under the hatch. The van didn't stop. She held onto the hatch with both hands.

Through the hatch window, she could see four people inside. Two were armed with submachine guns. One of them was Val. And another was tending to Val, who lay still with closed eyes, and another carried a tablet. On the back of the tablet there was a small logo that looked like a DNA strand.

Taking one hand off the handle, Olesya aimed her pistol through the glass, at the nearest armed passenger. He lunged for the hatch, but she put one round into his head. It shattered the window and tore through his skull. The hatch popped up, lifting her with it. Tverskaya Street became a smear of cars and buildings. Wind howled through her ears.

Olesya landed on top of the van, then tumbled over the side. She grabbed a roof rack and hung with one hand. The van was surrounded by traffic that roared around her.

There was a truck on one side and a bus on the other. She hung to the roof rack while the passengers in the bus beside her watched in disbelief.

Her Gyurza pistol was near the front of the van, wedged under the roof rack. She extended one hand and—

The van rammed a car in front, almost knocking Olesya free. She held on, then climbed toward the van's driver. He exposed his arm, pistol in hand. She closed the gap fast, snapping her legs in a scissor motion and breaking his elbow. The passenger sitting in the cabin next to him was quick to react. She took the wheel and tried to aim a pistol of her own. With the driver's head planted on the wheel—horn blaring—she aimed over his shoulder at Olesya.

Olesya's legs were still clamped over the driver's arm. She drew them in, pulling the driver back and blocking the passenger's aim. The passenger fired and blew a hole through the driver's head. The driver slumped on the steering wheel, hitting the horn.

The van steered into the bus. The bus driver saw them coming and tried to get clear. Olesya released her driver's arm and quickly pulled herself over the roof racks. The van smashed into the side of the bus, metal on metal. Olesya slipped and rolled off the roof. The horn drowned everything else out. She went flying over the road and— slammed into the side of the truck. Her hip took the impact and she bounced off, back onto the roof of the van. But she wasn't going to make it. The road rushed to meet her.

Olesya reached out. She grabbed a roof rack and hit

the side of the van, crushing air from her lungs. She didn't let go. The new driver glared through the side mirror.

One driver down, another to go.

Olesya climbed along the side of the van, hands moving quickly across the roof rack, and made her way to the passenger's side of the cabin. She reached into her boot for the only knife she had left—her survival knife.

But this driver saw her coming. She steered into the truck.

Olesya still had time. She held the roof rack with one hand, knife with the other. She struck the knife's hilt into the cabin window. The window crystallized. She struck again. The laminated glass caved in.

A flash of movement behind her, from the open hatch.

Submachine gun.

Olesya flung her survival knife at the shooter. He pulled back. The knife missed. He aimed again, then suddenly retreated. The van went crashing into the truck again. Olesya saw it coming and kicked off the side of the truck. She landed on top of the van and braced herself. The van grazed the truck and almost lost control. Olesya went for her pistol. The hatch bobbed open behind her.

Rounds punched through the roof, narrowly missing her. The van roared through a busy intersection. Horns and cars blasted in their wake.

Olesya turned over onto her back and slid to the rear of the van. She slammed her heel on the open hatch. It whipped down, struck the shooter and sent him tumbling from the van. Motorists behind them hit their brakes.

The van struck a curb and Olesya lost her grip on the roof. She slid down the closed hatch, twisting to grab for the broken window. Her pistol flew over her head and her boots grazed the road. She hung on by the window frame with one hand. She reached up with her other hand and pulled herself toward the window. Inside, Val lay with one remaining passenger. That passenger aimed a submachine gun at her. The van took a corner. Hard. In that split second, Olesya made her decision.

She let go.

CHAPTER TWENTY-TWO

Barranquilla, Colombia

DAMIEN LISTENED for the two intruders. Silence. The intruders paused outside the ward a little too long. They were coming inside.

Nasira folded her knife and gave it to Jay, then took him by his other arm.

Damien grabbed a nurse by the shoulder. 'Is there another exit?' he asked in Spanish.

'No, no, just through the glass door.'

'Hide,' Damien said.

The nurse did as instructed, hiding behind a hospital bed. Damien did the same. A dazed patient looked down at him. He heard the glass door breaking.

On the other side of the ward, Nasira tucked Jay in behind the staff desk. Damien peered over the bed. A masked woman aimed her suppressed carbine at the first bed in the ward. She fired a short burst. People screamed.

Fear rose inside Damien, cold and sickly.

They weren't here for Jay. They were here for everyone.

There was a second burst. Then gunfire from other wards. In chorus, it echoed through the building.

Damien risked another glance. Now there were two masked shooters in the ward with them. One was shooting while the other walked over to where Damien was hiding. Damien unlocked the bed wheels and shoved the bed into the aisle. It crashed into the masked shooter, but didn't stall him long. He pushed forward and aimed at Damien—

The back of his head sprayed the wall. He slumped against it.

Nasira stood behind the desk, pistol in both hands, but the first shooter dived for the glass door and escaped.

Jay collected the dead shooter's suppressed carbine— an FN Scar Mark 17 with a compact 13-inch barrel. Jay looked ready to move, but the sedatives slowed him a fraction.

Damien stepped around him. 'On me.'

Nasira knew the drill. She didn't have Damien and Jay's enhanced healing and regeneration abilities, so she stacked behind them. They entered the corridor quickly, Damien aiming left, Jay right. Jay was the first to fire. He discharged a short burst of suppressed rounds.

'Shooter down,' Jay said quietly.

They never said 'Clear' because it never was.

Suppressed gunfire and screams echoed from every

direction. Nasira broke formation and moved away from the elevator. Damien checked behind and saw the crumpled body Jay had shot. He considered running over to the body and stealing the carbine, but the distance in open ground wasn't worth it.

Nasira was running ahead. Damien followed her and Jay took up rear security. Nasira hit a t-intersection and went left, bringing them to another glass door. She swiped her stolen ID and pushed through into what looked like an administration wing. There was no one here. The desks were scattered with breath mints and coffee, but there were no bodies. The staff had evacuated very recently. Nasira kicked a chair from her path and kept moving. Damien followed, making sure Jay didn't slow.

It took them a very long minute to make it to the staff vehicle bay. Damien searched for older cars to steal, but they were all new. On foot, Nasira took them across the vehicle bay and toward a ramp, then she stopped and swore.

Three masked figures walked down the ramp, suppressed barrels aimed at them. Two 4x4s crawled behind the figures, their engines rumbling and windshields dark. The figures wore white armbands above their elbows.

Nasira lowered her pistol. There was no other option. Damien and Jay did the same.

'Don't shoot!' Damien called out in Spanish, then English. 'We came here to find you.'

Damien honestly had no idea where to go from here, but it was worth a shot. He searched the vehicle bay for more options as he talked, but there was nothing to help.

The masked figures approached, suppressors trained on Nasira, Damien and Jay. At least they weren't shooting —yet.

'I know you don't have any reason to trust us,' Damien said, speaking in English. 'But we want to join you.'

One masked figure stepped forward, speckled green eyes on Damien. He aimed his carbine at Damien. 'How can you join something you know nothing of?'

'One word.' Damien struggled to remember the word from Cartagena. 'Aberrations.'

The masked gunman lowered his carbine. 'Those without faith are cursed with terrible powers of trickery and deception. They take the gift of the angels and give nothing in return.'

Damien heard footsteps behind them. He turned his head only a fraction, just enough to see a new pair of masked figures moving quickly through the vehicle bay.

'Then we understand each other.' Damien lowered his hands slowly to his sides.

'I understand deception,' the masked gunman said.

The new pair of figures ignored Damien, Nasira and Jay and went for the vehicles. One of them carried a black armored carry case. She reached the rear 4x4 and hurled the case into the back seat. The pair climbed in the 4x4 and reversed it up the ramp, leaving the original three figures and one vehicle to face Damien, Nasira and Jay.

'Listen pal,' Jay said, 'we're not standing in your way.'

The masked figure fired a single round into Jay's chest.

Jay collapsed on his knees, mouth open.

Damien lunged over and pressed his hand over the

entry wound. He found the exit wound and pressed on that too. Blood ran from his fingertips. He took his hand off the exit wound so he could quickly tear through his belt pouch and find the sachet of hemostatic combat gauze. He ripped the sachet open with his teeth and packed Jay's exit wound with gauze. Blood oozed and bubbled over his hand. He kept some of the squares for the entry wound.

'What do you want?' Nasira asked, voice wavering with anger.

The figure smiled through his mask. 'This is just the beginning.'

Jay leaned on Damien and groaned. The smell of Jay's blood mixed with gasoline. Damien kept his fingers inside the exit wound, making a ball from the combat gauze and maintaining pressure. On anyone else, this was life and death. But Jay's enhanced healing would save him. His pseudogenes would keep him alive. Damien just needed to stem the blood flow.

'There's something you need to know,' Jay said, struggling to breathe.

Damien risked a glance at the masked gunman. 'I'm working on it.'

'Listen to me.' Jay gripped his arm. 'They didn't just copy my pseudogenes.'

Damien leaned in, taking over the pressure for both wounds.

Jay's breathing slowed. 'They stole them.'

HELIX: EPISODE 2

EXILE

CHAPTER ONE

Six years ago
Location: Classified

THE DOOR to the control room hissed open, revealing three enemy soldiers in mid-rescue. Damien sighted his first target, a masked soldier. The soldier, standing in front of the captive they were attempting to rescue, turned quickly to shoot Damien.

Damien was quicker. He shot him and kept moving. Jay was behind him, moving and firing in tandem. Jay dropped a second soldier and Damien dropped a third. A moment later, their squad leader entered the control room and lowered her pistol.

'Three down,' Sophia said.

Her helmet concealed most of her dark brown hair, but her gray eyes were visible through her goggles. They sent shivers through some, but reminded Damien of marbles.

Sophia ignored the soldiers lying on the floor. Her attention was on the captive soldier they'd attempted to rescue. She sat calmly in a chair, her hands bound behind her back.

Sophia shot her in the chest.

Damien's eyes widened. 'What was that for?'

Sophia said nothing as the soldier slipped from her chair, her arms free and a pistol concealed in one hand. 'The idea is you don't get shot.'

He stared at the pistol. 'We almost fell for that.'

Denton, the Project GATE director, was already standing in the doorway. Fluorescent light curved over his shaved head. 'Reset and swap.' He paused, then spoke into his handheld radio. 'Give Helldiver some reinforcements.' With that, he walked out.

The Helldiver Squad soldiers climbed back to their feet, recovering slowly from the electro-rounds. Their leader, Nasira, removed her helmet with a growl.

Jay whistled. 'Guess that's a failed rescue.'

'You'll be a failed rescue in a minute.' Nasira shouldered him on the way out. 'Let's see how far your Firebird Squad gets this time.'

AFTER THE RUSSIAN and Chinese recruits were withdrawn from Project GATE—rumors suggested they were disqualified for treason—Damien had noticed smaller squads everywhere. At that time, there were only four modestly sized squads in Special Operations Training, and his was one of them. The instructors still referred to them as recruits, which annoyed him.

He still didn't know what GATE stood for, but he knew his scholarship was part of it. He'd been told to expect military training, but he hadn't expected anything like this. Everyone here had come from around the world; gifted children with special genes, who Denton had carefully tested and selected. Damien's test results had come back with a green star and a gold star. The green star was for outstanding results. The gold star was for genetics.

The gold star got you into Project GATE.

As Damien's squad approached the end of their Special Operations Training, Denton merged the four squads into two: Firebird and Helldiver. The rest of Project GATE's squads were months behind schedule, still working through Combat Training; all the while newly minted squads channeled recruits through the Education Module. Denton's plan to train recruits wasn't a one-off project, it was just the beginning. That's what he kept telling them at their monthly briefings.

All of this was leading to something big, Damien could feel it. Sure, once he completed the training he could visit his family for the first time in years—and he missed them terribly, especially his mother and his dog, Primo—but then their career would begin, and with that came options. His skin prickled at the thought. What lay in store for him?

Not much, if he failed to qualify.

Now that the Russian recruits, Ark, Val and Olesya, were disqualified from Firebird, Jay had hoped for a promotion to squad leader. He wasn't impressed when

Denton promoted some recruit they'd never heard of: Sophia.

Now he and Jay stood with Sophia in the loading zone. This time, they were the rescue party. Damien's hand twitched over his holster. He couldn't screw this up.

There were no windows in the loading zone, just three scratched gray walls and a blast door fringed with yellow and black caution stripes. There was a flashing red light and a speaker on either side of the door. Damien ignored the red light. Above it were security cameras with wide lenses and a jeweled cluster of infrared sensors. Standing on a catwalk above them, Denton. He watched them, probably waiting for Damien to screw up. Damien's fingers trembled, so he curled them into fists.

Jay tapped Sophia on the shoulder. 'What's the go?' he said through his mask. 'You're supposed to be our leader.'

Sophia adjusted her protective goggles. The red lights flashed in silence, making her pale eyes dark and her brown hair darker.

'How many are we up against?' Damien asked.

'We don't know. I'll go in the room alone,' Sophia said, her voice muffled by her mask.

Damien didn't know whether to relax or freak out.

Jay's eyes looked ready to pop. 'What?'

'Otherwise they'll seal us all inside,' she said. 'And then we lose.'

The speakers made their customary *boop* sound. Damien's pulse raced. On the third *boop*, he drew his compact pistol.

The doors opened. Damien and Jay closed on Sophia's shoulders. Damien checked again for the access card in his pocket. They'd need it to enter the room and rescue the detained Firebird recruit. He was breathing too fast, he had to slow it down.

'If they seal me in the room,' Sophia said, 'count to ten and open the door again.'

They didn't have time to argue, Sophia was already moving down the corridor. Damien kept on her shoulder until she turned left into the next corridor. He stacked behind her, and Jay behind him. In single file, they moved for the control room.

Damien took up position on one side of the door, Jay on the other. Sophia stood between and gave Damien a nod. He pressed the access card against the reader. It blinked green and the door slid upward.

Sophia fired, sidestepped.

'I'm counting at least four!' she yelled over the pop of gunfire.

Electro-rounds filled the air between them and snickered off the corridor wall.

Jay returned fire. 'Make that three.'

Damien expected the Helldivers to wait until they'd rescued their prisoner, but they played their hand early.

Sophia was already adjusting to the situation. 'Close the door. Now!'

Damien gripped the access card, his hand damp with sweat. He pressed it against the reader. The door slid back down. Sophia knelt in the corridor and leaned forward, her helmet to the ground.

'Jay, stay where you are. Shoot anything in your arc,' she said.

'With pleasure.'

'Open the door,' she said.

'Are you sure?' Damien asked.

She glared at him. He opened the door.

As it slid upward, Sophia was already firing from her low position.

More Helldivers appeared at the end of the corridor.

'Behind us!' Damien yelled, opening fire.

The Helldivers took positions on either corner, avoiding his shots.

'On me!' Sophia yelled.

Jay was behind her, so Damien stacked behind them, his pistol trained at the end of the corridor. Quickly and aggressively, they moved inside. Rounds cracked behind Damien from the soldiers outside, narrowly missing him. Mid-step, he swapped hands to take aim inside the control room. By then, Sophia and Jay had taken out three more Helldiver soldiers with their electro-rounds. They shuddered on the floor around them.

Damien closed the door with his access card. 'How many are we supposed to be fighting here?'

'As many as Denton wants us to.' Sophia marched to their own prisoner, Xiu.

Xiu was tied to a chair, mouth covered with duct tape. Jay ripped it off her legs and then her face.

'Ow.' Xiu kicked him and almost knocked him over.

'Guys, watch the door.' Sophia moved behind Xiu and worked a flat piece of metal into her plasticuffs, then cut the duct tape from her wrists.

The Helldivers on the floor could do nothing except remain there. Their pistols were disabled and as per the rules, they were to remain in position until the exercise finished. Damien checked each of them carefully, making sure their pistols all had red LEDs—disabled from combat.

Damien heard the door click. The red light on the card reader started to blink.

'I'm guessing that's not a door malfunction,' Jay said.

'Locked remotely.' Damien took a step toward it. 'I could try my card again.'

'No.' Sophia removed her blue vest and reached for one of the Helldiver's purple vests, pulling it over his helmet. In an instant, she was Helldiver.

Jay went for the nearest Helldiver while Damien kept his pistol trained on the sealed door. Sophia tossed a purple vest in his direction. He caught it and, keeping a hand on his pistol at all times, pulled it on. Xiu was wearing a Helldiver vest too. With their faces still concealed by masks and goggles—no one was the wiser.

Sophia nodded to Damien, so he tried his access card. The door flashed red.

Denton was testing them.

'Now what?' he asked.

'We play dead,' she said.

'They're gonna talk, you know.' Jay jabbed his thumb at the Helldivers sitting on the ground. 'We should tape them up.'

Sophia looked at him. 'Good idea.'

Jay grinned and retrieved the duct tape they'd taken from Xiu's mouth and wrists. He sliced both pieces in half and used them to tape the Helldivers' mouths shut, then put their masks back on. They could mumble, but they couldn't talk very well.

Just in time too; Damien heard an access card being swiped. Sophia gave a hand signal. All four of them dropped to the ground as though they'd been shot.

The door slid upward.

'What the hell?' Nasira said.

Before she could ask where Firebird were, Sophia pointed north, down the corridor.

'They took *eight* of you down? So much for reinforcements.' Nasira turned to the other Helldivers. 'Go! Go!'

Damien counted just three of them. They hurried back into the corridor, their boots taking them in the direction Sophia had pointed.

Xiu was on her feet. 'Nice trick, but you just sent them in the direction we need to escape.'

'It's the only direction they'll believe. We're not exactly swimming in options here.'

Damien, Jay and Xiu followed Sophia out of the control room and in the direction of Nasira's team. A corridor took them right and down into a stairwell. They stacked on Sophia and she took them to an underground parking lot. It was empty. The only exit was up a ramp and into open ground. It was a great place to get shot.

Beyond that, a forest. And just inside the forest, a perimeter with two beacons. To complete the exercise they would need to make it through those beacons.

'Their best strategy now is to wait for us in the forest,' Xiu said.

Damien nodded. 'And hit us from there.'

'We've taken out most of their team, they only have three left.' Jay shrugged. 'We could use Xiu as a shield and blast our way to the beacons.' He turned to Xiu. 'No offense.'

'Xiu is our objective, that's a dumb idea,' Sophia said.

'Fine, use me as a shield,' Jay said.

Sophia chewed her lip. 'How about making a break for it? By yourself.'

'I was joking.' Jay sighed. 'You're going to get me shot, aren't you?'

'It's what you wanted,' Xiu said. 'And since you're going, can I use your pistol?'

Jay gripped his weapon. 'Not a chance. If I'm doing this, I'll need it.'

'He's right,' Sophia said. 'If he's going out there unarmed, Nasira will smell a rat. Then she'll just dig in and wait us out.'

Jay frowned. 'If I get shot, it's your fault.'

'I'm comfortable with that.'

He holstered his pistol. 'Tell me what to do.'

JAY HIT the ramp at full speed, pistol in hand. He shunted all his energy into both legs and made for the forest. He wanted to get close enough so he could at least get a shot. Even if he could take one of them down, he'd be satisfied.

He sprinted across the open ground. Ahead of him, the gray sky bled color from the forest. The beacons were deep inside the trees. He watched the brush and tree trunks for movement, deciding where he would place his own three soldiers if he were setting the ambush.

He lined his pistol on a patch of foliage and slowed his pace, giving him finer control over his aim. There: a purple vest. But he was still too far away for an accurate shot. Instead, he swapped hands and checked the other side. The other two Helldivers. He recognized Nasira and another Helldiver trying to hide in the undergrowth. They saw him too.

Jay dived and hit the ground on his side. Before they could fix their aim, he fired his pistol through the undergrowth at the other Helldiver. Then he shifted his aim to Nasira—

An electric current jolted through him.

He fell onto his back, his muscles contracting. Gray sky and treetops. The current stopped and his limbs relaxed.

'That went well,' Jay said.

He heard another Helldiver, Loren, curse to herself. At least he'd taken her out with him.

Tilting his head back, he met Nasira's gaze. She was behind him, lying on her stomach. She wasn't wearing her vest at all, she'd placed it to one side as a decoy.

With a wry grin, she tapped the end of her barrel on his helmet. It made an annoying clonking sound.

Jay groaned. 'Why are you doing that?'

'This is my applause. My tiny applause for your tiny performance.'

The other Helldiver, Tetsuya, was still operational. He crouched near a tree and waited.

'And this is why you should wear your vest,' Jay said.

He arched his back, drew Damien's pistol from where it was tucked into his waistband, and fired into Nasira's armpit. She roared in pain. Jay arched some more, aimed at Tetsuya and fired again. Tetsuya rolled clear. Jay's electro-round struck a nearby tree.

Nasira elbowed his arm, knocking his aim off.

'You're not playing by the rules.' She leapt on top of him and pinned his arms to the ground. Tetsuya grabbed his wrist and wrestled the pistol from him.

'Yeah, well you know me and rules.' Jay grinned.

'Here's a rule for you.' She stood over him and fired Damien's pistol into his vest.

The electric shock rippled through him. He slobbered inside his mask and Nasira laughed. She sat back down on him again, her knees in his armpits. Her russet skin was shiny with sweat, and a single ringlet of hair brushed against her visor.

'Nice try, though,' she said.

The forest around them cracked with electro-rounds. Tetsuya returned fire, but was hit. He spasmed to the forest floor. Nasira lurched forward on top of Jay. An electric current surged through her, courtesy of Sophia's pistol. But then it surged through him, too. He lay under her, his body rigid as the current numbed his fingertips. Their goggles clinked and finally the current stopped.

Jay drew breath again. 'I don't care. That was still worth it.'

Nasira exhaled, fogging her goggles. 'I hate you.'

Sophia sprinted past them, through the beacons. Xiu and Damien were a few steps behind. They made it.

Nasira winced, lifting herself off him.

'Was it good for you too?' Jay asked.

She ignored him and walked off.

'HOW DID Firebird Squad survive that last exercise?' Denton asked.

He walked the floor of the dimly lit debriefing room at a crisp pace. The room, temperature controlled to keep everyone cold and awake, smelt of stale carpet. All of the Firebird and Helldiver recruits sat in the front row, holding standard-issue pens and notebooks. Sophia didn't really know how to explain their survival. She did what she had to for Firebird Squad, it was as simple as that. But that wasn't really an answer. Not one Denton would accept.

'Jay was technically dead,' Nasira said. 'They cheated.'

Denton raised an eyebrow. 'Did they really? *Technically*, they made it past the beacons. Three of them, including their prisoner. Their objective was successfully completed.'

'But in the real world, Jay was toast,' Nasira said.

'In the real world, you cheat.' Denton started pacing. 'If that's what gets you across the line. They broke the rules, sure. But they broke them to complete the objective. And this could all have been avoided if you did one simple thing.' He stood in front of Nasira. 'Do you know what that is?'

Nasira folded her arms, wincing from the bruises. 'No, sir.'

'If you searched the enemy, as you always should, you would have found Jay's concealed weapon,' Denton said. 'The secret to their success was your lack of awareness.'

He pivoted on one heel and stared right at Sophia. She

stopped taking notes and straightened in her chair. He looked down at the notes on her page—they were sparse but she'd written the important things.

'Sophia, you issued two pistols to Jay,' he said. 'Which left only one usable weapon between the three of you. You put *everything* on him. That's a big gamble.'

Sophia looked over at Jay, who was sitting next to her. 'Yes sir.'

'Why?' he asked.

'I trust him.'

'Why do you trust him?'

'Because he could do it.' She cleared her throat. 'Once the Helldivers see Jay running through the forest by himself they'll know he's a decoy.' Sophia eyed Nasira. 'They're smart, they'd focus on the rest of us and anticipate an attack. So I used that to our advantage. It was the only move that made sense.'

Jay nodded and wrote something in his notebook. From where Sophia was sitting, there didn't seem to be any writing on his page. Instead, he drew a squiggle.

Sophia waited for Denton to explain her mistakes to everyone, but he didn't.

'Nasira, you removed your vest in the forest,' he said. 'It's a small rule, but you broke it. In the previous exercise, you gave your pistol to the prisoner you were supposed to rescue. It was an attempt to trick Firebird Squad. And it almost worked.'

Denton smiled. It wasn't often Sophia saw that.

Denton surveyed the debriefing room. 'Why does it work?'

Both squads were silent.

'Deception?' Damien asked. He was sitting next to Jay, his page was crammed with notes.

'And why does deception work?' Denton asked.

Sophia played the scenario in her head. She didn't know why she'd made the decisions she had, but now it was starting to make sense. 'It exploits our preconceived assumptions,' she said.

'Explain,' Denton said.

'In the first exercise, we expected Grace to be unarmed. We did not expect her to be a threat. We expected Nasira to be using her own weapon. With all these assumptions, we almost missed what was really happening.'

'But you didn't miss it,' Denton said. 'For the rest of your team, the battle seemed to be over. Yet when you entered the room, you did so in a heightened state of awareness. You saw it immediately. And this is why *every one of you* needs to be aware at all times.'

Everyone nodded, some taking notes.

'You never switch off,' he said. 'By the time I'm done with you, you won't be able to.' He paused, in case there were any questions.

Damien raised his hand, but Denton turned to Jay instead.

'Nasira's team expected a certain type of attack from you. So you changed your approach,' Denton said. 'You subverted their preconceptions. That is the art of deception.'

Nasira glared at Jay, but he paid her no attention and drew another squiggle.

'Firebird and Helldiver Squads, your Special Operations Training is now complete,' Denton said. 'You are no longer recruits, you are no longer soldiers. You are now specialists.' He eyed each of them carefully. 'The fourth and final phase of your training begins tomorrow: Intelligence Training.'

He focused on Sophia. She refused to blink, not while he was looking at her.

'And your first class for Intelligence Training will be *Full Spectrum Surveillance*.' Denton cast a final gaze over the squads. 'Dismissed.' He walked out.

Sophia scooped up her canteen bottle and notebook. She made for the door, but Nasira cut her off.

'You won,' Nasira said. It was more of a statement than congratulations.

Sophia wasn't expecting that. 'I learned it from you.'

'I'm flattered,' Nasira said, straight faced.

'I'm not sure if you're being sarcastic or you're only capable of two facial expressions,' Sophia said. 'But I guess you still dislike me.'

Nasira stepped aside, letting her pass. 'No, that's one facial expression. Besides, you're Firebird's new squad leader. I'd have to join the line to dislike you.'

'I'm just trying to qualify. Like everyone else.'

'That's what everything is, right? Qualifying.' Nasira turned to leave. 'See you 'round, Soph.'

Sophia watched her go.

Jay was suddenly beside her, arms folded. 'Got a nice ring to it.'

'Disliking me?' she asked.

Jay's eyebrows creased. 'No, you're all right. I meant Soph. One syllable, rolls of the tongue.'

'Call me that and I'll send you into the forest without a pistol,' she said. 'Or clothes.'

Damien joined them, trying not to laugh. 'He'd probably enjoy that.'

'So-phi-a. Three syllables.' Jay shrugged. 'That works too.'

'Thanks for getting us through,' Damien said. 'So-phi-a.'

CHAPTER TWO

Today
Moscow, Russia

THE HOODED OPERATIVE moved soundlessly across pink and white marble. She paused mid-step and appeared to tune into the sound. The Metro station was evacuated, but the operative knew someone was there. She drew her pistol and pivoted.

Sophia stepped out of the shadows, already aiming. But she didn't shoot.

They trained their pistols on each other. Sophia wielded the same Glock as the operative, only hers was modified. She met the operative's gaze over her pistol's sights.

'You're quieter than most.' The operative's voice echoed across the subway tunnels and vaulted ceilings.

'You're sensitive,' Sophia said.

'Forty decibels, if you're wondering.'

'Hyperaudition. That's the Pepsi gene, right?'

'*Prestin* gene.' The operative leaned into her pistol. 'I have a sensitive trigger finger too, so you might want to lower your weapon.'

'I was enjoying our little chat,' Sophia said. 'Might be cut short if I do that.'

'If you're trying to stall me, I've already placed the explosives.'

Sophia raised an eyebrow. 'If you're trying to detonate them, I imagine you'll want to get clear first.'

'I never mentioned they were here.'

'I can smell your fear,' Sophia said. 'And it's not the fear of my pistol, or me.'

There was the slightest twitch around her left eye. 'You're Sophia, aren't you? The te—'

'Terrorist,' Sophia finished for her. 'I also go by the title of insurgent and traitor. And occasionally the person who stops people like you from detonating explosives in Russian train stations and killing a whole lot of people.'

'Not long ago, you were the one doing our killing,' the operative said. 'Just down the passageway, right?'

'A long time ago,' Sophia said. 'I'm not on your side anymore. You could say I'm reformed.'

'I'm curious,' she said. 'How can you smell my fear when you don't even have an ability? You're useless.'

'I was a late bloomer,' Sophia said. 'These days, I smell pheromones. It really messes with your appetite, by the way.'

'Depends on which appetite.'

'So we're a hundred feet underground and your

anxiety is steadily building,' Sophia said. 'I'm guessing the explosives are on a timer.'

'Don't waste your last few minutes trying to brain-wash me,' the operative said. 'If you even try to turn me into one of your zombies, I won't be able to tell you where the explosives are.'

'That's a problem, because Moscow's Special Rapid Response will be crawling through this station any minute now,' Sophia said. 'The Fifth Column don't have much control over Russia these days. They might have a hard time pulling you out of custody. In fact, they'll prob-ably just cut their losses and leave you there. That's the whole point of a deniable operation, right?'

'You should know. You were like me, once.'

'Once,' Sophia said. 'If we're caught—'

'If we're caught, I'm the one with valuable intelligence to trade and you're the terrorist mastermind caught in the act.'

'Tell me where the explosives are and I'll get you out unscathed,' Sophia said. 'Relatively speaking.'

'With me as your prisoner.'

'Better than being dead.'

'It's me or the explosives,' the operative said. 'You can't have both.'

'Actually, there's a third option.'

Someone new had appeared from behind the opera-tive. Fluent English, Russian accent. No uncertainty in her tone. That bothered Sophia the most.

The newcomer moved from behind a column, her calcite-blue eyes focused on Sophia more than the opera-tive. She was noticeably taller than the operative, and she wore a charcoal gray coat that ran seamlessly from her neck to her legs. Frost blond hair touched her shoulders and her black boots were laced with paracord.

Operative.

That could only mean one thing: the Fifth Column. The covert multinational agency that had once trained Sophia. And yet Sophia had never seen this woman before. Perhaps she was deprogrammed? Perhaps she too was a rogue?

The newcomer aimed at Sophia with some sort of Russian pistol, difficult to identify at this distance. But her blue eyes locked onto Sophia, her nose and cheeks flushed pink and her lips, almost as white as her face, chapped and slightly parted. She breathed heavily. She must have sprinted here.

'I can drop you both without even calling for backup,' she said. 'If you want out of this alive, then I suggest you slowly point your weapons to the ceiling and remove your magazines.'

Neither Sophia nor the operative broke their aim.

'Listen to me,' Sophia said. 'This operative has placed explosives on the platform.'

The operative spoke in Russian, which Sophia roughly understood.

Don't listen to her, I'm the one stopping her.

'Last chance.' The newcomer watched them with a measured glance. 'Both of you: aim your pistols at the ceiling.'

Sophia made the first move. Slowly, she turned her barrel upwards, her finger out of the trigger guard. She released the magazine. It didn't drop so she shook it from the well and it clattered on the patterned marble. She still had one round in the chamber.

'Who are you?' the newcomer asked.

Sophia wondered if this woman had heard of her. Was she Sophia the terrorist or Sophia the freedom fighter? There was only one way to find out.

'My name is Sophia. You might have heard—'

'No, I haven't.'

Sophia didn't know whether to be relieved or offended, so she spoke to the operative. 'Your turn.'

The operative kept her aim on Sophia.

'Remove your magazine!' the newcomer said, speaking to the operative.

The operative's trigger finger shifted.

'Children three that nestle near,' Sophia said quickly.

The operative's trigger finger relaxed.

'Eager eye and willing ear, pleased a simple tale to hear,' Sophia said.

The operative twitched, seemed to stare through her and then refocus. 'Access permitted.'

The newcomer stood there too, her interest growing. The command hadn't worked on her, so she couldn't be an operative. She didn't even recognize Sophia's name. That didn't leave many options, but Russian intelligence was one of them.

'Ask her again,' Sophia said, this time in the best Russian she could manage. 'She will obey basic commands.'

The newcomer kept her aim on the operative for now. 'Point your barrel to the ceiling, remove your magazine and clear the chamber.'

Without hesitation, the operative did as instructed. The magazine bounced across the marble floor. She stared blankly ahead.

The newcomer spoke in English now. 'How did you do that?'

Sophia aimed at her. 'It's a long story.'

The newcomer covered her. 'You only have one round.'

'I can work with that,' Sophia said. 'Who are you? GRU? SVR?'

'FSB. Maybe that was your third guess.'

Sophia knew she was lying. 'Maybe.'

'Speaking of threes, how many of you are there—here in Moscow?'

'You tell me,' Sophia said.

Using her supporting hand, the newcomer touched the pressel switch on her jacket collar. 'I have two operatives.'

'You have one of them.' Sophia nodded to the operative nearby. 'And it's not me.'

She glared, unblinking. 'You're one of them. I remember you.'

Sophia felt her anger. The newcomer was losing control.

'Whatever you think I've done, that wasn't me,' Sophia said. 'I can explain.'

The newcomer's finger curled over her trigger. 'Give me one good reason why I don't shoot you right now.'

'Because I'm not like them,' Sophia said.

'Why should I believe anything you say?'

'I'm not programmed. Not anymore.'

The newcomer shook her head. 'That's not possible.'

'Then how would you explain what I just did?'

Holding down her switch, the newcomer said, 'Unreadable, say again.' Her expression shifted. She took her phone from her pocket and answered. 'Yes.'

'Let me guess,' Sophia said, 'you have to run?'

'My team know exactly where we are. If you were to make the wrong move.'

'Understood,' Sophia said.

The newcomer lifted her finger from the trigger. She wasn't interested in shooting Sophia. Although there was really only one way to be sure.

Sophia lowered her pistol. 'I take it you want me to disarm the explosives.'

The newcomer holstered her weapon. 'Whatever you do with that operative, do it fast.'

Without another word, she broke into a run. Past Sophia, to the southern entrance of the subway station. She raced up the escalator and disappeared.

'Well, that makes things simpler.' Sophia adjusted her aim to the operative. 'Where is the detonator?'

'I do not know,' the operative said.

'You placed the explosives, where is the detonator?' Sophia asked.

'This information is not accessible.'

Sophia cursed. 'Execute parapsyche designation Lycaon.' *Slave mode.*

'Command not recognized.'

'Fine.' Sophia didn't have time to dig around the operative's programming. She had to bring her back and ask directly. 'Execute parapsyche designation Ares.'

'Ares loaded.' The operative blinked, then focused on

Sophia. Her face contorted with anger. 'How long have I been out?'

'Where's the detonator?' Sophia asked.

The operative spotted her unloaded pistol near her foot. She had to know she couldn't get to it in time. 'There is no detonator. How long have I been out?'

'Almost five m—' Sophia said.

The explosion tore through the northern end of the subway, shearing stone columns and raising the station platform in a seismic wave of undulating marble. Sophia hit the ground behind the nearest column, protecting herself from the blast cloud and debris. She crawled to her hands and knees, collected her pistol, and noticed her earpiece roll past. She caught it, blew the dust off and shoved it back into her ear. She heard the concerned calls of her own team: Czarina and Ieva.

'I'm here.' Her own voice sounded dull, underwater.

Pistol in hand, Sophia checked around the column for the operative. She was standing right there, pistol aimed, magazine missing.

Sophia didn't raise her pistol. Like her, the operative had a round in the chamber.

'Weapon down,' the operative said.

Sophia laid her pistol on the marble.

'Slide it over.' The operative kept checking the southern end of the subway, her eyes wide.

Sophia heard it too. Special Rapid Response making their way down the stairs, perhaps accompanied by a specialized demolition team. Any moment now they could approach from the southern entrance, trapping Sophia and the operative inside.

Neither had much time.

'Slide your pistol over!' the operative said.

Sophia looked her in the eyes. 'No.'

The operative broke into a run. Off the platform, into the subway tunnel.

Sophia went for her pistol. 'Operative is gone.'

'Copy that,' Czarina said in her ear.

'Any other detonations?' Sophia asked.

'Negative,' Ieva said. 'We have only the one. Are you hurt?'

Sophia patted herself down, feeling for anything wet. No blood. 'I'm fine.'

'Get out of there,' Czarina said. 'I see a team moving from the south.'

Sophia picked herself up. Her head spun, then things sharpened around her. Boots hit the staircase on the south end. She ran for the platform's edge and leapt onto the tracks. Moving along the rocky surface, she kept low, heard the boots of more Special Rapid Response arriving. She crouched, keeping her head under the lip of the platform.

They moved swiftly past her. Once they were far enough behind her, she slipped into the darkness.

CHAPTER THREE

Barranquilla, Colombia

'NO ONE CAN ESCAPE THEIR DESTINY,' the lead shooter said.

Three masked gunmen aimed suppressed carbines at Damien and Nasira. There was nowhere in the underground parking lot to run; the shooters had blocked the ramp to the surface. Behind Damien and Nasira, the vehicle bay led back to the facility, now swarming with more shooters who seemed intent on burning the place down.

The leader stood ten meters in front of Damien, too far to close on him unarmed. Damien was on his knees, desperately packing Jay's wounds to stem the blood loss. Jay was pale and barely conscious. Damien wanted to roll him onto his side, but it was too late.

Over the sound of the idling engine, Damien's

enhanced hearing picked up on a new pair of footsteps. Feather-light across concrete, moving around the 4x4. For a moment he thought he imagined it.

'Fire,' the leader said.

A ribbon of blood spilled from the leader's neck. Something moved past him, slashed open another shooter, who collapsed on his side. An artery squirted blood into the air.

The driver opened fire—seemingly at nothing— drilling small holes through the windshield. Nasira rolled left to avoid the shots. The third shooter tracked her with his sights, but Damien saw the glint of a blade. The gunman dropped to his side, bleeding onto concrete.

All three masked gunmen—their necks cut.

The leader clutched his throat, his carbine hanging from its sling. He finally dropped to his knees, face to face with Damien.

The driver opened his door and stepped out. He aimed over the hood at Nasira. Damien was on his feet, running. He reached the kneeling leader and grasped the hanging carbine. He twisted the weapon on the driver, who ducked behind the vehicle's door. Damien punched three rounds through the door and the driver slumped.

'Go!' Nasira yelled.

Damien saw the third gunman, bleeding from his neck and lying flat on his stomach. He tried to aim his carbine, but Damien finished him off.

Behind the door, the driver stirred; he'd collected the rounds in his armored vest. Damien charged toward him and kicked the door. It struck the driver in the head and he sprawled onto his back, out cold. Damien checked for the unseen intruder but saw no one. He ran back for Jay.

Nasira reached over a dead gunman and cut his sling with a knife. She slid the carbine out from under his chest. 'Get him in!' she yelled, her barrel sweeping the parking lot.

Damien slung one of Jay's arms over his shoulder and lifted him to his feet. Damien dragged him to the 4x4. As they approached the side, he saw movement behind the vehicle.

'Look out!' Nasira yelled.

Damien saw the unseen intruder. 'Nasira, stop!'

The intruder was gone.

'Who the hell was that?' she asked.

The skin on Damien's neck prickled. 'Someone we owe our life to.'

He opened a rear door and lifted Jay onto the seat, resting him on his side. Jay's skin felt clammy. This 4x4 might be traceable and the unseen intruder might be hostile, but right now Damien didn't care.

Nasira pivoted on her knee, firing through the parking lot as more shooters poured from the facility and took cover behind concrete pillars.

Shit.

He snatched the driver's carbine and fired through the open door, covering Nasira as she ran for the vehicle. She threw herself across to the driver's seat and took the wheel. Damien took the back seat, beside Jay.

'Keep shooting!' she yelled.

Damien fired from the back seat, through the windshield. The shooters returned fire.

Nasira reversed the 4x4 up the ramp, her foot to the floor. Rounds punched finger-sized holes in the windshield and Damien ducked. He checked himself, then Jay for wounds. Nasira whipped them up the ramp so fast they went airborne. Damien held onto whatever he could. They hit the ground again and she lined up their escape.

'Are you hit?' Damien asked.

With one hand on the wheel, Nasira checked herself.

'I'm good.' She accelerated.

Damien gripped his carbine and inspected their path ahead. Four 4x4s and two vans were stationed outside the front entrance. Nasira drove right through. Damien kept his barrel trained on the vehicles as they passed, but no one stood guard. All the shooters were inside the facility —where the action was.

Once they hit the open road, Damien remembered to breathe again. Nasira kept watching her mirrors while Damien kept an eye on Jay. He'd lost consciousness and his pulse was fast and erratic.

At least it was pumping blood, Damien thought.

He inspected the exit and entry wounds. The gauze was still packed in and Jay wasn't bleeding through. That was something, at least. But Jay had already lost a lot of blood, and then there was the damage he'd taken from the round, which Damien hoped hadn't fragmented inside his chest.

A moment later Nasira pulled to a stop on cracked asphalt. Their own vehicle—well, their own stolen vehicle —was right where they'd left it, three blocks from the facility: a gray Daewoo sedan. Yet another vehicle that could be traced.

He quickly searched the 4x4 for medical supplies and salvaged a small first aid kit littered with bandages and tape. Jay was going to need a little more than that.

Nasira helped him transfer Jay to the back seat of the Daewoo, then took the wheel again. She put as much distance between them and the facility as possible.

Jay was in shock and he needed blood now.

'We have to find a hospital,' Damien said. 'Jay needs a transfusion.'

Nasira ignored him. She took another corner and swerved to avoid an oncoming car. 'Too dangerous.'

They could report the shooting as loosely connected to the raid on the facility. They would be questioned by police, but at least it'd give Jay time to be patched up by surgeons.

'He's dying,' Damien said.

'He won't die,' Nasira said.

'His pseudogenes are gone.'

She accelerated harder. 'What? What do you mean *gone*?'

'They're switched off,' Damien said. 'He told me.'

'He told—shit.' She shook her head. 'How much blood has he lost?'

'Before I packed the wounds, one, maybe two liters.'

'How much?' Nasira yelled. 'Exactly?'

'I don't know!' Damien yelled back. 'They were going to shoot us, I wasn't—'

'He won't make it,' Nasira said.

'But you just—look, he has to.'

Her fingers were white on the steering wheel.

'You have Jay's Brazilian passport,' he said. 'We can buy him enough time at the hospital until he's stable.'

'Those people will come searching for us. If we go to the nearest hospital they'll find us there and kill us all.'

'That's what we have to do,' Damien said.

'You want to get us all killed?' she asked.

'We go for one further away. One they won't look in immediately. Buy us a little time.'

She tossed her phone at him; her way of agreeing. He switched to maps and ran a search for hospitals, then chose a hospital beyond the nearest one.

Nasira hit her horn and swerved around another vehicle. 'Found one?'

'Twenty minutes out,' he said.

'Twenty, my ass.' Nasira looked over at the phone. 'I'll do it in five.'

Damien navigated for her. 'Five hundred meters, take a left.'

Nasira risked a glance over her shoulder. Tears streaked her face. 'How's he doing?'

Damien felt Jay's pulse. 'Still out. Still in shock.'

'Hang in there,' she said. 'Just a little longer.'

They tore through the night.

NASIRA KICKED the emergency doors open. Together, they hauled Jay inside.

'He's been shot!' Damien said in Spanish.

A pair of nurses ran from behind the glass. Another

nurse pushed a stretcher toward them. They laid Jay on it and wheeled him away. Damien let them go.

'They'll call the police,' Nasira said quietly.

By the time another nurse could question them, Damien had settled on a new story. They'd heard gunshots at a nearby factory, then Jay was on the ground. Damien struggled with his Spanish, so Nasira explained why they'd stuffed Jay with combat gauze.

The nurse left them in emergency. Damien stood, unmoving, aware of people watching him. Nasira pulled him by the arm, picking a spot in the corner to sit. He didn't feel like sitting but she locked his arm and forced him down.

Finally, Nasira spoke. 'They'll be putting blood into him now.'

Damien swallowed. 'Do you think the surgeons can save him?'

Nasira's hands were trembling. 'They got to.'

CHAPTER FOUR

Moscow, Russia

SHADOWS DARKENED ILLARION'S FACE, under his eyes and aquiline nose. The lines in his face were deeper today. He stared down at the briefing room table, at their notes and photos, barely acknowledging Olesya and Ark, and ran a hand over his shaved graying hair.

Olesya inspected their world map on the table. It was peppered with photos of Fifth Column operatives, each of them pinned to their last known location. Many were located in Russia, Eastern Europe and Central Asia; the rest were outdated, still children in their photos. These were pinned to the edge of the map, unknown and untracked. Olesya checked each of them with Ark, trying to identify new operatives. They did this after every encounter, but this time she took a bit longer than Ark.

When she finished, she took notes in her notebook, something Illarion always encouraged.

Ark didn't bother with that. 'What's the point? They could look like anyone now.'

'Just to be sure,' she said.

Of all the children pinned to the side of the map, none were called Sophia. It probably wasn't even her real name. But her manipulation of that operative's programming seemed very real.

Who was she? And how could she do that?

Olesya's gaze always came to rest on Xiu's face, but never for too long. Today her gaze rested on a new face, an adult face. Val's. She wasn't supposed to be on the map, and seeing her there made Olesya's stomach turn.

'Olesya?' Illarion was watching her. His silver whiskers were cropped shorter than usual. 'Is there anything else you have to share, or is that all?'

There was something. 'Maybe I'm not good enough.'

Illarion let out a slow breath. 'Is that what you believe?'

Ark started to talk, but Illarion raised his hand. He wanted her to answer.

She swallowed. 'I don't know.'

'It's not what I believe,' Illarion said.

That will change soon, she thought.

Illarion checked his papers. 'Val is the third hunter to go missing this week.'

'Wait, there were two others?' Ark blinked back tears. 'Why didn't you tell us?'

'Because it doesn't concern you,' Illarion said evenly.

'It does now,' Ark said.

Illarion met his stare. 'Would you like to run operations? Shall I take my leave and promote you in my stead?'

'No.' Ark brushed a curl of hair from his face.

'Then until I do, this concerns me,' Illarion said. 'You have your own responsibilities and they are burden enough. As of now, you both carry tracking devices. On and off duty.'

Olesya's gaze wandered to the photo of Xiu, with her brown eyes and ink-black hair.

'In the event you are captured, we will be able to track and recover you,' Illarion said. 'Is that clear?'

Xiu wasn't smiling in her photo—no one was—but Olesya remembered her smile. She wondered if Xiu was still alive and where she might be.

'Olesya?' Illarion said. 'Is that clear?'

She looked up to find he was watching her.

'Very clear.' Olesya closed her notebook.

From the table, she picked out the only piece of evidence they had. A business card she'd found on the man who she'd knocked off the van. He was dead by the time she'd reached him, and he was clean except for the card.

She held it up so both Illarion and Ark could see. It was white on both sides with a small logo on the front. It looked like two arrows intersecting each other, but there were no contact details. Illarion and Ark had seen it already, and no doubt Illarion had looked into it.

'So who are these people?' Olesya asked. 'Are they a Fifth Column proxy or do we have a new player in town?'

'Previous incidents point to the Fifth Column.' Illarion

cleared his throat. 'This is the first time another faction or group has been implicated.'

'Isn't that obvious?' Ark said. 'Fifth Column proxy.'

'The men in the van weren't Fifth Column operatives or soldiers,' Olesya said. 'This isn't some Fifth Column proxy like the Islamic State. These people were totally different.'

'And what tells you that? A stupid scribble on a bit of paper?' Ark said.

Illarion raised his voice only a fraction. 'Gleb has already identified the logo.'

'That was quick,' Olesya said.

'That's because they aren't hiding,' Illarion said. 'Intron Genetics Incorporated has been around for a long time, with a long line of respectable accomplishments in genetic engineering. If it's a proxy, then it's a very well established one.'

'And with a unique interest in Val's DNA,' Olesya said.

Ark grunted. 'Or the Fifth Column is framing them.'

'There are many possibilities,' Illarion said. 'And I will be exploring all of them.'

'We can help.' Ark pushed off the balls of his feet. 'Assign us to search, we can find them.'

'I can't spare you for that,' Illarion said. 'We have too many Fifth Column operatives crawling the region and you're our last line of defense.'

'Then how do we find her?' Ark's fists struck the table. He looked down, barely aware of the impact.

'Arkadiy,' Illarion said sharply. 'You need to control

yourself or I'll have no choice but to pull you from service. And trust me, I don't want to do that.'

Ark retreated from the table, his eyelids red. 'You can't *afford* to do that.'

Illarion's eyes glimmered in the dull light. 'We have specialists assigned to find the missing hunters, your sister included.'

Ark swallowed. 'Are they hunters, or are they—'

Illarion's deep voice stopped him mid-sentence. 'They are experts in their field. We're all upset and we all want her back. But you need to remain focused.'

Ark muttered an apology.

Olesya tried to think of a solution, something Illarion had trained her to do. But nothing came to mind. Not this time.

'Mark my words,' Illarion said. 'We will get them back. But until then you two continue working. Right now, the most important thing is making sure you don't become the next victims.'

Olesya nodded. 'Understood.'

Ark mumbled the same.

Illarion walked to the door. His assistant, Gleb, was standing patiently outside, his head visible through the glass.

'What happens if they are Fifth Column? They'll interrogate Val and the others?' Ark asked.

'This has always been a risk,' Illarion replied. 'And that is why I limit your operational knowledge. The less you know, the less you can reveal.'

'But what happens after that?' Ark asked. 'They just kill her and move on to the next hunter?'

'They won't harm her,' Olesya said. 'Think about it. Val is a highly trained weapon with unique genetics. Either way she's more valuable alive than dead.'

'Until we know more, there is little point in theorizing,' Illarion said. 'Right now I'm afraid we have graver concerns.'

Illarion opened the door and motioned Gleb inside. The intelligence officer hugged a folder of print-outs and a tablet to his chest.

'OK, so Eastern Europe.' Gleb said, stepping inside.

'Eastern Europe?' Ark said.

Gleb opened his folder and cleared his throat, but Illarion spoke first.

'A large number of Fifth Column operatives are shifting east. What does that tell you?'

'They're coordinating—' Gleb said, before Illarion waved his hand.

Gleb fell silent and let Olesya and Ark answer.

'For something larger,' Olesya said. 'Something in Eastern Europe.'

'Those other hunters were abducted from this region,' Illarion said. 'We're relocating there to assist. Gleb will brief you.'

Illarion stepped out and closed the door behind him, leaving his assistant to take over.

Gleb handed out papers, which Olesya skimmed quickly before folding and inserting them into her notebook. The Fifth Column were far more active in Eastern Europe than she thought. Not that she paid much attention; the operatives moving through Moscow were enough to keep her busy.

'You can just tell us,' Ark said. 'We screwed up and we're being transferred out.'

'Read the brief, Ark,' Olesya said. 'They need us out there.'

'It's your fault we're going there.' He threw the papers on the table. 'How am I supposed to find my sister if I'm in some backwater oblast?'

He got to his feet. Gleb stumbled over a response, but Ark was already opening the door and walking out.

Olesya leaned on the table. 'We've had a rough day.'

'It's not your fault.' Gleb blinked. 'What he said, it's not your—'

'And why do you think that?' she asked.

'This was a coordinated capture,' Gleb said. 'Just like the other two. Even if you were both there when she was taken, you may not have been able to prevent it.'

'OK. So who do you think is responsible?'

'I don't know, but I don't think—' Gleb paused and cleared his throat again.

'You don't think it was the Fifth Column?'

'I'm not in a position to give an opinion on that.'

'Then what's your position?' she asked.

'I've been tasked with monitoring new operatives as they enter Eastern Europe.'

'Have you heard the name Sophia before?' Olesya asked. 'She's a Fifth Column operative.'

Gleb looked at the map. 'Is she one of the children in those photos?'

Olesya shook her head. 'I just heard the name. It's probably nothing.'

'Nothing is nothing,' Gleb said. 'You should tell Illarion.'

'He has enough on his plate. You're new in this directorate, aren't you?'

'I was assigned this week from Analysis. It seems very stressful—'

'I think you're doing an excellent job so far,' Olesya said.

'Thank you, but we still need to go over—'

'Already read it.' Olesya opened her notebook to reveal his brief neatly folded inside.

Gleb stepped forward to inspect her notes further, but she closed them quickly.

'We all fly out in the morning,' she said. 'Ark and I deploy the very next day with a new batch of hunters. Don't worry, I'll make sure he pulls together. You can trust us both.'

'Yes, I know that I can, but the operation is in—'

'Poland.' She picked up the white card with the logo and flicked it across the map. It landed near his tablet. 'So Illarion has assigned you to look into Intron, I'm guessing.'

Gleb blinked. 'No, I have other responsibilities, but I'm sure—'

'He doesn't think it's Intron, does he?' she asked.

Gleb's gaze fell to the map. 'We're focusing on the Fifth Column.'

'Sorry if that's out of your'—Olesya let the word linger —'range.'

Gleb inspected the card. As he did so, she carefully placed her notebook over Xiu's photo.

'I'm afraid I can't dedicate any time to this without authorization. You'll need to speak to Illarion.' Gleb paused. 'Do you think Intron abducted Val?'

'That's something I'd like to find out.' She collected her notebook and held it against her chest. 'I want her back.'

'So do I.' Gleb cleared his throat. 'I mean, we all want her back.'

Olesya thought for a moment. 'Illarion won't give you authorization.'

'Perhaps not.' Gleb pocketed the card. 'If I come across something, I'll let you know. And Ark too.'

CHAPTER FIVE

Taganga, Colombia

JAY WOKE to the distant sound of gridlocked taxis and a barking dog. He was lying in a hammock, wearing his hospital pants and a t-shirt he didn't recognize. He tried to move but a sudden stabbing pain in his chest made him grasp for a phantom blade. It took him a moment to catch his breath and figure out where the hell he was.

The hammock was tied between two posts on a wooden balcony. Through the gaps in the railing he could see a bay of aquamarine water peppered with thin fishing boats, and a gritty beachfront strewn with plastic, garbage and people sprawled across beach towels. Some sort of sleepy fishing town. The water was calm and the distant voices were Spanish.

There was a strange noise beneath him. He peered over the hammock to see a very dirty duck who cast a disapproving look in his direction before waddling past. It took a wide circle around a short-haired dog chewing on a plastic cup.

'Where the fuck am I?' Jay said under his breath.

'Somewhere no one can find you,' Nasira said.

He looked in her direction but his chest flared with pain again. The hammock rocked slightly in the breeze. 'How's tricks?'

'Tricks are for kids.' Nasira stepped into view. The Colombian sun shimmered over her bronze skin. 'How you feeling?'

'I feel … alive,' he said.

She couldn't take her eyes off him and he wondered how awful he looked after being trapped in that facility as their guinea pig. He swallowed and felt his throat stick.

'You noticed, huh?' Nasira said.

'Highly trained ex-operative at your service.' He attempted a salute and wobbled in the hammock. 'Wait, how long have I been out?'

'Two days, five hours,' she said. 'Roughly.'

'How did you—'

'You're not gonna shut up until I tell you everything?' Nasira said. 'You got yourself shot, remember?'

'Yeah, I won't be forgetting that anytime soon.'

'Someone attacked those armed crazy people, then we got out of there,' she said. 'Took you to a hospital under your Brazilian passport. They did what they could. But—'

'But what, I died?'

'Clinically.' Nasira moved closer. 'And then you kicked in again. No brain damage. Uh, no more brain damage.' She forced a smile.

Jay touched where he'd been shot. Under his t-shirt the entry wound was stitched and dressed.

'How did I make it?' he asked. 'I don't have the pseudo things anymore.'

'Remnants, maybe. Hell if I know,' she said. 'Enough to rebuild your lung by the look of things. I ain't complaining.'

'You and me both.' Jay smiled, but felt it dissolve. 'I'm sorry.'

Nasira crossed her arms. 'Don't be.'

'You found me.'

'You didn't think I would?'

'Only thing that got me through,' he lied.

He wasn't about to tell her he'd given up on anyone coming for him.

Nasira reached forward and took his head in her hands. He'd seen her rupture someone's ear drums with the same motion, but this time she was relaxed, her fingers moving through his matted hair. She pressed her forehead against his and was silent for a moment, as if making sure he was real and he wasn't going anywhere. When she let go, he wished she'd held on a bit longer.

'It's my fault,' he said. 'I walked into a trap. I'm better than that, I shouldn't have—'

'Don't matter. Not anymore.' Her voice was soft. He wasn't used to that and it made him feel worse.

'Yeah, but I screwed up. And I almost didn't come back.'

'We almost didn't find you,' Nasira said. 'There were these ... mercenaries, dunno what they were but they were coming at us. Wanted us dead. I thought they were Fifth Column, you know, so they could reprogram and use us again—but they don't seem to be Fifth Column at all.'

'We need to find their headquarters,' Jay said.

'The mercs?'

'No,' he said. 'The people who abducted me, stole my suede jeans.'

'Pseudogenes.' She let out a slow breath.

He hauled himself upright. 'Right, whatever.'

'You're not going in there half cocked.'

Jay laughed nervously. 'They didn't touch that.'

His chest burned in protest but he swung his body around and lowered his feet to the wooden floor.

Nasira stopped him. 'Slow down, you ain't exactly in peak condition right now. You're not going anywhere.'

'I woke up like this,' Jay said. 'I'm flawless.'

'The hell you are.' Nasira held him down by his shoulders. 'For a dead guy, you—'

'Say I look so good tonight,' Jay said.

Nasira's eyes narrowed. 'Are you quoting Beyoncé?'

'No.' He sat back in the hammock. 'Look, I've been out of it a while. And they played a lot of music.'

'You're not going anywhere.' She helped him recline. 'We got time.'

'No, we have a duck,' he said.

Nasira looked down to see the duck waddling between her legs. It quacked angrily at her, then continued on its way.

'These people who took me,' Jay said. 'I think their headquarters are in Rio.'

Nasira ran a hand through her dark coiled hair. 'Why you telling me that?'

'They turned things off inside me. That means they can turn it back on.'

'So you wanna go to Rio?' she asked.

Jay shrugged. The movement made his chest burn. He winced and breathed slowly. 'I was supposed to go there to confess my sins. Now I guess I have two reasons to go.'

Nasira folded her arms. 'You were going to Rio?'

Jay swallowed. 'I was thinking about it. A little.'

'Those people who took you, you even know who they are?'

'No,' he said.

'You know where in Rio exactly?'

'No.'

Her shoulders dropped. 'Great. How we supposed to find them?'

Damien appeared on the balcony. 'I know someone who can help.' He flashed a goofy smile. 'Oh hey, you're alive.'

Jay shook his head. 'Everyone's so surprised.'

'At least it's a good surprise, unlike everything else right now,' Damien said.

'So who can help us?' Jay asked.

Damien ran a hand through his scruffy hair and side-stepped the duck underfoot. 'I know someone. And she knows computers.'

Nasira didn't blink. 'You want to bring *her* into this?'

'What other option do we have?' Damien asked.

Nasira thought for a moment. 'Fine, but she's still in

America. You really think she can help us find these people?'

'Whoa, hold up,' Jay said. 'There's no way I'm going back to America.'

'Why not?' Nasira asked.

'Because I'm like the most wanted terrorist in the United States,' Jay said.

Nasira snorted. 'You're top ten if you're lucky.'

Damien counted his fingers. 'And we're kind of top ten in every country, so—'

'Where she at now?' Nasira asked.

'Las Vegas,' Damien said.

'Vegas?' Jay cleared his throat. 'We could … yeah, we should definitely go.'

CHAPTER SIX

Vilnius, Lithuania

'WHERE'S THE OPERATIVE?'

Sophia ignored the question and put the kettle on the stove. But Czarina wasn't going anywhere. She pulled up the collar on her ruby red jacket and slid a chair out, but she didn't sit.

'She got away, didn't she?' Czarina's eyebrows were barely visible under the sharp edge of her bangs. 'You haven't said a word since we got back.'

'That's because you keep talking,' Sophia said.

Czarina sighed loudly. 'It works better when you talk back.'

Sophia's mind was elsewhere. She thought of the Russian intelligence agent who'd confronted her in the Moscow subway station. How much did that agent know? She wasn't Fifth Column, Sophia knew that much.

But she was something. And that something seemed very well trained.

Ieva joined them in the kitchen and took a seat. She carefully placed her modified Glock on the table and rested a hand on each knee. 'Don't mind me.' Unlike Czarina, there was no sarcasm.

'See, we both want answers.' Czarina offered a stick of gum to Ieva, who politely declined.

'It was one or the other,' Sophia said. 'The Fifth Column operative or the explosives. I didn't have time for both.'

'You really need to stop blowing up subway stations.' Czarina popped gum between her wine-red lips.

'That's not funny,' Sophia said.

'We stopped the other one for you!' Ieva smiled and tucked a lock of ash gray hair behind her ear. 'But we didn't have time to adopt an operative. Sorry.'

'No, it's best you leave that to me,' Sophia said. 'For now.'

'You are training us, yes?' Ieva asked. 'So we can do it ourselves!'

'It's dangerous,' Sophia said.

The kettle whistled in agreement.

'You don't have to capture and deprogram every operative who crosses your path, you know,' Czarina said. 'Takes too long anyway.'

'If I didn't deprogram anyone, you wouldn't be here,' Sophia said.

Normally, Czarina was grateful Sophia had rescued her in New York last year, but sometimes she needed a reminder.

Sophia plucked the kettle from the stove and poured boiling water into three mugs of tea. She added a touch of cold water to Ieva's because she didn't like to wait. Sophia carried their mugs to the table. Czarina took one and sat beside Ieva. Although compared to Ieva's upright posture, it was more of a slouch.

'Here's an idea.' Czarina chewed her gum loudly. 'These operatives shooting at you ... maybe shoot back? Trying to deprogram them with all your fancy codes and phrases, that's just—'

Sophia raised an eyebrow. 'What?'

Czarina mumbled now. 'Dangerous.'

Ieva wrinkled her small nose. 'But she didn't *try* to deprogram anyone. Sophia was stopping them from blowing up the station.'

'Yeah, and look how that worked out,' Czarina said.

Sophia looked out the kitchen window. Behind the old Lithuanian mansion, the backyard disappeared into a centuries-old oak forest. There was something about that Russian agent, but Sophia couldn't put her finger on it.

'I should've started teaching you how to deprogram earlier,' Sophia said. 'We're behind schedule.'

Czarina grunted. 'I don't think I want that responsibility just yet.'

'I do!' Ieva raised her hand. 'You can teach me. I wouldn't be as good as you though.'

Czarina pressed her chewing gum against the side of her mug.

'That's gross,' Ieva said.

'You are.' Czarina left the gum there. 'Maybe we just need a Plan B.'

'This is Plan B,' Sophia said.

'So what was Plan A?' Ieva asked.

'A tropical island.' Czarina slurped her tea. 'That was my Plan A.'

'I don't like tropical islands,' Sophia said.

Czarina lowered her lipstick-stained mug. 'So let me get this straight. One Fifth Column operative wants to shoot another Fifth Column operative, and you care because…?'

'Because one wasn't Fifth Column,' Sophia said.

'How do you know that?' Czarina asked.

'She thought *I* was Fifth Column.'

'OK, now I'm confused,' Czarina said.

Ieva's nose twitched in disapproval. 'Then what is she?'

Sophia thought for a moment. Czarina and Ieva were former Fifth Column operatives. Like her, they'd spent most of their lives in Project GATE. American accents aside, they still spoke their native languages.

'Czarina, do you speak Sri Lankan?' Sophia asked.

'I'm from Sri Lanka, but I speak Sinhala.'

'Right,' Sophia said. 'And Ieva, do you speak Lithuanian?'

Ieva nodded. 'And Russian and German and—'

'Yes, but my point is that a lot of us speak English in addition to our first language. And the Fifth Column never squandered that. We were all deployed to our home countries for operations because we could blend in and operate best there.'

Ieva nodded some more. 'I was here in Lithuania when you found me.'

'Exactly. So have you ever had a run-in with a Russian operative?' Sophia asked. 'Light blond hair, pale blue eyes?'

'You just described half the population on the largest supercontinent in the world,' Ieva said. 'But no, I haven't seen any Russian operatives. Not here.'

'Why didn't you just take a photo of her?' Czarina asked.

'She had me at gunpoint.'

'That's what they all say,' Czarina said. 'You're trying to tell us that you had a Fifth Column operative at gunpoint, and then some blond girl just swishes in, takes over and then leaves. And you let her?'

'She was very careful,' Sophia said. 'The circumstances made it hard for me to stop her. And besides, she ran really fast.'

'Made it hard for you to stop the station from blowing up,' Czarina said.

Ieva sipped her tea. 'Mayakovskaya was a lovely station too.'

Sophia shook her head. 'The thing is, I put the Fifth Column operative into slave mode right in front of this Russian, and she didn't even blink.'

'So she's Fifth Column then,' Czarina said. 'Maybe a diversion. And it worked, you lost both of them.' She leaned over her mug of tea. 'Now the Fifth Column knows we were in Moscow. Something I'm not all that cool with.'

'What are you trying to say?' Sophia asked.

'All I'm saying is less talking'—Czarina mimed a gun with her finger—'more action.'

'I wasn't going to shoot them in the back,' Sophia said. 'And neither will you.'

'You know they won't hesitate to do the same to you, right?' Czarina shrugged. 'Better you shoot first, I say.'

'She didn't shoot me,' Sophia said.

'Not this time.'

Ieva elbowed Czarina. 'Grumpy pants.'

'I told you not to call me that,' Czarina said.

Sophia allowed herself a smile. Outside, the forest grew dark, the treetops fringed with silver from the moon.

'They're programmed to believe we're the enemy,' Sophia said. 'It's not their fault.'

'It doesn't change the fact they can shoot you.' Czarina turned to Ieva for support. 'Right?'

Ieva looked down at her tea. 'Um, I guess.'

'I've killed enough operatives.' Sophia tapped her phone and pulled up a map of Eastern Europe with various dots, each representing a live operative. Thanks to her friend who was very good with computers, Sophia had secret access to the Fifth Column's satellites.

'So?' Czarina asked.

'It's about time we start saving them,' Sophia said.

'That's not working out so well. I mean'—Czarina glanced at Ieva—'no offense, we have Ieva now. But that's three of us. And the rest of your little gang is on the other side of the world somewhere.'

'Is there anyone on the radar for us?' Ieva asked.

Sophia nodded. 'We have three operatives moving west.'

'Three?' Czarina said. 'We can barely handle one.'

'So we isolate and take one operative,' Sophia said. 'Play it safe.'

'Does your map say their destination?' Ieva asked.

'Berlin. We leave tonight.'

Sophia's phone chirped.

'Proximity sensors.' Czarina drew her pistol from the holster in the waistband of her jeans.

On her phone, Sophia opened the video feed for one of her IR cameras. Someone walked through their front yard with a high posture and crisp stride she'd recognize anywhere.

'Ding dong, Navy SEAL calling,' Czarina said in a sing-song voice, holstering her pistol.

'He took his time,' Sophia said.

'Perhaps he knows the Russian agent?' Ieva asked.

Sophia thought for a moment. 'Don't mention her. Not yet.'

'But he might—' Ieva said.

Czarina leaned over the table, grinning. 'Hang on, you don't even trust him yet, do you?'

Ieva dragged Czarina out of the kitchen, but not before Czarina pulled the gum from her mug and shoved it back in her mouth.

'Maybe this time get a room,' Czarina said with a wink.

Sophia shot her a glare, but Czarina was already creeping down the hall with Ieva. Sophia stood and slipped her pistol into her waistband holster. Then she changed her mind—she didn't want to look armed—so she shoved it down the back of her waistband, hidden under her jacket.

The floorboards creaked beneath heavy boots. A moment later, DC stepped cautiously into the kitchen. A thin pink scar on his obsidian knuckles glinted like silver under the kitchen lights.

'Nice place,' he said.

'Here for a good time, not a long time,' Sophia said. 'Would you like to stand in the doorway and not drink the tea I'm not making for you?'

'I don't drink tea or—' DC noticed her smile. 'Oh.' He cleared his throat. 'So what brings you to this neck of the woods, still chasing operatives?'

'I go where the business is,' Sophia said. 'And you?'

'The Fifth Column is crumbling.'

'That wasn't nearly dramatic enough,' she said. 'You need to work on your delivery.'

He folded his arms, his brown jacket pulling taut over his wide shoulders. 'You don't believe me?'

'I'll believe it when I see it.'

Still in the doorway, he remained irritatingly still. 'They're making a desperate push. It could be their last.'

'Could be?'

'This is bigger than just operatives, Sophia. I'm talking with some people. People who could help us end them.'

'You know what happened last time I tried that,' she said. 'So you can see why I have trouble coming around to this idea. Especially when you're pitching it.'

DC's gaze shifted to the floor. 'I'm sorry.'

'You don't need to tell me, I can smell it from the ecto-hormones you're secreting through your skin.'

'Huh. I bet you say that to all the guys.'

'Sure, if they don't shower.'

245

His smile disappeared. 'Look, I don't expect you to trust me.'

'I don't,' she said. 'And I won't be played.'

'So you think I'm playing you?'

'I hope you're not,' she said. 'And I definitely don't want outsiders involved.' Her words came sharper than she'd intended. Maybe *outsider* was a bit harsh.

'But that's exactly what you're doing.' DC stepped into the kitchen, finally. Only a small step, it almost didn't count. 'You didn't score an operative today.'

'You were watching us,' she said. 'I knew I had a stalker.'

'There will be more. You can see their movements, even now.'

He was right. Activity was ramping up. It was why she was here in the first place.

'Not all their movements,' she said.

'Maybe you should stop and catch your breath.' He took another careful step toward the table. 'Look at what you have around you.'

Frustration built inside her. 'The Fifth Column has an extensive network of operatives. I have two.'

'You have two *here*, sure. But you also have Nasira. And you have Damien and Jay.'

'They've sacrificed enough,' she said.

His scent evoked a particular combination of emotions in her that attracted and repelled at the same time. It made the hair on her arms prickle.

'And you have me,' he said.

She smiled. 'Not yet.'

CHAPTER SEVEN

Las Vegas, United States

'I WOULD OFFER YOU A CHAIR,' the suited man said, taking a seat in the hotel room. 'But you're a spring chicken who can make do with the floor. Plus, I really must compliment you on your hair. What color do you call that, chili red?'

'Scarlet,' Aviary said.

He wasn't even looking at her. 'Close enough.'

Aviary sat near the bed, her wrists and ankles cuffed. The green-tinted window cast an appropriately radioactive haze over the man before her.

Not long ago, this hotel was for guests. Now it was under the control of the US Marines Corps.

The suited man was regular in almost every respect. His skin was taut around his eyes and mouth, crinkled across his forehead and scarred below his lips. His nose seemed slightly askew, or perhaps his face was slightly askew. His suit was crease-free and his hands were well moisturized. She could smell the light fragrance of his hand cream.

He seemed in a much better mood than anyone else in this building, which wasn't hard; the marines lingering outside were on double shifts, wavering between restlessness and fatigue.

'My name is Hal,' he said. 'With an *a*, not an *e l l.*'

What was his strategy? Aviary thought. *To irritate people into a confession?*

He laughed to himself and removed a tablet in a hideous leather casing from his briefcase. He placed it upon the table, cracked his fingers and wiggled them.

'Okie dokie, let's get this chat rolling.' Hal smiled at Aviary. She felt ill. 'Now, you have been questioned a bit already. And I do apologize for that. I mean, you're barely an adult and you're thrown into this horrible mess. You will be relieved to know that I won't be covering the same line of questioning as the United States Marine Corps.'

He flopped his badge open, almost an afterthought.

'I'm with the National Clandestine Service of the CIA.' He took a moment to rub his thin nose. Even at this distance she could see the pores. 'Make of that what you will. Now, let's get to the meat of this.'

Hal seemed excited by the prospect. Aviary wasn't.

His fingers tapped the surface of his tablet. Each tap was heavy and she wondered if the screen might break under impact. Already she was starting to prefer his talking.

'All righty, so let's get one thing super-duper clear, shall we?' Hal said. 'This resistance you're part of? Not a big fan. I mean, the United States Marine Corps don't care for them folks either. But—'

Oh God, now he was waggling his finger.

'I care a great deal less,' Hal said. 'You see, they keep the marines busy and all, but I'm here to have a conversation with you. A good old-fashioned conversation between a gentleman and a lady.' He gestured to her cuffs. 'Alas, the lady is tied up right now—'

He rubbed his hands together and leaned forward, his gaze firmly on Aviary.

'More than likely, everything I say to you will go in one ear and out the other. Chances are, you won't be interested in what I'm yakking about,' Hal said. 'So I'll keep it brief. Five minutes of my waxing lyrical. I don't expect we'll be talking much beyond that.' He raised a hand. 'However, this is always the most interesting part. *For me*, anyway.'

He paused and sucked at something between his teeth.

'You know the gravity of your situation. I'm sure the kind marines—while short on humor—have informed you of your status as a terrorist, subject to indefinite detention. Listen to me, talking like a politician. To put it simply, we're not calling an alligator a lizard, are we? You know you're going away for a very long time.'

Aviary nodded slowly.

'Excellent! I mean, not excellent. Terrible. Very terrible.' He pursed his lips, thinking for a moment. 'This is interesting because I can do certain things to change that.' He held out both hands to inspect them. 'Now, before you question my moral status, there are limits to my powers of persuasion, but they are not to be underestimated. While I can't change the fact that you're a terrorist and all the nasty stuff that comes with your unfortunate life choices and personal … *style*, I can change how we handle you.'

He launched to his feet, almost knocking his chair over. He apologized to no one in particular, maybe the chair, and paced the narrow space around the hotel bed.

'Down to brass tacks. Your best case scenario is where your value outweighs,'—he shook his fist as he formed the thought—'gosh, your value is really valuable. That might well be enough to keep you from detention altogether.' He halted and locked his gaze with her. 'Now wouldn't that be something? Wouldn't that be something worth talking about?'

Aviary scratched an adhesive bandage on her palm. 'Sure, why not?'

'You see, Miss Aviary Keli'i.' His tongue tripped over her Hawaiian surname. 'I couldn't give two hoots about your involvement with this resistance. I mean, what started all this business anyway? A pesky nationwide firearm ban?'

'Or programmed shooters,' Aviary said. 'Take your pick.'

'That sounds a bit silly.' Hal almost smiled. 'You see, the resistance are not the reason I'm here.'

Hal leaned over and tapped on his tablet. This time, he wasn't typing. He lifted the tablet over so Aviary could see the screen. She recognized the woman in the photo.

'Sophia. Born Zofia Novotný, Czech Republic,' he said. 'Do you know her?'

'Does she still keep her surname?' Aviary crossed her legs on the carpet. 'Or is it just a mononym like Björk or Madonna?'

'See, I was hoping you could tell me.'

'Or Sting,' Aviary said.

'This is one of the many questions about Sophia that keep me up at night. Which is not that hard because you were aiming a little low there. No offense.'

'Some taken,' Aviary said.

'You have three options. Option one: you tell me everything you know of Sophia's whereabouts, activities and operational capabilities. You know, all the good stuff that people like me really love to know.'

'I thought you don't care about the resistance,' she said.

He smiled. 'Sophia is not the resistance. She is not even connected to the resistance. She is merely a woman. And I want all the dirt on her. In return, you have your freedom. Under one condition: you leave this country and you never come back.'

Aviary frowned. 'Cher? No surname.'

His smile faded. 'Option two: you work with us. All the aforementioned dirt on Sophia, sure. But you become our little spy. You pretend to join her, only you're on our side. Once she's taken care of, we can broker a deal between the resistance and the government. Something to your satisfaction.'

'My satisfaction?' she asked.

'Civil war ends and we all go back to fighting climate change. And you go back to whatever you like. Just not more terrorist stuff, because that would be awkward.'

'See, I thought terrorism was *your* specialty.' She smiled. 'Awkward.'

Hal took a seat again. 'Bless your little heart, Aviary, but I really don't think you're giving this the attention it deserves.'

'You're right,' Aviary said.

Hal drew his pistol and placed it on the table, the barrel facing her. It was large and clunky, and there was a small red diode on the pistol grip.

Weapon retention system.

Even if she could get to it, she wouldn't be able to fire it.

Hal nodded to his pistol. 'It's big.'

'I doubt that,' she said. 'You haven't told me option three.'

'Option three is you don't play ball. And then it's prison for a very long time.'

'Listen,' Aviary said, 'There's a reason why I don't have much faith in your options. I get what you're trying to do, but if you're looking for the threat to our country you need only look up.'

Hal looked up at the ceiling.

'Figuratively speaking.' She sighed. 'I'm wasting my breath.'

'You probably are,' Hal said. 'But please, continue.'

'You want to stop the bloodshed, right?'

He gestured with open hands. 'It's why I'm here.'

'But you won't. You'll keep killing,' she said. 'Bloodshed is where we started and it's where we end.'

'Do you want the end?' Hal asked softly.

'The end is never the end though, is it?' Aviary said.

'All things come to an end. Even you.'

'There are billions of us,' she said. 'And we're all programmed to execute an infinite loop. Our conditions are never met. And so we are doomed to reset.'

He sucked on his teeth again. 'You might be surprised to know I have thought of this on many occasions. A little less melodramatically and without your programming lingo. But sure as God made little green apples, I've considered this dilemma at least once. Possibly even twice.' He cleared his throat. 'This infinite loop, do you want to change it?'

'No, it's the conditions that need to change,' Aviary said. 'They don't account for one bug in the program. We don't even know how to debug it. And it destroys us every time.'

Hal smiled. 'Are you the bug, Aviary?'

'No,' she said. 'You've been the bug from the moment you were born.'

'Curious.' He clasped his fingers together, as one might to indulge a child. 'How can you tell?'

'You run a different loop,' she said. 'You have parameters missing.'

'Are you suggesting I have some sort of brain damage?' Hal asked. 'That's quite an accusation for a terrorist to make to an employee of the Central Intelligence Agency.'

'It might be, except you're not from the CIA. In case you're wondering why I have little faith in your options.'

He waved his CIA badge in one hand. 'And if you're

wondering why they *are* options, it's because your suspicions are correct.'

Aviary's heart raced.

'Final boarding call,' he said.

'I've been waiting for you.' Aviary released her handcuffs and launched to her feet.

Hal took up his pistol. 'Not so fast. Sit down this instant.'

Aviary squeezed the palm of her hand, triggering the implant under her skin.

A faint whining sound came from his pistol. A tiny red diode blinked on the pistol grip, above his thumb. She'd just denied him fingerprint access to his own weapon. He looked back at her and realization washed over his face.

'I don't think you've thought this through,' he said.

Aviary approached the table. 'Three interviews. Two interrogations. What does it take to get the Fifth Column's attention around here? I mean, come on.'

'Let's remember that you're in a building filled with soldiers who like to shoot first and ask later,' Hal said. 'And my partner is due any moment. Doesn't help you, now does it?'

'Bitch, please. Doesn't help you either,' Aviary said. 'And besides, you don't even have a partner.'

Hal stiffened. 'Sit down this instant, or you'll face charges for assaulting a federal officer.'

'Why aren't you calling for help?' Aviary asked.

Hal blinked. 'If I call this in, there's no going back. They'll give you one heck of a beating.'

She raised an eyebrow. 'Shame you won't be alive to see it.'

'You don't have combat training.'

'Neither do you,' she said.

'I'm a reasonable fellow. We might just put some options back on the table.'

Hal carefully reached for his tablet.

She slammed her fist on his fingers. They crunched. He lashed out with his other fist. She stepped back, kicked the table into his legs. He stumbled into the wall. She vaulted over the table—narrowly avoiding a kick as Hal fought back—and jammed the edge of the tablet into his neck.

Hal's gasp was explosive.

He slid down the wall, hands over his neck, trying to breathe. Aviary took his pistol from the holster. It was black and heavy.

'Do you penetrate yourself with this?' she asked.

Hal coughed, tried to reach for it. She retreated, taking the tablet and pistol with her. She placed the tablet on the bed and peeled the adhesive bandage from her palm, revealing stitching that hadn't dissolved yet. Under the bandage, she peeled off a strip of sticky tape and applied it to the slide of Hal's pistol, where his supporting thumb rested. Then she—

Hal's elbow caught her across the face. Light sparked around her. She dropped to both knees, one hand on the carpet to brace herself. Hal took the tablet and was about to crack it across her face, then hesitated. He discarded the tablet and his fist came crashing down instead.

Aviary narrowly dodged the blow.

She whipped her knuckles into his ribs, but his knee caught her in the chest and sent her reeling back across

NATHAN M FARRUGIA

the carpet. She crashed into the lamp beside the bed. Hal was on his feet, wheezing.

Aviary struggled to draw breath. She panicked, clutched at the bedside table behind her, grasping little more than the room service menu. She slipped to the floor.

'What were you saying about'—Hal coughed —'combat training?'

She kicked him, but he sidestepped and lowered his knee to her chest, pinning her.

'You must bring so much shame to your parents.' He loosened his tie. 'Does that make you sad?'

She wanted to spit in his face but she could barely breathe under the weight of his knee. He pinned one of her wrists under his other knee and grabbed her free hand. Now she couldn't fight back.

'Is it because of your brother?' His lips twitched into a grin. 'Because of what you did?'

She struggled to fill her lungs. '*Your* people did that.'

'It doesn't matter who laid the trap.' He leaned over her. 'Because you sent him right into it.'

Aviary tried to lift his knee from her chest, but he pushed all his weight into it. She strained to speak. 'I didn't ... kill him.'

Hal clamped a hand over her mouth, pushed her head against the bedside table. 'You know the truth. You can't lie to yourself about this.'

She shouted, but his hand muffled her.

'You're disgusting.' He inched closer and whispered, his breath sour. 'You must hate yourself.'

His hand moved to her neck and clamped hard. She

writhed under him, but there was no escape. Darkness settled over her.

She passed out.

When she opened her eyes, he wasn't astride her. Now, he lay next to her. The lamp's power cord wrapped around his neck. She was holding both ends of it.

Reeling back, she bumped into the bedside table. The lamp fell on her shoulder, its shade popping free. Hal coughed and opened bloodshot eyes. She smashed the lamp stem over him. He roared and clutched his arm. She swung the lamp again, catching him in the neck.

He dropped onto her, spluttering. Blood stained his teeth.

She grabbed both ends of the cord and pulled until his saliva dripped on her face, then scrambled away, across the carpet. She found his pistol. The red diode still glowed on the pistol grip.

'You little bitch.' Hal crawled to his knees. His neck was red. A vein rippled across his crinkled forehead.

She pressed twice into her palm and the red diode on his pistol shifted to green. She aimed the pistol. 'Back up, cowboy.'

He growled, but raised both hands. One eye twitched.

There was a muffled thud outside, followed by another. She listened for a moment, but there were no voices, no sudden movements.

Retrieving the tablet, she peeled the sticky tape from the slide of his pistol and placed it over the tablet's fingerprint sensor. It unlocked.

Hal's eyes swiveled between her and the tablet. 'Put that down this instant.'

Aviary changed his tablet's fingerprint to her own, then disabled the remote wipe feature.

'Need I remind you, I'm a federal officer,' he said.

She met his stare. 'I don't think you've thought this through.'

CHAPTER EIGHT

Kaliningrad, Kaliningrad Oblast

OLESYA AND ARK padded through the snow toward a young Central Asian woman. She was no older than Olesya and wore a black headscarf, watching them from outside a gray, unremarkable bunker. Olesya presumed this would be their new home for a while. The bunker probably had more levels underground than above. Set into the side of a snow-coated hill on the outskirts of Kaliningrad, it was a forgotten remnant of the Soviet Union from decades past.

After a less than comfortable ride on a turboprop from Moscow, Olesya wasn't looking forward to being thrown in with another bunch of hunters she'd never met. The young woman pressed a cigarette between her lips, its tip glowed hot.

'New hunters?' she asked.

'I'm Olesya, this is Ark.'

'And I am Marina,' she said. 'Welcome to the Kaliningrad Special Region.'

'What's special about it?' Ark asked.

'It's special because you're trapped between the Black Sea and a sea of black operatives.' She exhaled smoke and didn't smile. 'That was a joke.'

'I got it,' Olesya said. 'It was very funny.'

'Good. How many more of you?' Marina asked.

'Commanding officer and his assistant.' Ark gestured to Illarion and Gleb, treading through snow a short distance behind them.

Marina eyed them. 'But how many more hunters?'

'Just us,' Olesya said.

'With all the chaos the Fifth Column have been stirring up in the Middle East, I'm surprised they didn't send you there.' Marina inhaled more smoke. 'That's where they send everyone. Except us.'

'How many hunters are posted here?' Ark asked.

Marina's gaze drifted from his boots to his face. 'How many were stationed here or how many are there now? Because they have very different answers.'

Olesya could see fresh pain in Marina's eyes. She'd lost something.

'In the beginning, we had twelve,' she said. 'Now we have three.'

'I'm sorr—'

'You must be Marina.' Illarion reached them, his hand extended in greeting.

'Commander.' Marina extinguished her cigarette and shook his hand. 'This way, please.'

They followed her inside, where she showed Illarion and Gleb to their offices—or office, since there was only one to share. Then she led Olesya and Ark down the hall to their quarters.

'Olesya, you're with me.' Marina pointed to their bedroom.

Olesya stepped inside. There was a chest of drawers with an old record player on top and a row of records held up by an ammunition box. On one side of the room there was a single bed with a long plush toy that resembled a giant fish on the bedhead.

'Is that an anchovy?' Olesya asked.

'Yes,' Marina said. 'His name is Frank.'

On the other side of the room, there was a second bed and bedside table. The bed was made, and looked like it hadn't been touched for a while. Another door led to a private bathroom.

Ark stood in the doorway. 'Do we get a Frank too?'

'No.' Marina folded her arms. 'Where were you transferred from?'

'West Strategic Command, Moscow District.'

'I see. What's the capital like?' Marina asked.

'Busy.' Olesya placed her rucksack by her new bed. 'Where are you from?'

'Aralsk,' Marina said. 'A fishing port in Kazakhstan.'

'I was born in Belarus,' Olesya said. 'We're both a long way from home then.'

'Not really. Home is where the work is.'

Olesya didn't agree, but nodded anyway. 'Operatives.'

Marina frowned. 'Your—*our*—commander hasn't told you?'

'Told us what?' Ark asked.

'You're not here to hunt operatives.'

Ark blinked. 'Uh, so what are we here for?'

'You're here to help us stop the uprising.'

'Which uprising would that be exactly?' Olesya asked.

'You are Muscovites, after all.' Marina sighed. 'You don't have a clue.'

'I'd appreciate a hint,' Olesya said.

'They call themselves Purity. As we speak, their popularity expands rapidly.' Marina looked her up and down. 'And if there's one thing they don't like, it's those with genetic … differences.'

'So what about all the Fifth Column operatives?' Ark asked. 'They're crawling across Eastern Europe and stealing our hunters. We're just supposed to let them take what they want?'

'Purity are doing more damage to Eastern Europe than the Fifth Column ever could,' Marina said. 'Fanatics, the lot of them.'

She walked around Ark, into the corridor. Standing outside another bedroom door, she knocked. A young man opened it immediately. Standing behind him, a young woman. They looked about Olesya's age, barely in their twenties.

'This is Andrey and Nika,' Marina said. 'Meet Olesya and Ark.'

Andrey gave a curt nod and ran a hand over his shaved head. He stood taller than Olesya, with straw-colored stubble that glinted across his jawline.

'Ark, you bunk with Andrey,' Marina said.

Nika pushed past Andrey. With amber hair and gray

eyes, she was small and unassuming, yet jumped forward and shook their hands vigorously.

'Hunters?' she said. 'We can use more of you.'

'Won't be enough.' Andrey spoke over Nika's head. 'We're screwed either way.'

'How many were you expecting?' Olesya asked.

Andrey snorted. 'None. They don't give a shit about us. Sometimes I think they forget we're here. And now it sounds like they've forgotten you.'

Ark dropped his ruck by his feet. 'They haven't forgotten us.'

'Then why are you here? To stop the operatives?' Andrey didn't wait for an answer. 'Of course not.'

'We're being brought up to speed on Purity,' Olesya said.

'Purity are bringing *us* up to speed,' he said. 'They took over Ukraine last month and we can't do a damn thing about it.'

'We are doing something about it,' Nika said, her hand on his.

'Sitting around here?' Andrey asked. 'Waiting for a bunch of modern-day Nazis to take over the world. Yeah, good plan.'

'They're not Nazis,' Nika said.

'She's right,' Marina said. 'They're much worse.'

'But now that we have more hunters and a new commander,' Nika said, 'maybe we can do something about it.'

'What happened to your old commander?' Olesya asked.

'Discharged,' Andrey said quickly.

263

'They took my best friend too,' Marina said.

'I'm sorry,' Olesya said.

Marina crossed her arms. 'Do you Muscovites know what it's like to lose your best friend?'

'They took my sister,' Ark said.

Marina gave a sincere nod. 'And what have you lost in this war, Olesya?'

'Everyone.'

CHAPTER NINE

Las Vegas, United States

DRESSED AS US MARINES, Damien and Nasira stepped into the elevator at the MGM Grand Hotel & Casino, which was now a USMC operational base. Damien stood in the corner while Nasira hit the button for Level 26.

Jay was their getaway driver, mostly because Nasira didn't want him in harm's way. Jay didn't listen to Damien much but he listened to her. And she was right—Jay could barely breathe and walk at the same time. He was in no shape to be helping them spring someone from a fortified military operating base.

The doors slid shut, then stopped as a hand slipped between them.

Damien went for the USMC-made pistol in his holster.

The doors parted and a suited man joined them. He was tall and slender, with a weathered face and graying hairline. Under his arm, his jacket bulged slightly. He gave Damien and Nasira a polite smile before making a comment.

'There's nothing worse than missing an opportunity,' he said.

Damien smiled, but decided to say nothing. The less, the better.

The man turned to the gold panel near the doors and selected his floor. But Damien had already pressed it. The man withdrew his finger and straightened himself.

'Now there's quite the coincidence,' he said. 'Saves me the trouble.'

The elevator doors finally closed.

Level 6.

The suited man's hands, curled into fists with his thumb on the outside, an involuntary action that suggested a military background. Damien wondered what role the man filled now.

Level 11.

'Half the city on high alert and marines every which way. But folks are still out there, playing the darn slot machines.' The man shook his head. 'Sometimes I get to thinking we don't deserve the lives we're given.'

Level 17.

'Life used to be so precious,' he said. 'Now everyone thinks they can live forever. That they're born to be stars.' He adjusted his tie. 'That we all have a great destiny waiting for us. We used to look down upon that kind of delusion.' He looked over his shoulder at Damien. 'Do you know what it is now?'

Damien shrugged.

'Heck, now it's a God-given virtue.'

Level 23.

In the gold panel, Damien watched the warped reflection of the man's face. It seemed to shift. Damien tensed, ready to block the man's draw.

'There's no lessons anymore, no consequence,' the man said. 'Just one big spear of destiny. You hear what I'm saying?'

Damien struggled for words, but Nasira was quicker off the mark.

'There's always consequence,' she said.

'Exactly.' The man gave them a second glance, lingering on Damien. 'You know, you look a mite familiar.'

'You must be thinking of someone else,' Damien said.

Hurry up, you piece-of-shit elevator.

Level 26.

The doors opened, but the man didn't budge, blocking their exit. He stepped to one side and extended a hand.

'After you,' he said. 'Your service to our nation is appreciated.'

Damien's heart was pounding. Nasira thanked the suited man and stepped out. Damien followed. Nasira checked the numbers in the elevator lobby. She was quicker than he was to orient herself, which he wanted to put down to her enhanced navigational abilities—magnetoception—but she was probably just paying more attention.

Nasira led the way. They walked in tandem across the carpeted floor, through to the north tower. The corridor continued in a straight line, so far into the distance that it seemed endless. Damien followed her lead. She checked the hotel room numbers while he kept his attention on the suited man who walked a short distance behind them.

Ahead, there were six marines carrying carbines and pacing the same area of corridor.

Guarding.

Damien gave one of the marines a nod. He didn't return it, and the others just tracked them with their eyes. Nasira kept him on course. They passed more hotel room doors on both sides. Damien still couldn't see the end of the corridor. The walls, ceiling and floor simply converged into a distant point ahead.

With his enhanced hearing, he listened as behind them the suited man identified himself to the marines.

'Hal Claycomb, NCS.'

An element of the CIA.

Someone swiped an access card and he heard Hal step inside. The door closed behind him.

'NCS,' Damien said under his breath.

Nasira kept walking. 'My ass he is.'

Denton often used an NCS identity while operating in the United States, and sometimes in allied countries. And Denton wouldn't be the only one. A fresh surge of epinephrine prickled Damien's fingers. His phone told him that Aviary's location matched the room the marines were guarding.

'I think Hal Claycomb is here to see Aviary,' he said.

'He could be here for any of those resistance people,' Nasira said. 'Maybe a leader. We don't know it's Aviary yet.'

'We need to stop him,' Damien growled under his breath.

'From what?' she asked. 'Talking to her?'

'Taking her,' Damien said. 'If he leaves this building with her, we lose her for good.'

'Here's how we roll,' Nasira said. 'We walk out of sight and then we double back. If the marines are still chilling, we keep walking. We don't grab her until she's out of the room. You got that?'

'They'll escort her.'

Nasira matched his stride. 'Better still.'

They walked for a moment longer, then spun and started back the way they'd come. A pair of marines walked inside the room.

'Faster,' Damien said. 'That isn't looking good.'

'You're getting reckless, just like Jay,' Nasira said.

'Sorry, I'm just anxious.'

'Not saying it's a bad thing,' she said. 'But if we take them, we take them on my cue.'

'What's your cue?'

She moved faster. 'When you hear a bone break.'

They drew level with the marines.

'Wrong floor?' one of them asked.

Damien paused in front of the correct room. 'Is this level twenty-six?'

'That's us,' the marine said.

Another intervened, a hand outstretched. 'Sorry dude, we gotta keep this area clear. We have a job to do.'

'Yeah,' Nasira said, 'me too.' And broke his wrist.

That would be my cue, Damien thought.

He launched for the marine behind him, grasped the

barrel of her gun and twisted it up, tangling her trigger finger. The scope broke her nose, blood spattering the door of the room.

He kicked her legs out and took her carbine. They all had weapon retention systems—programmed to fire only with the owner's fingerprint—so he couldn't fire it, but he could use it for other things. Like hitting her with it.

He whipped the stock of the carbine into the marine's nose, then stepped behind her, carbine rail under her neck, keeping her between himself and the third marine, who was lining up a shot on him.

Nasira twisted the carbine over and out of his grasp, whipped it back so the butt caught him on the chin. The marine stumbled against the wall, and Nasira brought the end of the carbine down, cracking it over his kneecap, then slamming it into his groin. He folded in on himself.

Damien took the access card from the marine's pocket and gave it to Nasira, then together they bound the marines with their own plasticuffs. One of them stirred, and Nasira banged his head against the wall, hard enough to knock him out.

'Let's roll,' she said.

CHAPTER TEN

Berlin, Germany

IN THE DEAD of the night, the Nightcrawler was a gray oppressive block that could have passed for a disused Ministry of Defense building. The bass from the night-club's music pulsed toward nearby factories and graffiti etched walls.

Sophia killed the engine and stepped out onto gravel. 'Do we have their faces yet?'

Ieva climbed from the car, her breath visible under the street lights. 'One of them, yes. But the other two … all I can find are photos of them as kids.' She nodded in the direction of the Nightcrawler. 'All three of them are outside.'

They were somewhere among the long line of hopeful patrons in shimmering dresses and vests, wrapped in winter coats. The line was carefully funneled between temporary wire fences weighted with cinder blocks.

'Maybe they're just having a dance on their night off,' Czarina said. 'Operative summer break. Except in, you know, winter.'

'I doubt that,' Sophia said.

Czarina glared at her. 'I was joking.'

'You're always joking,' Ieva said, offering her phone.

Sophia took Ieva's phone. Onscreen was a young girl, Priya, with wide eyes, thick dark hair that spilled over warm sienna cheeks, and the hint of a smirk. Sophia flicked to the next photo. Also as a young girl, Loren had a pink, pointed nose and wavy ash hair. It wasn't much to go on, but it was a start. The third photo was of Tetsuya as an adult. He had eyebrows like black feathers and a soft, rounded chin, but his dark amber eyes carried a quiet confidence. If Sophia could find him, she could find the others.

'That seem weird to you?' Czarina asked. 'If this place was their operation, they'd take an alternate entry.'

Their operative tracking map did just that—track the location of all the Fifth Column operatives, but it didn't divulge any details of their operations. They had to figure that out on their own.

'Cache your weapons in the car,' Sophia said. 'We're lining up.'

Czarina and Ieva exchanged a glance.

'You want us to line up and go in there?' Ieva asked.

'It will be quicker than sneaking in. Do you have an objection?'

'Yeah.' Czarina leaned against the car. 'My objection is this is a super bad idea.'

Sophia stashed her pistol and knives under her seat. 'Then what do you suggest, we go home and drink tea?'

'Yes!' Ieva nodded enthusiastically. 'I like that idea.'

Czarina sighed. 'She was joking.'

'But Sophia never jokes,' Ieva said.

'I joke,' Sophia said. 'Sometimes.'

Czarina pointed to the line. 'Us lining up out there, that's a joke, right?'

'No.' Sophia shut her door. 'I hope you two brought dancing shoes.'

Czarina and Ieva stared at her.

'*That* was a joke.'

THE DANCE HALL resembled some sort of Medieval cathedral. Looming before them, concrete walls and metal staircases with hard lines and rough edges. With their phones tagged and bagged by the cloakroom attendant, they were granted access to the depths of the Night-crawler. The lower half of the nightclub shivered a fiery red, while the upper level pulsed a cool blue.

'So,' Czarina said into Sophia's ear. 'Have you ever been to a place like this?'

Around them, the hall rippled with face-pounding electronica and dazed patrons whirling over each other. A selection of dancers and performers, elevated above the crowd, stretched and contorted on square concrete platforms.

'Of course I have,' Sophia said as they stepped through a dark curtain.

Before them, a uniformed woman knelt behind a man wearing nothing but his mustache, and fisted him with a lubricated hand.

'Maybe not quite like this,' Sophia said.

Ieva squeezed between Sophia and Czarina, saw the mustached man brace himself. 'Oh. So I guess tonight isn't Bingo night.'

Sophia retreated from the room with her. 'Have you seen them yet?'

Ieva shook her head. Czarina was still watching from behind the curtain.

Sophia pulled her by the arm. 'Hey, are you with us?'

Czarina looked mesmerized. 'Uh, I think so.'

'Stay together,' Sophia said. 'We check everyone.'

Blending in was difficult when the crowd was a disconcerting jumble of shirtless glittering patrons dressed in a variety of uniforms. Sophia weaved around them, checking every face and evading their erratic, unapologetic dancing.

The dance hall was large, but it trickled off into dark alcoves. She led the impatient Czarina and unwilling Ieva deep into the lower level. On a raised stage, under a lighting rig, a DJ wore bug-eyed goggles. Dancers writhed around Sophia, scented with perfume and sweat. A woman dressed as Peter Pan blew glitter into the air. Sophia felt it settle on her lips.

The music swelled and the dance floor became a frenzy of elbows and hips. She wiped her face.

'You need to start dancing,' Czarina said.

Czarina was already moving in rhythm with everyone, her limbs jerking awkwardly.

If dance moves could kill, Sophia thought.

Ieva found herself in a competitive dance-off with an energetic young man in knee socks, shorts and a red feather in his hat. His bony elbows were a blur. Nearby, Czarina joined a pair of women in suits, one with purple hair tied in a ponytail and the other with short brown hair and burgundy lips that matched the handkerchief in her breast pocket. They smiled at Czarina and parted to accept her.

Sophia felt suddenly awkward, so she slipped to the edge of the crowd to have a better look around. In the blue level above, balconies overlooked the dance hall. Not a bad place for an operative to identify someone, but only a few people lingered for more than a moment. Smoke machines poured tangerine clouds overhead and Sophia saw nothing more from above.

When she looked at the people around her, she was surprised to discover she could not only smell their emotions with her inherent ability—she could now *see* them. Color overlapped and bled from the dancers, washing over her. Their psychoactive euphoria looked to her like dusted sugar. It floated past, tasting sweet on her lips. Whatever Peter Pan had blown in her face, it wasn't glitter. Something was messing with her enhanced senses, but it wasn't dulling them. It was sharpening *everything*.

What the hell was in that glitter? DMT?

She tried not to panic, turned her body in increments, seeking the operatives. If they were close, she would find them. Their emotions would be different. They would shimmer with cortisol, only without the softened edge of alcohol. Standing on the perimeter of the dance floor, Sophia searched for their sharp edges. Only now she would see instead of smell it.

There.

Above her, two figures watched from the mezzanine. One cradled a drink.

The music dropped low and strobe lights pulsed fiercely, making everything stutter. Sophia focused on the pallid face of a middle-aged man wearing an ill-fitted white shirt—or pale blue, she couldn't be sure in the fluorescence—and a little black bow tie. He danced with his eyes closed, glitter smeared across his cheek.

A pair of women in naval uniforms— blue, gold and silver—slinked around him. One was taller, her movements gentle and enchanting. She had ash brown hair, but it wasn't wavy. Three silver stars on her shoulder made her a Vice Admiral.

Her shorter counterpart had shortly cropped hair and short sleeves that revealed sienna arms. She danced boldly in front of Bow Tie Man, with parted lips and a gold bar on her shoulder, making her an Ensign. Sophia didn't see a soft edge on the women, but strangely she didn't see a serrated edge either.

Smoke poured through the hall, obscuring the women on the dance floor. On the mezzanine above, a lone figure still watched.

The lighting shifted and suddenly Sophia could see those weird auras again. From their heads to their fingertips, everyone was luminous at their core, half of them carrying different hues and shapes. She looked down at her own arms. Blues, oranges and purples crackled off her fingertips, and her chest quivered brightly.

Something was wrong.

Her awareness pushed back, and she shouldered her way through the crowd, stumbled, almost knocked someone over. Czarina.

Her colleague held her up, mouthed the words: *They're here.*

Sophia nodded. Ieva appeared beside her. Sophia felt everything begin to congeal around her. She had her world together again.

Smoke poured through the crowd, obscuring faces and movement. Sophia breathed, focused. They couldn't stand here forever. She remembered the Vice Admiral and Ensign dancing with Bow Tie Man and cut a path back toward them. The women danced with him, but he barely acknowledged them.

Ieva's former dancing partner—the young man in knee-socks and shorts—shimmied through the smoke. He circled around Bow Tie Man, paused for a moment, then switched to the Vice Admiral and Ensign. He brushed his back against the Admiral's, his legs lightly touching hers. Through the smoke, Sophia saw a small movement: the dancer's hand slipped between their backs and—in the space of a single strobe pulse—removed a fold of Euro bills from her uniform pocket.

Sophia knew a talented pickpocket when she saw one. She'd learned a few tricks herself as a kid, courtesy of the Romanies in outer Prague. The pressure between their bodies would've made the man's grab undetectable, and the Admiral wouldn't have noticed.

Except she did.

The Vice Admiral turned on her heel. Her arm weaved around him. The pickpocket's mouth popped open like the mouth of a milk carton and he tumbled forward. The Vice Admiral pocketed her money, but she took a moment to apologize and help him to his feet. The pickpocket recovered and flashed her a smug grin, then disappeared —unaware he'd been pickpocketed in return.

Czarina and Ieva appeared on either side of Sophia. Together, they watched the Admiral and Ensign resume their dancing. Their noose around Bow Tie Man constricted just a bit more.

Up on the mezzanine, that single figure was still looking down. A drink no longer in hand, not even a pretense at moving in time with the music. He didn't look self-conscious, just focused. Sophia tried to pick out detail in his silhouette, but all she could see was his thin jacket, which he hadn't shed in the cloakroom.

You only wear a jacket inside if you expect to be leaving in a hurry.

'We have them,' Sophia said.

CHAPTER ELEVEN

Las Vegas, United States

'DAMIEN?' Aviary lowered her pistol. 'What are you doing here?'

'Rescuing you?' Damien said.

Two marines stood in the room with Aviary, but they weren't there to capture her. Schofield and Gunn served with Aviary's brother in the USMC's Force Reconnaissance, but now they were with the resistance. They stood guard over Hal, the suited man from the elevator. He was bound, gagged, blindfolded and breathing slowly. He appeared to be taking a nap.

'You're alive!' She lunged for Nasira and hugged her. 'So glad you're OK.'

Nasira closed the door behind them and shot Damien a puzzled glance. He pretended not to notice.

Aviary released Nasira, but her eyes were wide. 'What about Jay?'

Damien looked over at Hal.

'He's sedated,' Schofield said. 'And don't worry, we won't kill him.'

'I wasn't worried,' Damien said.

'Jay's here in Vegas with us,' Nasira said.

Aviary relaxed. 'Good.'

'You missed the party,' Gunn said.

Schofield slapped Damien's shoulder. 'Welcome back.'

'Is someone going to tell us what's going on here?' Damien asked.

'Short version: they kidnapped me.' Aviary wiped blood from her septum ring. 'Long version: I'll explain later.'

Gunn stepped behind Aviary and half unzipped the small backpack on her shoulders. It was a black military-grade rucksack Damien had modified for her when he last visited. It was water-resistant and low profile, holding a modest sixteen liters and a bombproof compartment against her back for concealing a laptop or tablet. Like most special forces medical rucks, it opened flat to reveal several rows of webbing lined with cables and devices.

Gunn zipped it back up, leaving a small hole for a slender rubber antenna to protrude.

'Before you ask, there aren't any operatives floating around,' Aviary said.

'You don't know that,' Nasira said. 'We gotta move.'

Aviary held up a finger. 'One sec.'

'Tablet's a bit scuffed but it's secure,' Gunn said.

Aviary chewed her lip. 'Yeah, I kinda beat him with it.'

Damien nodded. 'Tablets are good improvised weapons.'

'You get the database encryption keys?' Gunn asked her.

'Hell and yes.' Aviary took a silver watch from Gunn and slipped it over her wrist.

'You're accessorizing?' Damien asked.

'It's a modified smartwatch. Which controls my modified phone.' Aviary eyed his marine uniform. 'Says the guy constantly stealing other men's clothes.'

'Dressing up is a liberating experience,' Schofield said, inspecting their stolen marine uniforms. 'Right, Damien?'

'Yeah. Wait, what database?' Damien asked.

'I'll explain later.'

'Good to see you're all right,' Nasira said.

Aviary fist-bumped her. 'Yeah, I'm pretty pleased about that too.' She glowered at Damien. There was no fist bump for him.

'Look, it was dangerous in Central America,' Damien said.

Nasira sighed. 'Colombia's not Central America.'

Gunn pointed to the sedated Fifth Column agent, Hal. 'Want us to finish him off?'

'No,' Aviary said. 'We got what we came for. We don't need to do that.'

'We *haven't* got what we came for,' Schofield said.

'Represent,' Gunn said.

Aviary gripped Schofield's elbow. 'You will. We're not leaving until you do.'

'So I guess you didn't need us then,' Damien said.

'I needed you a while ago.' Aviary opened the door.

Schofield and Gunn moved into the corridor, pistols aimed at the bound marines as they wriggled across the carpet. There was a protrusion across Schofield and Gunn's shoulder blades where they carried concealed swords.

Aviary led them down the corridor, back to the elevator lobby. She stepped inside an open elevator and called out, 'Get in!'

Damien stepped in beside her and Nasira, while Schofield and Gunn took the other corners.

'Marines will be waiting for you on the first floor,' Gunn said.

'We're going below ground,' Aviary said.

Schofield gave a sharp nod. 'You can drop us at twenty-two.'

'Special occasion?' Nasira asked.

'Got some friends who need fresh air,' Gunn said.

Aviary nudged Nasira. 'Part of the plan, don't worry.'

'Not worried at all,' Damien said, worried.

From the back of his vest, Gunn unsheathed what looked to be a dark angular sword with teeth and handed it to Damien.

Nasira stared at it. 'What the hell is that? A medieval chainsaw?'

It was shorter than a broadsword and made of hard-wood. Embedded in the blade, fragments of super-sharp obsidian glinted under the elevator light.

'Maquahuitl sword.' Schofield handed his sword to Nasira. 'Aviary can take care of their firearms, but you need to do the rest. Word of advice, these are sharper than any steel blade.'

'The obsidian sometimes snags on armor, though, so you can keep it in the sheath and beat them down,' Gunn said. 'That way no brother's gonna die.'

Damien slipped the sword over one shoulder to test it. He didn't want to dismember himself as he ran, but the sheath felt firm and secure. 'We can stay up here. Help you guys first.'

'Aviary's risked enough for us,' Schofield said. 'But you can help get her out of here. And if I were you, I'd do that now.'

'Alive would be good,' Aviary quipped.

'See you on the other side,' Schofield said.

Schofield and Gunn nodded to Aviary and stepped out at Level 22. Aviary hit the button and the doors closed, then switched her attention to her smartwatch. The elevator plunged downward.

'What are you doing?' Damien asked.

'Locking the other elevators,' she said. 'And giving us priority movement to the basement. From there we can move to the next building. All the different buildings are connected here, so I'm thinking we can escape through a casino or something.'

'That could work. We got Jay on wheels,' Nasira said. 'He can extract.'

The elevator levels ticked down. 'Are Schofield and Gunn going to be OK?' Damien asked.

Aviary nodded. 'Only way I could convince them to let me be captured by the Fifth Column. So they could rescue *their* friends.'

'Wait, you *wanted* to be captured?' Damien asked.

'A tablet like Hal's isn't easy to come by.' Aviary

turned to face him. 'So why are you back? You rescued Nasira and Jay, you didn't need to—'

'Hold up.' Nasira glared at Damien. 'You told her you were rescuing *me*?'

'I told you I'd come back,' Damien said to Aviary, pointedly ignoring Nasira.

'Yeah, but it's not like you were serious,' Aviary said. 'We both know I'd slow you down.'

'You should've brought her with you,' Nasira said.

'And do what?' Damien asked.

Aviary snorted. 'I can do things.'

'Nasira, you're not helping.' He turned to Aviary. 'It was dangerous.'

Nasira arched an eyebrow. 'And this isn't?'

Damien held his hands up in defense. 'I didn't know you were going to voluntarily sacrifice yourself to the Fifth Col—'

'Damien, shut your mouth,' Nasira said, turning to Aviary. 'We need your skills. That's why we're back.'

'Right, so the only reason you want me is so I can crack my way through something.'

'I thought that's what you wanna hear?' Nasira said. 'That we need you?'

'You need me?'

'We do.'

'What for?'

'The people who took Jay,' Nasira said. 'They're a company based in Brazil. They stole something from him and we need it back.'

The elevator reached the basement, but Aviary

jammed her finger on the button to keep the doors closed. 'What did they take?'

'His abilities,' Damien said.

'They can do that?'

Damien handed Aviary his pistol. 'Ask Jay yourself.'

Aviary looked down at the weapon. 'Sure you're feeling OK?'

'You might need it,' he said.

'Fine, whatever. Hold this button.'

Damien held the doors closed while Aviary fished her phone from her pocket and checked security camera footage outside the elevator. Damien was impressed, but he kept it to himself and watched over her shoulder. There were four thumbnails onscreen. He could make out six marines.

'Look at their placement. They're ready for us,' Nasira whispered.

'I can only disable their carbines' weapon retention systems,' Aviary said. 'But they can still use their pistols.' She pressed her palm.

'What are you—' Damien clutched his ears. The whining sound cut through him, almost taking him to the ground. He steadied himself. 'I'm fine.'

'Sorry,' she said. 'Forgot about your sensitive hearing.'

Nasira unsheathed her sword. 'I ain't taking chances.'

Damien kept his covered. 'These marines are cogs in the Fifth Column's machine, just like us. And your sword could catch on their armor.'

'Spare me your idealism.' She sheathed it. 'But I'm only doing it because I don't want it getting snagged.'

Aviary took a small flashlight from her rucksack. 'I have a plan. I hope you like it.'

Under her breath, Nasira said, 'What is it?'

'I open the doors to another elevator, which distracts them. Then, I open our doors,' Aviary said with a smile, 'and strobe the crap out of them.' She pressed briefly on her flashlight and almost blinded Damien. 'Sorry.'

Nasira nodded in approval. 'You'll need to cut—'

The elevator went dark, lit only by Aviary's phone.

Damien had to admit, she was handy in an escape. Maybe he could've used her in Guatemala after all. 'OK, now we just need—'

The doors opened.

Nasira slipped from their elevator, her obsidian sword in one hand, sheathed.

Damien followed. He counted the silhouettes of ten marines facing the other lift, more than the six he'd seen on the feed. Hearing boots on marble at last, the soldiers turned. There were five on Damien's side, and as he closed on the first, a thought hit him.

What if Aviary's disabler didn't work?

Behind him, Aviary's flashlight strobed. The marines held their ground through the frenzy of rapid flashes, their carbines aimed in all directions.

Damien cut across the first marine's carbine with his sword, tearing it from his grasp, then brought the sheathed blade across the marine's face. It struck him on the chin and lifted him from his feet.

Under the aggressively flashing lights, Damien could see a stop-motion performance of Nasira tearing her way through marine after marine. She slashed their weapons clear, cracked her sword across their arms and scooped their legs out from under them.

Damien closed on his second marine, taking out one of his legs with his sword. Then he slammed the hilt into the marine's chest. The marine toppled backward, and Damien grabbed his carbine by its rail. He stepped toward the remaining cluster of three marines. Their muzzles tracked him in the strobing glare.

With his sword in one hand, and carbine in the other, like an ax, Damien slipped between a pair of marines, using both weapons to redirect their barrels into each other. Ducking, he struck out with both hands, dropping them.

The last marine he kicked in the hip, spinning her away. He swung the carbine into her shoulder. She collapsed.

A noise behind him: one of the downed marines must have recovered. Moving from the marine's firing line, Damien swung the sword into his knee guards. The marine dropped to his knees and, sliding behind him, Damien slammed the carbine rail into the back of his helmet. The marine splayed forward.

Boots struck marble in the distance.

More marines.

'Aviary!' he yelled.

A new squad of marines appeared and opened fire. Damien lifted the collapsed marine to shield himself. Three marines closed on him, carbines aimed. Even through the strobing, they didn't fire on his human shield.

There was only one way out of this—and that was without the sheath.

One of the new marines tried to pull his human shield away for a clear shot, but Damien shoved his shield into the new marine. They collapsed in a heap. The left and right marines moved in fast. Damien's sword was free, dark and jagged. It glittered brilliantly in the strobe light.

The right marine ran into the sword. She stopped and collapsed, bleeding on the marble. Damien whipped the sword overhead, slicing the left marine, then flicked the blade forward. The front marine was on his feet again, carbine in both hands. The maquahuitl sword went smoothly through his neck, missing the spinal column. He dropped his weapon. Hanging from Damien's sword, his carotid artery squirted blood like a garden sprinkler.

Aviary stopped the strobe and Damien's eyes adjusted to the dark again. The marine's gaze was fixed on him. There was no fear or anger, just a blank stare of disappointment.

The marine Damien had used as a shield was moving again, scrambling for a nearby weapon. Nasira shot him in the head.

Damien withdrew his sword from the marine's neck. The marine stood there for a moment, then collapsed.

'You're goddamn lucky,' Nasira said.

He stooped, picked up a radio wire and transmitter. 'Let's move.'

Aviary stood in the elevator, still, staring into space. She gave no sign she'd heard him.

Damien strode over to her. 'We need to go. Aviary? We have to move.'

She blinked and focused on him. 'Yeah, of course.'

With Aviary moving again, she took them from the lobby and into a passageway.

'Aviary, get us to the monorail station,' Nasira said.

She was pale in the gloom, her fingers shaking as she used her smartwatch. 'Um, keep going, not far.'

Nasira overtook her and led the way, taking them underground. They passed a candy store and pretzel parlor, both shuttered and dark.

'Take a left,' Aviary said.

Nasira reached a split in the passageway and went left. There was a distant echo of boots behind them. Damien just hoped there weren't any marines ahead as Nasira took them to the underground monorail station. He speed-vaulted over the turnstiles—one hand on a turnstile and legs out to the side.

Nasira tucked her legs in and monkey vaulted over. Behind them, Aviary slid across the marble on her hip, under the turnstile gate. She was back on her feet and moving after them, color slowly returning to her face.

They sprinted up the disabled escalators, emerging at last onto the above-ground monorail platform.

Empty.

'The trains won't stop here,' Damien said.

'They will now, bitches,' Aviary said.

Nasira turned slowly. 'What did you just call us?'

'Glitches.' Aviary pointed down the tunnel. 'Look.'

A four-carriage monorail train slowed as it reached their platform. Painted black and green, it advertised a gritty energy drink that Jay probably drank when it was too early for alcohol.

'You saying you can control that with your fancy watch?' Nasira asked.

'I'm saying I already am.'

The train drew to a halt beside them, and automatic doors opened on all three carriages, aligning with the platform doors that kept people from falling onto the rail. The carriages were shaped like capsules, big enough to fit only a handful of passengers, and there were a few already seated inside. Nasira pushed her way through, clearing the doorway. Damien and Aviary stepped in after her.

'Make it go,' Nasira said. 'Now!'

Aviary was tapping her watch. 'I am, I am!'

Half a dozen marines hauled themselves over the turnstiles and sprinted for the train as the doors slid shut.

'Go, go,' Nasira said.

The marines raised their weapons.

Damien hit the floor, hauling Aviary with him. Nasira was beside them, pistol ready. Aviary pressed a finger hard into the bandage on her hand. No shrill frequency.

'Damn, it's out of juice,' she said.

'What?' Damien asked. 'How do you charge it?'

The train moved and through the glass doors Damien watched the marines disappear. A tunnel swallowed their train. They were safe, for the moment.

'Chill, it's piezoelectric.' Aviary shook her hand vigorously. 'My arm movements recharge it kinetically.'

'How much movement?' Nasira asked.

'Walking pace, thirty minutes. Running—about ten,' Aviary said. 'Or I can just keep shaking my hand like this.'

The other passengers inside the carriage—two young

men, and a trio of women about the same age—were watching Aviary shake her hand. As far as they could see, a pair of US Marines had kidnapped a small woman with an implant in her hand, and dragged her on the monorail to escape. Damien eyed the men, their sizes and builds. Their shirts and fitted jeans.

He pointed his pistol at one of them. 'Take your shirt off, now.'

The man looked at his shirt, a white button-down with charcoal pinstripes. 'Are you for real?'

'See what I mean?' Aviary said, figuring out Damien's play. 'You're taking men's clothes again.'

One of the women—tall, and wearing enough eyeliner for both of her friends—snorted with laughter.

'You. Raccoon face.' Nasira took aim at her. 'Your jacket and top.'

The woman quickly shed her jacket. She handed it to Nasira, who snatched it off her.

'I suppose you want my scarf too?' she asked.

'No, it looks like shit.' Nasira handed the jacket to Aviary.

'For me?' Aviary said. 'You shouldn't have. Now if you had something for my hair…'

Nasira handed her a plasticuff cable tie. 'I made it pretty for you.'

While Nasira watched the passengers, Damien unbuttoned his uniform. The train left the tunnel and slowly ascended, following the monorail track as it snaked north through Las Vegas. The city was aglow with light, burning away the last of Damien's night vision.

'Keep the train going,' Nasira said. 'Don't stop.'

Aviary tapped her smartwatch. 'You got it.'

Like Nasira, Damien wore a singlet and jeans underneath his uniform. While Nasira pulled her new glittering top on, Damien took the man's pinstriped shirt and slipped his arms through. The train passed another platform and patrons caught a glimpse of three half-naked fugitives as they changed clothes.

Damien checked his phone. Three missed calls from Nasira. That would be Jay.

'Aviary, call Nasira's phone,' he said.

Aviary called him on her watch. It rang once and he picked up.

'We're on the monorail,' Damien said immediately.

'Good. Stay the fuck on it,' Jay said.

Nasira and Damien locked gazes. That didn't sound good.

'Why?' Nasira asked.

'Marines are swarming the strip on the southern—' Jay said.

The call dropped out.

'Jay?' Nasira said.

Aviary cursed. 'I'll get him again.'

The train slowed as it reached the next stop: Bally's/Paris station.

Nasira pulled her coiled hair and retied it into a ponytail. 'Keep the train moving.'

Aviary tapped her smartwatch. The tiny square screen rippled with color as she accessed a variety of shortcuts she'd programmed into it. The train picked up speed again and whipped past a platform swarming with marines.

'Change of plans,' Nasira said. 'Take us two more stops and we bail.'

'What about Jay?' Damien asked.

'What about him?' she snapped. 'Give him a new RV.'

'A recreational vehicle?' Aviary asked.

'No, RV means rendezvous point,' Nasira said.

The train continued along the elevated monorail track. The shimmering lights of the replica Eiffel Tower blurred past. With two more stops to go, Damien unlaced and removed his boots, then shed his digicam pants down to his jeans. Nasira did the same.

'Just like real spies,' Aviary said.

Damien re-laced his combat boots. He could've stolen the man's shoes, but he wanted something he could run and fight in, not something that would slip on polished marble or fall off in mid-sprint. He slung the sheathed sword over his head. Opposite him, Aviary pulled the hood on her jacket.

'I'm the leader of the assassins now,' Aviary said in her best deep voice.

'What are you doing?' Nasira asked.

'The assassin video game, hello? You wear a hood.'

The topless man raised his hand. 'I got that one.'

'See, Nips got it,' Aviary said.

The man folded his arms over his nipples.

'You know what kind of assassin wears a hood that cuts off their peripheral vision?' Nasira pulled Aviary's hood down. 'A dead assassin.'

'But my hair's bright red,' she said. 'They'll see me a mile away.'

Nasira reached over and snatched the scarf from the

woman in the middle, who now sat awkwardly in just her bra and jeans. Nasira used the scarf to make a bandana and fastened it over Aviary's head.

'Fixed.' Nasira reached for her sheathed sword.

'Leave them here,' Damien said.

'We can haul them,' Nasira said. 'Aviary, take off your ruck.'

Aviary removed the rucksack from her back. Nasira slung her sheath over Aviary's shoulder, then gestured for Damien's. He understood and handed it to her. With both swords sheathed on Aviary's back, Nasira slipped her rucksack over them, concealing all but the hilt of each sword.

'Feel OK? Can you run with that?'

Aviary shrugged. 'I guess so.'

Nasira nodded her approval. 'Trying to keep a low profile, y'know.'

The passengers remained silent as the monorail train pulled into the next station: Harrah's/The LINQ. There hadn't been any marines at the previous two stations and Damien was pleased to find none here either. Their luck was starting to improve. But he knew if they stayed on this train any longer, it would run out.

The doors opened and Nasira was the first onto the platform, pistol in one hand. She ran down an escalator, Damien and Aviary close behind her.

'Do you need a map?' Aviary called out as they ran.

Nasira paused to tap her own forehead, but gave Aviary no explanation.

'Magnetoception,' Damien said, running beside her. 'She knows the turns before she takes them.'

'How does that work?'

'No idea,' he said. 'Like a compass in your head, I guess.'

'Oh, Magneto-Girl. Cool.'

'Probably don't call her that.'

They hit the shopping area inside The LINQ Hotel and ran past a candy store, a high-end clothing store for pets and a flashy looking sports car on display.

Nasira stopped, and Damien drew to a halt beside her. 'What?'

She was peering through a glass balcony at the hotel lobby below. Past that was the casino, their way out. Now it was filling with marines barking orders, steering panicked patrons out onto the boulevard.

Nasira cursed. 'A minute earlier and we could've made that.'

Damien rolled up his sleeves. 'I have a plan.'

But Nasira was already running for the display car—a blood orange Mustang with gunmetal spoked wheels. Aviary was two steps behind, tapping something on her watch. The Mustang's doors unlocked.

'Or we can go with your completely insane plan,' Damien said.

Nasira got behind the wheel. Aviary jumped in the front passenger seat, leaving Damien to dive quickly in the back. Aviary handed him a sheathed sword. She jammed the other one behind her ruck, both wedged in her footwell.

'If you don't want to die, get your seatbelt on,' Nasira said.

Damien hurriedly complied as the engine rumbled.

Nasira looked over at Aviary. 'How did you start the engine?'

'I'm really good at touching things.' Aviary tapped her watch. 'Wait. That came out wr—'

Nasira floored it.

The Mustang crashed through the balcony, soared through the air and plunged into the hotel lobby. Damien's fingers dug into the front headrest. Miraculously, the Mustang landed wheels down. Marines scattered. One rolled over the hood, spiraling in the air. Another snapped off a side mirror as he dived clear.

Marines and patrons rolled from the car's path. Nasira took the Mustang in a wide sweep across the lobby, deeper into the casino. This level was decorated to look like the streets of Paris, the ceilings painted with vanilla skies and the pathways decorated with old-fashioned street lamps.

'Watch out for the lamps!' Damien cried.

Nasira tore through them like they were made of foam and plaster, and that's when he realized they were.

'No magnetic fields,' Nasira said. 'I can tell.'

She corrected their path and grazed a row of slot machines. Patrons threw themselves clear of the speeding Mustang.

'Hey, I just cracked the car,' Aviary said.

'What does that mean?' Nasira asked. 'Can you plot us a route?'

'Hang on, I'm working on something. There.' Aviary tapped her watch and their hazard lights flashed. 'So you don't hit anyone.'

'Why would I need that? They have plenty of time to get out of the way,' Nasira said.

A man in a tuxedo tumbled over the Mustang with a trailing high-pitched scream.

'Except that one,' she said.

Nasira weaved through the winding pedestrian path. On either side they were flanked by clusters of panicked gamblers, slot machines, blackjack tables and monstrous chrome-and-glass leviathans that promised million dollar jackpots.

Damien checked their rear. Marines were cutting through the disarrayed crowd, but they were on foot and struggled to keep up. He reached for his sword, just in case.

'Aviary, get back on to Jay,' Nasira said. 'Tell him to meet us at the Venetian.'

'I'm on it, Magneto-Girl.'

'I'll pretend I didn't hear that.'

Something landed on the rear of the Mustang: a man, plain-clothed, eyes locked on Damien with calm determination as he clung to the trunk.

'Operative,' Damien whispered. He scrabbled for his pistol, raising it to fire through the rear window.

But the operative was already gone.

Then he heard it: climbing the roof. He fired upward, the sound of each shot making his ears ring.

The Mustang clipped another slot machine. Coins splashed over the hood, followed by a man in a blue hedgehog costume.

'I think you killed Sonic,' Aviary said.

'Gotta go fast,' Nasira muttered.

The rear window collapsed and fell away in large pieces around the operative, clinging to the trunk. Damien took aim, but the operative caught his firing hand and held tight. He turned Damien's wrist inward, tearing the pistol from his grasp, then aimed Damien's pistol at him and fired. Damien ducked and the round went through the windshield.

'Seriously!' Nasira yelled. 'I'm trying to drive through a casino here!'

Aviary looked over her shoulder and saw the operative. 'Oh crap oh crap oh crap.'

Damien reached for his sword, but the operative gripped his hand and held it away from the hilt.

'A little help here,' Damien said.

'Hang on.' Aviary worked her smartwatch.

An airbag deployed from the other rear door, doing absolutely nothing to help.

Damien elbowed the operative in the face, stunning him. He leaned forward, unsheathed and stabbed the sword behind him.

The operative rolled across the trunk to avoid the thrust, then clamped his knee on Damien's wrist, pinning the sword to the trunk. The operative drove his other knee into the back of Damien's head, but Damien raised his elbow to deflect it.

The operative wrapped his leg around Damien's neck and clamped hard. Damien couldn't breathe, couldn't get oxygen to his brain.

A sword sliced past, cutting the operative's leg and severing Damien's seatbelt. Aviary was wielding Nasira's sword from the front seat.

That helped.

The operative's hold around his neck relaxed. Blood from his leg soaked Damien's shirt. His own sword was free now. He slashed it across the trunk. The operative leapt over the blade, bounced off the trunk and disappeared. Damien gripped his sword, lungs burning for air. In the Mustang's wake, the operative tumbled across the casino floor and slammed into a mock lamppost.

'Are you OK?' Aviary asked.

'I am now.' He sheathed his sword. 'How about you?'

'I'm having constant anxiety attacks,' Aviary said. 'Pretty good.'

'Next stop, Harrah's Las Vegas,' Nasira said. 'Hold on.'

She plunged the Mustang down a flight of stairs, into a palace-like atrium.

'What's that?' Aviary asked, pointing to something near Damien's feet.

A flat plastic donut lay in the footwell.

The flashbang blasted to life. Unlike the standard pyrotechnic version, this device flooded the Mustang with a high-density array of LEDs, all strobing while a loud high-pitched whine filled Damien's head.

The Mustang shuddered and turned. Nauseated from the effects, unable to see or hear, Damien clung to his severed seatbelt. His ears rang and the world seared white. The Mustang lurched sickeningly through the air and then smashed into something hard at high speed.

CHAPTER TWELVE

Berlin, Germany

SOPHIA FOCUSED ON THE MEZZANINE, on the figure watching from above. She was certain now. He was an operative.

She tapped Czarina on the shoulder. 'Stay on the Navy women.'

Czarina read her lips and gave an almost imperceptible nod.

Sophia darted across the dance floor and climbed the metal stairs to the mezzanine. The operative was coming the other way when he locked eyes with her. She recognized him.

Tetsuya matched his photo, with slightly longer hair. He wore loose denim jeans, a charcoal t-shirt and a slender leather jacket that crinkled over his triceps and shoulders. The upper level's light glinted blue in his eyes.

Without breaking his stride, he altered course and plunged deeper into the azure lights. Sophia followed, pushing past patrons and spilling plastic cups of vodka. She lost him in the center of the mezzanine floor, then a moment later caught the shimmering back of his jacket. He entered a small room.

She darted for the room and stepped inside.

No Tetsuya. A dark curtain at the end, rippling. Someone had been through.

On her left, three faucets and three mirrors surrounded by electric blue light globes. The globes dimmed slowly, then illuminated again in a slow pulse. Opposite the faucets, cigarette smoke curled over writhing bodies. Sophia ignored them and strode for the curtain. She stood to one side and carefully pulled the curtain. Inside, she found a slender man patiently wrapping rope in a geometric Shibari style around the freckled body of an undressed woman.

'You're not in control.' She met Sophia's gaze. 'Let it go.'

Tetsuya, hiding among the bodies behind her, kicked her leg out. Sophia fell to the floor, entangled in the curtain. She got back onto one knee, but he wrapped the curtain over her head and pulled hard. She couldn't see through the material. Instead, she inhaled through it. Yelling her programming trigger words, she couldn't draw breath.

Still entangled in the hanging curtain, she kicked behind, hoping to catch him. Something—an elbow?—cracked hard on her spine and the air shot from her lungs. The curtain wrapped tighter around her chest. Her feet barely touched the floor and hands closed over her neck.

Sophia relaxed, let her body slump. Tetsuya's hands slipped. Her feet brushed the floor. She kicked and connected with a soft part of his body. He exhaled sharply.

She unwound from the curtain but was still blinded and entangled. Instead, she spun into it and wrapped herself further. Lifting off the ground, she kicked him. He crashed into something, startling the nearby patrons.

The curtain tore from its rings. Sophia landed in a crouch and could see again. The man with the rope paused, then resumed his rigging. Sophia faced Tetsuya. The blue lights dimmed and the room slowly went dark. She needed a weapon, so she grabbed the nearest object she could find and brought it down on his face. He spluttered, kicked for her legs in darkness.

The blue lights glowed again, revealing Sophia's improvised cosh. It was a Magic Wand, a sex toy shaped like an oversized microphone, except that it was white and sported a silicone head. Tetsuya gave it a moment's thought, then kicked low. She sidestepped and brought the wand down on his hyperextended knee, forcing him wider still. Then she coshed him with the wand. Across his arm. His face. His ribs. His neck.

He rolled backwards, out of the splits and to his feet. He was almost in the doorway, ready to flee. She lunged, stepped on his foot, pinning him. He reacted with a barrage of strikes—open handed, closed fists, elbows— each of which she deflected with the wand.

The wand's silicone head suddenly buzzed to life.

Tetsuya stared at it, then tried for another strike. Sophia deflected his strike and retreated. She shouted the trigger words at him, but the music rolling in from the upper level dance floor and washed them away.

She struck him again, but he countered with a punch that should have crushed her airway. She turned from the strike—his fist only brushing her shoulder—then turned back into the joint of his elbow and coshed him under the chin. His head went back. She snapped the wand across his neck. He spluttered and fell.

The blue lights dimmed again, and when they brightened he was still on the floor.

From the wall of patrons, a large, bearded man in aviator sunglasses stepped carefully toward Sophia, extended an open hand.

'Sind sie fertig?' he asked. *Are you finished*?

Sophia slapped the buzzing sex toy into his palm.

She checked Tetsuya's breathing. He was out cold, so she rolled him onto his side and plucked a pair of plasticuffs from her jeans, drawing them tight over his wrists.

Security officers rushed past the doorway in front of her. They were heading right for the balustrade. She left Tetsuya for the moment and gave chase. As she suspected, they led her back to the lower level dance floor. Between the gaps in the balustrade, she saw the Vice Admiral and Ensign lunge across the dance floor, targeting Ieva. Their limbs were sharp and precise under the strobe lights. In an instant, Ieva was down. They hunted for Czarina next. Czarina was vicious in close quarters, but even she couldn't engage two operatives at once.

Sophia needed to intervene now, except the stairs were

blocked with panicked patrons. Bow Tie Man was sandwiched somewhere in the middle, eyes wide. Under her balustrade was the goggle-wearing DJ and the lighting rig. She leapt over and landed on the lighting rig, then swung from it, kicking the DJ into a pillar.

On the dance floor in front of her, the Vice Admiral and Ensign flanked Czarina, their movements furious and quick. Too many of their strikes made it through. Blood sprayed from Czarina's smashed mouth. Strobe lights blazed red.

Sophia cut the music and grabbed the microphone.

'Children three that nestle near, eager eye and willing ear. Pleased a simple tale to hear.'

The Ensign moved for Ieva, who was recovering on the ground, then shuddered. The Vice Admiral, wielding a knife, halted where she stood. Czarina took the knife and cut the operative's throat.

Sophia cursed, then leapt off the DJ's platform. She landed on the cleared dance floor and went for Czarina, but security got to her first. Czarina released her knife and let the security officers seize her. One bent her wrist forward until she complied. She relaxed, then with her free hand she pulled her wrist back the right way. With her heel into the side of his knee, she broke his stance and he collapsed. At the same time, she straightened out the other officer's arm and forced him head-first on the dance floor.

When Sophia reached them, Czarina paused. She tilted her head. 'I can hear sirens. Not police.'

Blue light glinted off a leather jacket.

The third operative.

He was conscious and moving, shoved Bow Tie Man through the doors with him.

Sophia pushed her way outside, but she was too late. The stolen ambulance tore into the night.

In her wake, Czarina and Ieva emerged dazed and bloody from the Nightcrawler.

'Are you both OK?' Sophia rushed toward them.

'We're fine,' Czarina said. 'I could use a drink though.'

Someone else slipped behind them. Sophia lunged forward and grabbed the collar of a young man with knee-high socks. He struggled, and screamed for security. She slapped both hands over his ears. Stunned, he lost his balance and slumped to the ground. She knelt beside him and searched his pockets, retrieving his earnings for the night.

Bow Tie Man's wallet. She flipped it open and dug out the driver's license. Evgeny Sporyshev. He was the operatives' target, and now they had him.

CHAPTER THIRTEEN

Las Vegas, United States

AVIARY HUNG UPSIDE DOWN.

She shoved the airbag from her face and reached for her seatbelt. She couldn't get to it with the airbag in the way. She punched it, but that didn't help. Blood rushed to her head and she felt dizzy, pressure building behind her eyes. She had to think.

The entire Mustang was upside down and her rucksack was resting below her, on the roof. She reached down and unzipped the ruck, then clawed for her multitool. She flicked the large blade open and punctured her airbag, then used the blade to cut through her seatbelt.

She crashed down on the inside of the Mustang's roof, her arms protecting her head. She was glad Damien couldn't see her terrible crash-landing—he'd taught her a hundred times how to do it properly. But he wasn't conscious, and neither was Nasira.

Aviary's heart pumped faster. She reached over and punctured Nasira's airbag. Through Nasira's window and past a large fountain, Aviary watched marines enter the atrium.

'Nasira!' she yelled, her voice dull and distant from the flashbang.

Cutting Nasira's seatbelt would mean Nasira would fall on her head, but Aviary had no choice: it was that or leave her for the marines. Aviary wriggled under Nasira and cut her free. She braced to absorb Nasira's fall, but Nasira slid down slowly, her legs caught under the steering wheel. She slumped onto Aviary, pinning her there.

Well, I didn't think that through.

Aviary shook Nasira. Hard. No reaction. She checked her neck. Still a pulse—strong too.

That's a good sign, right?

Damien was sprawled in the back seat. His sheathed sword was lying in the center of the Mustang, the hilt resting by her knee. Damien's chest was rising and falling, but blood was leaking from his ears.

The marines circled the overturned Mustang.

Wriggling her way out from under Nasira, Aviary crawled back to the passenger side, her knee pressing on the sword. That wasn't going to help her now. She tossed her multitool back into her ruck and slipped it over her shoulders. She thought about making a run for it, but the marines were already pointing their weapons at her.

Seeing she was unarmed and her friends were out cold, they closed in.

The leading marine yelled something at her but she still couldn't hear properly. Something about hands? The marine had two stripes so he was ranked higher than the others and was probably a Gunnery Sergeant or Sausage or something.

'Hands ... in front!' Gunnery Sausage yelled.

Her hearing was returning—she understood most of that. She reached out for the sun visor in front of her. Through the broken windshield, a figure appeared in the distance.

The operative.

Not a great time, dude. Seriously.

Aviary placed one hand on the sun visor, but the other landed on something else. It was the handle to Damien's shiny black sword. She closed her grip over the handle and felt the satisfying click as her implant transmitted a signal. That signal would be picked up by the retention systems installed on each of the marines' carbines, disabling their own fingerprints. Finally, her implant had recharged.

She kneeled harder on the end of the sword and drew it from its sheath. The marines fired. Dry clicks. She reacted without thinking, thrusting the sword through her window. The jagged obsidian cut through Gunnery Sausage's vest, then stopped, impeded by ceramic. Not enough to wound him, but enough to take him off guard.

She kicked her door open, knocking him back. She pried her sword free and climbed out of the overturned Mustang. The operative in the distance was gone.

What the hell am I doing? she asked herself. *Oh nothing, just facing a squad of marines with nothing but a sword I don't even know how to use.*

One of the marines switched to his pistol and took aim—

His leg buckled, the knee shattered.

Nasira was awake and shooting. She fired more shots, hitting two marines in the face. The marine nearest Aviary drew his pistol. They all went for their sidearms.

Shit.

Aviary swung her sword at the nearby marine, knocking the pistol clear and slicing his hand. He screamed and dropped to his knees. A cold chill washed over her.

She ran around the Mustang and tripped, almost toppling into the fountain. Rounds cracked over her head. She dived into the fountain and crawled behind the ornamental centerpiece. Nasira was out of the Mustang, holding a knife to the Gunnery's throat and her pistol aimed at one of the marines. The marines converged on her, their pistols aimed. She retreated slowly through the atrium, past the fountain and Aviary's hiding spot. Damien was still in the Mustang.

Aviary had an idea. Nasira didn't have Jay's enhanced vision, but she could detect the electrical and magnetic fields of the marines. Maybe that was enough to see them. From behind the centerpiece, Aviary focused on her smartwatch. She found the power grid inside the casino and isolated a nice family of circuits.

'It's over!' one marine yelled. 'Lower your weapons.'

Aviary pressed the crown on the side of her watch.

The atrium went dark. Everyone started shooting. With loud pops, their muzzle flashes dazzled the atrium. Keeping low, Aviary grabbed her sword and waded through the fountain to the Mustang. She felt for Damien's door—

Something pulled her feet from under her. She hit the marble floor, her sword clanging beside her.

The lights came back on and the atrium burned fiercely with an array of chandeliers. With short blond hair and ice blue eyes, the operative loomed over her— knife in hand and ready to strike where she'd been standing.

Damien kicked his door open, disarming the operative. With a free hand, the operative drew his pistol and, taking a knee, aimed at Aviary. At the same time, he tossed her sword out of reach.

From inside the car, Damien lunged for him. He pivoted, aiming at Damien.

Aviary hit the crown on her watch and the door's airbag deployed. It smacked into the operative's head, knocking him sideways. He landed in front of her with a smack. Out cold.

Nasira helped Aviary up and aimed her pistol at the downed operative, but her pistol's slide was locked to the rear. She loaded a new mag as she moved for Damien, pulling him out of the Mustang. He was wobbly, but could walk.

More marines poured into the far end of the atrium.

'There's more of them!' Aviary yelled.

Damien snatched something up from a fallen marine—

a radio—then stumbled toward a flight of stairs, up to the next floor. Nasira, soaking wet, jockeyed Aviary ahead of her.

'Run!' she barked.

By the time she caught up with Damien, he was awkwardly jamming the radio halfway into his jeans pocket and pushing an earphone into his ear.

Nasira steered her into the cover of a maze of slot machines and gambling tables. To her surprise, this casino's floor was still bustling with patrons and staff. Some of the patrons looked at her, their expressions shifting slowly from confusion to alarm.

'Where's Jay?' Nasira asked between breaths.

Aviary raised her watch to her lips and gave it a voice command. 'Call Nasira.'

Jay had her phone, but he didn't pick up.

Why wasn't he answering?

Nasira was gaining ground on her, and she hurried to keep up. There was a dark blood stain on Nasira's shoulder; an exit wound that marred the silver shimmer of her top yet didn't appear to slow her down.

Aviary sprinted on, touching her body, arms, even her legs as she ran. Damien had taught her that she wouldn't register pain in a situation like this, so she needed to know if she was bleeding. She wasn't—none of the blood staining her stolen, shredded jacket was hers.

Her call connected.

'They're locking the whole strip down!' Jay yelled. 'Had to turn the car around.'

Nasira slowed to a fast walk. She took Aviary's wrist

and spoke into it so Jay could hear. And so could most of the startled patrons, but Nasira seemed past the point of caring.

'Where are you?' Nasira yelled.

'North, just passing the Eiffel Tower,' Jay yelled.

Nasira ripped off her shimmering top, down to her black singlet. Aviary followed suit and tore off her blood-soaked jacket. Damien was beside her now. He took her jacket and flung it onto a passing roulette table. The dealer and players froze in shock.

'Thirty-three black,' Damien said, removing his own shirt.

Aviary flushed at the sight of Damien tearing his blood-soaked shirt off with both hands, then flushed deeper at the idea that it could still have that effect given their situation. He plugged his earphone back in and caught up.

From Aviary's watch, Jay yelled, 'Find a way to the strip and I'll get you out.'

'You better,' Nasira said. 'Don't do anything stu—'

Jay ended the call.

'Get us out of here, Aviary,' Nasira said.

Aviary was generally familiar with these casinos, but panic and adrenaline had robbed her of her bearings. Now her hands trembled. 'I don't know where!'

'Then get knowing,' Nasira said.

Aviary pointed. 'OK. That way.'

She directed them to a bridge, its two long moving walkways a quick way of ferrying patrons between this building and The Venetian next door. Aviary sprinted across, weaving around the occasional patron. Nasira and Damien fell in behind her.

Her watch bleeped. Jay, calling again. She hit the crown to answer.

'Hey!' Jay said. 'You're riding me! I mean, uh, you're right on top of me!'

Aviary looked over the side of the walkway and spotted Jay's getaway car beneath her. 'Don't go far!' she said. 'We'll find a way down!'

At the end of the bridge was a large open-air plaza. Gondolas floated under arched walkways and along canals of turquoise water. They'd arrived at The Venetian.

'The fuck is this place?' Nasira asked, slowing to a fast walk.

'Can't get through!' Jay yelled through Aviary's watch. 'Security fences everywhere!'

'Can you make it to arrivals at the Venetian?' Aviary asked. 'It's the closest access by car.'

'That's a whole other casino,' Damien said. 'We won't make it.'

'Give me a map.' Nasira extended her hand. 'We have to make it. Are they closing on us?'

Damien was listening to their radio. 'Still behind, but they're catching up.'

Nasira took one look at the map on Aviary's phone, then started running. She tore through the Gold Club Lounge and into the central casino. Nasira ran for a particular corner, catching puzzled glances from nearby patrons. Lungs burning, Aviary finally caught up.

'Through Walgreens,' Nasira said.

'Nope, nope, nope.' Damien was listening to his earphone.

Nasira hesitated. Aviary saw why.

Half a battalion of marines poured down the escalators in front of Walgreens.

CHAPTER FOURTEEN

Kaliningrad, Kaliningrad Oblast

OLESYA OPENED her notebook and Xiu's photo slipped into her hand.

She wasn't smiling in the picture, but Olesya could remember how she looked when she did, and the way she wrinkled her nose when she was concentrating.

Even here in Kaliningrad, she couldn't escape her feelings of loss.

There was a light knock on the door.

Ark stepped inside. 'Gleb called a meeting.'

'Right now? Where?'

Ark made way, and the intelligence officer entered the room. Gleb stood awkwardly in his neatly pressed combat fatigues, hands clasped behind him. 'Here, if that is no issue.'

'There's no room here for everyone,' Olesya said.

Ark closed the door. 'This meeting's just for us.'

She glared at both of them. 'What about Illarion?'

Gleb cleared his throat. He hadn't shaven today, which she found unusual. Now he looked his age, which she estimated only a few years more than the rest of them.

'It's best we keep this between ourselves for the moment,' Gleb said.

'I'm not sure how I feel about that,' she said.

'If you'll hear me out, then you can make your decision.'

'And if I don't?'

'Then I will brief Illarion.'

Olesya folded her arms. 'Fine. What's this about? And can you sit down? It's unsettling having you both stand there.'

Gleb sat on the very end of Marina's bed, shifting the fluffy anchovy from under him with a perplexed expression. Ark helped himself to Marina's chair.

'How long does it take?' Ark asked.

She blinked. 'For what?'

'He means deprogramming.' Gleb clasped his hands. 'How certain are you that it can be done successfully?'

She met his gaze. 'I *know* it can be done. Otherwise Ark and I wouldn't be here.'

'You weren't completely programmed by the Fifth Column, is that correct?' Gleb asked.

Olesya raised an eyebrow. 'Is that why you're here? To *evaluate* us? Who exactly do you report to?'

'Normally I report to Illarion,' Gleb said. 'Tonight, I report to you.'

'What are you talking about?'

'Gleb is here because we can help each other,' Ark said.

The intelligence officer unfastened a button on his uniform and removed a large envelope from inside, which he handed to Olesya. 'You're not supposed to see this. And I didn't give it to you.'

The envelope contained a stapled collection of papers and a small thin book—a standard firearms manual. The papers were printed with the Intron logo, the two arrows intersecting like a misaligned X.

'Check the next page,' Gleb said.

Olesya turned over the top sheet. At the head of the page there was a code: *M165.*

'What do you see?' Gleb asked.

'An invoice.'

She looked closer. The buyer was obscured. Everything was in numbers except for the description of the product. Height in centimeters, weight in kilograms, eye color, hair color, nationality: Russian.

'Looks like human trafficking to me.' She looked at Gleb. 'You haven't shown this to Illarion yet, have you?'

He shook his head.

She pointed to a word on the invoice. 'Tetrachromacy.'

'Ultraviolet vision,' Ark said. 'The ability that Val was born with.'

At the bottom of the invoice, she noticed the word *cancelled* and a date beside it. The date was recent. 'Whoever they are, they cancelled the order.'

'That date is the night when the Fifth Column raided an Intron facility in Belarus.'

'What did they raid it for?' she asked.

'They abducted some of the patients,' Gleb said.

'Val,' Olesya whispered.

Ark nodded. 'Exactly what I'm thinking.'

'This invoice tells a story.' Olesya wet her lips. 'Of Intron abducting Val and conspiring to sell her. Until she was abducted.'

'At this very moment, I'm tracking a new operative in Eastern Europe,' Gleb said. 'She is marked for an operation tomorrow.'

'A *new* operative? So that's our operation in Poland tomorrow?' Olesya asked.

Gleb shook his head. 'Poland is running federal elections tomorrow and Purity's political party are in the running. We have sources who suspect they might spike their popularity with something ... traumatic. You're dispatched to make sure that doesn't happen.' He paused. 'However, the new operative is in Estonia.'

Olesya handed back the papers. 'We can't be in two places at once.'

'I have the authority to declare you unfit for duty. I can choose to classify you—both of you—as suffering from post-traumatic stress. That means temporary leave.'

'You're going to lie?' she asked.

'It's the truth.'

Ark leaned forward in his chair. 'Olesya, this operative has a fresh tag.'

'They're training new recruits?'

'We have no reports of that,' Gleb said. 'Look at the firearms manual. Please.'

Olesya opened the book and found page after page of scrawled handwritten notes in English. Each page looked to be a photocopy, and not a great one either. She leafed through, skimming the words.

Her heart raced. 'This is a deprogramming manual.'

Gleb nodded. 'The only one of its kind.'

'Where did you get it?' she asked.

'It's best I don't answer that.'

She glared at him. 'If you want us involved, I need to know.'

'This stays between us,' Gleb said. 'This document was on the bed of the abducted patient in Belarus.'

Olesya considered that for a moment. 'So you're saying that Intron abducted Val, and then the Fifth Column stole her?'

'It's possible that the abduction was a condition of the sale,' Gleb said.

'It wasn't cancelled at all,' Olesya said. 'The new operative is Val.'

'I have no doubt,' Ark said.

'It's probable,' Gleb countered.

Or perhaps not, Olesya thought. *It could be Xiu.*

'I know it's a big ask, going to Estonia,' Ark said. 'But we can let the others take care of the election. Gleb can put us on the bench.' He shrugged. 'At least look like we're on the bench.'

'And then what?' Olesya said.

'I've already issued you with Estonian passports and driver's insurance—that's standard procedure,' Gleb said. 'But I can also book you flights.'

'That's not standard procedure,' she said. 'Why should we trust you?'

'I just handed you a deprogramming manual that's not

supposed to exist.' His eyes were glassy now. 'My career is on the line. And Val…'

Olesya watched him for a moment. 'You care about her.'

'She's one of our hunters, it's essential that I care about her,' Gleb said.

'No,' she said softly. 'It's more than that.'

A tear spilled down his cheek. 'It's foolish. I'm not—I know there's no chance that anything could…'

Ark stared at him. 'What are you saying? Were you guys…'

'What Gleb is saying, is we all care for her very much.' Olesya glared at Gleb. 'Right?'

Gleb stood and brushed creases from his shirt. 'And that is precisely why I'm here.'

Ark turned to Olesya. 'Gleb wants to help get Val back. Do you?'

'On one condition.' She closed the deprogramming manual. 'I run this operation.'

CHAPTER FIFTEEN

Devil's Mountain, Berlin

SOPHIA LOOKED through the torn shell of the radar dome.

Once an NSA spy station during the Cold War, the surface of the golf ball-shaped structure had peeled away, and was laced with graffiti. Below it, thick forest sprawled toward Berlin.

She didn't want to take their newly captured operative back to the old mansion in Lithuania. Not yet. This forgotten spy station was the perfect location for the first stage of deprogramming, even if it meant risking impalement by wild boar just to get here.

She checked her phone in case DC had made contact—nothing—then turned her attention to the woman in Naval uniform. Her name was Priya and Sophia had sat her in an old red bathtub. The woman's hands were unnaturally still, resting on the lip of the tub as she stared ahead, unfocused. She'd been locked in slave mode since the nightclub.

Czarina and Ieva stood at a safe distance, near the ladder they'd used to climb into the dome. While they'd made it out of the club mostly unscathed, Czarina sported a cut lip and Ieva a dark bruise that swelled across her jaw. Ieva held her phone, tapping notes into the screen. Czarina hovered, eyes on the prisoner, hand over her pistol grip. Sophia felt responsible for their injuries, but it could've been a lot worse had she not used the DJ's microphone in time.

'Priya, my name is Sophia.' Her voice reverberated off the dome's interior, sounding like she was in a philharmonic hall. 'Confirm neopsyche designation: Alcyone.'

Priya stared through Sophia. 'Alcyone confirmed.' Her voice was not hers anymore. It was even and smooth. She was a world away.

Sophia crouched in front of the bathtub. 'Where are you, Priya?'

'I'm playing Pachisi with Grandma.' She smiled. 'I think she's letting me win.'

'Are you safe?'

She nodded enthusiastically. 'You can call me Pri-Pri, like Grandma. But it's your turn to roll.'

'Sure, give me a moment.' Sophia stood and turned to Ieva and Czarina. 'It's important we ground her before continuing.'

Ieva raised her hand. 'Question.'

'You don't need to raise your hand, Ieva.'

'Which one is Alcyone?'

'Alcyone is the neopsyche—her false personality,' Sophia said. 'Denton programmed this into each of us.'

'So that lives alongside the arky ... archeo—'

'Archeopsyche,' Sophia said. 'That's the real you. It's always there, but it's not in control. Only when you are deprogrammed can the real *you* return.' Sophia regarded Czarina. 'Are you taking notes?'

Czarina tapped her head. 'All up here.'

Ieva grinned. 'At least something is.'

Czarina elbowed her, but kept her attention on Priya.

'Any other questions?' Sophia asked.

'No, more of a general complaint really,' Czarina said. 'This stuff is hard to get my head around.'

'Maybe you should write it down,' Ieva said.

'It's not your head you need to get around, it's Priya's,' Sophia said. 'Priya, execute Alcyone, confirm parapsyche listing.'

Priya didn't say anything for a moment.

Sophia knelt in front of the bathtub. 'Pri-Pri?'

'Alcyone loaded. Listing'—Priya frowned —'unknown.'

Sophia paused. *Interesting.*

Czarina's fingers twitched over her pistol. 'Everything OK?'

Sophia checked her handwritten deprogramming manual, noticed her bookmark was in the wrong place. She stuffed it in her jacket pocket and approached Priya.

Priya's hands were steady, her emotions simmered flat. Sophia hoped she remained that way. She'd stressed to Czarina and Ieva on many occasions that the early stages of deprogramming were often the most dangerous. For the deprogrammer and the subject.

But Sophia hadn't really started. Not yet. 'Pri-Pri, I need you to answer a few questions.'

Priya didn't blink. 'But it's your turn Sophie, have you rolled your shells?'

Sophia cleared her throat. 'Yes, I have rolled.'

Ieva whispered loudly. 'You rolled a six!'

'I rolled a six,' Sophia said.

'You can leave the *Charkoni* now.' Priya moved the invisible piece from the center of the invisible board, her hand waving over the bathtub. 'Your journey begins. It's your turn again.'

Sophia shifted closer to the bathtub. 'Already? OK. But first, can you please tell me about your target in the Berlin nightclub?'

'Evgeny Sporyshev,' Priya said. 'He dances funny.'

'What were you doing with him?'

'We took him away, Sophie. We took him far away.' Priya tilted her head. 'What did you roll?'

'Three,' Sophia said. 'Where do you take him?'

Priya sang, 'I'm late, I'm late, for a very important date!' She moved Sophia's invisible piece, then said, 'He has an important meeting in east Berlin and we can't be late.'

'What is the meeting for?' Sophia asked.

Priya's gaze fell to the inside of the bathtub. 'I don't know, Sophie.'

'Why does the Fifth Column want Evgeny?' Sophia asked.

'Kill … kill.' Priya's fingers quivered. 'Turn it off,

please! It's too loud.'

'Turn what off?'

'All of us! We're too loud.' Priya's body jerked in the bathtub, limbs twitching. 'I don't want to play anymore.'

Too far. Sophia raised her hand. 'Disregard question.'

'Pri-Pri is tired. Can I sleep now?'

'Soon.' Sophia stepped away from her, to where Ieva feverishly took notes and Czarina stood in silence. 'It's important to know the tolerances of the programmed operative. In fact it's not just important, it's crucial.'

'What sort of tolerances?' Ieva asked.

'Truth,' Sophia said. 'It's the same for an operative as any person. Our minds can only abandon so many lies at once. We can only accept so much reality.'

'There's a capacity for her?' Czarina asked.

'She can only be stretched so far,' Sophia said. 'And you're no different.'

Back to the questions, while she had the chance. 'Priya, do you know what will happen to Evgeny now that you've taken him to his important meeting?'

Priya seemed not to hear the question at first, but then, hesitatingly, her lips moved. 'Put them on ice,' Priya said. 'Put them on ice and melt them to dust.'

'*They?* How are they melting?' Soft waves of anxiety emanated from Priya, curled around her. Sophia was pushing too hard. 'Disregard.'

'OK, Sophie.'

Sophia spoke low to the others. 'If you take a programmed operative too far, too close to the edge of reality, they will reject it. They'll reject you. And they'll reject themselves. When that happens, they become dangerous.'

'To us or themselves?' Czarina asked.

'Both,' she said. 'Priya, do you know why there have been a lot of Fifth Column operatives in Eastern Europe recently?'

'They're planning,' Priya said. 'Like busy bees. It's a very big operation.'

Czarina and Ieva exchanged a nervous glance.

'That's some grim shit,' Czarina said. 'How big is she talking?'

Sophia spoke softly. 'Can you tell us about the operation?'

'What if I get in trouble?' Priya asked.

'You won't get in trouble anymore, I promise.'

'Maximum collateral.' Priya's words were whispers. She gripped the edge of the bathtub.

The serrated edge of Priya's pain slashed at Sophia, stealing the breath from her. Her legs weakened and she dropped to one knee.

'Sophia, you good?' Czarina called out. 'You still got this?'

'I'm in control.' Sophia moved closer to the bathtub. 'It's all right, Priya.'

Priya relaxed her grip and started to breathe slowly again.

'Where is the operation?' Sophia murmured.

Priya's stare was unfocused again. Only this time, she shook her head. Sophia didn't want to push through those obstacles too hard, but needed to know about this operation before it was too late.

'What is the location?' Sophia asked, more firmly than she'd planned. 'Is there a date for this?'

Priya's head transitioned from shaking to nodding. Lots of nodding. She was agreeing. But agreeing to what? She muttered to herself in another language Sophia couldn't understand, then stopped and looked at her. Not through her, *at* her. For a moment, Priya's archeopsyche came to the surface.

'Destiny,' Priya said.

Czarina took a step forward. 'She doesn't know shit. There's no big operation.'

'This takes time though, right?' Ieva asked.

'It's all about the right question.' Sophia leaned in closer. 'What is the Fifth Column planning to do in Eastern Europe?'

'I'm sorry, Sophie, I lost the game,' Priya said.

'It's OK.' Sophia reached out to touch her hand. 'I'm here now.'

'No. You lost too.'

Priya launched from the bathtub, her foot clipping Sophia across her head. Sophia recovered, but Priya was running along the concrete floor and leaping through a hole in the radar dome. Czarina drew her pistol.

'Don't shoot her!' Sophia yelled.

'But she's trying to escape!'

Sophia jumped through a torn section of the dome. She rolled, came to her feet. Priya was on a flat rooftop, moving for the railing around it.

She wasn't trying to escape.

'No!' Sophia cried.

She ran at Priya and dived, caught hold of the woman

as she leapt over the railing. Sophia held onto the collar of her uniform. Pulled the struggling Priya back up, across the metal railing and onto the concrete. Priya tore out of her Navy jacket, kicked Sophia in the ribs and was running again. Sophia pulled herself to her feet. Czarina sprinted across the rooftop, cutting off Priya's escape.

She had nowhere left to run.

Sophia approached her, close enough to hear Priya whisper, 'Are you really in control?'

Then she sprinted, back to the radar dome. Sophia gave chase. Pain flared in her ribs, slowing her down.

Ieva ran to cut Priya off, but the woman didn't even change course. Instead, she sprinted right for one of the torn edges of the radar dome…

And ran her throat into a jagged piece of metal.

The shard nicked an artery. Blood pumped from her neck with the power of a garden hose. Sophia arrived at her side, but it was too late. Covered in Priya's blood she sensed Czarina and Ieva looking to her for orders, but she didn't have any. She wasn't in control.

Pri-Pri bled out.

CHAPTER SIXTEEN

Las Vegas, United States

AVIARY STRUGGLED to keep pace with Nasira and Damien as they moved across the casino floor. The marines hadn't spotted them yet, but they blocked a potential escape route through the side entrance. Now, a new cluster of marines emerged in the casino center.

'Got any more tricks?' Nasira asked.

Aviary's stomach coiled tightly. 'I think I'm about to throw up.'

'Now's probably not the time.' Nasira pulled them deeper into the crowd before they were spotted.

'Wait a second,' Aviary said. 'Casinos use servers to program their slot machines, right?'

Nasira glared at her. 'You asking me?'

While they concealed themselves in the crowd—most of whom were too distracted by slot machines to pay them any attention—Aviary used her smartwatch to comb through the servers in the building until she found the one she was looking for.

'They're covering all angles except the plaza outside,' Damien said.

Nasira's gaze flickered from one direction to another. 'Trying to flush us into the open.'

'Aviary, we need that distraction,' Nasira muttered. 'They're gonna see us any second now.'

'Working on it.'

'Call Jay,' Nasira said.

'I'm still here.' Jay spoke through Aviary's watch. 'What's the go?'

Nasira leaned in. 'We're coming out the front entrance.'

'Through the plaza?' Jay said. 'You crazy?'

'Aviary?' Damien asked.

'It's just like your lockpicking,' Aviary said. 'Once you're in, you can go almost anywhere. Especially if their cyber security is basically zero. And it is.' She tapped her watch. 'Jackpot.'

Around them, rows of slot machines sang triumphantly. Coins fired from dispensers. People watched in disbelief. Ignoring the marines—whose presence wasn't that unusual these days—they went for it.

Aviary covered her ears to drown out the discordant slot machine music and people screaming with excitement. Everyone pushed in to the slot machines, clogging the casino floor.

A young man with a septum piercing and an aggressively tailored suit hauled a bucketload of coins in his shirt. An elderly man tripped him with his walking stick. The coins shimmered across the floor; three marines slipped on them and fell. They climbed to their feet again, only to be brutally clotheslined by a rotund lady in a vibrant floral dress.

'Outta my way!' she yelled, opening her handbag so coins could pour in from two slot machines at once. 'It's pay day.'

'Go! Go!' Nasira yelled.

Aviary bolted for the glass doors. Through the frenzied crowd, Aviary saw the marines converging on them.

'Oh crap,' Damien said.

Her thoughts exactly.

Jay was yelling something on her watch. 'Don't go outside! They have the plaza surrounded!'

'Damien!' Aviary yelled.

He kicked the door open and stepped through. Aviary lunged toward him, reaching for his hand, but someone grabbed her ruck, pulling her back into the crowd. A trio of marines secured her, holding her wrists. She tried to relax and twist from their grasp, as she'd been taught, but their grip was already solid and pistols jammed in her face.

Two of the marines forced her wrists together behind her back and wrapped plasticuffs around them, while the third forced her to her knees. He kneed her in her ruck, knocking the air from her and driving her face down onto the floor. As she fell, she turned, wrists wrenching from their grasp. A giddy patron with handfuls of coins tripped over her, showering the marines with money. The marines scrabbled in the confusion, one marine managing to grab her ankle. She kicked him in the face and rolled to her feet, coming face to face with the guy holding coins.

It was Sonic the Hedgehog.

'Gotta go,' she said.

Then she was running. Through the coins. Through the feverish patrons. The marines knocked Sonic aside and gave chase, but the crowd closed between them.

Aviary headed for the entrance, burst through ... and skidded to a halt.

'Well, if it isn't Miss ... Aviary,' Hal said.

He stood atop a mock Venetian bridge over a mock Venetian canal, arms folded in equally mock impatience. Another man in a suit—ten years younger and minus the scar tissue—stood beside him.

He really does have a partner, Aviary thought.

Flanking the two Fifth Column men, an entire platoon of marines were aiming at her with carbines. Damien and Nasira were already out of play, dozens of weapons trained on them. Aviary pressed the implant in her hand. It was charged enough to trigger again, taking care of the carbines. But then she glanced around and her heart sank.

One marine operated a fold-out tripod topped by a radar dish the size of a buffet tray. It seemed oddly familiar. She thought back to all the files she'd stolen from the Fifth Column but nothing clicked. Nothing like this. It was a threat for which she had no response.

She stepped forward again, purposely in front of Damien, her heart racing.

'Did you really think you could just run away from us?' Hal asked.

'Um, I guess my hands are tied,' Aviary said.

Behind her back, the plasticuffs pinched around her wrists, and her skin tingled with heat. Just as she'd hoped, Damien was using his thermogenesis to melt the loop. An instant later, the tension in her cuffs disappeared.

'Hands above your heads,' Hal said. 'You will pay for your crimes against humanity.'

'What about yours?' Nasira raised her hands. 'You get a promotion for those?'

Hal turned to the marine wielding the tripod dish. 'Activate.'

The dish hummed softly, but did nothing else.

'Hey,' Nasira said. 'I think the sperm count's a bit low on your toy over here.'

'Don't say that,' Damien said.

Aviary's face and arms grew hotter, but it wasn't Damien causing it. She got warmer and warmer, the sensation building until it felt like she was on fire. She howled, and behind her, Damien moaned and collapsed. Nasira fell to her knees.

Hal nodded. 'Give it more juice.'

Suddenly it was like Aviary was falling into the sun itself. She collapsed, too agonized to touch her smart-watch, to see Damien and Nasira writhing beside her, even to scream.

All she could do was lay there as she and her friends burned alive.

HELIX: EPISODE 3

INTERCEPTOR

CHAPTER ONE

Berlin, Germany
26 April 1945

DENTON DROVE his knife between the SS-Sonderkom-mando's clavicle and scapula, cutting the subclavian artery. With his hand over the soldier's mouth and the blade still in his neck, Denton lowered him softly to the attic floor. The soldier's heart stopped pumping blood and Denton withdrew his knife.

The old building was mostly intact, but someone had intentionally torn a hole in the brick wall, connecting the attic of this building with the next. Stepping carefully over the body, Denton leapt through the hole and caught the next SS-Sonderkommando by surprise. The soldier aimed his rifle at Denton's chest, but Denton stepped around it and ran his knife across the Sonderkommando's throat. He hooked the knife behind the neck, spinning the Nazi by his elbow. Blood sprayed and the soldier slumped. Denton grasped the rifle so it didn't clatter to the floor, and placed it carefully on the body.

A sliver of moonlight lit the dusty attic. Denton used the faint light to locate Colonel Wolfram Sievers in the shadows. The former administrator of the Ahnenerbe institute stood at the other end of the attic, surveying the mortar-torn street below through a tiny, dirty window. He wore his black beard trimmed and his hair precisely combed with Brylcreem. Under his overcoat, he was impeccably dressed.

Denton checked the darker corners of the attic, then leveled his suppressed Tokarev pistol at Sievers. The man didn't reach for his own weapon, but he watched Denton with dark, glistening eyes.

'Lieutenant Denton,' Sievers said. 'I was starting to think you would miss your opportunity.'

'Then you know why I'm here.'

'You must have worn every uniform in this war by now,' Sievers said. 'Do you have a favorite?'

'Hugo Boss does a good Nazi,' Denton said. 'But I wouldn't waste your breath with small talk.'

'You're impulsive yet adaptable,' Sievers said. 'Perhaps this is how you have survived so long in this war, where other spies might have perished.'

Denton kept his aim on the bearded man. 'Call me lucky. If you knew I was coming, why are you still here?'

'We have a lot in common, I thought we might talk,' Sievers said.

Denton shook his head. 'We already have all your research.'

'Then why are you here?'

'Suspicion.'

'I would be gravely concerned were you not,' Sievers said.

There was a moment's silence, quickly followed by the distant crack of gunfire. Soviet forces were breaching the city.

'I presume you came here under ... less than official circumstances.'

'My entire job is less than official,' Denton said. 'That's the whole point.'

'Likewise, the offer your superiors made me. I'm on your side,' Sievers said, his voice a pitch higher. 'How do you say, *in cahoots*? My work is now yours.' He reached slowly inside his coat.

Denton's trigger finger flexed.

Sievers turned his lapel out so Denton could see him reaching for a small, slender tin. He crouched and opened the tin on the floorboards, then stepped back. Inside, a large stainless steel and glass syringe. The liquid inside the syringe burned with the colors of molten lava.

'You already know what this is,' Sievers said. 'And you'll need it, if you intend to live long enough to find what you're really looking for.'

Denton took a step toward him. 'You're using my people to get what *you* want.'

For the first time, Sievers smiled. White teeth flashed between his black beard. 'And you are doing precisely the same.'

Footsteps creaked from the adjacent attic. Denton aimed his pistol, ready to fire on the SS soldiers. But they weren't SS at all. They aimed their own submachine guns through the hole at Denton.

'Lower your weapon!' the SAS commander ordered, first in German, then in English.

Despite their Soviet overcoats, he recognized their British accents. First SAS.

Denton lowered his pistol. 'It's all right, you don't have to pretend you don't recognize me.'

The soldiers relaxed, then crawled through the hole to join Denton and Sievers. First SAS were here to escort Sievers from Berlin, and Denton had accomplished little except get in the way. Sievers walked toward them, empty-handed, and they encircled him.

'Leave the tin, it's for our friend here,' Sievers said to the soldiers, before turning to Denton. 'Perhaps we can continue our conversation in a new world. If you live long enough.'

'You can count on that,' Denton said.

Sievers almost smiled, then the soldiers ushered him through the hole in the wall. The SAS commander took a moment to double-check Sievers had left nothing behind.

'Weren't expecting you on this outing, sir,' he said.

Denton stared at the syringe. 'Neither was I.'

CHAPTER TWO

Kiev, Ukraine
Today

DENTON ENTERED the parliamentary session hall, now being used as the battalion headquarters. The hall was lit from above by a large, multi-colored glass dome and a crystal chandelier shaped like a sunflower. Denton walked the aisle of wooden stalls, his soft leather shoes striking the floorboards and catching the attention of the men at the front stall: the newly appointed general, Vitali Sych, and four buzz-cut associates. Fortunately, Denton had brought four operatives of his own, dressed to match in fitted suits.

The general and his men appeared to be holding their own official session, and they did so while dressed in forest green combat uniforms that smelt of sweat and tobacco. Purity flags hung from the wall behind them, charcoal with a white dove under a single red diamond. There was an open space where the aisles converged at the front stall, which Vitali had fashioned into his new meeting area. It was cluttered with desks, papers, office chairs and ashtrays.

Vitali sat between two desks, watching Denton and his operatives approach.

'I must say it's a pleasure to meet you in person,' Denton said in English, his words echoing through the hall.

'Who are you?' Vitali asked. 'We are not expecting visitors.'

'I'm not your usual liaison.' Denton gestured to their desks. 'Is this where you talk? What's wrong with your office?'

'I like open space.' Vitali stood and adjusted his belt. There was an AK-74 rifle resting against his desk, within arm's reach. 'Why are you here? Is there problem?'

'The weapons you have requested,' Denton said, taking an educated guess.

Denton could see Ukrainian words inside Vitali's head but he couldn't understand them. Some people 'saw' their words in their head, some 'heard' them, while others felt them or processed them abstractly. Depending on what kind of person he was dealing with, Denton could tune into a non-English speaker's thoughts and interpret them. But it didn't work on everyone. If only there were pseudo-genes to activate a universal translator in his head.

All he could see and understand in Vitali's head were images of soldiers in white combat armor marching through columns of fire and smoke.

'The soldiers you have requested,' Denton corrected himself quickly. 'We have made arrangements.'

'How many?' Vitali watched Denton with tiny eyes. His face was large and soft as dough.

He reminded Denton of a pufferfish.

Denton took a chair and wheeled it to Vitali's desk. Ignoring the buzz-cut men in uniform, he sat before Vitali. His own operatives took up positions and surrounded the uniformed men.

'How many do you need?' Denton asked.

'Five thousand,' Vitali said. 'We want special forces only.' Slowly, but not subtly, he thrust his chest outward—along with his stomach, regrettably.

The pufferfish inflates.

'I can give you six hundred paratroopers from Italy to train your newly formed Purity Guard,' Denton said. 'We would prefer you engage your enemy with your own soldiers though. As a matter of policy.'

Vitali shook his head. 'There are not enough of us to stop the deviants and aberrations. We need more men—pure men—to join us as we take back Europe.'

'We cannot directly engage with your enemy. It would not be appropriate,' Denton said.

Vitali's nostrils enlarged. 'How can this not be appropriate?'

Good, Denton thought. He had him in the right place and the right emotional state. It hadn't taken much.

'We have given you a great deal,' Denton said. 'Power over your government. Funding, equipment, intelligence, and most importantly—opportunity. And yet we are behind schedule.' He leaned forward. 'Let me make this clear: you are underperforming.'

'I am not an idiot,' Vitali said. 'And we are not underperforming.'

Denton leaned back in his chair. 'You should know that my general is not pleased with your failure thus far.'

'I have talked with your general many times,' Vitali said, finally sitting behind his desk again. 'He is very happy with our campaign against the aberrations.'

Sievers' face flashed through Vitali's mind. Denton's heart rate quickened. He was close.

Sixty years and Sievers is still alive.

'*Was* happy,' Denton said. 'In your last meeting, what did you speak of?'

Vitali swallowed. 'The Fifth Column's commitment to Purity in Europe. In our country. And our historic mission to recover our nation. Glory to Purity!'

The four men in fatigues echoed Vitali. 'Glory to Purity!'

Denton cleared his throat. 'My superior's last visit, a few weeks ago...'

'Two weeks ago,' Vitali said.

'That's right,' Denton said. 'He traveled all the way here, I'm sure he was tired and short-tempered.'

Vitali nodded. In his mind, Denton saw the city of Prague. Now he had Sievers' semi-permanent location. That would be helpful.

'When he returned, he told me about your next strategy,' Denton said.

Vitali blinked, but said nothing.

Denton frowned. 'He didn't tell you?'

'Of course.' Vitali reached for the metal briefcase on the table and pushed it toward Denton. 'Tell your general we want only soldiers. We have no interest in your filthy needles.'

Denton didn't need to look inside the briefcase, he caught a glimpse in Vitali's mind of the syringes filled with milk-colored liquid. 'Why don't they interest you?'

Vitali snorted. 'You cannot make someone pure. They are dogs, you can only put dogs down.' He pointed to the crates stacked against the far wall, behind the rear stalls. 'The rest of your shipment is over there.'

In Vitali's mind, Denton saw images of prisoners— executed instead of injected with syringes. Denton stood and reached for the briefcase. The visions of violence faded. Vitali put his hand back, holding the briefcase there.

'You are not Fifth Column.' Vitali reached for the rifle behind his desk. His men raised theirs. 'You are Russian spies!'

Denton kicked the desk forward, pinning the bulging general between his desk and the wall. Around Denton, his own operatives aimed their Czech submachine guns —*Scorpion EVOs* with attached suppressors—and peppered Vitali's four associates with subsonic rounds. They collapsed in tatters, face-down on desks and floorboards.

Between the two desks, Vitali tried to free his AK-74, but the curved magazine hooked under the desk. Denton drew his own USP pistol and aimed at his face.

'You know,' Denton said, 'the Purity Party in the United States is very different to your people. They're forgiving and evangelical, but here it's all doom and gloom. I just find it really boring.' He turned to his operatives. 'Tie him up.'

Denton stepped back and let a pair of his operatives drag the desk out and disarm Vitali. Using duct tape, they wrapped him to his own chair, his hands behind his back.

'Tape his mouth,' Denton said. 'You look very dashing in your suits, by the way,' he said to his team. 'We should do this more often.'

The operatives said nothing. One pair took defensive positions while the other covered the hall entrance. Denton walked around the desk and sat on the edge, staring down at Vitali.

'You need to look to your American Purity pals and stay on brand,' Denton said, rubbing a fingerprint off the black nitride finish of his pistol. 'They just want to be pure. And yes, slaughter all the deviants and aberrations. But you get my point.'

Vitali remained motionless.

Denton leaned over him. 'Oh, but you'll never be pure, will you?'

Vitali said something, muffled behind the duct tape. Denton enjoyed that.

'You're very, very filthy,' Denton said. 'You look like a pufferfish. Don't you think? In Japan, they're called *fugu*. You have the eyes of a fugu.' He pressed the barrel of his USP into the general's nose, forcing it upward so it looked like a snout. 'You have the mind of a fugu.'

Vitali struggled to breathe.

Denton shook his head. 'No. You're not a fugu. You're something quite … I wouldn't use the word "remarkable" because you're not. You might be a hired mercenary or a professional killer. You might be an overweight, overcompensated general with no real skill to speak of. Yet you are quick to take up arms with no regret or remorse to inhibit your performance. You're a *jackal*.'

Vitali mumbled something through the duct tape. Denton saw the violent image in Vitali's mind and struck him across the ear with his pistol grip. Not too hard though, he wanted the general to be conscious. Just in a bit of pain. Pain was good. Besides, he had what he'd come here for. He had Sievers' location and, as a bonus, this suitcase with some interesting samples he will most certainly have tested. Who knows, they might be useful. And now he could at least enjoy himself for a short, controlled moment.

'You're the bottom of the food chain,' Denton said. 'You feed off the scraps. You slaughter people in their homes. Yes, we all enjoy a bit of bloodletting from time to time. It gets the blood pumping—yours, and theirs. But you, you live and breathe it. You roll in it. There is nothing more to you than violence. I find that very boring.'

Vitali breathed slowly now. His eye twitched.

'And yet, you cannot even succeed at that,' Denton said.

The general looked up at Denton, then his operatives. There was fear in his tiny pufferfish eyes. Denton liked that. He enjoyed the satisfying curve from predator to sashimi.

'When some people are fired, they clear out their desks and maybe steal a stapler.' Denton laughed. 'I already had a stapler, so I stole these operatives.'

Vitali's gaze moved from one operative to another with wide, bloodshot eyes.

'I'm not a Russian spy. And I'm not Fifth Column anymore.' Denton leaned in close to the general's ear—swollen and red from the pistol whip—and pressed the barrel to his temple. 'I'm much worse.'

Vitali whined, his plea muffled through the tape.

'You don't mind if I destroy your brain, do you?' Denton asked. 'It's not like you're using it.'

Denton squeezed the trigger.

CHAPTER THREE

Las Vegas, United States

JAY DROVE THROUGH THE FENCE.

With the car radio pumping, he crashed into the casino plaza and took a panel of metal fence with him. He kept going, accelerating over the bridge.

Jay drove through a string of marines and a pair of men in suits. They saw him at the last moment and dived into the canal. At the other end of the bridge, Nasira, Damien and Aviary were on the ground, twitching and turning. There was a heat ray dish aimed at them.

Guess they made a portable version.

Jay hit the brakes hard. The fence flew from his windshield and knocked over a row of marines. He accelerated again, down the bridge and toward the heat ray. He turned the wheel hard and pulled the handbrake, clipping the dish with the side of his car. It toppled, and his friends stopped convulsing.

'Get in!' he yelled.

Aviary rolled to her feet and jumped in next to him, barely breathing. 'I cracked the power grid,' she gasped.

The marines recovered and reached for their carbines, aiming for Damien and Nasira out in the open. Others aimed for Jay. He had no chance, but he drew his pistol anyway.

'Jackpot,' Aviary said.

The canal and streetlamps turned black. He couldn't see the marines on the bridge. Through his window, the casino's lights—level by level—shut down. Around him, in an expanding radius, Las Vegas went dark.

Nasira and Damien moved through the darkness and jumped in the back.

'What the hell—did you do that?' Jay asked.

Aviary had her flashlight out, her finger touching the strobe for a moment. 'Get us out of here!'

Jay took off the handbrake and roared up the bridge, radio pumping. 'Get ready to use that … now!'

Aviary hit the strobe and blasted everyone on the bridge with dizzying flashes. The only lights Jay could see were the headlamps of cars on the boulevard ahead. Where they needed to go.

From the back seat, Nasira leaned forward to switch on his high beams. 'Are you playing Taylor Swift?'

'No idea.' Jay drove off the bridge and toward the boulevard. 'Aviary, did you just black out a whole city?'

'Uh, I was running out of ideas,' she said.

He gripped the steering wheel. 'Good job.'

A new vehicle crossed the boulevard and cut off their escape. It was large and sharp, the size of a tank with the maneuverability of a 4x4.

Marauder.

Jay took a hard right, racing between the canal and the boulevard. He just hoped he wasn't driving into a dead end. In his rear-view mirror, the Marauder smashed through the bollards and metal fence with an unsettling ease. Jay didn't want to be the next bollard.

'Fifty cal,' Damien said, describing the Marauder's mounted M2 machine gun.

Aviary hit Jay's horn, forcing stray pedestrians in the plaza to scatter.

Jay's chest tightened, stealing his breath. 'Hold on.'

Ahead of them, there was an old white building and a small length of pavement without a barrier. That was his way out. He downshifted, took the left, scraping across a metal fence and smashing through a signpost. He held his breath and punched through. The car roared off the plaza, crashing onto the boulevard and narrowly missing a black pickup. The pickup swerved and corrected itself.

'Take that, Marauder!' he yelled, making Aviary cover her ears.

The Marauder exploded through a concrete wall behind them.

'Fuck.'

'I think it's angry now,' Damien said.

'Faster!' Nasira said. 'And turn off the radio.'

Jay shook his head. 'Taylor Swift helps me focus.'

In the rear-view mirror, he saw a marine climb behind the machine gun.

Shit.

Jay jerked the car, narrowly avoiding a white van in front of them. The machine gun lit up the boulevard. The sound of gunfire drowned everything out. The white van shredded into curled metal, then veered right for them. Jay pulled sharply to avoid it, flying over a bump and into oncoming traffic.

Breathe. You can do this.

He steered between oncoming vehicles with all the focus he could muster, humming softly to the music. There was a concrete barrier separating both sides of the boulevard, at least until the Marauder exploded through it *right in front of them* and rammed a gray SUV head-on. Jay swerved around the Marauder as it sent the SUV into the air. It tumbled and came crashing down, narrowly missing Jay's car. The Marauder was four lanes across from them, but not far behind. It ploughed through two more cars, growling hungrily. The machine gun operator turned the barrel in Jay's direction.

Jay cut between lanes. Horns blared, drivers swerved to avoid him. The Marauder smashed across lanes to catch up. Jay checked his side mirror. The M2 operator was taking aim.

'Shit shit shit shit shit,' Aviary said.

Jay pulled in behind a white 4x4, waited a moment, listened to the Marauder roar toward them. Then he hit the brakes. The Marauder overshot, clipping the 4x4 and ploughing right into a Treasure Island-themed bar and grill. Jay watched the Marauder disappear inside a faux pirate ship. Its rear wheels spun, but it was firmly embedded.

Jay hit the gas again, lurching them ahead.

'Get us the hell outta here,' Nasira said.

'We're clear,' Damien said. 'But we should switch cars soon.'

Jay's breathing became short and suddenly he couldn't fill his lungs properly. He gripped the steering wheel and hunched over, breathing faster. Panic rushed through, freezing him in place. The car slipped into another lane.

'Jay?' Nasira's hand was on his back. 'What's wrong?'

He corrected the wheel and forced himself to slow each breath, drawing deeper. 'I'm fine.'

Aviary was staring from the passenger seat. 'Are you sure?'

'Of course,' he said. 'Anyone hungry? There's a drive-through up ahead.'

CHAPTER FOUR

Tallinn, Estonia

OLESYA WALKED the snow-swept cobblestoned street and kept a close eye on Karamysheva, the Russian intelligence officer she was tracking. She'd followed him from the train station through the ancient barbicans of Tallinn. He hadn't stopped for even a moment, barely glancing at his phone. He hunched forward, a gray scarf looped around his brown collar while long arms swayed with each step.

Olesya kept as much distance as she could while holding a good eye. She wore sunglasses under today's weak sunlight and did most of her checks on him through the corner of her vision. Two girls weaved past her on mopeds, their wide tires rumbling loudly over the cobbles. The girls split up, steered around a group of German students, and again around the officer. Unlike the students, he didn't look startled; he knew they were coming long ago.

To the ordinary passerby, Karamysheva's eyes were taking in the architecture, the Gothic spires and medieval markets; or perhaps he was people-watching, observing the locals and business folk enjoying the ale and public Wi-Fi. But Olesya knew it wasn't any of these things. He walked with out-of-breath purpose under iron street lamps, drinking in details through his subconscious and looking for unexpected bumps in the scenery —someone or something that was out of place. Out of baseline.

Someone like her.

Olesya kept her attention on the Russian officer, but like him she was looking for someone else. A Fifth Column operative. And like her, this operative would know what train this officer arrived on, and that he was here in Estonia to meet someone. They planned to abduct them both.

But Olesya and Ark weren't going to let that happen.

The officer changed direction. It wasn't a slow turn toward the corner, it was sudden and precise. As he did so, he cast an innocent glance back in the direction he'd come.

Counter-surveillance.

Karamysheva would have noted everyone in the crowd behind him, Olesya included, but he wouldn't have seen anything remarkable about her. With her winter coat, linen-blond hair and fair complexion, she blended in with the Baltic locals. Being noticed was OK; being noticed too many times wasn't.

'Turning left on Olevimäi,' Olesya said into her throat mike.

She kept her communication plain and sparse. One of the first things Illarion taught her about surveillance was to stop talking like a soldier and start talking like a civilian. This meant relaxed speech that won't sound strange in public places.

'That's a one-way street,' Ark said. 'I'm a block away and circling.'

Ark was Olesya's backup. He was out of sight but in range, driving a small coupe Gleb had signed off on.

Olesya casually followed the German students around the corner. She stretched her distance some more, putting a block between her and the cautious officer. If he looked at her again, even indirectly, she would need to swap places with Ark. And she really didn't want to do that. She wanted Ark behind the wheel so that she could handle the operative when she—

Someone moved past Karamysheva, smoothly, off axis. A woman with long, dark hair, straight, unlike Val's natural curls. She wore white trainers on the cobblestones and a navy coat with no loose straps or belts; nothing that would get tangled if she needed to run. She brushed past the officer and kept going. With a slight turn of his head, he noticed.

Olesya's heart rate spiked. 'Possible.'

'What does she look like?' Ark asked.

Olesya thought about what to say. 'Straight hair. Navy coat.'

The woman walked ahead, sifting through clusters of slow walkers, matching their movements. She was taller than most of the people, so Olesya followed her head in the crowd, dividing her attention between Karamysheva and this new target.

The woman stepped inside a bar, two couples heading in alongside her, and Olesya lost sight of her. She tried to keep her eyes on the bar entrance while focusing on the officer.

'Possible is ahead, in a bar,' Olesya said. '*He* is still moving.'

Olesya had both the bar entrance and the officer in sight, so she dropped back a little.

'What's the name of the bar?' Ark asked.

'Pudel Baar,' she said.

There was a pause. 'So is this a bar for people ... or poodles?'

'*Pudel* means bottle,' she said.

The woman left the bar and walked purposefully across the street. Not much of her face was visible to Olesya: a hard jawline, small mouth and fine eyebrows. She didn't look Russian or Kazakh. Perhaps Chinese.

It could be her.

'So it's a bottle bar?' Ark asked. 'A bar with bottles?'

The woman turned slightly, checking traffic.

'It's her,' Olesya whispered.

Ark heard her. 'Val?'

'No.' Olesya's heart beat faster. 'Operative.'

'Talk to me,' Ark said. 'What's she doing?'

Olesya checked everyone on the street, every vehicle. There were no vans, no SUVs, nothing that might conceal a small grab team. Karamysheva still walked ahead, his attention diffused across the entire street. He passed Pudel Baar.

The operative crossed the street ahead of him, maybe fifty meters, and kept going. Olesya increased her pace, taking long strides on the opposite side of the street.

'I'm doing a pass now,' Ark said. His unremarkable charcoal coupe appeared, heading toward her.

Olesya stopped. The woman had looked the wrong way to cross a one-way street.

She was looking at Karamysheva.

Olesya crossed Pudel Baar and picked up her pace to pass Karamysheva. She didn't speak to Ark again until she was out of earshot.

'I'm going for her,' she said softly. 'You stay on him.'

'What?' he asked. 'But it's not Val, is it?'

'I don't think so,' Olesya said. 'But I need to stay on her. Can you stay with *him*?'

'I can't!' Ark said. 'I'd have to go on foot!'

Ark drove past. In his wake, the operative changed direction and took a small alley.

'Then go on foot!' Olesya said, breaking into a run.

In her ear, Ark cursed.

She rounded the corner. Ahead of her, the operative walked briskly down the alley. There was a road at the end; the operative could only go in one of two directions.

Olesya ducked under an open window frame and kept moving, slowly now. She busied herself with her phone, bringing up Google Maps. She didn't want direct eye contact with the operative.

'Passing him now,' Ark said. 'Son of a bitch looked straight at me though. I'm just looking for a place to park.'

The operative took a right at the end of the alley. She wanted to run after her, but instead she kept to a brisk walk. When she reached the corner, she turned and kept her face angled toward her phone. Over the phone's edge, she caught sight of the operative. She walked alongside a blue building, passing café tables decorated with potted flowers and umbrellas.

Olesya consulted her phone's map. The operative was heading down a blind alley. And at the next corner, Olesya would have to do the same. But the rules of surveillance were clear in her head.

Never follow your target into a dead-end. Dead-ends are the perfect places to be spotted. And for your target to confront you...

Olesya slowed as she reached the alley. Her heart was racing, and not just because she was about to face the operative. It was more than that. She knew it wasn't Val.

After all these years, it could be Xiu.

CHAPTER FIVE

DAMIEN OPENED HIS EYES. He was sitting in a metal chair in front of White. Right there on the table, in front of the border patrol officer, was Jay. He lay with his eyes closed, not breathing.

White's eyes burned. 'Rise and shine.'

Damien pulled at the cuffs on his wrists. 'What have you done to him?' he shouted.

'What have you done, Damien?' White asked.

Damien gripped the metal armrests and poured heat into them. His arms shook. He wanted to kill White, and his two officers standing in the shadows. But first he had to get free.

'Blessed is he who reads.' White's eyes were glowing embers.

'Get away from him!' Damien yelled.

White's hands hovered over Jay. 'And those who hear the words of the prophecy.'

Blood rushed to Damien's cheeks. His hands clenched white

over the armrests. They weren't heating fast enough. They weren't burning through.

'And keep those things which are written in it,' White said.

Fire burst from White's hands and engulfed Jay in flames.

Damien cried out. Pulled at his chair. Other officers appeared from behind Damien and held him down, pressed their weight onto him. He couldn't breathe. The table caught fire, burning through Jay.

'No one can escape their destiny,' White said. 'He's one of us now.'

Somewhere in Mexico

DAMIEN WOKE SUDDENLY, smacking his head against the car window.

'Bad dream?' Aviary asked.

She was curled up on the other side of the car, one eye open. There was no White or interrogation room. Just traffic and the car radio.

'He gets those dreams,' Jay said.

Damien closed his hands until his fingers stopped trembling.

A scratchy voice came from a radio under the dash-board. It was the marine's radio he'd stolen.

'Blessed is he who reads and those who hear the words of this prophecy—'

Half-asleep, Nasira reached over and—with the butt of her pistol—cracked the radio. Then she rolled back and started snoring.

Jay was driving southeast to Mexico City now—
Damien had slept through most of Phoenix and parts of
the border crossing into Mexico. Last time he was awake,
Aviary had been keeping an eye on military channels and
the media. At the time, nothing had been mentioned
about the Las Vegas mayhem, except for reports of a
training exercise running at the exact same place and
time. It was almost as though the authorities were trying
to cover it up rather than spark a genuine manhunt for
them.

Damien's stomach grumbled. Nasira had only allowed
Jay to stop for fuel, which meant they'd been running on
gas station food for most of the night. Apart from that, the
only break was so Damien could do a clothesline run
through an Arizona suburb to find everyone a change of
clothes. Aviary now wore a gray beanie that was too big
for her head. She pulled it over her eyes and resumed
her nap.

Even medical help was out of the question. Jay was
still recovering from his damaged lung and Nasira
sported a gunshot wound through her shoulder, but she'd
made it very clear she wasn't stopping for stitches until
they were out of the country. They had morphine and a
clotting agent with sterile bandages, and that would have
to do for now.

'Are you OK?' Aviary peeked out from under her
beanie.

Damien nodded. 'Yeah, I'm OK.'

'Good.' She stretched her legs over his, her purple
socks resting on his knees.

'You should keep your shoes on,' he said.

She sighed. 'I know, I know. Always have your feet out the end of the bed. Always keep your shoes on, so you can move straight away when there's danger, right?'

'No,' he said. 'Your feet smell.'

IT SEEMED like forever to Aviary, but finally they reached Mexico City—or Distrito Federal as Nasira called it. Damien had taken over driving the last leg so Jay could rest, and Aviary wasn't happy about it because he snored louder than Nasira.

Distrito Federal was a spirited city of turbulent structures and twisting alleys, splashed with Spanish colonial architecture and murals that coated entire facades. There was little urgency here and the traffic slowed their path to a crawl. When they finally made it to the street Nasira was looking for, Aviary still didn't know what they were doing there.

She followed the group along a cracked sidewalk, past a food cart wrapped in plastic tarp, and through the rear of a house—or restaurant, she couldn't be sure—covered in cement tiles and blistered paint.

Damien ruffled his short hair. 'Keep your beanie on.'

'It is on.' Aviary knew it was to conceal her dyed red hair, which she tucked under her jacket collar.

Nasira led them through the kitchen. Aviary's stomach grumbled as she passed a row of prepared dishes. The chefs were in t-shirts and sweatpants, which made her want to wear a t-shirt and sweatpants too.

One of the chefs, an older woman with short curled

hair and a Ninja Turtles apron, greeted Nasira with a bear hug, which Nasira tolerated for at least a moment. If it hurt her shoulder wound, she didn't show it. The chef wiped sweat from her brow and led them to a front room where the locals ate, and a concealed alcove reserved for private gatherings.

They sat at the table and Aviary shot Nasira a grin.

'You have friends?' Aviary asked.

Nasira bristled. 'I got ... people I know.'

'Yeah, she knows the owners,' Jay said. 'We ate here this one time and we didn't shoot anyone, so that was good.'

Nasira passed the menu over to Damien. He seemed intent on hiding his terrible Spanish, so he just nodded in agreement. The chef took their order—Aviary made sure to add mezcal—then left them alone in the alcove.

Damien turned to Aviary. 'How many exits?'

She stared at him. 'Two.'

'How many people sitting out there?'

Aviary turned.

'Without looking,' he said.

She sighed and counted with her fingers. 'A couple in the front left, awkward. Family with two kids on the right. Weird man with glasses reading the menu and drinking water.' She paused. 'Two girls, one dude on the right.'

Damien smiled. 'Wrong. Two men, only one woman.'

She sighed. 'He looked girly.'

Nasira tied her crimped hair into a tight bun, wincing when she used both arms.

'How's the wound?' Aviary asked.

'Yeah,' Damien said. 'We still need to find a doctor to clean and dress it.'

'We eat first,' Nasira said. 'And drink.'

'Are you sure that's a good idea?' Damien asked.

'A drink is always a good idea,' Nasira said.

'Hear, hear,' Jay said.

'I can find a black market doctor,' Aviary offered. 'In Mexico City, if you want.'

'How?' Jay asked.

'This new thing called the internet.'

He glared at her. 'I know what an internet is.'

'Seriously though, you can do that?' Damien asked. 'Just find someone on the black market?'

'Yeah, on the list by that Craig dude,' Jay said.

'Craig's List?' Aviary glanced between them. 'Did they keep you in caves during your training?'

'No,' Damien said. 'We had bunk beds.'

'Top or bottom?' she asked, then regretted it immediately. 'You know what, I'd rather not know.' Instead, she pulled her laptop from her ruck and perched it on the floral plastic tabletop.

'I liked it better when the black market was in the real world,' Jay said. 'They were always in bars. And bars always had alcohol.'

'So, you have a problem,' she said. 'With your mojo.' Nasira had filled her in while Jay took a shift snoring in the back seat.

Jay cleared his throat. 'Nothing wrong with my mojo.'

'That's libido,' Nasira said. 'Aviary's talking about your pseudogenes.'

'Oh,' Jay said. 'Gotcha. Yeah, so I need your help.'

365

'Finding the headquarters of the people who kidnapped you, I know,' she said. 'But I think you're better off finding their research center. That's where you'll find your answers.'

Jay shrugged. 'Sounds good. But we don't know where that is.'

Aviary sighed. 'They do teach you Google Maps in Operative School, right?'

Everyone stared blankly at her.

She shook her head. 'What's it even like there? Hogwarts for soldiers?'

Damien looked disgusted. 'It's nothing like a strip club.'

Aviary planted her face in her hands. 'OK, how about you tell me everything you know about these people?'

'That ain't much,' Nasira said.

'Hey, I'm staying positive here,' Jay said.

A waitress approached, dropped off glasses and a bottle of mezcal. Nasira went to pour, but gritted her teeth in pain. Aviary took the bottle and poured for everyone.

'We have a name,' Damien said. 'They're called Intron.'

He and Jay looked at Aviary expectantly.

'Have you looked them up?' she asked.

'They're public, but nothing on their research center, not even their headquarters are listed,' Nasira said.

'Plus, we need to find out what they're doing with my abilities,' Jay said. 'That's ... that's the most important part.'

Aviary drank her mezcal in one hit. This was going to

be a long night. She opened her laptop and pinched a nearby wireless connection.

A different waiter arrived with plates of food. Jay scooped up something wrapped in soft tortilla and started munching.

'All I know is they're in Rio,' Jay said between mouthfuls. 'Somewhere.'

Nasira sighed. 'That should narrow it down.'

Aviary scooped up a taco. It was simple, just a slice of beef in a tortilla. She spooned on one of the salsas and added some chilies, then got to work. 'Give me a moment while I do something awesome.' Her phone buzzed. She quickly shoved the taco into her mouth and picked up. 'Message from Sophia.'

Nasira noticed. 'She need us?'

'Nah, just asked me to ID someone,' Aviary said. 'Some Russian dude from Berlin.'

'She doing all right?' Nasira asked.

Aviary raised an eyebrow. 'Why don't you ask her yourself?'

Nasira shrugged. 'She's not one for small talk. Even on an encrypted network.'

'Bingo,' Aviary said. 'Found him, that was easy.'

'Anything on these guys we're trying to find?' Jay asked.

'Give her a chance, Jay,' Nasira said. 'They'll be tough to find.'

'I'll find them,' Aviary said.

Jay raised something wrapped in a tortilla. 'I have a good feeling about this,' he said, taking a bite. 'This is really good. Nopales y queso. Cheese on ... what's nopales?'

'Cactus,' Aviary said.

Jay eyed the tortilla uncertainly.

Damien leaned over to read her screen.

'Can you not? That's really annoying,' Aviary said.

'Evgeny Sporyshev,' Damien said. 'Russian diplomat, agricultural attaché.'

'You know him?' Aviary said. 'That's the guy Sophia asked about.'

'Nope.' Damien pulled her laptop closer. 'But you know what agricultural attaché means, right?'

'I'm guessing ... he doesn't grow corn?'

Damien shook his head. 'Do you still have access to the Fifth Column—'

Aviary didn't wait for him to finish. She pulled her laptop back and opened a file.

'They're not gonna track us here, I hope,' Nasira said.

'Nope.' Aviary petted her laptop. 'Now that I finally have the encryption keys for the Fifth Column database, I can do it all on here. Do you know how long it's taken—'

'Fifth Column database?' Nasira asked.

'Oh right, yeah,' Aviary said, gesturing to the files she stole from Hal's tablet. 'I've kind of been stealing the Fifth Column's database from their Department of Research. I call it the Mad Scientist Wing.'

No one laughed.

Aviary sighed. 'That joke is literally funny to *everyone* in the world except you guys. Anyway, I have records from all their divisions: cyber, microsystems, defense and

—most importantly—their Tactical Tech Division.' She wiggled an eyebrow.

'I don't even know what that means.' Jay turned to Nasira. 'Am I meant to know what it means?'

'High-risk, high-payoff, advanced military research,' Aviary said. 'You name it, they're working it. Hybrid air-ground vehicles, quadruped combat units, cognitive threat warning systems, soft exoskeletons—they're still years behind the Chinese by the way—oh, and *Special Projects* is where you came from. Project GATE.'

Nasira shook her head. 'Why the hell you messing with that? It's dangerous shit.'

'Exactly,' Aviary said. 'And it's going to help us sooooo much. Let me just run a search on this Russian diplomat and we'll see what comes up.'

She typed in his name and ran a search, which instantly pulled a match on her database. 'Well that explains his incomplete LinkedIn profile. All top secret, baby.'

Damien took one glance. 'He's Fifth Column.'

'*Was*,' Aviary said. 'Last entry in 2001.'

'So he ... quit? Retired?' Jay asked.

Aviary skimmed his record. 'Doesn't say anything. But guess who gave the order to collect him. Our old friend Hal from Las Vegas.'

'Huh,' Damien said. 'What was this guy into?'

'He was working under the Fifth Column's Department of Research. Microsystems Technology Division. Nothing crazy though. No mind control or super soldiers. Just lasers, electronics, photonics, signals,' Aviary said.

'He did a bit of time in Project GATE, while you guys were getting your Hogwarts training.'

Nasira leaned forward. 'So why did Hal grab this guy? Is he cleaning house?'

'He was working on something for Project GATE called TERMORD,' Aviary said.

Damien looked nervous. Across the table, Jay and Nasira stiffened.

'Uh, I take it that's bad,' Aviary said.

Damien nodded slowly. 'Could be.'

'Super soldier bad? Mind control bad?' Aviary asked. 'Where on the scale of bad are we talking here?'

'Sophia found this guy in Berlin?' Nasira asked. 'What happened?'

'She didn't say.'

Damien poured more mezcal, but didn't drink. 'TERMORD usually stands for termination order.'

'They're going to kill him?' Aviary asked.

'Not him,' Damien said. 'And it's not like when you just assassinate someone. This sounds like a different kind of termination.'

'It sounds like a kill switch,' Nasira said. 'A kill switch for operatives.'

CHAPTER SIX

Vilnius, Lithuania

'NEOPSYCHE, DESIGNATION ALCYONE,' Sophia said.

She took a seat opposite Ieva in the living room and put her pistol down on the table, beside her phone.

'Hmm.' Ieva leaned forward in her chair and absently touched the scab on her split lip. A strand of ash gray hair lingered over one eye. She blew it aside and thought for a moment. 'That's the false personality.'

Sophia nodded. 'Very good. How many neopsyches are there?'

Ieva wrinkled her nose, then smiled. 'Trick question. Only one neopsyche, the one the Fifth Column installs into their minds with all those parapsyches.'

'Which is what they did to us,' Sophia said. 'But what else is there?'

'Archeopsyche!' Ieva said quickly. 'That's the real personality.'

She's learning fast, Sophia thought. *Maybe Ieva can deprogram an operative by herself one day. And one day soon.*

'If the operative isn't blinking when you first encounter them, what does that tell you?' Sophia asked.

'Um, they're in one of the parapsyches,' Ieva said. 'Intense focus. I can't remember ... wait! Ares parapsyche.'

'Good. But that's just a hint. You need to confirm which parapsyche is enabled. What do you do?'

'You access the listing.'

'OK. So how do you do that?'

'I know this one,' Ieva said. 'Um, you just request the parapsyche listing. Simple.'

'And what happens if the listing is restricted?' Sophia asked. 'What do you do?'

'I go direct. Start debugging.'

Sophia shook her head. 'You missed a step.'

'Oh.' Ieva thought for a moment. 'I need the parapsyche that gives me the debugging mode. The ... um ... I can't think of it without my notes.' She reached for her phone but Sophia put her hand over it.

'No notes,' Sophia said. 'I want you to remember.'

Ieva shook her head. 'I can't. I'm not good at this.'

On the table, both phones buzzed. Sophia checked hers: their perimeter cameras had picked up Czarina returning to the mansion, bags on each arm.

'You're doing fine,' Sophia said, putting her phone down. 'You need to execute the code architecture parapsyche if you want to start debugging. It's called Calaeno.

I just remember C for code, it's easier that way. Then you can start debugging.'

'Shouldn't I take the operative somewhere else first?'

'Yes, but not here,' Sophia said. 'You disable their tracking device first, so the Fifth Column can't follow them to this mansion.'

'Right, of course,' Ieva said.

The front door opened downstairs and Czarina's sneakers creaked across the floorboards.

'Tomato soup.' Ieva sniffed the air. 'Sausages, fried potato. Cheese and garlic sauce.'

Ieva's innate ability was *hyperosmia*, a heightened sense of smell.

'Oh, bacon and sour cream!' Ieva added. Her brow furrowed, a thought occurring. 'Sophia, what if the para-psyche is unknown and they—'

'Try to kill themselves?' Sophia asked.

Ieva nodded. 'Yeah. Sorry.'

'Don't be sorry. That's what went wrong in Berlin,' Sophia said. 'Once you're in, there isn't much room for playing around. You need to execute a command or they can become unstable. Worst case scenario, put them in slave mode until you get back to me and we do the rest together.'

Czarina appeared at the top of the stairs, a bag of takeout in the crook of her arm. She was still wearing her ruby leather jacket, even though Sophia had tried to convince her to wear something less conspicuous. At least her bruised jaw—reduced to a blotch of purple on brown skin—was healing up.

'Seriously,' Czarina said. 'You guys know how hard it

is to find Lithuanian food that isn't ninety-nine percent potato? One more week here and I'm gonna turn into an actual potato.'

'With red lipstick,' Ieva said.

'Shut up and eat.' Czarina dumped the bags of food on the table, then shrugged her rucksack to the floor.

Ieva disappeared into the kitchen, returning with plates and glasses.

'All civilized, huh?' Czarina opened the containers of food. 'You know, why can't we have an operative diet that is just carbs? Would be so much easier.'

Ieva set out the plates and glasses. Almost as an afterthought, she held up a credit card. 'You forgot this.'

Czarina grunted, already shoveling food into her mouth. Ieva disappeared into the kitchen again to retrieve some bottled water. She opened it, but Czarina waved her off.

'You pick-pocketed again,' Sophia said.

Czarina shrugged. 'I forgot the card, OK? Relax.'

The card was one of Aviary's little inventions, which helped them steal money from automatic teller machines.

'You don't need to steal unless you have no choice,' Sophia said.

'I had no choice,' Czarina said, food falling from her mouth. 'I forgot the card. And I had to get rations.'

Sophia noticed the bottle of Polish vodka. 'What sort of ration is that?'

'The good kind.' Czarina cracked open the bottle and took a swig, freezing with it still on her lips as their phones lit up again.

Sophia collected her phone. This time it wasn't a camera sensor.

'Active!' Ieva shouted excitedly. 'Active! Active!'

Sophia pressed her thumb against her phone's fingerprint scanner and accessed the restricted content. A map came up, showing an operative in Kraków, Poland. She was on the move, and instead of gray—the color denoting a dormant agent—the dot was yellow.

'Stand by.' Sophia grabbed her pistol. 'Pack up your food, we'll take it with us.'

Czarina grimaced. 'Aw, come on.'

Ieva tapped on the yellow dot to read the operative's status. 'Not going green until tomorrow morning. See the twelve-hour timer ticking down? That means standby for another twelve hours.'

'It will take us ten to get there,' Sophia said.

'Eight if *I* drive,' Czarina mumbled, cramming a final few bites into her mouth.

'all right,' Sophia said. 'Eat fast.'

They finished their meal and took their rucks. When they reached the front gates, Ieva re-activated the motion sensors they'd rigged inside the mansion.

'We'll need wheels,' Sophia said.

'I got us a fresh set,' Czarina said. 'I'll take first shift.'

She walked them to her latest steal—a white 90s Fiat sedan. Sophia took the passenger seat while Czarina started the engine.

'You know, if we get there early,' Czarina said, 'we could just grab the operative *before* they go live. Hit them while they're in their pajamas watching cartoons.'

'One, I'm pretty sure they don't have pajamas,' Sophia said.

'I have pajamas,' Ieva said.

'Two, if we start grabbing them while they're on standby, the Fifth Column will catch on pretty quick,' Sophia said. 'We do it my way for a reason: we stay under the radar and they never suspect we have access to their satellites. If they find out, they'll lock us out and we're back to square one.'

'And this is better how?' Czarina said. 'The Fifth Column will still suspect us.'

'Not if the operatives are active and in mid-operation. Disappearing on a high-risk operation could be down to any number of things. But "stolen by rogue operatives" is going to be pretty low on their list. And we need to keep it that way.'

'They'll eventually catch on,' Czarina said.

'And that's why we need as many operatives on our side as possible, before that happens,' Sophia said. 'Because when it does, they're *our* army. And it will be us against all the other operatives.'

'Um, so that's over a hundred operatives, according to this map,' Ieva said.

Sophia focused on the road ahead. 'Then we have some recruiting to do.'

CHAPTER SEVEN

Tallinn, Estonia

OLESYA TOOK a breath and stepped into the alley.

No operative.

The alley ended where two buildings merged. Olesya's boots crunched over snow as she reached the dead end. The operative's footsteps ended here.

The building on her right was old and pink, paled almost white. Its entrance was sealed off and the intercom appeared out of service. Against the rundown façade, a new drainage pipe stood out. The building on her left was in a worse state. Its walls were peeling layers of peppermint green and the windows were worn, the frames rusted. A chunk of rendering was missing from the wall, revealing bare brick. Moss grew between crevices.

The only place the operative could go was over the roof on Olesya's left, above the missing chunk in the wall.

It was possible she had swung off the street lamp that was fixed to the wall and climbed onto the roof, walked over the tiles to a balcony in the corner, almost within arm's reach. The balcony was decorated with withering potted plants and a single drainage pipe. But there was no evidence of disturbed snow on the roof.

'I see the operative,' Ark said.

'That can't be right,' Olesya said. 'Where?'

ARK WATCHED the woman make a move toward Karamysheva. She didn't have curly hair, but it could still be his sister. She approached the officer. This had to be the operative Olesya was tracking.

'Closing on her right now,' Ark said. 'Black leather jacket, shoulder-length hair.'

'I said navy coat and long hair. What about her face?' Olesya asked. 'Describe her face.'

'Can't see, but definitely a black jacket. Are you sure it was navy?' Ark asked.

'Of course I'm sure.'

The woman passed Karamysheva and her arm slipped behind his neck. Her hand closed into a fist and she jabbed him with something, then walked on without breaking her stride.

Karamysheva staggered against a dark blue van.

'She sedated him!' Ark said under his breath.

'Don't engage,' Olesya said. 'Keep walking.'

Maybe Val straightened her hair…

The van was a high-roofed Ford with no windows. Its

rear doors opened and two plain-clothed men jumped out, followed by two more. The van's engine turned over as they lifted Karamysheva by his shoulders. The officer couldn't fight them off, he couldn't even use his legs. They hauled him from the pavement and into the van. It was down the street before anyone seemed to notice, and disappeared around a corner.

'They have the officer,' he said under his breath.

'Keep looking,' Olesya said.

A few curious onlookers stared blankly at the space where the van had been. The woman in the black coat was farther ahead; she made a quick left at Pudel Baar and disappeared. Ark rounded the corner after her.

'I'm going for the black jacket,' he said.

Olesya sounded out of breath. 'Don't lose her!'

The operative walked under an archway and into a T-intersection. Ark crossed the road, cutting in front of a champagne BMW coupe. The driver hit the horn, and the operative looked over her shoulder at the noise, saw Ark and broke into a run. She fled under an archway and went right.

'Olesya!' Ark said as he sprinted down the road. 'Can you hear me?'

He accelerated under the archway and turned after her. This alley was extremely narrow, barely wide enough for one vehicle. One side was centuries old—a castle wall of the old town. Ahead, the operative was nowhere to be seen. He tore off across the cobblestoned road.

He wasn't letting this operative go.

He wasn't letting Val go.

At the next intersection he paused, scanned the streets.

No sign. He dug into his pocket for his monocular. Through its magnified scope, he saw a couple holding hands on one street and absolutely nothing on the other.

He'd lost her.

For a while, he stood there. Stood there and felt nothing.

'Ark?' Olesya approached him from behind, catching her breath.

Anger burned from him. 'Where were you?' He grabbed her by the collar of her jacket. 'I needed you!'

With one smooth motion, she brushed his arms off.

'Why weren't you there?' he yelled, shoving her.

She absorbed the blow, taking two steps back. 'I told you, I was following the operative in the navy coat.'

'No, you were chasing ghosts,' he said. 'The operative who sedated the officer, she wore a black coat. I saw it with my own eyes! And now he's gone.'

'He doesn't matter,' Olesya said.

'I know that!' Ark said. 'But I lost both of them. *We* lost both of them.'

The energy slipped from him. He propped himself up against the castle wall. 'I tried to get her but...' He couldn't finish what he was saying. It meant failure and he couldn't accept that.

Olesya moved closer. 'The operative in the black jacket. Was it Val?'

He breathed slowly through his nose, calming himself. But there was so much disappointment and shame inside and he had nowhere to move it.

Our only goal was to identify the operative, and we couldn't even do that.

'Do you think it could be her?' Olesya asked.

'If she had a haircut. She was the same height, but I couldn't really see her face,' Ark said. 'I couldn't get close enough.'

'It's possible,' she said.

He pressed both hands up against the wall. He shook his head. 'No, it wasn't her. I just wanted it to be.'

'I'm sorry.'

Tears filled his eyes and he couldn't be bothered wiping them away. 'I've lost her, haven't I? Forever.'

'You can't give up,' Olesya said.

He saw a tear roll down her cheek, but he knew it wasn't for his sister.

'I already have,' he said.

CHAPTER EIGHT

JAY RAN.

Over the satellite dishes and under the thick cables of Rocinha. Over a tin roof and through a broken window. His younger brother struggled to keep pace.

The building they were running for wouldn't be empty for long. BOPE, Rio de Janeiro's Police Special Forces, were inbound to raid it. This was no place for young boys to be exploring. Jay had a few moments to grab anything of value before the police confiscated it. Illegal cable broadcast equipment, ammunition, anything he could sell on the street.

He hurried across the second level, slowing to step around a large hole in the floor. Catching up, Jay's brother almost tumbled through the window, startling a nearby rabbit as it scampered over the concrete. Jay did a quick sweep, finding only a bottle of soda and a fireworks cylinder. He opened the fireworks cylinder and grinned to find live ammunition.

'BOPE!' his brother screamed.

Gunfire cracked past the building. Jay froze. His brother had stumbled on something. Jay stepped out into the main room and saw shadows of soldiers moving past the windows. Fear riveted him where he stood. He looked back. His brother was hanging from the edge of the hole.

It was a long drop to the concrete floor below.

'Jay!' his brother yelled.

He wanted to run to his brother, but gunfire echoed around them and he couldn't move. His brother's fingertips slipped from the edge.

Jay heard him land on the concrete below.

~

Quito, Ecuador

JAY JOLTED AWAKE.

The same goddamn dream every time, ending the same way.

He covered his sudden flinch with a hearty clearing of his throat and sat upright. Nasira was in the driver's seat beside him, but the car was stationary. Beside him stood the fishing rod Aviary had insisted they purchase. He peered through the windshield. There was nothing in front of them except flat ground. Grass gave way to metal and concrete, slicked by rain. With his infrared vision stolen from him, he couldn't make out much beyond the muddy haze and downpour, but he could see the capital city. Old and new towns intertwined between volcanic peaks, rolling into the horizon and through the interandean valley. Nasira had parked them on one of those volcanic peaks.

Aviary sat in the back of the car. Her dyed hair hung over her face as she pecked away at her laptop's keyboard. Damien sat next to her, pretending to understand what she was doing.

'Oh, cool,' he said.

Aviary gave him a sidelong glance, then continued.

'Is this the place?' Jay asked.

Aviary chewed her lip. 'We're here. This is … unofficially … an Intron Genetics Incorporated data center.'

Jay inspected the flat surface before them. 'Did someone take the data center? And run away with it?'

Aviary focused on her laptop. 'It's inside the mountain, dummy.'

Jay sighed, loudly. 'Who puts a data center inside a mountain?'

She counted her fingers and said, 'Ambient temperature, low risk of natural disasters, physical security—'

'OK, OK, I get it,' Jay said.

'So do we have to infiltrate another facility?' Damien asked. 'Because we don't have a great track record with that.'

'Nope,' Aviary said. 'I can get access from up here. Hopefully.'

'Hopefully?' Damien said.

'If you want to find out where they're hiding their research, this is the place,' Aviary said.

'We could just go in there and punch someone important,' Jay said. 'Ask them where it's at.'

'Even I think that's a stupid idea,' Nasira said. 'And I like punching people.'

Jay slouched in his seat. 'Do you have a better idea?'

'Look, chances are the location of their research center isn't their most protected secret,' Aviary said. 'I'm sure they've got all sorts of sensitive things going on they'll keep nicely locked up. We don't need that; we just need an address. I'm hoping that won't be as hard to find as their really classified stuff, like Top-Secret-Project-for-Sucking-Powers-from-Poor-Suckers.' She met Jay's gaze. 'No offense.'

'No, you're right,' Jay said. 'I'm a sucker for letting this happen.'

'Could've happened to anyone,' Nasira said. 'Even stubborn people, like you.'

He exhaled loudly. 'Can we just get this over with?'

'Do you want my help or not?' Aviary asked.

'Yeah, I do,' he said.

'I need to show you something first.' Aviary reached into her ruck and removed her stolen tablet. 'I was digging around Hal's tablet for more about this TERMORD thing. Sounds like only two people knew about it. Hal—obviously—and Cecilia McLoughlin. She proposed the whole thing.'

'She's also dead,' Nasira said.

Aviary shrugged. 'Yeah, but she wanted to secretly inject the kill switch into operatives, along with the pseudogene activators. It's still possible she did that.'

'So everyone who got a jab,' Nasira said, 'got the kill switch?'

'Including us,' Damien said.

'Yeah,' Aviary said. 'And the only reason Hal knows about this is because he ran a test on one of his operatives. For a whole other reason.'

'What reason?' Nasira asked.

'I'm working on that,' Aviary said. 'But I have these emails written by Hal—they're encrypted, but I can read some of them.'

'Is there proof?' Damien asked.

'No, just these emails,' she said.

'That makes Hal the only person who knows about this,' Aviary said. 'Not even Denton seemed to know, and he was running Project GATE.'

'Do the emails tell you how this kill switch works?' Damien asked.

'Hang on,' she said. 'All I have is an email addressed to Hal. They identified what they first thought was a harmless protein, but it's actually an endotoxin that she smuggled in there. With the right trigger, the protein self-destructs and the endotoxin is released. Multiple organ failure within one hour, then death.'

'But how is it triggered?' Damien asked.

'That's in the proposal.' She flicked back to it. 'The signal is delivered by radio waves, through base stations. So that's pretty much everywhere with cell phone coverage.'

'Great,' Nasira said. 'They can find and target any operative.'

'Hey,' Jay said. 'Playing devil's adjective here—'

'Advocate,' Damien said.

'Wiping out all the operatives,' Jay said. 'Not a bad thing?'

'It is when it includes us.' Aviary grabbed her phone. 'If the Fifth Column figure out how to trigger this, you guys are—'

'Dead,' Nasira said.

Aviary swallowed. 'I'll send Sophia a message. She's in Lithuania this week.'

Nasira reached over and lowered her phone. 'Wait, don't you want to read Hal's emails first? If we go to Sophia, we need the full picture.'

Aviary nodded. 'If you say so.'

Nasira stared through the windshield. 'So, how close do we need to get?'

CHAPTER NINE

Kraków, Poland

SOPHIA WATCHED THE OPERATIVE. Valeria knelt in the attic and peered through the scope on her MPX submachine gun, both eyes open. She was watching the market square below. According to the Fifth Column's Assetrac system, Valeria was newly assigned to this region.

Below them, tourists and locals sprinkled across the market square. Large parasols sheltered tables of patrons sipping Polish beer with shots of grenadine or eating sausages, ham and cheese. Beyond that, the square was the size of ten blocks, all paved surface and four-story Renaissance buildings, all peach and pastel yellow and pressed snugly against each other, except for the museum in the center.

Sophia took a step closer and an attic floorboard creaked.

Valeria shifted.

'Don't even try it.' Sophia leveled her pistol. 'Weapon down.'

Valeria did as she was told.

'Stand up slowly, hands in the air.'

Valeria complied. There was a slim rucksack on her back, likely where she stowed her MPX with its folding stock. She raised her hands, turned and eyed Sophia carefully.

Sophia spoke into her throat mike. 'I have the operative.'

'Copy that,' Czarina said. 'I'm downstairs in the café.'

'Congratulations,' Valeria said.

'Thank you,' Sophia said.

She knew exactly what sort of operation this was. And it wasn't a bombing. Not this time.

Valeria eyed Sophia carefully. She wasn't blinking.

Ares parapsyche. Assassination.

But for an assassination, the operative wouldn't choose a short-range weapon. She should be using something with a reasonable barrel length. And she wouldn't be confining herself to a small attic with minimal escape points and a limited field of view.

This position wasn't for shooting any *particular* target.

It was for shooting indiscriminately.

Sophia spoke into her microphone. 'Czarina, Ieva! Get outside now! There's a proxy in the market square.'

'Range?' Czarina asked.

'Fifty meters. A hundred, pushing it.'

'On it,' Czarina said.

Valeria couldn't hear the other end of the conversation, but she gave Sophia a tiny smile. 'Clever girl.'

Sophia grunted. A proxy was a programmed civilian, handled by a Fifth Column operative. Sometimes it was a suicide bomber and sometimes the proxy was a lone wolf. Sophia handled enough of each back when she was a programmed operative, both in the United States and across Central Europe.

She twitched her pistol, gesturing for Valeria to move away from the window and her MPX. Valeria retreated, her steps unsteady on the old attic floorboards. She would have a pistol on her body somewhere, but Sophia didn't trust the operative to disarm herself. Besides, Sophia had her under control, and she needed to focus on the proxy.

This particular proxy had to be a lone wolf.

The programming would be simple, at least compared to the operative now standing with her hands up in front of her. Proxies were not trained, they were disposable. If they managed to survive until the end, they were programmed to commit suicide so they weren't around to answer inconvenient questions.

Sophia had made it just in time. Another moment and Valeria would've made the phone call, issued the activation command. Then the proxy would open fire. On everyone.

Sophia's gaze fell to Valeria's weapon of choice. The MPX fired pistol rounds, and no one would question the trajectory of the rounds because no one would have any reason to look for a second, more competent shooter on higher ground.

Now the weapon seemed like a clever choice.

Sophia spoke into her throat mike. 'Got anything?'

Czarina replied, breathing quickly. 'Not yet. Every-one's wearing a jacket. Could be a hundred people here packing heat.'

Maybe, Sophia thought, *but only one will be jittery and focused.*

The proxy wouldn't be an operative, so they wouldn't know how to blend with the baseline. Czarina and Ieva should spot them in a heartbeat.

Sophia checked her phone's Assetrac map. Still only one operative in the area: Valeria. Sophia kept her pistol trained on her and watched for shifts in emotion. The edges of color around Valeria—ivory and ice-blue—were calm.

She isn't scared. Odd.

Sophia picked up the MPX by the pistol grip, using her left hand. She didn't want Valeria lunging for it. 'Remove your throat mike.'

Valeria plucked it from inside her collar and let it drop to the floorboards.

'Is your proxy in the market square?' Sophia asked.

'Perhaps.'

'What is your proxy wearing? Describe their clothes.'

Valeria swallowed. Her hostility crackled around her in orange bursts.

'Who are we looking for?' Sophia stepped forward to stomp on the microphone.

Valeria smiled. 'You really believe you're in control?'

Sophia hesitated. 'What are you saying, I'm the proxy?'

'No, I'm saying you're out of your depth. *Intercept!*' Valeria yelled the word.

The activation code. Through the microphone. Sophia crushed it under her shoe, but it was too late.

'Wireless mike.' Valeria smiled. 'Voice activated.'

Shit.

Shouts and screams came from outside. Valeria's fingertips shimmered an electric white. Her arms and legs buzzed, rippled. The operative's entire body was luminous.

Not again.

Sophia looked down at her pistol hand. It flared with brilliant color. She could feel Valeria's emotions shift and intersect like colors on a Rubik's cube. Sophia dropped the MPX. Staggered. Found herself on one knee.

It was happening, just like in the Berlin nightclub.

Valeria knocked the gun from her hand, then straightened Sophia's arm to break it. Sophia rolled forward, slipping free. She couldn't see what was happening or where she was going. She could only feel it.

She kicked out, knocked Valeria's leg away. Valeria staggered and her knee struck a floorboard. The operative drew a pistol from her hip, got off her knee.

The wood creaked as she moved. A loose board.

Sophia hammered her fist down on it. The other end lifted and struck Valeria's face.

Sophia rolled on her shoulder and sprang back to her feet. Her vision slowly returned. The MPX was right under her, but she didn't bother picking it up—it would be fingerprint encoded. The operative stood by the window, now open, her pistol missing. Sophia couldn't see it on the floor.

Valeria hurled herself out the window.

Sophia swore, ran to the window. Below her, Valeria missed a parasol entirely. She rolled across the pavement, still moving and uninjured.

That's not possible.

People stood around Valeria, but they weren't watching Valeria. Their attention was riveted on something else.

Shots rang out from the market square.

Sophia jumped from the window.

The parasol rushed to meet her, wrapping and entangling her. Her descent slowed, then she landed across the table. It knocked the air from her lungs. Around her, people were screaming. Fleeing in blind panic. But not from her. She launched to her feet and stared down the front of a suppressed pistol and a wry smile.

Valeria had found her pistol then.

There were five meters between them. Too far for Sophia to close on her.

'Children three that nestle near, eager eye and willing ear!' Sophia shouted over the distant screams. 'Pleased a simple tale to hear.'

Valeria smiled. 'No tales for the wicked, my love.'

Sophia's heart skipped. It couldn't be…

Valeria was firewalled.

The shots kept coming. Sophia needed to get out there and stop the proxy, help Czarina and Ieva. But she had to get through Valeria first. And Valeria was closing on her right now.

Sophia swallowed. 'Execute parapsyche, designation Lycaon!'

Valeria aimed her pistol.

Sophia pulled back into the café doorway. 'Echo parapsyche installations!'

She retreated, almost colliding with a waitress inside, frozen and holding a tray of coffee cups. Valeria's attention shifted for just a moment. The tray fell on Sophia and she grabbed it, flung it at Valeria. The edge of the tray knocked the pistol from her hand. Sophia drew her own.

Valeria used her knee to knock the tray up and into her grasp. She sliced it back at Sophia. It knocked Sophia's aim off. The operative stepped in closer and punched her in the sternum. The air rushed from Sophia's lungs. Her feet left the ground. She flew backward and crashed into a table. Plates and flatware crashed around her, loud and sharp. She smashed through another table—only the solid barrier of a wall stopped her.

She slumped to the floor, gasping for oxygen that didn't come.

That punch … Valeria must be using an exoskeleton.

Valeria stepped inside the café, heading straight for her. Sophia sucked in air, trying to breathe, to use her throat mike, call for help. But her words were soundless.

CHAPTER TEN

Quito, Ecuador

NASIRA MOVED FAST. Pistol in one hand, she searched the white fog that curled ahead, her magnetoception guiding her to the banks of cooling units. She could sense their cuboid shapes and cool metal surface. She led Aviary, Jay and Damien toward them.

'Stop,' Aviary whispered from under her hood.

Nasira pulled the covering from Aviary's head, exposing her vermillion hair to the rain. 'Peripheral vision,' Nasira reminded her.

'But I've got you guys to—' Aviary cut herself short. 'Fine.'

Nasira peered through the grill of a cooling unit. A large fan whipped air inward. Aviary pulled the laptop from her ruck and laid it on the ground. She struck a key and the fan slowed.

Nasira checked their surroundings while Jay and Aviary stepped away from the grill, allowing Damien to hold it. His hands heated the corners just enough for Jay to move in with wire cutters and snip the soft metal. Carefully, Damien and Aviary lifted the grate clear.

Nasira didn't like this one bit. She hadn't seen a single camera or sensor for Aviary to disable. *Did they care so little about the roof of their data center?*

She nodded to Damien, who moved far enough away so the other fans wouldn't interfere with his attuned hearing. Jay's infrared vision was gone and they were in open ground with no concealment save for the cooling units. Damien was their only early warning system.

Wearing gloves, Jay removed an altimeter and a fishing reel—minus the rod—from Aviary's ruck. He checked the knot on the heavy line and the attached wireless repeater. To Nasira, it looked like a stubby gray antenna. Jay took another repeater from her ruck and slapped it on the inside wall of the cooling unit, just above the fan.

'Go,' Aviary said.

Jay flipped the wire bail on the fishing reel. The line unspooled, plummeting the wireless repeater down the chute like a giant lure. Aviary tapped on her laptop keyboard, mining for wireless connections and devices she could hijack.

Nasira paced around them, her fingers resting on her pistol. She didn't want to be here a moment longer than necessary. She reached out into the fog, feeling for shapes or disturbances in the magnetic fields.

She walked past Aviary's laptop. On the screen, multiple connections blinked and console windows trickled with text. The repeater on the unit wall was talking to the repeater dangling from Jay's fishing line. And that was sending everything to the laptop.

'How's it going?' Nasira asked.

Aviary stared fixedly at her screen. 'Searching everything from any device. Keywords are "Rio" and "research." Getting a few things on Rio, but nothing else.'

Rio de Janeiro was the headquarters for many private, national and multinational corporations. If Jay was right —going off what he'd learned from his stay in Colombia —Intron's headquarters would be there. And maybe their research center would be too.

'How much longer?' Nasira asked.

'I don't know.'

The rain stopped. Nasira could only hear Aviary's quiet keystrokes and the light hum of other fans. Beyond them, white fog and unnerving silence. Nasira dropped to one knee and watched Damien, reading his expression. He was calm, just listening.

'You good?' Nasira asked.

Damien nodded. 'Just thinking about that cloaked operative from the parking lot in Colombia.'

'What about it?'

'Why'd she save us?'

Nasira raised an eyebrow. 'Why's the operative a *she*?'

He shrugged. 'Just guessing.'

Nasira did another three-sixty before checking on Aviary again.

Aviary spoke. 'Let it go.'

Jay was holding the fishing reel in one hand, leaning on the unit. He flipped the metal bail and the line unspooled some more.

'Stop,' Aviary said.

Jay flipped the bail back, holding the line in place. He read something off his altimeter. 'Forty-meter depth.'

Aviary's fingers rattled across her keyboard. 'I think I have something.'

Damien's voice was soft in Nasira's ears, speaking through his throat mike. 'Standby-standby,' he said.

Nasira and Jay went for their pistols.

'Could be nothing, but get ready,' Damien said.

Aviary typed hurriedly.

'Keep us posted.' Nasira turned to Aviary. 'Get ready to move.'

'Our luck about to run out?' Jay asked.

Nasira sighed. 'What luck?'

'This luck,' Aviary said. 'I have a possible address. Coming up as a research center *and* headquarters on a few devices down there.'

Google Maps filled her laptop screen. 'Presidente Vargas Avenue.'

'Business district,' Jay said. 'Financial sector, right near the ports.'

'I have movement.' Damien's words sent a chill through her.

'Pack it up,' Nasira said. 'Pack it up now.'

Aviary closed her laptop. 'Transferring to my watch.'

'Cut the wire,' Nasira said to Jay.

Jay drew his knife and cut the line. With no finger-prints, the repeater and the wire were safe to drop. Aviary reached for her repeater inside the unit.

'Leave it.' Nasira lifted the grill back with Jay.

Damien emerged from the fog and whispered, 'We're cut off. Go.'

They couldn't get back to their car from here. Pistol in hand, Nasira started running in the opposite direction. Her team fell in behind her.

Ahead in the fog, something shifted. Armed security closed on them from the front and, Nasira sensed, behind. If she headed right, she would fall off the data center and down the mountain. There was only one direction they could all take now. She pointed to their left. As one, they moved.

Then Damien slowed.

'What do you hear?" Nasira hissed.

Something shaped like a manta ray tore through the mist, heading straight for them. It descended from above and a dazzling laser flashed over her. Her vision turned green, pulsing. Damien and Jay became silhouettes that swirled into each other, then slowly the shapes of her friends sharpened. Another manta ray appeared—a small, lightweight drone. It spat something web-like over her.

The net wrapped around her, sticky and constricting, tightening over her arms and drawing her legs together. She pried at the net and stumbled forward. Beside her, Jay wrangled with another net.

Pain exploded across her body and a heavy weight pinned her down. She could smell the minted breath of a guard as he pulled her wrists together and bound them. Her hands went numb. A boot crunched down on her pistol and a knee across her back. Air shot from her lungs. She burned for more. Above her, a voice.

'We have them.'

CHAPTER ELEVEN

Kraków, Poland

ROUNDS CRACKED through the market square. People crashed into each other as they fled in all directions. Czarina weaved around them, listening carefully as the sound of shots reflected off the buildings. Using the reflected sounds, her echolocation—a kind of passive sonar for humans—helped her zero in on the proxy.

The sounds pulled her to a young man, tall and sinuous with shell-white skin. He wore a puffy red jacket with the sleeves rolled to his elbows, faded jeans and white sneakers, and held a pistol with one arm completely extended.

Czarina drew her pistol from the concealed holster in her jeans. She lifted the weapon to her chest, both hands over the grip. The proxy pivoted to shoot at anyone who caught his attention. He looked relaxed, almost bored.

Czarina extended both arms, angling for a clear shot. But as the crowd thinned, the proxy saw her coming, and lined up his own shot. He swiveled like the turret on a tank.

'Drop your weapon!' Czarina yelled, moving quickly sideways.

Even as she said it, she knew her words were useless. He wouldn't listen. He was activated.

How many more people will he kill?

How many would I have to kill to stop him?

The sound of gunfire cracked through her earpiece and echoed across the market square. The proxy stared at her, his eyes wide with surprise. Blood radiated from one side of his neck and torso. His red jacket grew darker, wet. He turned his barrel to the sky.

Off to one side, Ieva lay on her stomach with her arms out and pistol still aimed. She'd dropped flat to the ground and fired high to avoid shooting bystanders. Both shots had struck the proxy; she'd put the first under his rib cage to avoid ricochets, the second through his neck. She was likely aiming for his head on the second shot, but it still did the trick.

The proxy dropped to his knees, his glazed eyes locked on Czarina.

Then he shoved the pistol under his chin and fired.

Ieva's throat mike picked up the shot, making Czarina's ears sting. The proxy collapsed face down, revealing the large, wet exit wound at the top of his punctured skull. Blood pooled around him, bright and oxygenated.

$\sim$

SOPHIA STAGGERED AFTER VALERIA, into the center of the square and under the archway of a domed classical building. Inside, rows of market stalls stretched away. The operative was ahead, moving down a vaulted aisle. People lingered around her, slow and glaze-eyed, inspecting amber jewelry, wooden crafts and embroidered cloth. With the noise in here, no one had heard the gunshots outside. Sophia weaved through them, keeping an eye on Valeria. The operative changed trajectory and sprinted up a flight of stairs.

Sophia angled toward a flight closer by. She climbed them quickly to the next floor, hoping they would take her to the same place as Valeria. She stepped out into a large gallery, whisper-quiet with polished marble floors and skylights that cast afternoon light on sculptures and pastel walls.

Visitors quietly admired the art, barely registering Sophia's presence and the blood flowing from her lips. She kept her pistol close to her body and strode forward. Twenty meters ahead, Valeria appeared. She turned, looked over the shoulder of a passing man and saw Sophia.

Sophia raised her pistol in a snap motion—up her chest, then out. The man froze in place and Valeria grabbed him, used him as a shield. She jammed her pistol hard into the man's eye. She was careful, kept her head directly behind his. Sophia didn't want to kill Valeria, but if the programming triggers didn't work then what else could she do?

'If you shoot through his mouth, you'll kill me,'

Valeria said. 'Would you like that?' Under pressure, her accent slipped. It was no longer American.

Czarina appeared behind the operative, but Sophia knew she wasn't close enough. Sophia tried to hide her glance, but the operative saw it. She kept hold of her hostage and sidestepped behind a statue, then pivoted and aimed for Czarina.

Sophia needed to get closer for a clear shot.

But Ieva launched from nowhere, tearing the pistol from Valeria's hand. Valeria recovered, kicked Ieva away, sending her crashing into a wall. Then she turned to Czarina—who'd moved closer—and disarmed her, throwing the pistol across the marble floor.

The operative drove her fist into Czarina's throat. Czarina avoided the blow, barely. Sophia was close enough now, but Valeria sidestepped her pistol, kicking down on Sophia's knee and driving a fist into her midsection.

Pain flashed through Sophia, crushing oxygen from her. She was in the air for a moment, flying sideways. She floated across the polished floor and crashed into a tall wooden stand. A marble bust wobbled and fell from the stand, smashing in front of her. She lay on her side, pain slicing every breath. Unable to move.

Czarina and Ieva were on the ground too. Sirens wailed in the distance, approaching the market square. Paramedics and police would soon converge on the square. How long would it take for the police to think to come in here?

Valeria strode toward her. Along the way, she scooped

up Czarina's pistol. She stopped five meters short of Sophia and raised the weapon.

'This was fun,' Valeria said. 'Let's do it again sometime.'

Overhead, the skylight shattered. Instinctively Sophia covered her eyes, and when she opened them, a figure moved in front of her.

If nothing else, DC knew how to make an entrance.

Steel flashed. Czarina's pistol hit the wall. Valeria withdrew her hand just in time as DC moved swiftly, the blade of his tachi slicing and tearing her sleeve. The operative ducked and rolled, found an opening and struck DC in his chest. He went flying back through the air and smashed into the wall beside Sophia.

DC groaned. 'I didn't think that through.'

'She packs a punch,' Sophia said.

His sword landed nearby. Before the operative could scoop it up, Sophia was on her feet, and despite the pain, wielding it comfortably in both hands. Her Kali training wasn't a perfect match for this kind of sword, but it would do.

Valeria glared at Sophia, then at DC. He staggered, drew his pistol. The sirens were closer. The operative focused on Czarina's pistol, lying there on the ground, then gave Sophia a wry smile. DC eyed it off too.

Valeria went for it, diving across the marble floor and colliding with DC. He slid across the floor, his pistol knocked clear. Valeria was back on her feet and running, her sneakers crunching on skylight fragments. She was out of the museum before anyone could get in her way.

'Leave her.' Sophia said.

DC was already standing, flustered. 'I must be losing my edge.'

She handed him the tachi. 'No, that's here. Thanks for dropping in.'

He took his sword and struggled to stand upright. 'So … I think that went well.'

CHAPTER TWELVE

Kaliningrad, Kaliningrad Oblast

GLEB FLIPPED OPEN THE LAPTOP, lighting up a large display on the briefing room wall, then retreated to a corner. Olesya found herself staring at a grainy CCTV image. In the center, a lone shooter fired into the fleeing crowd. Everyone stared at the image in silence, including Ark and the other operative hunters—Marina, Andrey and Nika.

Marina's large green eyes were focused on the CCTV image. She wasn't wearing her headscarf today, and she stood apart from the other pair. Nika's eyes weren't as dilated as when Olesya had first met her, and Andrey stood unnervingly still.

Illarion rubbed at his silver stubble. 'This happened in Kraków.'

'So we were in the wrong city,' Andrey said.

'At least some of us were in the right country.' Marina shot Olesya an irritated glance.

'We wanted to be there,' Ark said quickly.

'Ark and Olesya weren't cleared for operations,' Illarion said. 'This is not *anyone's* fault. You all need to understand that.'

Olesya swallowed. Only Gleb knew where she and Ark had really been today. And that their secret mission had been a failure. She wasn't even sure if the woman in the navy coat was the same woman Ark had been chasing. All they knew for sure was that at least one of them was a Fifth Column operative and they'd successfully snatched a Russian intelligence officer from the streets of Tallinn.

Illarion hit a key on the laptop and the image changed. Ark launched to his feet, eyes wide. His mouth opened, but he didn't speak.

Now it was another image from a CCTV camera; a lone woman in a dark coat, moving fast across the market square in Kraków. Around her, people were running from something, looking back. But she was moving in a different direction. Only half her face was visible from the high angle of the camera, but it was enough. There was no uncertainty this time.

Val.

Olesya and Ark had been on the other side of Eastern Europe. And Val was right there. Right where *they* were supposed to be.

Ark took a deep breath and composed himself. 'My sister.'

'We believe so, yes,' Illarion said.

'How are we supposed to stop them if we're given the wrong details?' Marina asked.

'We don't always get intel on these operations,' Illarion said. 'We're fortunate to have agents inside the Fifth Column who can supply any information at all.'

Andrey threw his hands in the air. 'Our operation was a non-event. No bombs or attacks in Wrocław. Meanwhile you're telling us there was a goddamn proxy shooting up civilians in Kraków?'

'We should've been there to put that shooter down,' Marina muttered to herself. 'And his handler.'

Ark turned to her, eyes bulging. 'That's my sister you're talking about.'

'She's not your sister anymore,' Marina said. 'She's Fifth Column now, don't you get it?'

Ark's fist closed, but Andrey stepped between them.

'You want to do the Fifth Column's work for them and fight each other?' Andrey asked. 'By all means, knock yourselves out.'

Ark glared fixedly at Marina. 'Don't ever say that again.'

'That's what you Muscovites do, right?' Marina said, hands on her hips. 'Take them in all pretty and wrapped in absorbent cotton?'

Andrey turned to face her. 'Is there something wrong with that?'

'There's something wrong, all right,' Marina said. 'There's something very wrong with this, wouldn't you say?'

Andrey fell silent.

'Marina,' Illarion said. 'One more word and I'll pull you off the team, do you understand?'

She fell silent.

Olesya folded her arms. 'Let me guess, the shooter killed himself afterwards.'

'Correct,' Illarion said. 'But there was one difference this time.'

'What?'

Illarion cleared his throat. 'The proxy was Russian.'

'Shit.' Olesya should've been there.

'I bet the Western media are having a field day with this,' Marina said.

'Next image,' Illarion said.

Gleb hit a button on his laptop. The image changed again. This time, there were two women standing outside a café in the same square. Ark's gaze was transfixed on one woman, Val. But Olesya was focused on the other, whose back was facing the camera.

'Who's the other one?' Marina asked.

'Another operative,' Illarion said. 'We don't have a clear shot of her face, but we'll have her identity soon.'

The woman's black leather jacket, the cut of her shoulder-length hair, her sneakers. Olesya knew her; the operative with the gray eyes. Sophia.

You bitch, you're Fifth Column after all.

Sophia had to be behind the abductions. But Olesya couldn't reveal her suspicion. Doing so would mean admitting she'd withheld information on the Moscow operation. She needed to be absolutely certain before she brought this to Illarion.

Illarion leaned over the table, across his map of

Europe and the scattered photos of operatives. He'd taken the map with him from Moscow and now there was a new photo over Kraków, Poland. A photo of Val.

'Val is one of them,' Illarion said. 'For now.'

Ark turned away, hand over his mouth.

'This presents a problem for us,' Illarion said. 'The Fifth Column seem to have Val and the other kidnapped hunters under their control. We have to expect they now possess intimate knowledge of our operations and will be looking to exploit that.'

He slid the laptop over to Gleb, who removed the CCTV photo and switched to Polish news feeds. They played across the big screen with the audio muted.

'So what happens now?' Marina asked.

'We're assigned to deal with Purity, not the Fifth Column operatives,' Illarion said.

'What?' Ark said. 'We just found Val!'

'He has a point,' Olesya said. 'You trained us to hunt operatives and disarm nuclear warheads. You didn't train us to fight a bunch of street thugs.'

Illarion pointed to the screen. 'That bunch of street thugs just won Poland's presidential election.'

Onscreen, there was footage of Purity supporters celebrating their Purity candidate—a fragile man with wire-framed glasses and peppered hair—mouthing a silent speech.

'Purity are a bunch of lunatics,' Ark said. 'How could they win?'

'Their popularity is rising sharply across Eastern Europe and they have the public support of many governments around the world,' Gleb said. 'But they tap into a deep river of...'

Marina crossed her arms. 'Racism?'

'Fear,' Gleb said. 'Fear of outsiders, fear of those different to themselves. Fear of people who undertake gene doping or gene therapy.'

'People like us.'

He turned up the sound and the Purity leader's voice filled the room.

'Our thoughts are with those who have suffered the loss of their loved ones at the hands of this radicalized Russian soldier. Amid our prayers and our outrage, we cannot deny this is a brazen assault on the territorial integrity of our country—a sovereign and independent European nation.'

The video switched to a grainy image of Val from the CCTV. Beside this image, a close-up of her face as a child. A subtitle read *Accomplice in shooting—Russian spy program.*

The President continued. *'It is becoming clear to us that Russia's ruthless genetic engineering program, inflicted on innocent children, is connected to this senseless act of aggression. What happened today is a violation of what makes us pure. We will do everything in our power to bring purity and justice to—'*

Illarion hit pause. 'You get the idea.'

Ark shook his head. 'Is someone going to tell them who runs Project GATE?'

'Yeah,' Andrey said. 'Because it sure as hell isn't us.'

Gleb cleared his throat. 'Purity are adept at attributing blame to a certain type of people. And right now, that's you. And anyone else who is genetically ... diverse.'

'Let me make this clear,' Illarion said. 'Purity is our primary objective. The more power it absorbs, the more dangerous it becomes to us, and to the rest of the world.'

'Even if the world supports them?' Marina asked.

'Yes,' Illarion said. 'It doesn't matter how many people they enchant, if we don't stop them, they will kill many more. Dismissed.'

The hunters slowly gathered their notes and filed out. Only Olesya remained with Illarion as Gleb collected his laptop and notes. He gave her a brief nod as he left.

Alone in the room with Illarion, she turned to him. 'Why haven't we tried yet?'

The rings under Illarion's eyes were darker than usual, his stubble a bit longer. 'Tried what exactly?'

'Tried destroying the Fifth Column,' Olesya said. 'We both know they're financing Purity. Why don't we cut off the serpent's head?'

'We don't know that yet. And cutting off the head is not the solution.'

'I know what you've been doing,' Olesya said. 'Your strategy, from the beginning. We've been on the defensive. Every time, we react. You've trained us to be more than just a reactionary force, and yet we never truly take action.'

'Is that what you really think, Olesya?'

'You freed Russia of the Fifth Column and now you're so worried about them taking it back that all we ever do is sabotage *their* operations,' she said. 'We don't have our own. And I think we should.'

Illarion clasped his hands behind his back. 'What sort of operation are you proposing?'

'We bring the fight to the Fifth Column. We destroy them.'

Illarion surveyed the map and the operative photos scattered across it, some pinned, some unsorted. 'This doesn't sound like the Olesya I know.'

'The Olesya you knew hadn't lost ... as much.'

'The Fifth Column are much weaker, far more depleted, than they were when we severed our ties with them, that's true,' Illarion said. 'But they are still very powerful and they hold sway over many of the nations on this planet. Destroying something like that is no simple task.'

'But we have to start somewhere,' she said.

'As a matter of fact, you can start by avoiding all Fifth Column operatives,' Illarion said.

'*What?* Why?'

'We're receiving reports of operatives being selectively upgraded.'

Olesya chewed her lip. 'Upgraded with what?'

'Gleb is preparing a full briefing for everyone, but the Fifth Column call them HAC operatives,' Illarion said. 'Human Artificial Chromosome.'

'What, so there's a whole new chromosome now?'

'A microchromosome. Imagine an operative with the strength and power of a full-body exoskeleton—without the exoskeleton.'

The bruises Olesya picked up from her encounter in Moscow still ached. 'That does explain a few things.'

'Until we learn more, you keep your distance,' he said.

Olesya shook her head. 'This doesn't change the fact we need to hit them *hard*. We need to destroy the Fifth

Column once and for all. We're *still* picking up the pieces after their attacks in the Middle East. Not to mention they've been terrorizing Western populations for decades. It will take generations for people to recover from this.'

Illarion frowned. 'I don't deny it, but taking on the Fifth Column … even if you win, you lose.'

'What are you talking about?'

'The Fifth Column is run by the most cunning psychopaths on this planet. Denton is middle management at best. Or at least he was.'

'I don't understand. How do we lose?'

Illarion gestured across the map, over every continent. 'Let's say we put everything we have into fighting the Fifth Column. And we crush them. Let's say the psychopaths in power face certain defeat at our hand. Tell me, what do psychopaths do when they face certain defeat?'

'They get desperate.'

'And desperate psychopaths are the most dangerous kind. Rather than lose the game, they'll burn the entire chess board.'

'With us still on it,' Olesya whispered.

'If we destroy the Fifth Column, we face the psychopath's endgame,' he said.

'They'll go nuclear.'

'Precisely.'

Olesya exhaled slowly. 'So we just let the Fifth Column run the world because we're too scared they'll destroy it? That's the plan?'

'Psychopaths of all strains have run empires and nations on this planet for thousands of years,' Illarion said. 'I'm sorry, but evil has prevailed in our world for a very long time, and that won't change just because you want it to. At least not yet.'

Anger burned through her. 'How can you say that? You rescued me from the Fifth Column. You told me I could make a difference!'

'You still can.'

Olesya turned her back on him. The rest of the hunters —Ark, Marina, Andrey and Nika—were watching the argument through the windows. Her cheeks reddened.

'There *has* to be a way,' she said.

Leaning on the map, Illarion breathed for a moment. Without warning, he tore the map from the table and hurled the table across the room. It hit a wall, the photos fluttering in the air like confetti. 'If there is, I don't know it.'

Olesya's rage cooled. She felt only despair now. 'I'm sorry, I was just frustrated...'

'Do you think I asked for this?' Illarion inhaled sharply. 'Do you think I asked to mentor a bunch of kids in some long-shot hope of saving the world?'

'We're only *long shots*?'

Laptop in hand, Illarion strode for the door. 'That's the thing with long shots. They don't all work out.'

CHAPTER THIRTEEN

Vilnius, Lithuania

'NICE OF YOU TO DROP IN.' Sophia led DC into the kitchen. 'To what do we owe the honor?'

Before DC could reply, Ieva shoved a mug into his hands. 'Tea?'

He took the drink, and Ieva offered him a seat before tending to the other mugs.

DC sipped his tea. 'How you holding up?'

'Not bad, considering,' Sophia replied.

'Just her ribs.' Czarina said. She'd inspected Sophia for any critical wounds and found remarkably few.

'They'll heal,' Sophia said.

'You're lucky that you heal fast.' Ieva sat down with a mug of her own.

The sun set over the forest, casting a golden tint through the window. DC squinted and shifted his chair while Ieva's reaction was to produce her phone and take a photo. She had a library of sunset and dog photos. Right now, the dog photos were winning by a slight margin. Sophia didn't mind, as long as the shots were stripped of metadata and didn't reveal anything about their headquarters.

'She certainly knows how to throw a punch,' Sophia said. 'Have you crossed paths with her before?'

DC shook his head. 'If I had've known she was jacked up like that, I would've left it to you.'

'Why would you do that?' Sophia asked.

Czarina stifled a cough. 'He was joking.'

'I knew that.'

DC slumped in the chair and exhaled. 'I've seen a cloaked operative, I've seen an immortal operative, I've even watched a limb grow back. But *this* is something else.'

'Wonder Woman.' Ieva giggled. 'Because we're all sitting here *wondering*. Get it?'

'That was terrible,' Czarina said.

Sophia failed to hide her smile. 'The operative's accent,' she said. 'It was American in the beginning, but then it changed.'

'She was tagged on the Fifth Column Assetrac system,' Ieva said. 'We all saw it.'

'My deprogramming commands didn't work on her,' Sophia said.

'What did they change this time?' Ieva asked, her fingers poised over her phone, ready to note the new phrases.

Sophia shook her head. 'Everything. I couldn't get in at all. It's like—'

'Like she wasn't programmed?' DC said.

'What about that operative in Berlin?' Czarina asked. 'You told him about that?'

He looked at Sophia. 'What happened?'

'We ran into three operatives,' Sophia said. 'They kidnapped a civilian. Russian. His name was Evgeny Sporyshev.'

DC's shoulders stiffened.

'Do you know him?' she said.

'Doesn't ring a bell,' he said. 'So the Fifth Column have him now?'

Sophia nodded. 'We killed one operative and captured the second, but the third managed to get out of there with Evgeny.'

'What happened to the one you captured?' DC asked.

'She didn't make it,' Sophia said.

'The deprogramming seemed to work,' Ieva said, in a hopeful voice. 'In the beginning.'

'I got into the outer layer. I must have triggered something I shouldn't have.'

DC leaned over the table. 'What did she do?'

'She killed herself.'

'Ah, right,' DC said. 'Did she ... say anything before that? Give you anything at all?'

'Something about an operation in Eastern Europe with massive collateral. She used the word *destiny*.'

'Then she went bananas,' Czarina said.

'Does that mean anything to you?' Sophia asked him. 'Destiny?'

'No. You need to find a way through their new programming, and fast.' DC stood and excused himself from the table. 'Thanks for the tea.'

'And what are you doing?' Sophia asked.

He stood in the center of the kitchen for a moment, silhouetted by the sunset. 'Shake a few trees, see if anyone knows anything. I'll be in touch if I get lucky.'

Sophia already had her suspicions. The Russian agent from the subway—the one who lied about being FSB—had to be linked to this Kraków operative in some way and she was determined to prove it.

DC paused in the doorway. 'If you find anything more on that upgraded operative, let me know. But please, don't go after her. She'll kill you.'

'Not if I can deprogram her,' Sophia said.

'Even that's not a sure thing anymore,' he said.

'Wait.' Sophia held up one of their modified iPhones. 'You should take one of these. Join the twenty-first century.'

He waved his little black Nokia. 'I like the *Snake* game.'

'You can play on mine,' Sophia said. *That sounded awkward.*

'Um, I'll be in contact soon.' He disappeared down the creaking staircase.

'Oh, be still my heart,' Czarina said.

'Shut it,' Sophia said, 'or I'll put you back in slave mode.'

Czarina blinked. 'I don't ... still have slave mode, do I?' She looked at Ieva. 'Do I have slave mode?'

'Of course not. You're deprogrammed.' Ieva leaned in and lowered her voice. 'Or are you?'

Czarina jabbed a finger at her. 'Don't do that. Or I'll put you in *unconsciousness* mode. Even I can do that one.'

Sophia leaned back in her chair. The muscles around her ribs were burning and itching. Her *Regen* pseudo-genes were doing their thing, driving her accelerated cellular repair and regeneration.

'Maybe DC's right,' Ieva said. 'Maybe we need to slow down and be careful for a little while.'

'Until we figure out what the hell's going down,' Czarina said.

'That's the last thing we should be doing,' Sophia said. *Right now, we need help.*

Ieva folded her arms. 'You're going back out there, aren't you?'

Sophia pulled up the map on her phone. The operative was on standby now, sitting in northern Poland. Sophia stood and her ribs burned. 'I need a spare phone.'

'Why?' Ieva asked.

'I'm going out there again,' Sophia said. 'This time, I'm doing things differently.'

Czarina and Ieva stood together.

'Not without us, you're not,' Czarina said.

CHAPTER FOURTEEN

Vilnius, Lithuania

THE FIFTH COLUMN had Evgeny now.

DC couldn't get the thought out of his head. He wasn't sure how much the Fifth Column knew, or why after all this time they'd grabbed the Russian spy, but the fact Evgeny had played a crucial role in Project GATE was known to very few. Sophia didn't know. Not even Denton.

He reached the crest of the cobbled alley and looked down at Vilnius. In its twilight hour, the city was dotted with the honeycomb yellow of candle- and bulb-lit windows. The sharp spires of Orthodox and Catholic churches lined the horizon like barbed wire.

He'd stopped by a crumbling wall, inside which stood the remains of a factory. His vehicle was parked on the other side, next to a cemetery; he just had to cut through the remains of the factory to get to it. Moving through the rubble, he glanced behind him; a precaution.

Some small distance away, a man was walking toward him. Moonlight glinted off his shaved head and polished black shoes, but was absorbed by the dark suit and scarf. A chill washed through DC.

Denton wasn't even trying to hide. He stepped through into the remains of the factory with a smile. 'You're not an easy man to follow.'

'That's why you recruited me,' DC said. Denton was too far out of range to read DC's mind, but not too far to shoot him. DC's hand remained close to the pistol grip protruding from his waistband.

'What do you want?' DC asked.

Denton was the only figure DC could make out, but he was sure the man had backup. There'd be operatives here too, watching him.

'You ignored my LinkedIn invitation,' Denton said. 'And after everything I've done for you. Now I hear you're a double agent for no fewer than two resistance groups.' He shrugged. 'Then again, one group is extinct and the other … I'm not even sure existed in the first place.'

'The Sixth Column exists.' DC stepped carefully backward, facing Denton the whole time.

Denton frowned. 'Russia and China cut loose years ago. Doesn't sound like much of a *sixth* column to me. It sounds like a handful of rubble. It sounds like this place right here.'

DC said nothing. How much had Denton siphoned from his mind in the last few minutes as he walked the alleys of Vilnius? DC was well trained, but so was Denton. He didn't want to think about it as Denton took a step closer, so he thought instead of the Sixth Column and its potential.

'Is that what you've been doing all these years?' Denton asked. 'Hoping to rebuild an alliance that will never exist? The Sixth Column is dust, but at least you're alive. You're welcome, by the way.'

'You have nothing to do with my survival,' DC said.

'Oh, but every moment you stood against the Fifth Column, every moment you looked to destroy it, I was there to carve that path for you,' Denton said. 'I made it possible. Whether you choose to believe it or not, we're fighting on the same side.'

'You're the one who's lucky to be alive. The next time you cross Sophia, you might not be.'

Denton climbed over rubble, closing the distance between them.

'That's close enough,' DC said.

Denton halted, but his smile did not fade. 'Have you told her?'

'Told her that *you're* here?'

'No, that you can't be trusted,' Denton said. 'That you *will* betray her in the end. That you always do.'

DC swallowed his anger.

'Poor Sophia,' Denton said. 'Trying so hard to put it all together, but here you are, hiding pieces from her.'

'Why are you here, Denton?'

'Do you mean, why am I here talking, and not killing you?' Denton asked.

'Fine.'

'I'm here because something is coming,' Denton said. 'You can feel it, too. I see you do, in your step, in your eyes. It's coming off you in waves.'

'Big deal,' DC said. 'You can only smell emotions because you stole it from Sophia's DNA. But you'll never feel them, not the ones that matter.'

'And for that I am grateful.' Denton smiled. 'That and all the pseudogenes I'm collecting. Speaking of which, I hear the *Regeneration* pseudogene is on the market.'

'It doesn't exist,' DC said.

'It's already in my DNA, I think it does exist.' Denton took another step closer.

'Maybe.' DC's hand tightened over his pistol grip. 'But the samples don't exist. I made sure of that.'

Denton raised his hands in admission. 'Word on the street says otherwise.'

'If you're looking to upgrade your little squad of operatives, including the one with her scope on me through that dark window'—DC pointed to the building across the street—'the Fifth Column have their HAC thing going. I hear they pack a real punch.'

'Human Artificial Microchromosome.' Denton nodded. 'I've ordered the sampler.'

'Tell me why you're really here.'

'The Fifth Column general. He's planning something.'

'What generals do,' DC said.

'I know the patterns, the behavior. You see it too.'

'If you're such a genius, then what is it?'

'I was hoping you could tell me.'

DC stifled a laugh. 'You don't know anything, do you?'

'I know the general is making his final move. And whatever the outcome, it will end badly.'

'Define badly.'

'On a scale of genocide to extinction?' Denton wiggled his hand. 'It's a little flexible.'

DC sighed. 'Or melodramatic.'

'The Fifth Column doesn't like to lose.'

'Sorry, can't help you,' DC said.

'That certainly is a shame.' Denton turned sharply on his heel and walked away.

DC kept his hand on his pistol grip. He could've stepped clear of the operative's scope and taken the shot, put a round through Denton's skull. But Denton would've considered that possibility, and he would almost certainly have multiple operatives shooting DC the moment his gun cleared his waistband. If nothing else, Denton never doubted his own strategic value.

And neither did DC.

In the alley outside the destroyed factory, Denton turned and waved back at DC. 'See you at the Christmas party.'

CHAPTER FIFTEEN

Rio de Janeiro, Brazil

THE GLASS ELEVATOR shot Aviary skyward. Damien and Nasira stood beside her, their arms cuffed as tightly as hers. Intron's security had taken them into custody at the Ecuadorian data center and questioned Nasira. Whatever she'd said, it worked because their captors barely said a word after that, throwing them—sedated and under guard—onto a private jet bound for Brazil. And now here they were, on an elevator traveling to the very top of Intron headquarters. Aviary's stomach knotted.

'Centro Zone,' Jay said. 'We're downtown.'

As the elevator rose, it granted them a view of the lush, green mountains that encircled the city. Jay pointed to the beaches and mountainous islands that peppered the bay.

'That's the South Zone. Sugar Loaf Mountain.'

'You grew up here?' Aviary asked.

'Nah, in a slum on the other side of Super Jesus.' He pointed to their right, at a large forested mountain and the Jesus statue that loomed over the city.

Aviary didn't know exactly what was waiting for them, but when she tried to press a button for a level about halfway it ignored her request. 'Worth a try.'

'Welcome is Intron headquarters,' Nasira said. 'You wanted their research center, you got it.'

'Yeah, but can we do things in a way where I don't get captured all the time?' Jay asked.

'You're lucky they didn't kill us,' Nasira said. 'Thank me later.'

'What did you say to them?' Aviary asked.

Nasira positioned herself in front of the elevator doors. 'I told them there's a problem with their operatives, and we can help fix it.' She turned to Aviary, sweat beading on her forehead. 'We *can* help, yeah?'

Aviary swallowed. 'I ... I hope so.'

'What about getting my abilities back?' Jay asked.

'We'll get to that,' Nasira said. 'If we last that long.'

The elevator drew to a halt. The doors opened.

Seven employees stood before them, mostly security. Four of them—two on each side—wore vests and carried submachine guns. The centermost trio were dressed sharply in tailored suits. Two of them, a woman and a man, had room under their arms for shoulder holsters. Aviary was getting good at noticing those things. Unlike the others, the employee standing in the very center was unarmed. She clasped her hands behind her back.

'My name is Lívia.' She had a smoky, beige

complexion and bright, olivine eyes, which focused directly on Aviary. 'This way.'

Aviary stepped out of the elevator and under a gleaming white arch, beyond which it looked like a jungle had taken over the entire atrium. Curved glass walls leaned in from the sides, with foliage climbing the glass to a high ceiling and carefully pruned trees lining the perimeter.

'What is this place, a terrarium?' Nasira asked.

'Carbon neutral,' Lívia said, walking ahead of them. 'And completely self-sufficient.'

They followed Lívia up a staircase to a vine-wrapped mezzanine, drawing curious glances from the Intron employees they passed on the way. Wall-mounted panels showed colorful video presentations of different company projects: gene therapy with an adeno-associated virus breaching a host cell; *smart suits* that monitored health and increased mobility; or elegant, V-shaped drones coated in solar panels, gliding peacefully through the stratosphere. Under the panels, three words:

Your Destiny Awaits.

Lívia escorted Aviary and her group into a meeting room shaped like a large tea cup. In its center were two white, hexagonal tables that almost connected. Resting on top, a plastic water jug and plastic cups. Ergonomic mesh chairs were tucked around the tables, where Lívia gestured for the party to sit. Aviary took a seat first, followed by Damien. Nasira and Jay took longer, casing the room before finally lowering themselves into chairs. Both the suit and vest people—six security officers in total—took positions against the walls and the room's bank of windows, beyond which a rainforest cavity collected moisture.

Lívia clasped her hands on the table. 'You've come a long way to get my attention.'

Nasira reclined in her chair, crossing her legs. 'I think we already had it.'

'You seem oddly comfortable for someone caught trespassing *and* stealing.'

'Speaking of odd,' Nasira said, 'when were you planning on reporting our crimes?'

One of Lívia's eyebrows moved fractionally.

'You have something of a hard-on for genetics,' Jay said.

Lívia glanced sideways at him. If the change of subject irritated her, she didn't show it. 'We have an interest in many fields. Tomorrow, we launch our fleet of solar-powered drones. Project Destiny.'

Jay nodded. 'And what will Project Destiny be bombing?'

Lívia barely registered his question. 'Project Destiny will deliver high-speed internet to those who don't have it, which is two thirds of the population. Here, in parts of Latin America and in regions of Africa and Asia, we're partnering with local carriers to change that.'

'Must come with a hefty price tag,' Jay said. 'Like this place, right? Smack bang in Centro Rio … that's more expensive than New York City.'

'We're fortunate that our work has proven successful,' Lívia said. 'And we're always pursuing new areas to explore.'

'Such as?' Aviary asked.

'As your … friend mentioned, we're most interested in *life sciences*,' Lívia said. 'Now, you can imagine my curiosity after finding you poking around our data center in Ecuador. And you can imagine my suspicion when you claim our *life science* products are potentially faulty.'

'About that,' Aviary said. 'I mean, I was looking—'

Lívia raised her hand. 'And then you can guess how surprised we were to find serial numbers on particular genes'—she glanced between Nasira and Damien—'in both of your DNA.'

'You took blood samples without our consent,' Damien said.

'More importantly, we took it before deciding whether to press charges.' Lívia leaned over the table to whisper, 'We know what you are.'

'Pissed off,' Jay said. 'And a bit thirsty.'

Lívia gestured to the jug of water. 'You're from Project GATE. Rogue operatives, judging by the lack of tracking devices under your skin.'

'Guessing that's why you didn't press charges,' Nasira said.

'We do things a little differently around here.'

'Yeah, getting that vibe,' Nasira said. 'So let's cut to the cha—'

'Let's start with why *you're* here,' Lívia interrupted. 'You want something from us.'

'Your research center,' Nasira said. 'It's in this building, right?'

Jay shifted in his chair. 'You know, the kind of joint where you strap people down and scoop out their pseudogenes.'

'Not only is that unlikely, it is very much unlike our business practices.' Lívia studied him. 'Is there something you're not sharing?'

Jay stood suddenly. The security officers uncoiled like snakes from their corners. But Jay simply glared at her. 'Your people already kidnapped me and stole all my abilities. No point denying it, we both know. So yeah, don't think I have much else to share.'

'This is something we need to address.' Lívia's hand trembled over her phone. She moved her hand under the desk. 'I cannot express how truly sorry I am for what you endured. You've been a victim of an unauthorized black market operation—a despicable violation of human rights that is no way condoned by Intron.' She picked up her phone and started writing onscreen. 'I'm requesting our bioengineer join us.' She lowered her phone and focused on Jay. 'He can assist in answering your questions, but please know that, as we speak, we are bringing those responsible to justice. And if there's anything we can—'

Nasira leaned forward. 'Your justice sounds a little … internal to me.'

'We're dealing with corruption on an unprecedented scale, but we're making excellent progress,' Lívia said. 'What happened to your friend here, that exposed everything to us. And that means no one else will have to experience what he went through. As of this moment, we have shut down all unauthorized operations.'

'Because they were burned to the ground?' Nasira asked.

'Our facility in Barranquilla, yes,' Lívia said. 'The

terrorist group who attacked this facility did so in order to steal highly valuable research.'

'My genetics?' Jay asked.

'No,' Lívia said. 'They did not steal anyone's pseudo-gene profiles. Please, sit.'

Jay reluctantly sat down. 'They shot me. I'm lucky to be alive.'

'It's a miracle we can all be grateful for,' Lívia said.

Aviary cleared her throat. 'So what did they steal?'

'Sensitive research that unfortunately I cannot share,' Lívia said. 'Rest assured, it does not affect you in any way.'

The glass doors to the room parted to reveal three new faces. Two of the new entrants were armed with holstered pistols, a man and a woman in black vests and boots. The third pulled up short before the hexagonal tables. He looked younger than Lívia, his smooth, round face not a day older than nineteen. Unlike Lívia, he was dressed in sneakers and a gray t-shirt.

The bioengineer, Aviary thought.

He walked to Lívia's table and carefully sat beside her while his bodyguards took positions on either end of the table.

'Hélio Morgado is our lead bioengineer,' Lívia said. 'He specializes in gene resurrection.'

Hélio shrugged. 'I prefer the term biohacker.'

'I prefer the term *put my shit back where you found it*,' Jay said.

'Your bodyguards.' Damien spoke softly. 'Where did you find them?'

Unlike the security officers, the bodyguards' arms weren't folded or crossed.

Lívia blinked. 'I'm not sure I follow.'

Nasira sat upright and inhaled slowly. 'Now that you mention it, they look kinda familiar.'

Aviary recognized her "shit was going down" look. The security officers bristled, yet the bodyguards remained calm and still. Aviary concentrated on slowing her breathing, remaining calm.

'They look like a lot of people,' Hélio said quickly.

Nasira smiled. 'Helldiver Squad. One of them was under my command.' Her gaze fixed on the male bodyguard. 'Felix, right?'

He gave a stiff nod. 'Nasira. It's been a while.'

'Eight years,' she said. 'So there's one of two possibilities here. One—which would explain a hell of a lot—Intron is a front for the Fifth Column.'

Hélio snorted. 'Are you trying to insult us?'

'We just did,' Jay said.

'Two,' Nasira said, 'You're stealing Fifth Column operatives. Gotta be honest, I'm not sure which is worse.'

Felix twitched. 'We're Intron employees now. We choose to be here.'

Aviary's smartwatch pulsed, a luminous dot onscreen. Under the table, she rotated her bound wrists and tapped the display. The small screen lit up with data transfers. The watch was still running its data mining program from Ecuador; it must have found a new device to siphon.

'What about your abilities? Did Intron steal those?' Jay asked.

Hélio's expression hardened. 'We don't *steal* abilities.'

'But you take them,' Nasira said.

'We research their profiles,' Hélio said.

Aviary kept her attention on Lívia, but from the corner of her vision she watched emails, messages and browser history stream across her watch face. It was siphoning Lívia's phone. She looked down at her watch, concealed under the table, and pretended to think.

The first piece of captured information she noticed was a message Lívia had written only moments ago: *Bringing you into a meeting now with GATE operatives; one missing genes. Victim of Intron corruption.*

Adrenaline iced through Aviary.

'Whatever you did, you switched his pseudogenes off,' Nasira said. 'And now he wants them back on.'

Lívia folded her arms and leaned into her chair. 'Firstly, we didn't switch anything off. Secondly, if we're to come to any kind of arrangement, what exactly do you bring to the table?' She glanced at their bound wrists. 'So to speak.'

'We'll be saving that for the CEO,' Nasira said. 'Perhaps you can invite him to our little chat.'

'I don't think so,' Lívia said.

'How's that?' Nasira asked.

'I *am* the CEO.' Lívia gave her a thin smile. 'Now'—she turned to Aviary—'you mentioned something earlier about a faulty product. I presume this is your leverage.'

Lívia and Hélio watched Aviary from across the table. It was all on her.

'The problem is with Project GATE operatives.' Aviary glanced at Hélio's ex-operative bodyguards. 'Current and former.'

'And what's that, precisely?' Hélio asked.

'Well, we have reason to believe the Project GATE injections—the viral vectors—included more than you bargained for.'

'More than all of us bargained for,' Nasira said.

'If you're talking about genetic tracking devices, we're aware of those,' said Hélio. 'And rest assured, we have systems in place to disable and remove them.'

'No, I'm talking about a kill switch,' Aviary said. 'An endotoxin.'

The bioengineer fell silent.

Lívia turned slowly to him. 'Is that even possible?'

'Theoretically,' Hélio said. 'But we would've seen it.'

'You're stealing government tech,' Aviary said.

'Worse,' Nasira said. 'You're stealing Fifth Column tech.'

Hélio shook his head. 'Their tech is obsolete. Yes, we use their blueprints—that saves us decades of finding needles in haystacks—but they're still using zinc finger modules.' He chuckled to himself. 'Slow, obsolete technology.'

'So what makes yours so much better?' Nasira asked.

'We have our own patented system, the *Argonaute*, which works at any temperature,' Hélio said. 'It's a DNA sequence. Think of it like a pair of scissors with a little microchip inside. I tell the Argonaute where to go and what to do. It cleaves your DNA in the precise place I tell it to. Your little DNA police come running to fix it. That's the perfect opportunity for the Argonaute to alter your DNA to my exact specifications.' He smiled. 'That's one pseudogene resurrected. Imagine thousands of Argonautes doing this all at once, in every cell in your body. Gene expression is systemic in less than an hour. Voila, your new ability is activated. This blows the Fifth Column's process out of the water.'

'You sure about that?' Nasira said.

'There's no way anyone could sneak a kill switch in there. Not without me knowing about it.'

Aviary risked a glance at the emails downloading onto her watch. 'I think someone did.'

Hélio's face turned a slight shade of pink. 'Thinking isn't the same as knowing.'

'We do not engage with the Fifth Column,' Lívia said. 'No matter what sneaked in.'

'Yeah, well I'm betting they'll engage with you,' Jay said. 'Not many countries these days the Fifth Column can't strong-arm.'

'Not Brazil,' Lívia said.

'Wanna make a bet?' Nasira said. 'Take it from us, no one's safe.'

Aviary leaned forward, over the table. 'Are you using a Fifth Column virus to deliver your activator?'

'The virus is just a shell,' he said. 'An empty adeno-associated virus.'

'Are you sure they're empty?'

Hélio focused on the table, deep in thought. 'Oh.'

Lívia shot him an impatient glare. 'Do we have a problem, Hélio?'

'Holy crap.' He leaned back in his chair, eyes wide. 'It's possible the Fifth Column could have smuggled the endotoxin into the virus shell itself.'

'And you didn't notice this?' Lívia asked. 'You just said there was no way you'd miss it.'

'That's the wonderful thing about endotoxins,' he said. 'They can be masked as a perfectly normal protein. A protein that tells us'—he pointed to Nasira and Damien —'their unique serial numbers. The same protein we use for our serial numbers.'

Lívia's voice was low. 'It never occurred to you that this protein had a more sinister purpose?'

'There was no reason to. They fuse with the activated pseudogenes and don't do anything.' His gaze locked onto Aviary. 'Unless you specifically destroy them.'

Aviary felt her mouth go dry. 'And the endotoxin is released.'

'Clever approach,' he said. 'Even I hadn't thought of that.'

CHAPTER SIXTEEN

Prague, Czech Republic

THE HOTEL'S executive suite had everything: the regal sitting area, king-sized bedroom and walk-through shower with adjustable tinted glass. All things considered, specialist Hal Claycomb was surprised to find General Wolfram Sievers cross-legged on a sleeping bag in the middle of the floor, scooping beans from a tin. Whatever Hal expected of the six-star General, former head of the Subversion department and present director of the Fifth Column, this certainly wasn't it.

Sievers took his time uncrossing his legs and standing, his movements slow and considered. He wore an ink-black uniform, not the sort of full dress affair that gleamed with medals or brass. It was his service uniform, missing only the jacket and black wool greatcoat that hung by the door, and the high, polished boots standing by the bed. His uniform was so precisely designed that it outdid anything Hal had seen his superiors wear in full dress. Yet the uniform spoke of no rank or affiliation; in fact it might have passed for civilian winter clothing. The man was not one to grandstand.

This was the first time Hal had seen him in person, although he had seen a photograph of him once. Sievers looked a good ten years older now than he had in the picture. A picture taken seventy years ago.

Sievers nodded, inviting him closer. His mustache and beard were trimmed now, his hair combed and allowing for the tiniest of a cow lick on one side. He looked upon Hal with dark, decisive eyes.

'Specialist,' he said.

Hal had an inkling that Sievers had already evaluated him and the meeting was already over. 'General, might I say it is an honor to finally meet you.'

'The six stars are for ceremonial purposes only,' Sievers said, without a trace of his European accent. 'I am still very much a Colonel and I expect to be regarded as such.'

'Colonel.' Hal clasped his hands across his lower back.

Sievers stepped forward and brushed lint from Hal's collar. 'As of today you are a Lieutenant General, two stars.' He looked into Hal's eyes. 'Congratulations.'

Hal's mouth went dry. *Denton's old rank.* 'Much obliged, Colonel.'

'For ceremonial purposes only.'

'Understood, sir,' Hal said.

Sievers strode to the window. Before him, the rooftops of Prague were thorns rising to the sun.

'You are still a Specialist,' Sievers said, 'yet now we can discuss terms without my having to suffer dull courtesy and procedure.' He turned and eyed Hal for a moment. 'Drop the rank. Tell me why you think you are here.'

Hal's fingers tightened over one another. 'US marines captured an insurgent in Las Vegas. I was inbound, looking forward to interrogating the little scamp, when she was up and stolen by—'

'Sophia.'

'No,' Hal said. 'Not this time. But, a friend of hers.'

'Do you know where Sophia is?' Sievers asked.

'No, we don't I'm afraid,' Hal said. 'But don't worry—'

'I'm not worried. Why would you assume otherwise?'

'You asked to be notified immediately of anything that might be relating to Sophia and her rogue operatives,' Hal said. 'I thought this would be of some concern.'

'The tramp and her vermin are of *interest* to me, but no concern. Do not confuse the two.' Sievers returned to his view of Prague. 'You're here because of Denton.'

'He's been on his own for a year now,' Hal said. 'We haven't heard a squeak.'

'Until today,' Sievers said. 'Six months of ground work in Ukraine, unraveling. Denton is putting us behind schedule.' He took a comb from his breast pocket. 'You have a name for him, what do you call him again?'

'Chrome-dome,' Hal said.

Sievers smiled. 'Chrome-dome got his hair growth back some time ago. He simply prefers a shaved head now.'

'All the better to read minds, Colonel?' Hal asked.

Sievers ran his comb through the curl in his fringe, then turned to face Hal. 'You don't think he can.'

'To be frank, that's above my pay grade,' Hal said. 'But there are a few stories floating about. Some are particularly wacky.'

Sievers' gaze did not break this time. 'Under no circumstance is Denton—or any of the operatives he stole from us—allowed to come within one hundred meters of me, is that clear?'

'Without question, Colonel,' Hal said.

'There are things I know that he cannot,' Sievers said.

'So he can?' Hal asked. 'Read folks' minds?'

'The term is *silent spatialized communication*,' Sievers said.

'I don't follow, Colonel.'

'Back in 2003, we were able to discern imagined speech and intended direction from the electrical signals of our test subjects.' Sievers slipped the comb back into his breast pocket and breathed slowly. One of his nostrils whistled. 'These signals can be intercepted at a short distance and processed. It is unlikely—but not unfeasible —that someone can do this naturally.'

'Synthetic telepathy,' Hal said. 'I thought that was a myth.'

Sievers eyed him.

'Mistakenly,' Hal added.

'Only Denton's would not be synthetic.' Sievers cleared his throat. 'Moving along, did you recover the Russian spy from Project GATE?'

Hal took a moment to recall the name. 'Evgeny Sporyshev. Yes, I'm pleased to say we have him.'

Sievers' dark eyes flickered. 'Very good.'

'Shall I be resuming my assignment in Eastern Europe?'

'With renewed urgency,' Sievers said. 'You're dismissed.'

Hal turned to leave, his hand on the door when he heard Sievers speak.

'Specialist,' he said, without raising his voice. 'The Benefactors commend your work thus far.'

CHAPTER SEVENTEEN

Rio de Janeiro, Brazil

HÉLIO CHEWED HIS LIP. 'Do you have any proof of this kill switch?'

Aviary stretched her arms out—careful to keep her watch hidden inside the cuff of her jacket—so Felix could snip her plasticuffs. She rubbed her wrists. 'Do you have my laptop?'

Lívia nodded, then turned to one of her security officers. 'Bring in their possessions.'

'Can we just back up a second here?' Jay asked. 'So if you didn't take my abilities, how come they're gone?'

'It has nothing to do with our process of identifying pseudogenes,' Hélio said. 'Even under that unauthorized program, Intron employees didn't steal anything from you, they simply studied your DNA.'

'So who else could've taken them?'

'Biotechnologies to silence genes have been around for decades,' Hélio said. 'It's possible you've been exposed to something like that. But it certainly wouldn't be in an Intron facility.'

'You said if there's anything you can do for us … so?' Jay asked. 'What can you do?'

'We can offer you generous compensation,' Lívia said.

'I don't want your money,' Jay said.

'I was going to suggest switching on new abilities for you,' she said. 'Ones we have the blueprints for. How does *crypsis* sound?'

Jay folded his arms. 'Like a made-up word.'

'It's called adaptive infraspecific color camouflage,' Hélio said. 'Like the octopus, you blend with your surroundings. And we have the "smart suit" to match.'

'Why the hell would I want a smart suit?' Jay asked.

Hélio lifted the cuff of his jeans to reveal a thin, black material covering his leg. 'I was in a car accident when I was young. The Intron smart suit helps me walk.'

'Good for you, but that doesn't *suit* me,' Jay said. 'I'm here for what's mine.'

'But is it yours?' Hélio asked. 'Or did the Fifth Column give you a free pass?'

Jay stood suddenly, but held his temper. 'The electrogenic one was mine. I was born with it. Why do you think the Fifth Column recruited me?'

Nasira tugged on Jay's arm. He cleared his throat and sat down again.

'I don't know what to tell you,' Hélio said. 'We don't yet have the blueprints for that one.'

The security officer returned with a large metal case.

Another guard followed him in with a second case. They opened the cases, which Aviary realized were small Faraday cages, to reveal their gear. Each item from their rucks had been removed and stashed in these cases, no doubt inspected too.

Hélio retrieved the only laptop. 'Yours?'

Aviary nodded.

He opened it and passed it over to her. 'Show us what you have on this kill switch.'

She looked at Nasira, who gave her a nod. Aviary unlocked the laptop and logged into her concealed operating system—a Unix-based system she'd built herself—with just enough privileges to access the Fifth Column database.

'So what are you doing with these pseudogene profiles, anyway?' Damien asked Lívia. 'Selling them?'

'No. We only sell the complete solution,' Lívia said. 'We have our own trained people. Former special forces. We give them these abilities—if their genetics are complementary—and they sign a contract to work for us.'

'Army for hire,' Nasira said.

'*Specialists* for hire,' Lívia said.

'I have the proposal on TERMORD,' Aviary said quickly. 'This is the summary page. And there's more.'

She pushed the laptop across the table, then quickly withdrew her hands back under the table. Hélio read through the proposal and then stood. He started to pace, slowly, thoughtfully.

'When you're ready,' Lívia said to him.

'Do the Fifth Column know about this?' Hélio asked.

'Just Hal Claycomb,' Aviary said. 'And going by his

email correspondence, he's playing his cards close to his chest. That's good news, except for the part about him wanting to trigger the kill switch.'

Lívia raised an eyebrow.

'The proposal recommends an entire fleet of the Fifth Column's Low Earth Orbit satellites,' Aviary said. 'They'd transmit the trigger to base stations in the area you want to target. All operatives within range would be hit with that trigger, same way your phone communicates with a base or trunk tower. In this case, it's low-frequency radio waves—about one-hundred-and-fifty kilohertz. And then bye-bye operative.'

'Hal is definitely the only person who knows about this,' Nasira said.

'What makes you so sure?' Lívia asked.

'If the Fifth Column knew someone had spiked their punch—slipped this kill switch into all of us—they'd have killed us all by now,' Nasira said.

'You're certain they've made and deployed the switch?' Lívia asked.

Hélio pointed to Aviary's laptop. 'It's in the sample your Hal guy had tested.'

Aviary nodded. 'It seems he tested one of his operatives and found it, although he won't go into any sort of technical detail. But if that operative has it, you all do.'

Hélio turned to her. 'This Fifth Column database you now have in your possession, can we have a copy? To assist in our investigation.'

Aviary hesitated. 'If we have a deal.'

'Which we don't yet,' Nasira said.

Lívia pursed her lips. 'It seems that verifying the existence of this kill switch is in everyone's best interests. Perhaps we can arrange something.'

'Look, we're here for two reasons,' Nasira said. 'Three, if you count us being captured.'

'And they are?' Lívia asked.

'One: you stop capturing operatives,' Nasira said. 'Unauthorized activity, whatever you want to call it. Two: you find out what happened to Jay's dead pseudogenes.'

'You need to understand,' Hélio said, 'I can't activate something if I don't know where in your DNA it's located.'

'So locate it,' Jay said. 'You're the expert biofucker.'

'Biohacker,' he said. 'As I said, we don't have the blueprints for your missing ability.'

'Then you better get finding the blueprint,' Nasira said.

'Perhaps we can help you, *if* you help us,' Lívia said.

'How do you figure that?' Jay said. 'Gene Hackman over there says he can't do shit.'

Lívia tapped something on her phone and the surface of their table lit with a vibrant image, a frame from security camera footage. Aviary rose from her seat to see it properly. It showed two women, fighting outside a café. The camera showed the face of one clearly.

Sophia.

'A friend of yours, I presume,' Lívia said.

'We know of her,' Damien said, carefully.

'What do you want with her?' Nasira asked.

'We require some cooperation here,' Lívia said. 'If you want everyone to stop capturing operatives, this friend of yours needs to do the same. In the last two weeks, she's killed three.'

'I don't believe you,' Nasira said. 'She wouldn't do that.'

Lívia tapped her phone again and the image faded. 'Whatever the case may be, this is in all our best interests.'

Nasira nodded. 'Fine, agreed.'

'That image was taken in Kraków, Poland,' Lívia said. 'We have a talented virologist in Budapest, not terribly far away. She has worked closely with Hélio on improving our Argonautes. Together, they have the best chance of finding out where this kill switch is in your DNA and how to disable it.'

'Without releasing the endotoxin,' Hélio added. 'See, that's the tricky part.'

'We can set up a meeting for you,' Lívia said. 'The first step is for her to confirm whether this kill switch is in *your* DNA.'

'What about Jay?' Nasira said.

'Our virologist might be able to help him,' Lívia said. 'But I hope you understand, his inactive genes will take secondary priority. If you want our help with Jay, your friend in Poland needs to stop capturing or killing operatives. That's the deal.'

'So you have the market to yourself?' Jay asked. 'Is that what this is about? Gotta catch 'em all?'

'Jay, be cool,' Nasira said.

'If you agree to our terms, my offer still stands,' Lívia said. 'Your possessions will be made available to you.'

'You're letting us go?' Nasira asked. 'Just like that?'

'We *hire* operatives, we don't control them,' Lívia said. 'Not like the Fifth Column.'

But do you track them? Aviary wondered.

'I'll arrange a private flight for you to see your friend, the one in that photo from Poland,' Lívia said. 'Choose your destination and we'll get you there. Then you can proceed to meet with the virologist in Budapest.'

'That's not a bad plan, but I got one more question,' Nasira said.

'By all means.'

'We don't trust you. So why would you trust us?'

Lívia smiled and clasped her hands. 'I don't. Hélio and our two operatives here will accompany you. This will be a joint assignment.'

Hélio jumped in. 'My attendance isn't necessary. I can study the protein—'

'That's not your decision to make,' Lívia said. 'And your team can study it on your behalf while you attend to more pressing matters, such as meeting with the virologist. Will that be a problem?'

'I ... it's—' he stumbled.

'Good, well that's settled then.' Lívia smiled thinly. 'I wish you all luck. You'll need it.'

CHAPTER EIGHTEEN

Kaliningrad, Kaliningrad Oblast

'I APOLOGIZE, I didn't know we had a briefing.' Olesya slipped into the room and took a seat at the table.

Someone had put the table back upright with the map on top, and all the operative photos meticulously pinned to it. Illarion stood over it, studying the map. Ark was already seated, as were Marina, Andrey and Nika. Curiously, the only person missing was Gleb. Maybe no one had told him to come to the meeting either.

'This is not a briefing,' Illarion said. 'But we do have intelligence from no fewer than two sources inside the Fifth Column.' He paused. 'It indicates there will be a shooting in Wrocław. Six hours from now.'

'So it's another party in Poland,' Andrey said, 'and everyone's invited.'

'Except us,' Marina said. 'We're assigned to Purity now.'

'I will be briefing you on Purity, as per my orders,' Illarion said. 'But as I said, this is not a briefing. This is simply a *chat.*'

Olesya and Marina exchanged a glance.

'How many operatives are we ... *chatting* about?' Olesya asked.

'Just the one.' Illarion placed Val's photo on the map, over Wrocław.

Ark's gaze fixed on her photo. His lips moved, but he said nothing.

'You have two days before you're permanently assigned to Purity,' Illarion said. 'I expect everyone to be in attendance then. What you do between now and that time is entirely your own choice. Arkadiy, I have one last question for you.'

'What question is that?'

Illarion leaned over the map. 'Would you kill your sister? If you had to.'

Ark hesitated. 'I'd do what it takes.'

'The answer is not for me, it's for you,' Illarion said. 'This concludes our chat.' With that, he walked out of the briefing room, closing the door behind him.

Marina's gaze lingered on Olesya. 'So what are you going to do?'

'Why are you looking at me?' Olesya asked. All eyes in the room were on her.

'You're the leader,' Ark said.

You've never said that in your life.

Marina drew a fresh cigarette, moved it restlessly between her fingers, unlit. Andrey and Nika said nothing.

'I'm going to get your sister back,' Olesya said.

Ark let out a slow breath. 'I'll do whatever I can to help.'

'We're coming with you,' Marina said.

That surprised Olesya. 'This isn't your fight. She's Ark's sister.'

Marina frowned. 'Is she your sister too?'

'Yeah,' Olesya said. 'She is.'

'Well, then she's ours too.'

CHAPTER NINETEEN

Rio de Janeiro, Brazil

DAMIEN TOOK a seat in the private jet, opposite Nasira and Jay. Sitting with the operative bodyguards on the other side of the aisle, Hélio slouched in his seat and glowered at Jay.

'He really doesn't like you,' Damien said.

Jay shrugged. 'I get that a lot.'

Aviary sat down next to Damien, which surprised him. She brushed his leg momentarily, but she wasn't smiling. 'Got a lot of reading to catch up on. '

'You should sleep,' he said.

'I wasn't talking about me.' She handed him her laptop.

'Oh.' He opened it. 'Hal's emails?'

Aviary leaned over to Nasira. 'Do those bodyguards have enhanced hearing, like Damien?'

'Not unless Intron gave them freebies,' Nasira said. 'They can lip read though.'

Aviary turned to Damien so they couldn't see her mouth, then she spoke quietly. 'Don't get mad, but I kinda copied everything from Lívia's phone.'

Damien couldn't have heard her right. 'What?'

'It's cool.' Aviary leaned in more than enough. 'I didn't scrape her phone on purpose, it just happened while we were there.'

Damien sat upright. 'That's … not good. Really not good.'

'What's not good is that whole corruption story; it's for real. They're having problems.' Aviary purposely spoke under her breath so only he could hear. 'And in one of Lívia's emails, she mentioned the people who attacked her facility and stole something in a briefcase that was very important to her.'

Damien frowned. 'So is it Jay's abilities in the briefcase or not?'

'Dunno, but maybe you can find out.' Aviary flashed him a quick smile. 'Lívia has a lot of emails on there.'

Damien looked over his laptop lid, watching Nasira carefully run her hand—without touching—over her own arms and upper body.

'What's wrong?' Damien asked.

Nasira eyed him. 'Just checking for tracking implants.'

'You think they tagged us?' Jay asked.

'They had to,' Nasira said. 'I would've.'

'What if it's something you can't detect?' Aviary said. 'Genetic, like he said?'

Nasira let her hand drop into her lap. 'You should both be sleeping.'

'I have a bit of reading to catch up on,' Damien said.

Nasira held her tongue as the stewardess approached them with an enquiring smile.

'Whisky. Four,' she said.

Jay raised his hand. 'Double for me.'

Once she disappeared, Nasira leaned in some more and spoke in a low voice. 'Have you made contact with Sophia?'

Aviary shook her head. 'She was last online over a day ago, in Lithuania.'

Nasira blinked. 'Has she ... been offline that long before? What do you even mean by offline?'

Aviary sighed. 'It's the last time she's accessed the secret part of her phone, our messaging network. She hasn't checked it for a while.'

'That's not good,' Damien said.

'Can you stop saying that?' Aviary asked.

'Right,' Nasira said. 'Guess we wait until we land and go from there.'

Outside Damien's window, tarmac rushed by as the jet started for its assigned runway. It was the first time he'd been to an airport in a while, at least to board a plane. He was carrying a newly issued false passport, courtesy of Intron. According to their new passports, he was an Intron employee with a new Brazilian name.

The stewardess returned with their drinks. Jay sipped his while Nasira ran her hand over him, using her magnetoception to check for implants. To Damien it looked like some sort of sexy Reiki. The less he thought about that, the better.

'You're clear,' Nasira said.

Across the aisle, Felix rested his eyes while the other bodyguard busied herself reading a magazine. Hélio ordered a soda from the stewardess and cast another dirty look in their direction. Jay must have noticed, because he raised his glass.

Then the jet lifted off the runway, and Jay put his whisky down so he could clench his armrests. The city of shimmering skyscrapers, beaches and jungle was behind them now, and Damien wasn't quite sure what lay ahead.

CHAPTER TWENTY

Wrocław, Poland

A TRAM RATTLED across the main arterial. Sophia stepped off the pavement and through the shiny doors of a multi-level H&M store. On her phone, a single green dot pulsed. Valeria was already through the store and into the shopping mall, but two people moved quickly in her wake: a young woman with dark hair and gloved hands, and a tall man with a shaved head. Whoever they were, they were definitely following Valeria.

'Stop walking,' said a voice behind her. 'Turn around.'

It was the Russian woman with the calcite-blue eyes and charcoal coat. So she'd made it out of Moscow unscathed. Standing between two racks of sweaters, she aimed her pistol at Sophia, startling nearby staff and customers.

'It's a pleasure to meet you again,' Sophia said. 'I didn't catch your name.'

'No, you didn't. But you caught my friend.'

'It's what I do.'

'And hunting people like you is what I do,' she said. 'My name's Olesya.'

'If you're talking about Ieva, she's totally my friend now.'

'Don't play games,' Olesya said. 'I know you work for the Fifth Column.'

Around them, customers scrambled for the doors. A sales attendant retreated from the countertop, her back to the wall. Sophia kept an eye on her.

'I told you, not anymore,' she said.

'Then why did you abduct Val?' Olesya asked.

Sophia didn't hide her confusion. 'I didn't. I was hoping to, but she put me through a wall. And she'll do the same to your friends if we don't help.'

'I'm just the backup on this one. They can handle themselves,' Olesya said. 'Step aside.'

'I want to help you,' Sophia said.

'I don't want your help.'

'But you need it. You either take me in or you take me down.'

'I'm aiming a pistol at your head,' Olesya said.

Sophia nodded to the CCTV cameras on the ceiling. 'I'm sure that'll look great on the evening news. Execution style.'

Olesya moved fast. With her free hand, she reached down and drew something from her belt. It was black and cylindrical. But it slipped from her hand momentarily.

Sophia reached for the nearest clothing rack and flung it into her. The cylindrical object was lost in the pairs of sweaters, but Olesya launched over the rack, her knee catching Sophia in the chin. She fell into another rack and rolled to her feet.

Olesya's lips curled to flash teeth. 'I still hear their screams.'

She launched toward Sophia, sidestepped, then landed a blow across her face. Sophia moved her head with it, absorbing most of the impact. Olesya attacked again, but Sophia caught her arm inside a coat hanger. She twisted it, and kicked Olesya's leg out from under her.

Olesya stumbled, then kicked Sophia in the back of her knee. Sophia fell. Something wrapped around her neck and closed fast. Olesya pulled hard on a belt, its large metal buckle digging into Sophia's skin. Olesya yanked harder and circles of light popped across Sophia's vision.

'Tell me you blew them up,' Olesya said. 'Tell me it was you.'

Sophia slung a fist over her shoulder. It was loose and relaxed. She struck Olesya in the jaw, stunning her. Sophia moved clear.

'What are you talking about?' Sophia asked.

Olesya whipped her belt. The large metal buckle cracked across Sophia's ear and disturbed her balance. She tumbled, sprawled across the tiled floor.

'The Chechen suicide bomber,' Olesya said. 'You were the Fifth Column operative in charge. You triggered the blast and killed everyone.'

Olesya kicked low, catching Sophia under the ribs and

sending her flying into another rack of clothes. She rolled through the rack, over metal and through a pile of leather jackets. Gasping for air, she remembered. Like most operations the Fifth Column assigned to her, she never really forgot them.

Sophia crawled to her feet. 'That was four years—'

'I was ordered to stop you.' Olesya drew her pistol. 'And I failed.'

Sophia knew that look, she'd felt it many times. Olesya would never forgive herself.

'I was programmed,' Sophia said. 'I was Fifth Column.'

Before Olesya could respond, Sophia wrapped a jacket over her pistol, then elbowed her in the face. Olesya spat blood, then drove her knee into Sophia's side. Sophia felt a rib crack, again, and pain crawled through her in fiery tendrils. She tossed the jacket aside—with Olesya's pistol inside—and lost her footing. Olesya swept her legs from under her. She crashed down onto the rack of clothing.

Olesya came closer. 'You are Fifth Column.'

'That wasn't the real me,' Sophia said.

'Is there a difference?'

Sophia reached for anything she could find. She grasped the clothing rack and found a thin metal pipe. She swung it low, into the side of Olesya's leg. Olesya dropped to her knees. Sophia swung higher, aimed for her head. Olesya rolled clear, stealing her own pipe from the end of the clothing rack. Both on their knees, they attacked each other, metal clanging on metal.

On their feet, they attacked each other again.

Olesya matched her every move, and Sophia countered Olesya's. The pipes rang loudly, echoing to the upper levels of the store. Olesya twisted the pole from Sophia's grasp and kicked her backward. She slammed into the front of a countertop. The sales attendant screamed.

Olesya's eyes gleamed. Rage burned from her. 'What about you? Did you forgive yourself?'

Sophia plucked an umbrella from a rack nearby. 'I told you, I was programmed.'

Olesya came in with her metal pipe. Sophia cracked the umbrella down on Olesya's arm, sending the pipe across the tiled floor. She thrust the umbrella's metal tip into Olesya's stomach. Olesya turned her hips, taking the tip along her stomach and redirecting the strike. Sophia pressed the catch on the handle and the umbrella blasted open in Olesya's face. Sophia kicked the canopy, knocking Olesya into the counter. Her head struck the glass surface, but the glass didn't break.

'You lay a finger on Val...' Olesya dived and slid across the floor. She reached a rack of sweaters, where she found her black cylinder. Blood mixed with tears. 'Have you forgiven yourself now?'

'No,' Sophia said. 'It's what keeps me going.'

'Then maybe you should stop.' Olesya stood and walked over to a crumpled jacket. 'I can help with that.' She retrieved her pistol from inside, wielding a weapon in each hand.

'I meant what I said. I want to help.'

'In the Moscow subway, those code words you used on that operative,' Olesya said. 'Would they work on Val?'

'I already tried.' Sophia shook her head. 'I'm sorry.'

'Then you're of no use to me,' Olesya said, and fired.

THE END

Dear reader,

You can finally breathe. But only for a second.

Is this the end for Sophia?

If the kill switch is real, could it be the end of them all?

Olesya doesn't think so. If there was such a thing, someone would know, right?

Besides, she has a much bigger problem right now. And that problem is marching toward her with fire and rage.

They're called Purity and they're a paramilitary cult who want to burn people like Olesya at the stake.

Trapped in Riga and surrounded by Purity's forces, Olesya has no backup or escape plan. Just her wits and a Gyurza pistol.

Minute by minute, they're closing on her…

I hope you've enjoyed the ride, because it's just getting

started. If you've taken that breath, here's the link to the next boxset in the series.

Get it now:
Helix Boxset 2 (Books 4-6)

Cheers from down under,
Nathan

BY NATHAN M. FARRUGIA

ABOUT NATHAN M. FARRUGIA

Nathan M. Farrugia is the *USA Today* bestselling author of the *Helix* and *The Fifth Column* sci-fi thriller series.

Nathan is known for placing himself in dangerous situations, including climbing rooftops in Russia and being hunted by special forces trackers in the United States. He studies Systema, a little-known martial art and former secret of Russian special forces.

Beyond his army training, Nathan has trained under USMC, SEAL team, Spetsnaz and Defence Intelligence instructors, and the wilderness and tracking skills of the Chiricahua Apache scouts and Australian Aboriginals.

To stay up to date, follow Nathan here:
https://nathanmfarrugia.com

CREDITS

Edited by Tara Goedjen
Line edited by Pete Kempshall
Photography by Andrew Maccoll
Cover design by Stuart Bache, Books Covered
Olesya portrayed by Elke Bonner
Sophia portrayed by Haylee Collins
Costume design by Julianne Ting
Costume tailoring by Sam Melika
Hair and makeup by Kim Tavares and Janice Wu.

Expert beta reading by Neil Hawkins,
Jason Martin and Xavier Waterkeyn.

Proofreading by Sean Birkner, Fredrik Björk, Rachel
Collett, Jason Denness, Raissa E. Fedora, Jim Gabler,
Patricia Garner, Patti Holycross, Jessica Jocher, Evie

London, Elizabeth Love, Hilton J Mather, Katrina Mickle, Romano Robusto, Eric Vollebregt and Carolyn Walkden.

DISCLAIMER

This is a work of fiction. All fictional work by Nathan M. Farrugia takes place in a modern universe and is inspired by reality, however any unauthorized resemblance to actual events, real organizations or persons, living or dead, is coincidental.

The story, names, characters and events portrayed are for entertainment purposes only. No government agency has approved, endorsed or authorized the use of their name or the story.

Made in the USA
Monee, IL
12 February 2021